Rober

W
HEROES

Edited by Mike Ashley

Robinson Publishing
London

Robinson Publishing
11 Shepherd House
Shepherd Street
London W1Y 7LD

First published in this form in 1989
Previously published prior to 1936

Introductory material and this arrangement copyright © 1989
by Mike Ashley

Cover illustration © Chris Achilleos, 1988

ISBN 1 85487 001 7

Printed by Cox & Wyman Ltd., Reading

ROLL OF HONOUR

Born in Peaster, Texas in 1906, Robert E. Howard was a puny, shy child who took a body-building course that made him a muscle-bound youth, the image of the mighty heroes whose exploits he would later chronicle. Fixed on a writing career from the age of 15, rejections piled up until he sold a short tale about cavemen entitled 'Spear and Fang' in 1925.

By 1929, Howard's output included westerns, boxing stories, adventure and other fields, but it was his contributions to *Weird Tales* magazine which made him a legendary figure in fantasy fiction. From the late 1920s until his death in 1936 he invented a host of heroes, including Kull of Atlantis, Bran Mak Morn and Conan.

Howard was a surprisingly prolific writer, and long after his death a vast cache of unpublished manuscripts and unfinished drafts was discovered. These have been completed posthumously in some cases. His heroes have also continued to appear in new adventures at the hands of other writers.

This collection, however, presents Howard's heroes in their original forms, as he wrote them and as published during his lifetime.

FROM CONAN TO INDIANA JONES

On June 11th 1936 a young, muscular Texan, distraught at the impending death of his mother, walked out to his car and fired a bullet through his head. Thus ended the life of Robert E. Howard, a popular, though not especially successful writer for the American pulp magazines. There have been other writers and other suicides and, had Howard been like the hundreds of other pulp writers of his day, his passing would have been regretted but might also soon have been forgotten.

But Howard was not like most other pulp writers. Despite his youth (he was only 30 when he died) and his short career (he had sold his first story less than twelve years earlier), Howard had been astonishingly prolific and had created a wide range of memorable heroes in his stories. The most famous, and the one on which Howard's immortality rests, is the mighty-thewed Conan of Cimmeria. Long after Howard's death—he had no books published during his lifetime—the collections of Conan stories have sold in their millions and his adventures have been continued by other writers. Indeed, the sub-genre of sword & sorcery that Howard more or less created single-handedly, is thriving.

The success of the Conan stories has to some degree overshadowed Howard's other stories, and especially his other heroic, larger-than-life characters. Everyone has heard of Conan, but how many know of King Kull or Bran Mak Morn or Solomon Kane? Yet Howard wrote many stories featuring these and other heroes, every bit as fanciful and enjoyable as the Conan adventures, some even more so.

Collected here for the first time in a single volume are adventures of ten of Howard's mighty heroes. They follow an historical sequence and, if you believe in memories of past lives or reincarnation, as Howard himself liked to fancy, then you can follow through the adventures of Howard's eternal champion in his various incarnations.

We start in prehistoric times with the memories of a crippled James Allison who recalls his own past lives, starting with Niord Worm's-bane in 'The Valley of the Worm'. From the dawn of time we pass to the days of Atlantis, a hundred millenia ago where, in 'The Shadow Kingdom', we follow the adventures of Kull of Atlantis who flees to Valusia and sets his sights on the kingdom.

In Howard's historical canvas the Atlanteans gave way to their descendants, the Cimmerians in the Hyborian Age of twelve thousand years ago. This was the world of the mightiest hero of them all, Conan the Barbarian. In 'Jewels of Gwalhur', Conan seeks the fabled treasure of Alkmeenon.

Time passes and we enter known historical times—the days of imperial Rome, and its domination of Britain. In 'Worms of the Earth' we meet Bran Mak Morn, king of the Picts, who was descended from Brule, the friend and ally of Kull of Valusia. Bran also features in 'Kings of the Night', one of Howard's best stories, which introduces Cormac the Gael and also brings back to life the redoubtable Kull.

Centuries pass and Britain is now menaced by the Vikings. On to the literary stage stride Turlogh O'Brien in 'The Gods of Bal-Sagoth'. O'Brien was an Irish Celt of the eleventh century. Howard had a special fascination for the Picts and Celts feeling an affinity with these underdogs of history due to his own Irish descent on his father's mother's side.

The Crusades are the battle stage for 'Hawks of Out-remer' with Cormac FitzGeoffrey, a former comrade of Richard the Lion Heart but now in exile from his native Ireland.

Solomon Kane is perhaps Howard's most memorable hero after Conan. A Puritan adventurer in the reign of Elizabeth I, Kane features in a series of stories as he combats witchcraft and heathen magic across the African continent. 'Wings in the Night' was one of the best.

And so we come to the early years of the present century. Kirby O'Donnell and Francis Xavier Gordon are two of Howard's modern adventures, his own forerunners of Indiana Jones, soldiers of fortune in the near East.

Howard wrote of other heroes, and other heroines, but none so colourful or so magical as these. Enter the world of Howard's heroes.

Mike Ashley,
Walderslade,
June 1988.

NIORD WORM'S-BANE

The Valley of the Worm

I WILL tell you of Niord and the Worm. You have heard the tale before in many guises wherein the hero was named Tyr, or Perseus, or Beowulf, or Saint George. But it was Niord who met the loathly demoniac thing that crawled hideously up from hell, and from which meeting sprang the cycle of hero-tales that revolves down the ages until the very substance of the truth is lost and passes into the limbo of all forgotten legends. I know whereof I speak, for I was Niord.

As I lie here awaiting death, which creeps slowly upon me like a blind slug, my dreams are filled with glittering visions and the pageantry of glory. It is not of the drab, disease-wracked life of James Allison I dream, but all the gleaming figures of the mighty pageantry that have passed before, and shall come after; for I have faintly glimpsed, not merely the shapes that trail out behind, but shapes that shall come after, as a man in a long parade glimpses, far ahead, the line of figures that precede him winding over a distant hill, etched shadow-like against the sky. I am one and all the pageantry of shapes and guises and masks which have been, are, and shall be the visible manifestations of that illusive, intangible, but vitally existent spirit now promenading under the brief and temporary name of James Allison.

Each man on earth, each woman, is part and all of a similar caravan of shapes and beings. But they

cannot remember—their minds cannot bridge the brief,
awful gulfs of blackness which lie between those unstable
shapes, and which the spirit, soul, or ego, in spanning,
shakes off its fleshly masks. I remember. Why I can
remember is the strangest tale of all; but as I lie here with
death's black wings slowly unfolding over me, all the dim
folds of my previous lives are shaken out before my eyes,
and I see myself in many forms and guises—braggart,
swaggering, fearful, loving, foolish, all that men have
been or will be.

I have been Man in many lands and many condi-
tions; yet—and here is another strange thing—my line of
reincarnation runs straight down one unerring channel. I
have never been any but a man of that restless race men
once called Nordheimr and later Aryans, and today name
by many names and designations. Their history is my
history, from the first mewling wail of a hairless white ape
cub in the wastes of the arctic, to the death-cry of the last
degenerate product of ultimate civilization, in some dim
and unguessed future age.

My name has been Hialmar, Tyr, Bragi, Bran,
Horsa, Eric, and John. I strode red-handed through
the deserted streets of Rome behind the yellow-maned
Brennus; I wandered through the violated plantations
with Alaric and his Goths when the flame of burning villas
lit the land like day and an empire was gasping its last
under our sandaled feet; I waded sword in hand through
the foaming surf from Hengist's galley to lay the foundations of England in blood and pillage; when Leif the
Lucky sighted the broad white beaches of an unguessed
world, I stood beside him in the bows of the dragon-ship,
my golden beard blowing in the wind; and when Godfrey
of Bouillon led his Crusaders over the walls of Jerusalem,
I was among them in steel cap and brigandine.

But it is of none of these things I would speak.
I would take you back with me into an age beside
which that of Brennus and Rome is as yesterday. I
would take you back through, not merely centuries and

millenniums, but epochs and dim ages unguessed by the wildest philosopher. Oh far, far and far will you fare into the nighted Past before you win beyond the boundaries of my race, blue-eyed, yellow-haired, slayers, lovers, mighty in rapine and wayfaring.

It is the adventure of Niord Worm's-bane of which I would speak—the root-stem of a whole cycle of hero-tales which has not yet reached its end, the grisly underlying reality that lurks behind time-distorted myths of dragons, fiends, and monsters.

Yet it is not alone with the mouth of Niord that I will speak. I am James Allison no less than I was Niord, and as I unfold the tale, I will interpret some of his thoughts and dreams and deeds from the mouth of the modern I, so that the saga of Niord shall not be a meaningless chaos to you. His blood is your blood, who are sons of Aryan; but wide misty gulfs of eons lie horrifically between, and the deeds and dreams of Niord seem as alien to your deeds and dreams as the primordial and lion-haunted forest seems alien to the white-walled city street.

It was a strange world in which Niord lived and loved and fought, so long ago that even my eon-spanning memory can not recognize landmarks. Since then the surface of the earth has changed, not once but a score of times; continents have risen and sunk, seas have changed their beds and rivers their courses, glaciers have waxed and waned, and the very stars and constellations have altered and shifted.

It was so long ago that the cradle-land of my race was still in Nordheim. But the epic drifts of my people had already begun, and blue-eyed, yellow-maned tribes flowed eastward and southward and westward, on century-long treks that carried them about the world and left their bones and their traces in strange lands and wild waste places. On one of these drifts I grew from infancy to manhood. My knowledge of that northern homeland was dim memories, like half-remembered dreams, of blinding white snow plains and ice-fields, of great fires roaring in the circle of hide tents, of yellow manes flying in great winds, and a sun setting in a lurid wallow of crimson clouds, blazing on trampled snow where still dark forms lay in pools that were redder than the sunset.

That last memory stands out clearer than the others. It was the field of Jotunheim, I was told in later years, whereon had just been fought that terrible battle which was the Armageddon of the Aesir-folk, the subject of a cycle of hero-songs for long ages, and which still lives today in dim dreams of Ragnarok and Götterdämmerung. I looked on that battle as a mewling infant; so I must have lived about—but I will not name the age, for I would be called a madman, and historians and geologists alike would rise to dispute me.

But my memories of Nordheim were few and dim, paled by memories of that long long trek upon which I had spent my life. We had not kept to a straight course, but our trend had been forever southward. Sometimes we had bided for a while in fertile upland valleys or rich river-traversed plains, but always we took up the trail again, and not always because of drouth or famine. Often we left countries teeming with game and wild grain to push into wastelands. On our trail we moved endlessly, driven only by our restless whim, yet blindly following a cosmic law, the workings of which we never guessed, any more than the wild geese guess in their flights around the world. So at last we came into the Country of the Worm.

I will take up the tale at the time when we came into the jungle-clad hills reeking with rot and teeming with spawning life, where the tom-toms of a savage people pulsed incessantly through the hot breathless night. These people came forth to dispute our way—short, strongly built men, black-haired, painted, ferocious, but indisputably white men. We knew their breed of old. They were Picts, and of all alien races, the fiercest. We had met their kind before in thick forests, and in upland valleys beside mountain lakes. But many moons had passed since those meetings.

I believe this particular tribe represented the eastern-most drift of the race. They were the most primitive and ferocious of any I ever met. Already they were exhibiting hints of characteristics I have noted among black savages in jungle countries, though they had dwelt in these environs only a few generations. The abysmal jungle was engulfing them, was obliterating their pristine characteristics and shaping them in its own horrific mold. They were drifting into head-hunting and cannibalism was but a step which I believe they must have taken before they became extinct. These things are natural adjuncts to the jungle; the Picts did not learn them from the black people, for then there were no blacks among those hills. In later years they came up from the south, and the Picts first enslaved and then were absorbed by them. But with that my saga of Niord is not concerned.

We came into that brutish hill country, with its squalling abysms of savagery and black primitiveness. We were a whole tribe marching on foot, old men, wolfish with their long beards and gaunt limbs, giant warriors in their prime, naked children running along the line of march, women with tousled yellow locks carrying babies which never cried—unless it were to scream from pure rage. I do not remember our numbers, except that there were some five hundred fightingmen—and by fightingmen I mean all males, from the child just strong enough to lift a bow, to the oldest of the old men. In that madly ferocious age all were fighters. Our women fought, when brought to bay, like tigresses, and I have seen a babe, not yet old enough to stammer articulate words, twist its head and sink its teeth in the foot that stamped out its life.

Oh, we were fighters! Let me speak of Niord. I am proud of him, the more when I consider the paltry crippled body of James Allison, the unstable mask I now wear. Niord was tall, with great shoulders, lean hips, and mighty limbs. His muscles were long and swelling, denoting endurance and speed as well as strength. He

could run all day without tiring, and he possessed a
co-ordination that made his movements a blur of blinding
speed. If I told you of his full strength, you would brand
me a liar. But there is no man on earth today strong
enough to bend the bow Niord handled with ease. The
longest arrow-flight on record is that of a Turkish archer
who sent a shaft 482 yards. There was not a stripling in
my tribe who could not have bettered that flight.

As we entered the jungle country we heard the tom-
toms booming across the mysterious valley that slumbered between the brutish hills, and in a broad, open
plateau we met our enemies. I do not believe these Picts
knew us, even by legends, or they had never rushed so
openly to the onset, though they out-numbered us. But
there was no attempt at ambush. They swarmed out of
the trees, dancing and singing their war-songs, yelling
their barbarous threats. Our heads should hang in their
idol-hut and our yellow-haired women should bear their
sons. Ho! ho! ho! By Ymir, it was Niord who laughed
then, not James Allison. Just so we of the Aesir laughed to
hear their threats—deep thunderous laughter from broad
and mighty chests. Our trail was laid in blood and embers
through many lands. We were the slayers and ravishers,
striding sword in hand across the world, and that these
folk threatened us woke our rugged humor.

We went to meet them, naked but for our wolfhides,
swinging our bronze swords, and our singing was like
rolling thunder in the hills. They sent their arrows among
us, as and we gave back their fire. They could not match
us in archery. Our arrows hissed in blinding clouds
among them, dropping them like autumn leaves, until
they howled and frothed like mad dogs and charged to
hand-grips. And we, mad with the fighting joy, dropped
our bows and ran to meet them, as a lover runs to his love.

By Ymir, it was a battle to madden and make
drunken with the slaughter and the fury. The Picts were
as ferocious as we, but ours was the superior physique,
the keener wit, the more highly-developed fighting-brain.

We won because we were a superior race, but it was no easy victory. Corpses littered the blood-soaked earth; but at last they broke, and we cut them down as they ran, to the very edge of the trees. I tell of that fight in a few bald words. I can not paint the madness, the reek of sweat and blood, the panting, muscle-straining effort, the splintering of bones under mighty blows, the rending and hewing of quivering sentient flesh; above all the merciless abysmal savagery of the whole affair, in which there was neither rule nor order, each man fighting as he would or could. If I might do so, you could recoil in horror; even the modern I, cognizant of my close kinship with those times, stands aghast as I review that butchery. Mercy was yet unborn, save as some individual's whim, and rules of warfare were as yet undreamed of. It was an age in which each tribe and each human fought tooth and fang from birth to death, and neither gave or expected mercy.

So we cut down the fleeing Picts, and our women came out on the field to brain the wounded enemies with stones, or cut their throats with copper knives. We did not torture. We were no more cruel than life demanded. The rule of life was ruthlessness, but there is more wanton cruelty today than ever we dreamed of. It was not wanton bloodthirstiness that made us butcher wounded and captive foes. It was because we knew our chances of survival increased with each enemy slain.

Yet there was occasionally a touch of individual mercy, and so it was in this fight. I had been occupied with a duel with an especially valiant enemy. His tousled thatch of black hair scarcely came above my chin, but he was a solid knot of steel-spring muscles, than which lightning scarcely moved faster. He had an iron sword and a hide-covered buckler. I had a knotty-headed bludgeon. That fight was one that glutted even my battle-lusting soul. It was bleeding from a score of flesh wounds before one of my terrible lashing strokes glanced from his unprotected head. Ymir! Even now I stop to laugh and marvel at the hardness of that Pict's skull. Men of that age were assuredly built on a rugged plan! That blow should have spattered his brains like water. It did lay his scalp open horribly, dashing him senseless to earth, where I let him lie, supposing him to be dead, as I joined in the slaughter of the fleeing warriors.

When I returned reeking with sweat and blood, my club horribly clotted with blood and brains, I noticed that my antagonist was regaining consciousness, and that a naked tousle-headed girl was preparing to give him the finishing touch with a stone she could scarcely lift. A vagrant whim caused me to check the blow. I had enjoyed the fight, and I admired the adamantine quality of his skull.

We made camp a short distance away, burned our dead on a great pyre, and after looting the corpses of the enemy, we dragged them across the plateau and cast them down in a valley to make a feast for the hyenas, jackals, and vultures which were already gathering. We kept close watch that night, but we were not attacked, though far away through the jungle we could make out the red gleam of fires, and cloud faintly hear, when the wind veered, the throb of tom-toms and demoniac screams and yells—keenings for the slain or mere animal squallings of fury.

Nor did they attack us in the days that followed. We bandaged our captive's wounds and quickly learned his primitive tongue, which, however, was so different from ours that I can not conceive of the two languages having ever had a common source.

His name was Grom, and he was a great hunter and fighter, he boasted. He talked freely and held no grudge, grinning broadly and showing tusk-like teeth, his beady eyes glittering from under the tangled black mane that fell over his low forehead. His limbs were almost ape-like in their thickness.

He was vastly interested in his captors, though he could never understand why he had been spared; to the end it remained an inexplicable mystery to him. The

Picts obeyed the law of survival even more rigidly than did the Aesir. They were the more practical, as shown by their more settled habits. They never roamed as far or as blindly as we. Yet in every line we were the superior race.

Grom, impressed by our intelligence and fighting qualities, volunteered to go into the hills and make peace for us with his people. It was immaterial to us, but we let him go. Slavery had not yet been dreamed of.

So Grom went back to his people, and we forgot about him, except that I went a trifle more cautiously about my hunting, expecting him to be lying in wait to put an arrow through my back. Then one day we heard a rattle of tom-toms, and Grom appeared at the edge of the jungle, his face split in his gorilla-grin, with the painted, skin-clad, feather-bedecked chiefs of the clans. Our ferocity awed them, and our sparing of Grom further impressed them. They could not understand leniency; evidently we valued them too cheaply to bother about killing one when he was in our power.

So peace was made with much pow-wow, and sworn to with many strange oaths and rituals—we swore only by Ymir, and an Aesir never broke that vow. But they swore by the elements, by the idol which sat in the fetish-hut where fires burned for ever and a withered crone slapped a leather-covered drum all night long, and by another being too terrible to be named.

Then we all sat around the fires and gnawed meat-bones, and drank a fiery concoction they brewed from wild grain, and the wonder is that the feast did not end in a general massacre; for that liquor had devils in it, and made maggots writhe in our brains. But no harm came of our vast drunkenness, and thereafter we dwelt at peace with our barbarous neighbors. They taught us many things, and learned many more from us. But they taught us iron-working, into which they had been forced by lack of copper in those hills, and we quickly excelled them.

We went freely among their villages—mud-walled clusters of huts in hilltop clearings, overshadowed by

giant trees—and we allowed them to come at will among
our camps—straggling lines of hide tents on the plateau
where the battle had been fought. Our young men cared
not for their squat beady-eyed women, and our rangy
clean-limbed girls with their tousled yellow heads were
not drawn to the hairy-breasted savages. Familiarity over
a period of years would have reduced the repulsion on
either side, until the two races would have flowed together
to form one hybrid people, but long before that time the
Aesir rose and departed, vanishing into the mysterious
hazes of the haunted south. But before that exodus there
came to pass the horror of the Worm.

I hunted with Grom and he led me into brooding,
uninhabited valleys and up into silence-haunted hills
where no men had set foot before us. But there was one
valley, off in the mazes of the southwest, into which he
would not go. Stumps of shattered columns, relics of a
forgotten civilization, stood among the trees on the valley
floor. Grom showed them to me, as we stood on the cliffs
that flanked the mysterious vale, but he would not go
down into it, and he dissuaded me when I would have
gone alone. He would not speak plainly of the danger
that lurked there, but it was greater than that of serpent
or tiger, or the trumpeting elephants which occasionally
wandered up in devastating droves from the south.

Of all beasts, Grom told me in the gutturals of
his tongue, the Picts feared only Satha, the great snake,
and they shunned the jungle where he lived. But there
was another thing they feared, and it was connected in
some manner with the Valley of Broken Stones, as the
Picts called the crumbling pillars. Long ago, when his
ancestors had first come into the country, they had dared
that grim vale, and a whole clan of them had perished,
suddenly, horribly, and unexplainably. At least Grom
did not explain. The horror had come up out of the
earth, somehow, and it was not good to talk of it, since it
was believed that It might be summoned by speaking of
It—whatever It was.

But Grom was ready to hunt with me anywhere else; for he was the greatest hunter among the Picts, and many and fearful were our adventures. Once I killed, with the iron sword I had forged with my own hands, that most terrible of all beasts—old sabre-tooth, which men today call a tiger because he was more like a tiger than anything else. In reality he was almost as much like a bear in build, save for his unmistakably feline head. Sabre-tooth was massive-limbed, with a long-hung, great, heavy body, and he vanished from the earth because he was too terrible a fighter, even for that grim age. As his muscles and ferocity grew, his brain dwindled until at last even the instinct of self-preservation vanished. Nature, who maintains her balance in such things, destroyed him because, had his super-fighting powers been allied with an intelligent brain, he would have destroyed all other forms of life on earth. He was a freak on the road of evolution—organic development gone mad and run to fangs and talons, to slaughter and destruction.

I killed sabre-tooth in a battle that would make a saga in itself, and for months afterward I lay semi-delirious with ghastly wounds that made the toughest warriors shake their heads. The Picts said that never before had a man killed a sabre-tooth single-handed. Yet I recovered, to the wonder of all.

While I lay at the doors of death there was a secession from the tribe. It was a peaceful secession, such as continually occurred and contributed greatly to the peopling of the world by yellow-haired tribes. Forty-five of the young men took themselves mates simultaneously and wandered off to found a clan of their own. There was no revolt; it was a racial custom which bore fruit in all the later ages, when tribes sprung from the same roots met, after centuries of separation, and cut one another's throats with joyous abandon. The tendency of the Aryan and the pre-Aryan was always toward disunity, clans splitting off the main stem, and scattering.

So these young men, led by one Bragi, my brother-
in-arms, took their girls and venturing to the southwest,
took up their abode in the Valley of Broken Stones. The
Picts expostulated, hinting vaguely of a monstrous doom
that haunted the vale, but the Aesir laughed. We had
left our own demons and weirds in the icy wastes of
the far blue north, and the devils of other races did not
much impress us.

When my full strength was returned, and the grisly
wounds were only scars, I girt on my weapons and strode
over the plateau to visit Bragi's clan. Grom did not
accompany me. He had not been in the Aesir camp for
several days. But I knew the way. I remembered well the
valley, from the cliffs of which I had looked down and
seen the lake at the upper end, the trees thickening into
forest at the lower extremity. The sides of the valley were
high sheer cliffs, and a steep broad ridge at either end
cut if off from the surrounding country. It was toward
the lower or southwestern end that the valley-floor was
dotted thickly with ruined columns, some towering high
among the trees, some fallen into heaps of lichen-clad
stones. What race reared them none knew. But Grom had
hinted fearsomely of a hairy, apish monstrosity dancing
loathsomely under the moon to a demoniac piping that
induced horror and madness.

I crossed the plateau whereon our camp was pitched,
descended the slope, traversed a shallow vegetation-
choked valley, climbed another slope, and plunged into
the hills. A half-day's leisurely travel brought me to
the ridge on the other side of which lay the valley
of the pillars. For many miles I had seen no sign of
human life. The settlements of the Picts all lay many
miles to the east. I topped the ridge and looked down
into the dreaming valley with its still blue lake, its
brooding cliffs, and its broken columns jutting among
the trees. I looked for smoke. I saw none, but I saw
vultures wheeling in the sky over a cluster of tents
on the lake shore.

I came down the ridge warily, and approached the silent camp. In it I halted, frozen with horror. I was not easily moved. I had seen death in many forms, and had fled from or taken part in red massacres that spilled blood like water and heaped the earth with corpses. But here I was confronted with an organic devastation that staggered and appalled me. Of Bragi's embryonic clan, not one remained alive, and not one corpse was whole. Some of the hide-tents still stood erect. Others were mashed down and flattened out, as if crushed by some monstrous weight, so that at first I wondered if a drove of elephants had stampeded across the camp. But no elephants ever wrought such destruction as I saw strewn on the bloody ground. The camp was a shambles, littered with bits of flesh and fragments of bodies—hands, feet, heads, pieces of human debris. Weapons lay about, some of them stained with a greenish slime like that which spurts from a crushed caterpillar.

No human foe could have committed this ghastly atrocity. I looked at the lake, wondering if nameless amphibian monsters had crawled from the calm waters whose deep blue told of unfathomed depths. Then I saw a print left by the destroyer. It was a track such as a titanic worm might leave, yards broad, winding back down the valley. The grass lay flat where it ran, and bushes and small trees had been crushed down into the earth, all horribly smeared with blood and greenish slime.

With berserk fury in my soul I drew my sword and started to follow it, when a call attracted me. I wheeled, to see a stocky form approaching me from the ridge. It was Grom the Pict, and when I think of the courage it must have taken for him to overcome all the instincts planted in him by traditional teachings and personal experience, I realize the full depths of his friendship for me.

Squatting in the lake short, spear in his hands, his black eyes ever roving fearfully down the brooding tree-waving reaches of the valley, Grom told me of the horror that had come upon Bragi's clan under the moon.

But first he told me of it, as his sires had told the tale to him.

Long ago the Picts had drifted down from the northwest on a long, long trek, finally reaching these jungle-covered hills, where, because they were weary, and because the game and fruit were plentiful and there were no hostile tribes, they halted and built their mud-walled villages.

Some of them, a whole clan of that numerous tribe, took up their abode in the Valley of the Broken Stones. They found the columns and a great ruined temple back in the trees, and in that temple there was no shrine or altar, but the mouth of a shaft that vanished deep into the black earth, and in which there were no steps such as a human would make and use. They built their village in the valley, and in the night, under the moon, horror came upon them and left only broken walls and bits of slime-smeared flesh.

In those days the Picts feared nothing. The warriors of the other clans gathered and sang their war-songs and danced their war dances, and followed a broad track of blood and slime to the shaft-mouth in the temple. They howled defiance and hurled down boulders which were never heard to strike bottom. Then began a thin demoniac piping, and up from the well pranced a hideous anthropomorphic figure dancing to the weird strains of a pipe it held in its monstrous paws. The horror of its aspect froze the fierce Picts with amazement, and close behind it a vast white bulk heaved up from the subterranean darkness. Out of the shaft came a slavering mad nightmare which arrows pierced but could not check, which swords carved but could not slay. It fell slobbering upon the warriors, crushing them to crimson pulp, tearing them to bits as an octopus might tear small fishes, sucking their blood from their mangled limbs and devouring them even as they screamed and struggled. The survivors fled, pursued to the very ridge, up which, apparently, the monster could not propel its quaking mountainous bulk.

After that they did not dare the silent valley. But the dead came to their shamans and old men in dreams and told them strange and terrible secrets. They spoke of an ancient, ancient race of semi-human beings which once inhabited that valley and reared those columns for their own weird inexplicable purpose. The white monster in the pits was their god, summoned up from the nighted abysses of mid-earth uncounted fathoms below the black mold, by sorcery unknown to the sons of men. The hairy anthropomorphic being was its servant, created to serve the god, a formless elemental spirit drawn up from below and cased in flesh, organic but beyond the understanding of humanity. The Old Ones had long vanished into the limbo from whence they crawled in the black dawn of the universe, but their bestial god and his inhuman slave lived on. Yet both were organic after a fashion, and could be wounded, though no human weapon had been found potent enough to slay them.

Bragi and his clan had dwelt for weeks in the valley before the horror struck. Only the night before, Grom, hunting above the cliffs, and by that token daring greatly, had been paralyzed by a high-pitched demon piping, and then by a mad clamor of human screaming. Stretched face down in the dirt, hiding his head in a tangle of grass, he had not dared to move, even when the shrieks died away in the slobbering, repulsive sounds of a hideous feast. When dawn broke he had crept shuddering to the cliffs to look down into the valley, and the sight of the devastation, even when seen from afar, had driven him in yammering flight far into the hills. But it had occurred to him, finally, that he should warn the rest of the tribe, and returning, on his way to the camp on the plateau, he had seen me entering the valley.

So spoke Grom, while I sat and brooded darkly, my chin on my mighty fist. I can not frame in modern words the clan-feeling that in those days was a living vital part of every man and woman. In a world where talon and fang were lifted on every hand, and the hands of all men raised against an individual, except those of his own clan, tribal instinct was more than the phrase it is today. It was as much a part of a man as was his heart or his right hand. This was necessary, for only thus banded together in unbreakable groups could mankind have survived in the terrible environments of the primitive world. So now the personal grief I felt for Bragi and the clean-limbed young men and laughing white-skinned girls was drowned in a deeper sea of grief and fury that was cosmic in its depth and intensity. I sat grimly, while the Pict squatted anxiously beside me, his gaze roving from me to the menacing deeps of the valley where the accursed columns loomed like broken teeth of cackling hags among the waving leafy reaches.

I, Niord, was not one to use my brain over-much. I lived in a physical world, and there were the old men of the tribe to do my thinking. But I was one of a race destined to become dominant mentally as well as physically, and I was no mere muscular animal. So as I sat there, there came dimly and then clearly a thought to me that brought a short fierce laugh from my lips.

Rising, I bade Grom aid me, and we built a pyre on the lake shore of dried wood, the ridge-poles of the tents, and the broken shafts of spears. Then we collected the grisly fragments that had been parts of Bragi's band, and we laid them on the pile, and struck flint and steel to it.

The thick sad smoke crawled serpent-like into the sky, and turning to Grom, I made him guide me to the jungle wherein lurked that scaly horror, Satha, the great serpent. Grom gaped at me; not the greatest hunter among the Picts sought out the mighty crawling one. But my will was like a wind that swept him along my course, and at last he led the way. We left the valley by the upper end, crossing the ridge, skirting the tall cliffs, and plunged into the vastnesses of the south, which was peopled only by the grim denizens of the jungle. Deep into the jungle we went, until we came to a low-lying expanse, dark and dark beneath the great creeper-festooned trees, where our feet sank deep into the spongy silt, carpeted by rotting vegetation, and slimy moisture oozed up beneath their pressure. This, Grom told me, was the realm haunted by Satha, the great serpent.

Let me speak of Satha. There is nothing like him on earth today, nor has there been for countless ages. Like the meat-eating dinosaur, like old sabre-tooth, he was too terrible to exist. Even then he was a survival of a grimmer age when life and its forms were cruder and more hideous. There were not many of his kind then, though they may have existed in great numbers in the reeking ooze of the vast jungle-tangled swamps still farther south. He was larger than any python of modern ages, and his fangs dripped with poison a thousand times more deadly than that of a king cobra.

He was never worshipped by the pure-blood Picts, though the blacks that came later deified him, and that adoration persisted in the hybrid race that sprang from the Negroes and their white conquerors. But to other peoples he was the nadir of evil horror, and tales of him became twisted into demonology; so in later ages Satha became the veritable devil of the white races, and the Stygians first worshipped, and then, when they became Egyptians, abhorred him under the name of Set, the Old Serpent, while to the Semites he became Leviathan and Satan. He was terrible enough to be a god, for he was a crawling death. I had seen a bull elephant fall dead in his tracks from Satha's bite. I had seen him, had glimpsed him writhing his horrific way through the dense jungle, had seen him take his prey, but had never hunted him. He was too grim, even for the slayer of old sabre-tooth.

But now I hunted him, plunging farther and farther into the hot, breathless reek of his jungle, even when friendship for me could not drive Grom farther. He urged me to paint my body and sing my death-song before I advanced farther, but I pushed on unheeding.

In a natural runway that wound between the shouldering trees, I set a trap. I found a large tree, soft and spongy of fibre, but thick-boled and heavy, and I hacked through its base close to the ground with my great sword, directing its fall so that when it toppled, its top crashed into the branches of a smaller tree, leaving it leaning across the runway, one end resting on the earth, the other caught in the small tree. Then I cut away the branches on the under side, and cutting a slim tough sapling I trimmed it and stuck it upright like a prop-pole under the leaning tree. Then, cutting away the tree which supported·it, I left the great trunk posied precariously on the prop-pole, to which I fastened a long vine as thick as my wrist.

Then I went alone through the primordial twilight jungle until an over-powering fetid odor assailed my nostrils, and from the rank vegetation in front of me, Satha reared up his hideous head, swaying letally from side to side, while his forked tongue jetted in and out, and his great yellow terrible eyes burned icily on me with all the evil wisdom of the black elder world that was when man was not. I backed away, feeling no fear, only an icy sensation along my spine, and Satha came sinuously after me, his shining eighty-foot barrel rippling over the rotting vegetation in mesmeric silence. His wedge-shaped head was bigger than the head of the hugest stallion, his trunk was thicker than a man's body and his scales shimmered with a thousand changing scintillations. I was to Satha as a mouse is to a king cobra, but I was fanged as no mouse ever was. Quick as I was, I knew I could not avoid the lightning stroke of that great triangular head; so I dared not let him come too close. Subtly I fled down the runway, and behind me the rush of the great supple body was like the sweep of wind through the grass.

He was not far behind me when I raced beneath the deadfall, and as the great shining length glided under the trap, I gripped the vine with both hands and jerked desperately. With a crash the great trunk fell across Satha's scaly back, some six feet back of his wedge-shaped head.

I had hoped to break his spine but I do not think I did, for the great body coiled and knotted, the mighty tail lashed and thrashed, mowing down the bushes as if with a giant flail. At the instant of the fall, the huge head had whipped about and struck the tree with a terrific impact, the mighty fangs shearing through bark and wood like scimitars. Now, as if aware he fought an inanimate foe, Satha turned on me, standing out of his reach. The scaly neck writhed and arched, the mighty jaws gaped, disclosing fangs a foot in length, from which dripped venom that might have burned through solid stone.

I believe, what of his stupendous strength, that Satha would have writhed from under the trunk, but for a broken branch that had been driven deep into his side, holding him like a barb. The sound of his hissing filled the jungle and his eyes glared at me with such concentrated evil that I shook despite myself. Oh, he knew it was I who had trapped him! Now I came as close as I dared, and with a sudden powerful cast of my spear, transfixed his neck just below the gaping jaws, nailing him to the tree-trunk. Then I dared greatly, for he was far from dead, and I knew he would in an instant tear the spear from the wood and be free to strike. But in that instant I ran in, and swinging my sword with all my great power, I hewed off his terrible head.

The heavings and contortions of Satha's prisoned form in life were naught to the convulsions of his headless length in death. I retreated, dragging the gigantic head after me with a crooked pole, and a safe distance from the lashing, flying tail, I set to work. I worked with naked death then, and no man ever toiled more gingerly than I did. For I cut out the poison sacs at the base of the great fangs, and in that terrible venom I soaked the heads of eleven arrows, being careful that only the bronze points were in the liquid, which else had corroded away the wood of the tough shafts. While I was doing this, Grom, driven by his comradeship and curiosity, came stealing nervously through the jungle, and his mouth gaped as he looked on the head of Satha.

For hours I steeped the arrowheads in the poison, until they were caked with a horrible green scum, and showed tiny flecks of corrosion where the venom had eaten into the solid bronze. I wrapped them carefully in broad, thick, rubber-like leaves, and then, though night had fallen and the hunting beasts were roaring on every hand, I went back through the jungled hills, Grom with me, until at dawn we came again to the high cliffs that loomed above the Valley of Broken Stones.

At the mouth of the valley I broke my spear, and I took all the unpoisoned shafts from my quiver, and snapped them. I painted my face and limbs as the Aesir painted themselves only when they went forth to certain doom, and I sang my death-song to the sun as it rose over the cliffs, my yellow mane blowing in the morning wind.

Then I went down into the valley, bow in hand.

Grom could not drive himself to follow me. He lay on his belly in the dust and howled like a dying dog.

I passed the lake and the silent camp where the pyre-ashes still smouldered, and came under the thickening trees beyond. About me the columns loomed, mere shapeless heaps from the ravages of staggering eons. The trees grew more dense, and under their vast leafy branches the very light was dusky and evil. As in twilight shadow I saw the ruined temple, cyclopean walls staggering up from masses of decaying masonry and fallen blocks of stone. About six hundred yards in front of it a great column reared up in an open glade, eighty or ninety feet in height. It was so worn and pitted by weather and time that any child of my tribe could have climbed it, and I marked it and changed my plan.

I came to the ruins and saw huge crumbling walls upholding a domed roof from which many stones had fallen, so that it seemed like the lichen-grown ribs of some mythical monster's skeleton arching above me. Titanic columns flanked an open doorway through which ten elephants could have stalked abreast. Once there might have been inscriptions and hieroglyphics on the pillars and walls, but they were long worn away. Around the great room, on the inner side, ran columns in better state of preservation. On each of these columns was a flat pedestal, and some dim instinctive memory vaguely resurrected a shadowy scene wherein black drums roared madly and on these pedestals monstrous beings squatted loathsomely in inexplicable rituals rooted in the black dawn of the universe.

There was no altar—only the mouth of a great well-like shaft in the stone floor, with strange obscene carvings all about the rim. I tore great pieces of stone from the rotting floor and cast them down the shaft which slanted down into utter darkness. I heard them bound along the side, but I did not hear them strike bottom. I cast down stone after stone, each with a searing curse, and at last I heard a sound that was not the dwindling rumble of the falling stones. Up from the well floated a weird demon-piping that was a symphony of madness. Far down in the darkness I glimpsed the faint fearful glimmering of a vast white bulk.

I retreated slowly as the piping grew louder, falling back through the broad doorway. I heard a scratching, scrambling noise, and up from the shaft and out of the doorway between the colossal columns came a prancing incredible figure. It went erect like a man, but it was covered with fur, that was shaggiest where its face should have been. If it had ears, nose, and a mouth I did not discover them. Only a pair of staring red eyes leered from the furry mask. Its misshapen hands held a strange set of pipes, on which it blew weirdly as it pranced toward me with many a grotesque caper and leap.

Behind it I heard a repulsive obscene noise as of a quaking unstable mass heaving up out of a well. Then I nocked an arrow, drew the cord and sent the shaft singing through the furry breast of the dancing monstrosity. It went down as though struck by a thunderbolt, but to my horror the piping continued, though the pipes had fallen from the malformed hands. Then I turned and ran fleetly to the column, up which I swarmed before I looked back. When I reached the pinnacle I looked, and because of the shock and surprise of what I saw, I almost fell from my dizzy perch.

Out of the temple the monstrous dweller in the darkness had come, and I, who had expected a horror yet cast in some terrestrial mold, looked on the spawn of nightmare. From what subterranean hell it crawled in the long ago I know not, nor what black age it represented. But it was not a beast, as humanity knows beasts. I call it a worm for lack of a better term. There is no earthly language which has a name for it. I can only say it looked somewhat more like a worm than it did an octopus, a serpent or a dinosaur.

It was white and pulpy, and drew its quaking bulk along the ground, worm-fashion. But it had wide flat tentacles, and fleshy feelers, and other adjuncts the use of which I am unable to explain. And it had a long proboscis which it curled and uncurled like an elephant's trunk. Its forty eyes, set in a horrific circle, were composed of thousands of facets of as many scintillant colors which changed and altered in never-ending transmutation. But through all interplay of hue and glint, they retained their evil intelligence—intelligence there was behind those flickering facets, not human nor yet bestial, but a night-born demoniac intelligence such as men in dreams vaguely sense throbbing titanically in the black gulfs outside our material universe. In size the monster was mountainous; its bulk would have dwarfed a mastodon.

But even as I shook with the cosmic horror of the thing, I drew a feathered shaft to my ear and arched it singing on its way. Grass and bushes were crushed flat as the monster came toward me like a moving mountain and shaft after shaft I sent with terrific force and deadly precision. I could not miss so huge a target. The arrows sank to the feathers or clear out of sight in the unstable bulk, each bearing enough poison to have stricken dead a bull elephant. Yet on it came, swiftly, appallingly, apparently heedless of both the shafts and the venom in which they were steeped. And all the time the hideous music played a maddening accompaniment, whining thinly from the pipes that lay untouched on the ground.

My confidence faded; even the poison of Satha was futile against this uncanny being. I drove my last shaft almost straight downward into the quaking white mountain, so close was the monster under my perch. Then suddenly its color altered. A wave of ghastly blue surged over it, and the vast bulk heaved in earthquake-like convulsions. With a terrible plunge it struck the lower part of the column which crashed to falling shards of stone. But even with the impact, I leaped far out and fell through the empty air full upon the monster's back.

The spongy skin yielded and gave beneath my feet, and I drove my sword hilt-deep, dragging it through the pulpy flesh, ripping a horrible yard-long wound, from which oozed a green slime. Then a flip of a cable-like tentacle flicked me from the titan's back and spun me three hundred feet through the air to crash among a cluster of giant trees.

The impact must have splintered half the bones in my frame, for when I sought to grasp my sword again and crawl anew to the combat, I could not move hand or foot, could only writhe helplessly with my broken back. But I could see the monster and I knew that I had won, even in defeat. The mountainous bulk was heaving and billowing, the tentacles were lashing madly, and the antennae writhing and knotting, and the nauseous whiteness had changed to a pale and grisly green. It turned ponderously and lurched back toward the temple, rolling like a crippled ship in a heavy swell. Trees crashed and splintered as it lumbered against them.

I wept with pure fury because I could not catch up my sword and rush in to die glutting my berserk madness in mighty strokes. But the worm-god was death-stricken and needed not my futile sword. The demon pipes on the ground kept up their infernal tune, and it was like the fiend's death-dirge. Then as the monster veered and floundered, I saw it catch up the corpse of its hairy slave. For an instant the apish form dangled in midair, gripped round by the trunk-like proboscis, then was dashed against the temple wall with a force that reduced the hairy body to a mere shapeless pulp. At that the pipes screamed out horribly, and fell silent forever.

The titan staggered on the brink of the shaft; then another change came over it—a frightful transfiguration the nature of which I can not yet describe. Even now when I try to think of it clearly, I am only chaotically conscious of a blasphemous, unnatural transmutation of form and substance, shocking and indescribable. Then the strangely altered bulk tumbled into the shaft to roll down into the ultimate darkness from whence it came, and I knew that it was dead. And as it vanished into the well, with a rending, grinding groan the ruined walls quivered from dome to base. They bent inward and buckled with a deafening reverberation, the column splintered, and with a cataclysmic crash the dome itself came thundering down. For an instant the air seemed veiled with flying debris and stone-dust, through which the tree-tops lashed madly as in a storm or an earthquake convulsion. Then all was clear again and I stared, shaking the blood from my eyes. Where the temple had stood there lay only a colossal pile of shattered masonry and broken stones, and every column in the valley had fallen, to lie in crumbling shards.

In the silence that followed I heard Grom wailing a dirge over me. I bade him lay my sword in my hand, and he did so, and bent close to hear what I had to say, for I was passing swiftly.

'Let my tribe remember,' I said, speaking slowly. 'Let the tale be told from village to village, from camp to camp, from tribe to tribe, so that men may know that not man nor beast or devil may prey in safety on the golden-haired people of Asgard. Let them build me a cairn where I lie and lay me therein with my bow and sword at hand to guard this valley for ever; so if the ghost of the god I slew comes up from below, my ghost will ever be ready to give it battle.'

And while Grom howled and beat his hairy breast, death came to me in the Valley of the Worm.

KULL OF ATLANTIS

The Shadow Kingdom

1. A King Comes Riding

THE BLARE of the trumpets grew louder, like a deep golden tide surge, like the soft booming of the evening tides against the silver beaches of Valusia. The throng shouted, women flung roses from the roofs as the rhythmic chiming of silver hoofs came clearer and the first of the mighty array swung into view in the broad white street that curved round the golden-spired Tower of Splendor.

First came the trumpeters, slim youths, clad in scarlet, riding with a flourish of long, slender golden trumpets; next the bowmen, tall men from the mountains; and behind these the heavily armed footmen, their broad shields clashing in unison, their long spears swaying in perfect rhythm to their stride. Behind them came the mightiest soldiery in all the world, the Red Slayers, horsemen, splendidly mounted, armed in red from helmet to spur. Proudly they sat their steeds, looking neither to right nor to left, but aware of the shouting for all that. Like bronze statues they were, and there was never a waver in the forest of spears that reared above them.

Behind those proud and terrible ranks came the motley files of the mercenaries, fierce, wild-looking warriors, men of Mu and of Ka-nu and of the hills of the east and the isles of the west. They bore spears and heavy swords, and a compact group that marched somewhat apart were the bowmen of Lemuria. Then came the light foot of the nation, and more trumpeters brought up the rear.

A brave sight, and a sight which aroused a fierce thrill in the soul of Kull, king of Valusia. Not on the Topaz Throne at the front of the regal Tower of Splendor sat Kull, but in the saddle, mounted on a great stallion, a true warrior king. His mighty arm swung up in reply to the salutes as the hosts passed. His fierce eyes passed the gorgeous trumpeters with a casual glance, rested longer on the following soldiery; they blazed with a ferocious light as the Red Slayers halted in front of him with a clang of arms and a rearing of steeds, and tendered him the crown salute. They narrowed slightly as the mercenaries strode by. They saluted no one, the mercenaries. They walked with shoulders flung back, eyeing Kull boldly and straightly, albeit with a certain appreciation; fierce eyes, unblinking; savage eyes, staring from beneath shaggy manes and heavy brows.

And Kull gave back a like stare. He granted much to brave men, and there were no braver in all the world, not even among the wild tribesmen who now disowned him. But Kull was too much the savage to have any great love for these. There were too many feuds. Many were age-old enemies of Kull's nation, and though the name of Kull was now a word accursed among the mountains and valleys of his people, and though Kull had put them from his mind, yet the old hates, the ancient passions still lingered. For Kull was no Valusian but an Atlantean.

The armies swung out of sight around the gem-blazing shoulders of the Tower of Splendor and Kull reined his stallion about and started toward the palace at an easy gait, discussing the review with the commanders that rode with him, using not many words, but saying much.

'The army is like a sword,' said Kull, 'and must not be allowed to rust.' So down the street they rode, and Kull gave no heed to any of the whispers that reached his hearing from the throngs that still swarmed the streets.

'That is Kull, see! Valka! But what a king! And what a man! Look at his arms! His shoulders!'

And an undertone of more sinister whisperings: 'Kull! Ha, accursed usurper from the pagan isles'—'Aye, shame to Valusia that a barbarian sits on the Throne of Kings.' . . .

Little did Kull heed. Heavyhanded had he seized the decaying throne of ancient Valusia and with a heavier hand did he hold it, a man against a nation.

After the council chamber, the social palace where Kull replied to the formal and laudatory phrases of the lords and ladies, with carefully hidden, grim amusement at such frivolities; then the lords and ladies took their formal departure and Kull leaned back upon the ermine throne and contemplated matters of state until an attendant requested permission from the great king to speak, and announced an emissary from the Pictish embassy.

Kull brought his mind back from the dim mazes of Valusian statecraft where it had been wandering, and gazed upon the Pict with little favor. The man gave back the gaze of the king without flinching. He was a lean-hipped, massive-chested warrior of middle height, dark, like all his race, and strongly built. From strong, immobile features gazed dauntless and inscrutable eyes.

'The chief of the Councilors, Ka-nu of the tribe, right hand of the king of Pictdom, sends greetings and says: "There is a throne at the feast of the rising moon for Kull, king of kings, lord of lords, emperor of Valusia."'

'Good,' answered Kull. 'Say to Ka-nu the Ancient, ambassador of the western isles, that the king of Valusia will quaff wine with him when the moon floats over the hills of Zalgara.'

Still the Pict lingered. 'I have a word for the king, not'—with a contemptuous flirt of his hand—'for these slaves.'

Kull dismissed the attendants with a word, watching the Pict warily.

The man stepped nearer, and lowered his voice: 'Come alone to feast tonight, lord king. Such was the word of my chief.'

The king's eyes narrowed, gleaming like gray sword steel, coldly.

'Alone?'

'Aye.'

They eyed each other silently, their mutual tribal enmity seething beneath their cloak of formality. Their mouths spoke the cultured speech, the conventional court phrases of a highly polished race, a race not their own, but from their eyes gleamed the primal traditions of the elemental savage. Kull might be the king of Valusia and the Pict might be an emissary to her courts, but there in the throne hall of kings, two tribesmen glowered at each other, fierce and wary, while ghosts of wild wars and world-ancient feuds whispered to each.

To the king was the advantage and he enjoyed it to its fullest extent. Jaw resting on hand, he eyed the Pict, who stood like an image of bronze, head flung back, eyes unflinching.

Across Kull's lips stole a smile that was more a sneer.

'And so I am to come—alone?' Civilization had taught him to speak by innuendo and the Pict's dark eyes glittered, though he made no reply. 'How am I to know that you come from Ka-nu?'

'I have spoken,' was the sullen response.

'And when did a Pict speak truth?' sneered Kull, fully aware that the Pict never lied, but using this means to enrage the man.

'I see your plan, king,' the Pict answered imperturbably. 'You wish to anger me. By Valka, you need go no further! I am angry enough. And I challenge you to meet me in single battle, spear, sword or dagger, mounted or afoot. Are you king or man?'

Kull's eyes glinted with the grudging admiration a warrior must needs give a bold foeman, but he did not fail to use the chance of further annoying his antagonist.

'A king does not accept the challenge of a nameless savage,' he sneered, 'nor does the emperor of Valusia break the Truce of Ambassadors. You have leave to go. Say to Ka-nu I will come alone.'

The Pict's eyes flashed murderously. He fairly shook in the grasp of the primitive blood-lust; then, turning his back squarely upon the king of Valusia, he strode across the Hall of Society and vanished through the great door.

Again Kull leaned back upon the ermine throne and meditated.

So the chief of the Council of Picts wished him to come alone? But for what reason? Treachery? Grimly Kull touched the hilt of his great sword. But scarcely. The Picts valued too greatly the alliance with Valusia to break it for any feudal reason. Kull might be a warrior of Atlantis and hereditary enemy of all Picts, but too, he was king of Valusia, the most potent ally of the Men of the West.

Kull reflected long upon the strange state of affairs that made him ally of ancient foes and foe of ancient friends. He rose and paced restlessly across the hall, with the quick, noiseless tread of a lion. Chains of friendship, tribe and tradition had he broken to satisfy his ambition. And, by Valka, god of the sea and the land, he had realized that ambition! He was king of Valusia—a fading, degenerate Valusia, a Valusia living mostly in dreams of bygone glory, but still a mighty land and the greatest of the Seven Empires. Valusia—Land of Dreams, the tribesmen named it, and sometimes it seemed to Kull that he moved in a dream. Strange to him were the intrigues of court and palace, army and people. All was like a masquerade, where men and women hid their real thoughts with a smooth mask. Yet the seizing of the throne had been easy—a bold snatching of opportunity, the swift whirl of swords, the slaying of a tyrant of whom

men had wearied unto death, short, crafty plotting with
ambitious statesmen out of favor at court—and Kull,
wandering adventurer, Atlantean exile, had swept up to
the dizzy heights of his dream: he was lord of Valusia,
king of kings. Yet now it seemed that the seizing was
far easier than the keeping. The sight of the Pict had
brought back youthful associations to his mind, the free,
wild savagery of his boyhood. And now a strange feeling
of dim unrest, of unreality, stole over him as of late it
had been doing. Who was he, a straightforward man
of the seas and the mountain, to rule a race strangely
and terribly wise with the mysticisms of antiquity? An
ancient race—

'I am Kull!' said he, flinging back his head as a lion
flings back his mane. 'I am Kull!'

His falcon gaze swept the ancient hall. His self-
confidence flowed back. . . . And in a dim nook of the
hall a tapestry moved—slightly.

2. Thus Spake the Silent Halls of Valusia

The moon had not risen, and the garden was lighted
with torches aglow in silver cressets when Kull sat down
in the throne before the table of Ka-nu, ambassador of
the western isles. At his right hand sat the ancient Pict,
as much unlike an emissary of that fierce race as a man
could be. Ancient was Ka-nu and wise in statecraft,
grown old in the game. There was no elemental hatred
in the eyes that looked at Kull appraisingly; no Tribal
traditions hindered his judgments. Long associations with
the statemen of the civilized nations had swept away
such cobwebs. Not: who and what is this man? Was the
question ever foremost in Ka-nu's mind, but: can I use
this man, and how? Tribal prejudices he used only to
further his own schemes.

And Kull watched Ka-nu, answering his conversation
briefly, wondering if civilization would make of him a

thing like the Pict. For Ka-nu was soft and paunchy.
Many years had stridden across the sky-rim since Ka-nu
had wielded a sword. True, he was old, but Kull had
seen men older than he in the forefront of battle. The
Picts were a long-lived race. A beautiful girl stood at
Ka-nu's elbow, refilling his goblet, and she was kept
busy. Meanwhile Ka-nu kept up a running fire of jests
and comments, and Kull, secretly contemptuous of his
garrulity, nevertheless missed none of his shrewd humor.

At the banquet were Pictish chiefs and statesmen,
the latter jovial and easy in their manner, the warriors
formally courteous, but plainly hampered by their tribal
affinities. Yet Kull, with a tinge of envy, was cognizant of
the freedom and ease of the affair as contrasted with like
affairs of the Valusian court. Such freedom prevailed in
the rude camps of Atlantis—Kull shrugged his shoulders.
After all, doubtless Ka-nu, who had seemed to have
forgotten he was a Pict as far as time-hoary custom and
prejudice went, was right and he, Kull, would better
become a Valusian in mind as in name.

At last when the moon had reached her zenith, Ka-nu,
having eaten and drunk as much as any three men there,
leaned back upon his divan with a comfortable sigh and
said, 'Now, get you gone, friends, for the king and I
would converse on such matters as concern not children.
Yes, you too, my pretty; yet first let me kiss those ruby
lips—so; now dance away, my rose—bloom.'

Ka-nu's eyes twinkled above his white beard as he
surveyed Kull, who sat erect, grim and uncompromis-
ing.

'You are thinking, Kull,' said the old statesman, suddenly, 'that Ka-nu is a useless old reprobate, fit for
nothing except to guzzle wine and kiss wenches!'

In fact, this remark was so much in line with his
actual thoughts, and so plainly put, that Kull was rather
startled, though he gave no sign.

Ka-nu gurgled and his paunch shook with his mirth.
'Wine is red and women are soft,' he remarked tolerantly.

'But—ha! ha!—think not old Ka-nu allows either to interfere with business.'

Again he laughed, and Kull moved restlessly. This seemed much like being made sport of, and the king's scintillant eyes began to glow with a feline light.

Ka-nu reached for the wine-pitcher, filled his beaker and glanced questioningly at Kull, who shook his head irritably.

'Aye,' said Ka-nu equably, 'it takes an old head to stand strong drink. I am growing old, Kull, so why should you young men begrudge me such pleasures as we oldsters must find? Ah me, I grow ancient and withered, friendless and cheerless.'

But his looks and expressions failed far of bearing out his words. His rubicund countenance fairly glowed, and his eyes sparkled, so that his white beard seemed incongruous. Indeed, he looked remarkably elfin, reflected Kull, who felt vaguely resentful. The old scoundrel had lost all of the primitive virtues of his race and of Kull's race, yet he seemed more pleased in his aged days than otherwise.

'Hark ye, Kull,' said Ka-nu, raising an admonitory finger, ''tis a chancy thing to laud a young man, yet I must speak my true thoughts to gain your confidence.'

'If you think to gain it by flattery—'

'Tush. Who spake of flattery? I flatter only to disguard.'

There was a keen sparkle in Ka-nu's eyes, a cold glimmer that did not match his lazy smile. He knew men, and he knew that to gain his end he must smite straight with this tigerish barbarian, who, like a wolf scenting a snare, would scent out unerringly any falseness in the skein of his word-web.

'You have power, Kull,' said he, choosing his words with more care than he did in the council rooms of the nation, 'to make yourself mightiest of all kings, and restore some of the lost glories of Valusia. So. I care little for Valusia—though the women and wine be excellent—save for the fact that the stronger Valusia is, the stronger is the Pict nation. More, with an Atlantean on the throne, eventually Atlantis will become united—'

Kull laughed in harsh mockery. Ka-nu had touched an old wound.

'Atlantis made my name accursed when I went to seek fame and fortune among the cities of the world. We— they—are age-old foes of the Seven Empires, greater foes of the allies of the Empires, as you should know.'

Ka-nu tugged his beard and smiled enigmatically.

'Nay, nay. Let it pass. But I know whereof I speak. And then warfare will cease, wherein there is no gain; I see a world of peace and prosperity—man loving his fellow man—the good supreme. All this can you accomplish—*if you live!*'

'Ha!' Kull's lean hand closed on his hilt and he half rose, with a sudden movement of such dynamic speed that Ka-nu, who fancied men as some men fancy blooded horses, felt his old blood leap with a sudden thrill. Valka, what a warrior! Nerves and sinews of steel and fire, bound together with the perfect co-ordination, the fighting instinct, that makes the terrible warrior.

But none of Ka-nu's enthusiasm showed in his mildly sarcastic tone.

'Tush. Be seated. Look about you. The gardens are deserted, the seats empty, save for ourselves. You fear not *me?*'

Kull sank back, gazing about him warily.

'There speaks the savage,' mused Ka-nu. 'Think you if I planned treachery I would enact it here where suspicion would be sure to fall upon me? Tut. You young tribesmen have much to learn. There were my chiefs who were not at ease because you were born among the hills of Atlantis, and you despise me in your secret mind because I am a Pict. Tush. I see you as Kull, king of Valusia, not as Kull, the reckless Atlantean, leader of the raiders who harried the western isles. So you should see in me, not a Pict but an international man, a figure of the world. Now to that figure, hark! If you were slain tomorrow who would be king?'

'Kaanuub, baron of Blaal.'

'Even so. I object to Kaanuub for many reasons, yet most of all for the fact that he is but a figure-head.'

'How so? He was my greatest opponent, but I did not know that he championed any cause but his own.'

'The night can hear,' answered Ka-nu obliquely. 'There are worlds within worlds. But you may trust me and you may trust Brule, the Spear-slayer. Look!' He drew from his robes a bracelet of gold representing a winged dragon coiled thrice, with three horns of ruby on the head.

'Examine it closely. Brule will wear it on his arm when he comes to you tomorrow night so that you may know him. Trust Brule as you trust yourself, and do what he tells you to. And in proof of trust, look ye!'

And with the speed of a striking hawk, the ancient snatched something from his robes, something that flung a weird green light over them, and which he replaced in an instant.

'The stolen gem!' exclaimed Kull recoiling. 'The green jewel from the Temple of the Serpent! Valka! You! And why do you show it to me?'

'To save your life. To prove my trust. If I betray your trust, deal with me likewise. You hold my life in your hand. Now I could not be false to you if I would, for a word from you would be my doom.'

Yet for all his words the old scoundrel beamed merrily and seemed vastly pleased with himself.

'But why do you give me this hold over you?' asked Kull, becoming more bewildered each second.

'As I told you. Now, you see that I do not intend to deal you false, and tomorrow night when Brule comes to you will follow his advice without fear of treachery.

Enough. An escort waits outside to ride to the palace with you, lord.'

Kull rose. 'But you have told me nothing.'

'Tush. How impatient are youths!' Ka-nu looked more like a mischievous elf than ever. 'Go you and dream of thrones and power and kingdoms, while I dream of wine and soft women and roses. And fortune ride with you, King Kull.'

As he left the garden, Kull glanced back to see Ka-nu still reclining lazily in his seat, a merry ancient, beaming on all the world with jovial fellowship.

A mounted warrior waited for the king just without the garden and Kull was slightly surprised to see that it was the same that had brought Ka-nu's invitation. No word was spoken as Kull swung into the saddle nor as they clattered along the empty streets.

The color and the gayety of the day had given away to the eery stillness of night. The city's antiquity was more than ever apparent beneath the bent, silver moon. The huge pillars of the mansions and palaces towered up into the stars. The broad stairways, silent and deserted, seemed to climb endlessly until they vanished in the shadowy darkness of the upper realms. Stairs to the stars, thought Kull, his imaginative mind inspired by the weird grandeur of the scene.

Clang! clang! clang! sounded the silver hoofs on the broad, moon-flooded streets, but otherwise there was no sound. The age of the city, its incredible antiquity, was almost oppressive to the king; it was as if the great silent buildings laughed at him, noiselessly, with unguessable mockery. And what secrets did they hold?

'You are young,' said the palaces and the temples and the shrines, 'but we are old. The world was wild with youth when we were reared. You and your tribe shall pass, but we are invincible, indestructible. We towered above a strange world, ere Atlantis and Lemuria rose from the sea; we still shall reign when the green

waters sigh for many a restless fathom above the spires
of Lemuria and the hills of Atlantis and when the isles
of the Western Men are the mountains of a strange
land.

'How many kings have we watched ride down these
streets before Kull of Atlantis was even a dream in
the mind of Ka, bird of Creation? Ride on, Kull of
Atlantis; greater shall follow you; greater came before
you. They are dust; they are forgotten; we stand; we
know; we are. Ride, ride on, Kull of Atlantis; Kull the
king, Kull the fool!'

And it seemed to Kull that the clashing hoofs took
up the silent refrain to beat it into the night with hollow
re-echoing mockery:

'Kull—the—king! Kull—the—fool!'

Glow, moon; you light a king's way! Gleam, stars;
you are torches in the train of an emperor! And clang,
silver-shod hoofs; you herald that Kull rides through
Valusia.

Ho! Awake, Valusia! It is Kull that rides, Kull the
king!

'We have known many kings,' said the silent halls of
Valusia.

And so in a brooding mood Kull came to the palace,
where his bodyguard, men of the Red slayers, came to
take the rein of the great stallion and escort Kull to his
rest. There the Pict, still sullenly speechless, wheeled his
steed with a savage wrench of the rein and fled away in
the dark like a phantom; Kull's heightened imagination
pictured him speeding through the silent streets like a
goblin out of the Elder World.

There was no sleep for Kull that night, for it was
nearly dawn and he spent the rest of the night hours
pacing the throneroom, and pondering over what had
passed. Ka-nu had told him nothing, yet he had put
himself in Kull's complete power. At what had he hinted
when he had said the baron of Blaal was naught but a
figurehead? And who was this Brule who was to come to

him by night, wearing the mystic armlet of the dragon? And why? Above all, why had Ka-nu shown him the green gem of terror, stolen long ago from the temple of the Serpent, for which the world would rock in wars were it known to the weird and terrible keepers of that temple, and from whose vengeance not even Ka-nu's ferocious tribesmen might be able to save him? But Ka-nu knew he was safe, reflected Kull, for the statesman was too shrewd to expose himself to risk without profit. But was it to throw the king off his guard and pave the way to treachery? Would Ka-nu dare let him live now? Kull shrugged his shoulders.

3. They That Walk the Night

The moon had not risen when Kull, hand to hilt, stepped to a window. The windows opened upon the great inner gardens of the royal palace, and the breezes of the night, bearing the scents of spice trees, blew the filmy curtains about. The king looked out. The walks and groves were deserted; carefully trimmed trees were bulky shadows; fountains near by flung their slender sheen of silver in the starlight and distant fountains rippled steadily. No guards walked those gardens, for so closely were the outer walls guarded that it seemed impossible for any invader to gain access to them.

Vines curled up the walls of the palace, and even as Kull mused upon the ease with which they might be climbed, a segment of shadow detached itself from the darkness below the window and a bare, brown arm curved up over the sill. Kull's great sword hissed halfway from the sheath; then the king halted. Upon the muscular forearm gleamed the dragon armlet shown him by Ka-nu the night before.

The possessor of the arm pulled himself up over the sill and into the room with the swift, easy motion of a climbing leopard.

'You are Brule?' asked Kull, and then stopped in surprise not unmingled with annoyance and suspicion; for the man was he whom Kull had taunted in the hall of Society; the same who had escorted him from the Pictish embassy.

'I am Brule, the Spear-slayer,' answered the Pict in a guarded voice; then swiftly, gazing closely in Kull's face, he said, barely above a whisper:

'*Ka nama kaa lajerama!*'

Kull started. 'Ha! What mean you?'

'Know you not?'

'Nay, the words are unfamiliar; they are of no language I ever heard—and yet, by Valka!—somewhere—I have heard—'

'Aye,' was the Pict's only comment. His eyes swept the room, the study room of the palace. Except for a few tables, a divan or two and great shelves of books of parchment, the room was barren compared to the grandeur of the rest of the palace.

'Tell me, king, who guards the door?'

'Eighteen of the Red Slayers. But how come you, stealing through the gardens by night and scaling the walls of the palace?'

Brule sneered. 'The guards of Valusia are blind buffaloes. I could steal their girls from under their noses. I stole amid them and they saw me not nor heard me. And the walls—I could scale them without the aid of vines. I have hunted tigers on the foggy beaches when the sharp east breezes blew the mist in from seaward and I have climbed the steeps of the western sea mountain. But come—nay, touch this armlet.'

He held out his arm and, as Kull complied wonderingly, gave an apparent sigh of relief.

'So. Now throw off those kingly robes; for there are ahead of you this night such deeds as no Atlantean ever dreamed of.'

Brule himself was clad only in a scanty loin-cloth through which was thrust a short, curved sword.

'And who are you to give me orders?' asked Kull, slightly resentful.

'Did not Ka-nu bid you follow me in all things?' asked the Pict irritably, his eyes flashing momentarily. 'I have no love for you, lord, but for the moment I have put the thought of feuds from my mind. Do you likewise. But come.'

Walking noiselessly, he led the way across the room to the door. A slide in the door allowed a view of the outer corridor, unseen from without, and the Pict bade Kull look.

'What see you?'

'Naught but the eighteen guardsmen.'

The Pict nodded, motioned Kull to follow him across the room. At a panel in the opposite wall Brule stopped and fumbled there a moment. Then with a light movement he stepped back, drawing his sword as he did so. Kull gave an exclamation as the panel swung silently open, revealing a dimly lighted passageway.

'A secret passage!' swore Kull softly. 'And I knew nothing of it! By Valka, someone shall dance for this!'

'Silence!' hissed the Pict.

Brule was standing like a bronze statue as if straining every nerve for the slightest sound; something about his attitude made Kull's hair prickle slightly, not from fear but from some eery anticipation. Then beckoning, Brule stepped through the secret doorway which stood open behind them. The passage was bare, but not dust-covered as should have been the case with an unused secret corridor. A vague, gray light filtered through somewhere, but the source of it was not apparent. Every few feet Kull saw doors, invisible, as he knew, from the outside, but easily apparent from within.

'The palace is a very honeycomb,' he muttered.

'Aye. Night and day you are watched, king, by many eyes.'

The king was impressed by Brule's manner. The Pict went forward slowly, warily, half crouching, blade held low and thrust forward. When he spoke it was in a whisper and he continually flung glances from side to side.

The corridor turned sharply and Brule warily gazed past the turn.

'Look!' he whispered. 'But remember! No word! No sound—on your life!'

Kull cautiously gazed past him. The corridor changed just at the bend to a flight of steps. And then Kull recoiled. At the foot of those stairs lay the eighteen Red Slayers who were that night stationed to watch the king's study room. Brule's grip upon his mighty arm and Brule's fierce whisper at his shoulder alone kept Kull from leaping down those stairs.

'Silent, Kull! Silent, in Valka's name!' hissed the Pict. 'These corridors are empty now, but I risked much in showing you, that you might then believe what I had to say. Back now to the room of study.' And he retraced his steps, Kull following; his mind in a turmoil of bewilderment.

'This is treachery,' muttered the king, his steel-gray eyes a-smolder, 'foul and swift! Mere minutes have passed since those men stood at guard.'

Again in the room of study Brule carefully closed the secret panel and motioned Kull to look again through the slit of the outer door. Kull gasped audibly. For *without stood the eighteen guardsmen!*

'This is sorcery!' he whispered, half-drawing his sword. 'Do dead men guard the king?'

'*Aye!*' came Brule's scarcely audible reply; there was a strange expression in the Pict's scintillant eyes. They looked squarely into each other's eyes for an instant, Kull's brow wrinkled in a puzzled scowl as he strove to read the Pict's inscrutable face. Then Brule's lips, barely moving, formed the words:

'*The—snake—that—speaks!*'

'Silent!' whispered Kull, laying his hand over Brule's mouth. 'That is death to speak! That is a name accursed!'

The Pict's fearless eyes regarded him steadily.

'Look again, King Kull. Perchance the guard was changed.'

'Nay, those are the same men. In Valka's name, this is sorcery—this is insanity! I saw with my own eyes the bodies of those men, not eight minutes agone. Yet there they stand.'

Brule stepped back, away from the door, Kull mechanically following.

'Kull, what know ye of the traditions of this race ye rule?'

'Much—and yet, little. Valusia is so old—'

'Aye,' Brule's eyes lighted strangely, 'we are but barbarians—infants compared to the Seven Empires. Not even they themselves know how old they are. Neither the memory of man nor the annals of the historians reach back far enough to tell us when the first men came up from the sea and built cities on the shore. But Kull, *men were not always ruled by men!*'

The king started. Their eyes met.

'Aye, there is a legend of my people—'

'And mine!' broke in Brule. 'That was before we of the isles were allied with Valusia. Aye, in the reign of Lion-fang, seventh war chief of the Picts, so many years ago no man remembers how many. Across the sea we came, from the isles of the sunset, skirting the shores of Atlantis, and falling upon the beaches of Valusia with fire and sword. Aye, the long white beaches resounded with the clash of spears, and the night was like day from the flame of the burning castles. And the king, the king of Valusia, who died on the red sea sands that dim day—' His voice trailed off; the two stared at each other, neither speaking; then each nodded.

'Ancient is Valusia!' whispered Kull. 'The hills of Atlantis and Mu were isles of the sea when Valusia was young.'

The night breeze whispered through the open window. Not the free, crisp sea air such as Brule and Kull knew and reveled in, in their land, but a breath like a whisper from the past, laden with musk, scents of forgotten things, breathing secrets that were hoary when the world was young.

The tapestries rustled, and suddenly Kull felt like a naked child before the inscrutable wisdom of the mystic past. Again the sense of unreality swept upon him. At the back of his soul stole dim, gigantic phantoms, whispering monstrous things. He sensed that Brule experienced similar thoughts. The Pict's eyes were fixed upon his face with a fierce intensity. Their glances met. Kull felt warmly a sense of comradeship with this member of an enemy tribe. Like rival leopards turning at bay against hunters, these two savages made common cause against the inhuman powers of antiquity.

Brule again led the way back to the secret door. Silently they entered and silently they proceeded down the dim corridor, taking the opposite direction from that in which they had previously traversed it. After a while the Pict stopped and pressed close to one of the secret doors, bidding Kull look with him through the hidden slot.

'This opens upon a little-used stair which leads to a corridor running past the study-room door.'

They gazed, and presently, mounting the stair silently, came a silent shape.

'Tu! Chief councilor!' exclaimed Kull. 'By night and with bared dagger! How, what means this, Brule?'

'Murder! And foulest treachery!' hissed Brule. 'Nay'— as Kull would have flung the door aside and leaped forth—'we are lost if you meet him here, for more lurk at the foot of those stairs. Come!'

Half running, they darted back along the passage. Back through the secret door Brule led, shutting it carefully behind them, then across the chamber to an opening into a room seldom used. There he swept aside some tapestries in a dim corner nook and, drawing Kull with him, stepped behind them. Minutes dragged. Kull could hear the breeze in the other room blowing the window curtains about, and it seemed to him like the murmur of ghosts. Then through the door, stealthily, came Tu, chief councilor of the king. Evidently he had come through the study-room and, finding it empty, sought his victim where he was most likely to be.

He came with upraised dagger, walking silently. A moment he halted, gazing about the apparently empty room, which was lighted dimly by a single candle. Then he advanced cautiously, apparently at a loss to understand the absence of the king. He stood before the hiding place—and—

'Slay!' hissed the Pict.

Kull with a single mighty leap hurled himself into the room. Tu spun, but the blinding, tigerish speed of the attack gave him no chance for defense or counter-attack. Sword steel flashed in the dim light and grated on bone as Tu toppled backward, Kull's sword standing out between his shoulders.

Kull leaned above him, teeth bared in the killer's snarl, heavy brows ascowl above eyes that were like the gray ice of the cold sea. Then he released the hilt and recoiled, shaken, dizzy, the hand of death at his spine.

For as he watched, Tu's face became strangely dim and unreal; the features mingled and merged in a seemingly impossible manner. Then, like a fading mask of fog, the face suddenly vanished and in its stead gaped and leered *a monstrous serpent's head!*

'Valka!' gasped Kull, sweat beading his forehead, and again: 'Valka!'

Brule leaned forward, face immobile. Yet his glittering eyes mirrored something of Kull's horror.

'Regain your sword, lord king,' said he. 'There are yet deeds to be done.'

Hesitantly Kull set his hand to the hilt. His flesh crawled as he set his foot upon the terror which lay at their feet, and as some jerk of muscular reaction caused the frightful mouth to gape suddenly, he recoiled, weak with nausea. Then, wrathful at himself, he plucked forth his

sword and gazed more closely at the nameless thing that
had been known as Tu, chief councilor. Save for the reptilian head, the thing was the exact counterpart of a man.

'A man with the head of a snake!' Kull murmured.
'This, then, is a priest of the serpent god?'

'Aye. Tu sleeps unknowing. These fiends can take any
form they will. That is, they can, by a magic charm or the
like, fling a web of sorcery about their faces, as an actor
dons a mask, so that they resemble anyone they wish to.'

'Then the old legends were true,' mused the king;
'the grim old tales few dare even whisper, lest they die as
blasphemers, are no fantasies. By Valka, I had thought—I
had guessed—but it seems beyond the bounds of reality.
Ha! The guardsmen outside the door—'

'They too are snake-men. Hold! What would you do?'

'Slay them!' said Kull between his teeth.

'Strike at the skull if at all,' said Brule. 'Eighteen
wait without the door and perhaps a score more in
the corridors. Hark ye, king, Ka-nu learned of this
plot. His spies have pierced the inmost fastnesses of the
snake priests and they brought hints of a plot. Long ago
he discovered the secret passageways of the palace, and
at his command I studied the map thereof and came here
by night to aid you, lest you die as other kings of Valusia
have died. I came alone for the reason that to send more
would have roused suspicion. Many could not steal into
the palace as I did. Some of the foul conspiracy you have
seen. Snake-men guard your door, and that one, as Tu,
could pass anywhere else in the palace; in the morning, if
the priests failed, the real guards would be holding their
places again, nothing knowing, nothing remembering;
there to take the blame if the priests succeeded. But stay
you here while I dispose of this camon.'

So saying, the Pict shouldered the frightful thing stolidly and vanished with it through another secret panel.
Kull stood alone, his mind a-whirl. Neophytes of the
mighty serpent, how many lurked among his cities? How
might he tell the false from the true? Aye, how many of

his trusted councilors, his generals, were men? He could be certain—of whom?

The secret panel swung inward and Brule entered.

'You were swift.'

'Aye!' The warrior stepped forward, eyeing the floor. 'There is gore upon the rug. See?'

Kull bent forward; from the corner of his eye he saw a blur of movement, a glint of steel. Like a loosened bow he whipped erect, thrusting upward. The warrior sagged upon the sword, his own clattering to the floor. Even at that instant Kull reflected grimly that it was appropriate that the traitor should meet his death upon the sliding, upward thrust used so much by his race. Then, as Brule slid from the sword to sprawl motionless on the floor, the face began to merge and fade, and as Kull caught his breath, his hair a-prickle, the human features vanished and there the jaws of a great snake gaped hideously, the terrible beady eyes venomous even in death.

'He was a snake priest all the time!' gasped the king 'Valka! what an elaborate plan to throw me off my guard! Ka-nu there, is he a man? Was it Ka-nu to whom I talked in the gardens? Almighty Valka!' as his flesh crawled with a horrid thought; 'are the people of Valusia men or are they *all* serpents?'

Undecided he stood, idly seeing that the thing named Brule no longer wore the dragon armlet. A sound made him wheel.

Brule was coming through the secret door.

'Hold!' Upon the arm upthrown to half the king's hovering sword gleamed the dragon armlet. 'Valka!' The Pict stopped short. Then a grim smile curled his lips.

'By the gods of the seas! These demons are crafty past reckoning. For it must be that that one lurked in the corridors, and seeing me go carrying the carcass of that other, took my appearance. So. I have another to do away with.'

'Hold!' there was the menace of death in Kull's voice; 'I have seen two men turn to serpents before my eyes. How may I know if your are a true man?'

Brule laughed. 'For two reasons, King Kull. No snake-man wears this'—he indicated the dragon armlet—'nor can any say these words,' and again Kull heard the strange phrase: *'Ka nama kaa lajerama.'*

'Ka nama kaa lajerama,' Kull repeated mechanically. 'Now where, in Valka's name, have I heard that? I have not! And yet—and yet—'

'Aye, you remember, Kull,' said Brule. 'Through the dim corridors of memory those words lurk; though you never heard them in this life, yet in the bygone ages they were so terribly impressed upon the soul mind that never dies, that they will always strike dim chords in your memory, though you be reincarnated for a million years to come. For that phrase has come secretly down the grim and bloody eons, since when, uncounted centuries ago, those words were watchwords for the race of men who battled with the grisly beings of the Elder Universe. For none but a real man of men may speak them, whose jaws and mouth are shaped different from any other creature. Their meaning has been forgotten but not the words themselves.'

'True,' said Kull. 'I remember the legends—Valka!' He stopped short, staring, for suddenly, like the silent swinging wide of a mystic door, misty, unfathomed reaches opened in the recesses of his consciousness and for an instant he seemed to gaze back through the vastnesses that spanned life and life; seeing through the vague and ghostly fogs dim shapes reliving dead centuries—men in combat with hideous monsters, vanquishing a planet of frightful terrors. Against a gray, ever-shifting background moved strange nightmare forms, fantasies of lunacy and fear; and man, the jest of the gods, the blind, wisdomless striver from dust to dust, following the long bloody trail of his destiny, knowing not why, bestial, blundering, like a great murderous child, yet feeling somewhere a spark of divine fire. . . . Kull drew a hand acrosss his brow, shaken; these sudden glimpses into the abysses of memory always startled him.

'They are gone,' said Brule, as if scanning his secret mind; 'the bird-women, the harpies, the bat-men, the flying fiends, the wolf-people, the demons, the goblins all save such as this being that lies at our feet, and a few of the wolf-men. Long and terrible was the war, lasting through the bloody centuries, since first the first men, risen from the mire of apedom, turned upon those who then ruled the world. And at last mankind conquered, so long ago that naught but dim legends come to us through the ages. The snake-people were the last to go, yet at last men conquered even them and drove them forth into the waste lands of the world, there to mate with true snakes until some day, say the sages, the horrid breed shall vanish utterly. Yet the Things returned in crafty guise as men grew soft and degenerate, forgetting ancient wars. Ah, that was a grim and secret war! Among the men of the Younger Earth stole the frightful monsters of the Elder Planet, safeguarded by their horrid wisdom and mysticisms, taking all forms and shapes, doing deeds of horror secretly. No man knew who was true man and who false. No man could trust any man. Yet by means of their own craft they formed ways by which the false might be known from the true. Men took for a sign and a standard the figure of the flying dragon, the winged dinosaur, a monster of past ages, which was the greatest foe of the serpent. And men used those words which I spoke to you as a sign and symbol, for as I said, none but a true man can repeat them. So mankind triumphed. Yet again the fiends came after the years of forgetfulness had gone by—for man is still an ape in that he forgets what is not ever before his eyes. As priests they came; and for that men in their luxury and might had by then lost faith in the old religions and worships, the snake-men, in the guise of teachers of a new and truer cult, built a monstrous religion about the worship of the serpent god.

Such is their power that it is now death to repeat the old
legends of the snake-people, and people bow again to the
serpent god in new form; and blind fools that they are, the
great hosts of men see no connection between this power
and the power men overthrew eons ago. As priests the
snake-men are content to rule—and yet—' He stopped.

'Go on.' Kull felt an unaccountable stirring of the short
hair at the base of his scalp.

'Kings have reigned as true men in Valusia,' the Pict
whispered, 'and yet, slain in battle, have died serpents—
as died he who fell beneath the spear of Lion-fang on
the red beaches when we of the isles harried the Seven
Empires. And how can this be, Lord Kull? These kings
were born of women and lived as men! This—the true
kings died in secret—as you would have died tonight—
and priests of the Serpent reigned in their stead, no
man knowing.'

Kull cursed between his teeth. 'Aye, it must be. No
one has ever seen a priest of the Serpent and lived, that
is known. They live in utmost secrecy.'

'This statecraft of the Seven Empires is a mazy, monstrous thing,' said Brule. 'There the true men know that
among them glide the spies of the serpent, and the men
who are the Serpent's allies—such as Kaanuub, baron of
Blaal—yet no man dares seek to unmask a suspect lest
vengeance befall him. No man trusts his fellow and the
true statesmen dare not speak to each other what is in the
minds of all. Could they be sure, could a snake-man or
plot be unmasked before them all, then would the power
of the Serpent be more than half broken; for all would
then ally and make common cause, sifting out the traitors.
Ka-nu alone is of sufficient shrewdness and courage to
cope with them, and even Ka-nu learned only enough
of their to plot to tell me what would happen—what has
happened up to this time. Thus far I was prepared; from
now on we must trust to our luck and our craft. Here
and now I think we are safe; those snake-men without
the door dare not leave their post lest true men come here

unexpectedly. But tomorrow they will try something else, you may be sure. Just what they will do, none can say, not even Ka-nu; but we must stay at each other's sides, King Kull, until we conquer or both be dead. Now come with me while I take this carcass to the hiding place where I took the other being.'

Kull followed the Pict with his grisly burden through the secret panel and down the dim corridor. Their feet, trained to the silence of the wilderness, made no noise. Like phantoms they glided through the ghostly light, Kull wondering that the corridors should be deserted; at every turn he expected to run full upon some frightful apparition. Suspicion surged back upon him; was this Pict leading him into ambush? He fell back a pace or two behind Brule, his ready sword hovering at the Pict's unheeding back. Brule should die first if he meant treachery. But if the Pict was aware of the king's suspicion, he showed no sign. Stolidly he tramped along, until they came to a room, dusty and long unused, where moldy tapestries hung heavy. Brule drew aside some of these and concealed the corpse behind them.

Then they turned to retrace their steps, when suddenly Brule halted with such abruptness that he was closer to death than he knew; for Kull's nerves were on edge.

'Something moving in the corridor,' hissed the Pict. 'Ka-nu said these ways would be empty, yet—'

He drew his sword and stole into the corridor, Kull following warily.

A short way down the corridor a strange, vague glow appeared that came toward them. Nerves a-leap, they waited, backs to the corridor wall; for what they knew not, but Kull heard Brule's breath hiss through his teeth and was reassured as to Brule's loyalty.

The glow merged into a shadowy form. A shape vaguely like a man it was, but misty and illusive, like a wisp of fog, that grew more tangible as it approached, but never fully material. A face looked at them, a pair of luminous great eyes, that seemed to hold all the tortures of a million centuries. There was no menace in that face, with its dim, worn features, but only a great pity—and that face—that face—

'Almighty gods!' breathed Kull, an icy hand at his soul; 'Eallal, king of Valusia, who died a thousand years ago!'

Brule shrank back as far as he could, his narrow eyes widened in a blaze of pure horror, the sword shaking in his grip, unnerved for the first time that weird night. Erect and defiant stood Kull, instinctively holding his useless sword at the ready; flesh a-crawl, hair a-prickle, yet still a king of kings, as ready to challenge the powers of the unknown dead as the powers of the living.

The phantom came straight on, giving them no heed; Kull shrank back as it passed them, feeling an icy breath like a breeze from the arctic snow. Straight on went the shape with slow, silent footsteps, as if the chains of all the ages were upon those vague feet; vanishing about a bend of the corridor.

'Valka!' muttered the Pict, wiping the cold beads from his brow; 'that was no man! That was a ghost!'

'Aye!' Kull shook his head wonderingly. 'Did you not recognize the face? That was Eallal, who reigned in Valusia a thousand years ago and who was found hideously murdered in his throneroom—the room now known as the Accursed Room. Have you not seen his statue in the Fame Room of Kings?'

'Yes, I remember the tale now. Gods, Kull! that is another sign of the frightful and foul power of the snake priests—that king was slain by snake-people and thus his soul became their slave, to do their bidding throughout eternity! For the sages have ever maintained that if a man is slain by a snake-man his ghost becomes their slave.'

A shudder shook Kull's gigantic frame. 'Valka! But what a fate! Hark ye'—his fingers closed upon Brule's sinewy arm like steel—'hark ye! If I am wounded unto death by these foul monsters, swear that ye will smite your sword through my breast lest my soul be enslaved.'

'I swear,' answered Brule, his fierce eyes lighting. 'And do ye the same by me, Kull.'

Their strong right hands met in a silent sealing of their bloody bargain.

4. Masks

Kull sat upon his throne and gazed broodingly out upon the sea of faces turned toward him. A courtier was speaking in evenly modulated tones, but the king scarcely heard him. Close by, Tu, chief councilor, stood ready at Kull's command, and each time the king looked at him, Kull shuddered inwardly. The surface of court life was as the unrippled surface of the sea between tide and tide. To the musing king the affairs of the night before seemed as a dream, until his eyes dropped to the arm of his throne. A brown, sinewy hand rested there, upon the wrist of which gleamed a dragon armlet; Brule stood beside his throne and ever the Pict's fierce secret whisper brought him back from the realm of unreality in which he moved.

No, that was no dream, that monstrous interlude. As he sat upon his throne in the Hall of Society and gazed upon the courtiers, the ladies, the lords, the statesmen, he seemed to see their faces as things of illusion, things unreal, existent only as shadows and mockeries of sub-stance. Always he had seen their faces as masks, but before he had looked on them with contemptuous toler-ance, thinking to see beneath the masks shallow, puny souls, avaricious, lustful, deceitful; now there was a grim undertone, a sinister meaning, a vague horror that lurked beneath the smooth masks. While he exchanged courtesies with some nobleman or councilor he seemed to see the smiling face fade like smoke and the frightful jaws of a serpent gaping there. How many of those he looked upon were horrid, inhuman monsters, plotting his death, beneath the smooth mesmeric illusion of a human face?

Valusia—land of dreams and nightmares—a kingdom of the shadows, ruled by phantoms who glided back and forth behind the painted curtains, mocking the futile king who sat upon the throne—himself a shadow.

And like a comrade shadow Brule stood by his side, dark eyes glittering from immobile face. A real man, Brule! And Kull felt his friendship for the savage become a thing of reality and sensed that Brule felt a friendship for him beyond the mere necessity of statecraft.

And what, mused Kull, were the realities of life? Ambition, power, pride? The friendship of man, the love of women—which Kull had never known—battle, plunder, what? Was it the real Kull who sat upon the throne or was it the real Kull who had scaled the hills of Atlantis, harried the far isles of the sunset, and laughed upon the green roaring tides of the Atlantean sea? How could a man be so many different men in a lifetime? For Kull knew that there were many Kulls and he wondered which was the real Kull. After all, the priests of the Serpent merely went a step further in their magic, for all men wore masks, and many a different mask with each different man or woman; and Kull wondered if a serpent did not lurk under every mask.

So he sat and brooded in a strange, mazy thought ways, and the courtiers came and went and the minor affairs of the day were completed, until at last the king and Brule sat alone in the Hall of Society save for the drowsy attendants.

Kull felt a weariness. Neither he nor Brule had slept the night before, nor had Kull slept the night before that, when in the gardens of Ka-nu he had had his first hint of the weird things to be. Last night nothing further had occurred after they had returned to the study-room from the secret corridors, but they had neither dared nor cared to sleep. Kull, with the incredible vitality of a wolf, had aforetime gone for days upon days without sleep, in his wild savage days but now his mind was edged from constant thinking and from the nervebreaking eeriness of the past night. He needed sleep, but sleep was furthest from his mind.

And he would not have dared sleep if he had thought of it. Another thing that had shaken him was the fact that though he and Brule had kept a close watch to see if, or when, the study-room guard was changed, yet it was changed without their knowledge; for the next morning those who stood on guard were able to repeat the magic words of Brule, but they remembered nothing out of the ordinary. They thought that they had stood at guard all night, as usual, and Kull said nothing to the contrary. He believed them true men, but Brule had advised absolute secrecy, and Kull also thought it best.

Now Brule leaned over the throne, lowering his voice so not even a lazy attendant could hear: 'They will strike soon, I think, Kull. A while ago Ka-nu gave me a secret sign. The priests know that we know of their plot, of course, but they know not, how much we know. We must be ready for any sort of action. Ka-nu and the Pictish chiefs will remain within hailing distance now until this is settled one way or another. Ha, Kull, if it comes to a pitched battle, the streets and the castles of Valusia will run red!'

Kull smiled grimly. He would greet any sort of action with a ferocious joy. This wandering in a labyrinth of illusion and magic was extremely irksome to his nature. He longed for the leap and clang of swords, for the joyous freedom of battle.

Then into the Hall of Society came Tu again, and the rest of the councilors.

'Lord king, the hour of the council is at hand and we stand ready to escort you to the council room.'

Kull rose, and the councilors bent the knee as he passed through the way opened by them for his passage, rising behind him, and following. Eyebrows were raised as the Pict strode defiantly behind the king, but no one dissented. Brule's challenging gaze swept the smooth faces of the councilors with the defiance of an intruding savage.

The group passed through the halls and came at last to
the council chamber. The door was closed, as usual, and
the councilors arranged themselves in the order of their
rank before the dais upon which stood the king. Like a
bronze statue Brule took up his stand behind Kull.

Kull swept the room with a swift stare. Surely no
chance of treachery here. Seventeen councilors there
were, all known to him; all of them had espoused his
cause when he ascended the throne.

'Men of Valusia—' he began in the conventional manner, then halted, perplexed. The councilors had risen as a
man and were moving toward him. There was no hostility
in their looks, but their actions were strange for a council
room. The foremost was close to him when Brule sprang
forward, crouched like a leopard.

'*Ka nama kaa lajerama!*' his voice crackled through the
sinister silence of the room and the foremost councilor
recoiled, hand flashing to his robes; and like a spring
released Brule moved and the man pitched headlong
to the glint of his sword—headlong he pitched and
lay still while his face faded and became the head of
a mighty snake.

'Slay, Kull!' rasped the Pict's voice. 'They be all
serpent men!'

The rest was a scarlet maze. Kull saw the familiar
faces dim like fading fog and in their places gaped horrid
reptilian visages as the whole band rushed forward. His
mind was dazed but his giant body faltered not.

The singing of his sword filled the room, and the
onrushing flood broke in a red wave. But they surged
forward again, seemingly willing to fling their lives away
in order to drag down the king. Hideous jaws gaped at
him; terrible eyes blazed into his unblinkingly; a frightful
fetid scent pervaded the atmosphere—the serpent scent
that Kull had known in southern jungles. Swords and
daggers leaped at him and he was dimly aware that
they wounded him. But Kull was in his element; never
before had he faced such grim foes but it mattered little;

they lived, their veins held blood that could be spilt and they died when his great sword cleft their skulls or drove through their bodies. Slash, thrust, thrust and swing. Yet had Kull died there but for the man who crouched at his side, parrying and thrusting. For the king was clear berserk, fighting in the terrible Atlantean way, that seeks death to deal death; he made no effort to avoid thrusts and slashes, standing straight up and ever plunging forward, no thought in his frenzied mind but to slay. Not often did Kull forget his fighting craft in his primitive fury, but now some chain had broken in his soul, flooding his mind with a red wave of slaughter-lust. He slew a foe at each blow, but they surged about him, and time and again Brule turned a thrust that would have slain, as he crouched beside Kull, parrying and warding with cold skill, slaying not as Kull slew with long slashes and plunges, but with short overhand blows and upward thrusts.

Kull laughed, a laugh of insanity. The frightful faces swirled about him in a scarlet blaze. He felt steel sink into his arm and dropped his sword in a flashing arc that cleft his foe to the breast-bone. Then the mists faded and the king saw that he and Brule stood alone above a sprawl of hideous crimson figures who lay still upon the floor.

'Valka! what a killing!' said Brule, shaking the blood from his eyes. 'Kull, had these been warriors who knew how to use the steel, we had died here. These serpent priests know naught of swordcraft and die easier than any men I ever slew. Yet had there been a few more, I think the matter had ended otherwise.'

Kull nodded. The wild berserker blaze had passed, leaving a mazed feeling of great weariness. Blood seeped from wounds on breast, shoulder, arm and leg. Brule, himself bleeding from a score of flesh wounds, glanced at him in some concern.

'Lord Kull, let us hasten to have your wounds dressed by the women.'

Kull thrust him aside with a drunken sweep of his mighty arm.

'Nay, we'll see this through ere we cease. Go you, though, and have your wounds seen to—I command it.'

The Pict laughed grimly. 'Your wounds are more than mine, lord king—' he began, then stopped as a sudden thought struck him. 'By Valka, Kull, this is not the council room!'

Kull looked about and suddenly other fogs seemed to fade. 'Nay, this is the room where Eallal died a thousand years ago—since unused and named "Accursed".'

'Then by the gods, they tricked us after all!' exclaimed Brule in a fury, kicking the corpses at their feet. 'They caused us to walk like fools into their ambush! By their magic they changed the appearance of all—'

'Then there is further deviltry afoot,' said Kull, 'for if there be true men in the councils of Valusia they should be in the real council room now. Come swiftly.'

And leaving the room with its ghastly keepers they hastened through halls that seemed deserted until they came to the real council room. Then Kull halted with a ghastly shudder. *From the council room sounded a voice speaking, and the voice was his!*

With a hand that shook he parted the tapestries and gazed into the room. There sat the councilors, counterparts of the men he and Brule had just slain, and upon the dais stood Kull, king of Valusia.

He stepped back, his mind reeling.

'This is insanity!' he whispered. 'Am I Kull? Do I stand here or is that Kull yonder in very truth and am I but a shadow, a figment of thought?'

Brule's hand clutching his shoulder, shaking him fiercely, brought him to his senses.

'Valka's name, be not a fool! Can you yet be astounded after all we have seen? See you not that those are true men bewitched by a snake-man who has taken your form, as those others took their forms? By now you should have been slain and yon monster reigning in your stead, unknown by those who bowed to you. Leap and slay swiftly or else we are undone. The Red Slayers, true men, stand close on each hand and none but you can reach and slay him. Be swift!'

Kull shook off the onrushing dizziness, flung back his head in the old, defiant gesture. He took a long, deep breath as does a strong swimmer before diving into the sea; then, sweeping back the tapestries, made the dais in a single lionlike bound. Brule had spoken truly. There stood men of the Red Slayers, guardsmen trained to move quick as the striking leopard; any but Kull had died ere he could reach the usurper. But the sight of Kull, identical with the man upon the dais, held them in their tracks, their minds stunned for an instant, and that was long enough. He upon the dais snatched for his sword, but even as his fingers closed upon the hilt, Kull's sword stood out behind his shoulders and the thing that men had thought the king pitched forward from the dais to lie silent upon the floor.

'Hold!' Kull's lifted hand and kingly voice stopped the rush that had started, and while they stood astounded he pointed to the thing which lay before them—whose face was fading into that of a snake. They recoiled, and from one door came Brule and from another came Ka-nu.

These grasped the king's bloody hand and Ka-nu spoke: 'Men of Valusia, you have seen with your own eyes. This is the true Kull, the mightiest king to whom Valusia has ever bowed. The power of the Serpent is broken and ye be all true men. King Kull, have you commands?'

'Lift the carrion,' said Kull, and men of the guard took up the thing.

'Now follow me,' said the king, and he made his way to the Accursed Room. Brule, with a look of concern, offered the support of his arm but Kull shook him off.

The distance seemed endless to the bleeding king, but at last he stood at the door and laughed fiercely

and grimly when he heard the horrified ejaculations of
the councilors.

At his orders the guardsmen flung the corpse they
carried beside the others, and motioning all from the
room Kull stepped out last and closed the door.

A wave of dizziness left him shaken. The faces turned
to him, pallid and wonderingly, swirled and mingled in
a ghostly fog. He felt the blood from his wound trickling
down his limbs and he knew that what he was to do, he
must do quickly or not at all.

His sword rasped from its sheath.

'Brule, are you there?'

'Aye!' Brule's face looked at him through the mist,
close to his shoulder, but Brule's voice sounded leagues
and eons away.

'Remember our vow, Brule. And now, bid them stand
back.'

His left arm cleared a space as he flung up his sword.
Then with all his waning power he drove it through the
door into the jamb, driving the great sword to the hilt and
sealing the room forever.

Legs braced wide, he swayed drunkenly, facing the
horrified councilors. 'Let this room be doubly accursed.
And let those rotting skeletons lie there forever as a
sign of the dying might of the serpent. Here I swear
that I shall hunt the serpent-men from land to land,
from sea to sea, giving no rest until all be slain, that good
triumph and the power of Hell be broken. This thing I
swear—I—Kull—king—of—Valusia.'

His knees buckled as the faces swayed and swirled. The
councilors leaped forward, but ere they could reach him,
Kull slumped to the floor, and lay still, face upward.

The councilors surged about the fallen king, chattering
and shrieking. Ka-nu beat them back with his clenched
fists, cursing savagely.

'Back, you fools! Would you stifle the little life that is
yet in him? How, Brule, is he dead or will he live?'—to
the warrior who bent above the prostrate Kull.

'Dead?' sneered Brule irritably. 'Such a man as this is not so easily killed. Lack of sleep and loss of blood have weakened him—by Volka, he has a score of deep wounds, but none of them mortal. Yet have those gibbering fools bring the court women here at once.'

Brule's eyes lighted with a fierce, proud light.

'Valka, Ka-nu, but here is such a man as I knew not existed in these degenerate days. He will be in the saddle in a few scant days and then may the serpent-men of the world beware of Kull of Valusia. Valka! but that will be a rare hunt! Ah, I see long years of prosperity for the world with such a king upon the throne of Valusia.'

CONAN OF CIMMERIA

Jewels of Gwahlur

1.

THE CLIFFS rose sheer from the jungle, towering ramparts of stone that glinted jade-blue and dull crimson in the rising sun, and curved away and away to east and west above the waving emerald ocean of fronds and leaves. It looked insurmountable, that giant palisade with its sheer curtains of solid rock in which bits of quartz winked dazzlingly in the sunlight. But the man who was working his tedious way upward was already halfway to the top.

He came from a race of hillmen, accustomed to scaling forbidding crags, and he was a man of unusual strength and agility. His only garment was a pair of short red silk breeks, and his sandals were slung to his back, out of his way, as were his sword and dagger.

The man was powerfully built, supple as a panther. His skin was bronzed by the sun, his square-cut black mane confined by a silver band about his temples. His iron muscles, quick eyes and sure feet served him well here, for it was a climb to test these qualities to the utmost. A hundred and fifty feet below him waved the jungle. An equal distance above him the rim of the cliffs was etched against the morning sky.

He labored like one driven by the necessity of haste; yet he was forced to move at a snail's pace, clinging like a fly on a wall. His groping hands and feet found niches and knobs, precarious holds at best, and sometimes he virtually hung by his finger nails. Yet upward he went, clawing, squirming, fighting for every foot. At times he paused to rest his aching muscles, and, shaking the sweat out of his eyes, twisted his head to stare searchingly out over the jungle, combing the green expanse for any trace of human life or motion.

Now the summit was not far above him, and he observed, only a few feet above his head, a break in the sheer stone of the cliff. An instant later he had reached it—a small cavern, just below the edge of the rim. As his head rose above the lip of its floor, he grunted. He clung there, his elbows hooked over the lip. The cave was so tiny that it was little more than a niche cut in the stone, but it held an occupant. A shriveled brown mummy, cross-legged, arms folded on the withered breast upon which the shrunken head was sunk, sat in the little cavern. The limbs were bound in place with rawhide thongs which had become mere rotted wisps. If the form had ever been clothed, the ravages of time had long ago reduced the garments to dust. But thrust between the crossed arms and the shrunken breast there was a roll of parchment, yellowed with age to the color of old ivory.

The climber stretched forth a long arm and wrenched away this cylinder. Without investigation, he thrust it into his girdle and hauled himself up until he was standing in the opening of the niche. A spring upward and he caught the rim of the cliffs and pulled himself up and over almost with the same motion.

There he halted, panting, and stared downward.

It was like looking into the interior of a vast bowl, rimmed by a circular stone wall. The floor of the bowl was covered with trees and denser vegetation, though nowhere did the growth duplicate the jungle denseness of the outer forest. The cliffs marched around it without a break and of uniform height. It was a freak of nature, not to be paralleled, perhaps, in the whole world: a vast natural amphitheater, a circular bit of forested plain, three or four miles in diameter, cut off from the rest of the world, and confined within the ring of those palisaded cliffs.

But the man on the cliffs did not devote his thoughts to marveling at the topographical phenomenon. With tense eagerness he searched the tree-tops below him, and exhaled a gusty sigh when he caught the glint of marble domes amidst the twinkling green. It was no myth, then; below him lay the fabulous and deserted palace of Alkmeenon.

Conan the Cimmerian, late of the Baracha Isles, of the Black Coast, and of many other climes where life ran wild, had come to the kingdom of Keshan following the lure of a fabled treasure that outshone the hoard of the Turanian kings.

Keshan was a barbaric kingdom lying in the eastern hinterlands of Kush where the broad grasslands merge with the forests that roll up from the south. The people were a mixed race, a dusky nobility ruling a population that was largely pure Negro. The rulers—princes and high priests—claimed descent from a white race which, in a mythical age, had ruled a kingdom whose capital city was Alkmeenon. Conflicting legends sought to explain the reason for that race's eventual downfall, and the abandonment of the city by the survivors. Equally nebulous were the tales of the Teeth of Gwahlur, the treasure of Alkmeenon. But these misty legends had been enough to bring Conan to Keshan, over vast distances of plain, riverlaced jungle, and mountains.

He had found Keshan, which in itself was considered mythical by many northern and western nations, and he had heard enough to confirm the rumors of the treasure that men called the Teeth of Gwahlur. But its hiding-place he could not learn, and he was confronted with the necessity of explaining his presence in Keshan. Unattached strangers were not welcome there.

But he was not nonplussed. With cool assurance he made his offer to the stately, plumbed, suspicious grandees of the barbarically magnificent court. He was a

professional fighting man. In search of employment (he
said) he had come to Keshan. For a price he would train
the armies of Keshan and lead them against Punt, their
hereditary enemy, whose recent successes in the field had
aroused the fury of Keshan's irascible king.

This proposition was not so audacious as it might
seem. Conan's fame had preceded him, even into distant
Keshan; his exploits as a chief of the black corsairs, those
wolves of the southern coasts, had made his name known,
admired and feared throughout the black kingdoms.
He did not refuse tests devised by the dusky lords.
Skirmishes along the borders were incessant, affording
the Cimmerian plenty of opportunities to demonstrate
his ability at hand-to-hand fighting. His reckless ferocity
impressed the lords of Keshan, already aware of his
reputation as a leader of men, and the prospects seemed
favorable. All Conan secretly desired was employment to
give him legitimate excuse for remaining in Keshan long
enough to locate the hiding place of the Teeth of Gwahlur.
Then there came an interruption. Thutmekri came to
Keshan at the head of an embassy from Zembabwei.

Thutmekri was a Stygian, as adventurer and a rogue
whose wits had recommended him to the twin kings
of the great hybrid trading kingdom which lay many
days' march to the east. He and the Cimmerian knew
each other of old, and without love. Thutmekri likewise
had a proposition to make to the king of Keshan, and it
also concerned the conquest of Punt—which kingdom,
incidentally, lying east of Keshan, had recently expelled
the Zembabwan traders and burned their fortresses.

His offer outweighed even the prestige of Conan. He
pledged himself to invade Punt from the east with a host
of black spearmen, Shemitish archers, and mercenary
swordsmen, and to aid the King of Keshan to annex the
hostile kingdom. The benevolent Kings of Zembabwei
desired only a monopoly of the trade of Keshan and her
tributaries—and, as a pledge of good faith, some of the
Teeth of Gwahlur. These would be put to no base usage,

Thutmekri hastened to explain to the suspicious chieftains; they would be placed in the temple of Zembabwei beside the squat gold idols of Dagon and Derketo, sacred guests in the holy shrine of the kingdom, to seal the covenant between Keshan and Zembabwei. This statement brought a savage grin to Conan's hard lips.

The Cimmerian made no attempt to match wits and intrigue with Thutmekri and his Shemitish partner, Zargheba. He knew that if Thutmekri won his point, he would insist on the instant banishment of his rival. There was but one thing for Conan to do: find the jewels before the king of Keshan made up his mind, and flee with them. But by this time he was certain that they were not hidden in Keshia, the royal city, which was a swarm of thatched huts crowding about a mud wall that enclosed a palace of stone and mud and bamboo.

While he fumed with nervous impatience, the high priest Gorulga announced that before any decision could be reached, the will of the gods must be ascertained concerning the proposed alliance with Zembabwei and the pledge of objects long held holy and inviolate. The oracle of Alkmeenon must be consulted.

This was an awesome thing, and it caused tongues to wag excitedly in palace and beehive hut. Not for a century had the priests visited the silent city. The oracle, men said, was the Princess Yelaya, the last ruler of Alkmeenon, who had died in the full bloom of her youth and beauty, and whose body had miraculously remained unblemished throughout the ages. Of old, priests had made their way into the haunted city, and she had taught them wisdom. The last priest to seek the oracle had been a wicked man, who had sought to/steal for himself the curiously cut jewels that men called the Teeth of Gwahlur. But some doom had come upon him in the deserted palace, from which his acolytes, fleeing, had told tales of horror that had for a hundred years frightened the priests from the city and the oracle.

But Gorulga, the present high priest, as one confident in his knowledge of his own integrity, announced that he would go with a handful of followers to revive the ancient custom. And in the excitement tongues buzzed indiscreetly, and Conan caught the clue for which he had sought for weeks—the overheard whisper of a lesser priest that sent the Cimmerian stealing of Keshia the night before the dawn when the priests were to start.

Riding as hard as he dared for a night and a day and a night, he came in the early dawn to the cliffs of Alkmeenon, which stood in the southwestern corner of the kingdom, amidst uninhabited jungle which was taboo to common men. None but the priests dared approach the haunted vale within a distance of many miles. And not even a priest had entered Alkmeenon for a hundred years.

No man had ever climbed these cliffs, legends said, and none but the priests knew the secret entrance into the valley. Conan did not waste time looking for it. Steeps that balked these black people, horsemen and dwellers of plain and level forest, were not impossible for a man born in the rugged hills of Cimmeria.

Now on the summit of the cliffs he looked down into the circular valley and wondered what plague, war, or superstition had driven the members of that ancient white race forth from their stronghold to mingle with and be absorbed by the black tribes that hemmed them in.

This valley had been their citadel. There the place stood, and there only the royal family and their court dwelt. The real city stood outside the cliffs. Those waving masses of green jungle vegetation hid its ruins. But the domes that glistened in the leaves below him were the unbroken pinnacles of the royal palace of Alkmeenon which had defied the corroding ages.

Swinging a leg over the rim he went down swiftly. The inner side of the cliffs was more broken, not quite so sheer. In less than half the time it had taken him to ascend the outer side, he dropped to the swarded valley floor.

With one hand on his sword, he looked alertly about him. There was no reason to suppose men lied when they said that Alkmeenon was empty and deserted, haunted only by the ghosts of the dead past. But it was Conan's nature to be suspicious and wary. The silence was primordial; not even a leaf quivered on a branch. When he bent to peer under the trees, he saw nothing but the marching rows of trunks, receding and receding into the blue gloom of the deep woods.

Nevertheless he went warily, sword in hand, his restless eyes combing the shadows from side to side, his springy tread making no sound on the sward. All about him he saw signs of an ancient civilization; marble fountains, voiceless and crumbling, stood in circles of slender trees whose patterns were too symmetrical to have been a chance of nature. Forest-growth and underbrush had invaded the evenly planned groves, but their outlines were still visible. Broad pavements ran away under the trees, broken, and with grass growing through the wide cracks. He glimpsed walls with ornamental copings, lattices of carven stone that might once have served as the walls of pleasure pavilions.

Ahead of him, through the trees, the domes gleamed and the bulk of the structure supporting them became more apparent as he advanced. Presently, pushing through a screen of vine-tangled branches, he came into a comparatively open space where the trees straggled, unencumbered by undergrowth, and saw before him the wide, pillared portico of the palace.

As he mounted the broad marble steps, he noted that the building was in far better state of preservation than the lesser structures he had glimpsed. The thick walls and massive pillars seemed too powerful to crumble before the assault of time and the elements. The same enchanted quiet brooded over all. The cat-like pad of his sandaled feet seemed startlingly loud in the stillness.

Somewhere in this palace lay the effigy or image which had in times past served as oracle for the priests of

Keshan. And somewhere in the palace, unless that indiscreet priest had babbled a lie, was hidden the treasure of the forgotten kings of Alkmeenon.

Conan passed into a broad, lofty hall, lined with tall columns, between which arches gaped, their doors long rotted away. He traversed this in a twilight dimness, and at the other end passed through great double-valved bronze doors which stood partly open, as they might have stood for centuries. He emerged into a vast domed chamber which must have served as audience hall for the kings of Alkmeenon.

It was octagonal in shape, and the great dome up to which the lofty ceiling curved obviously was cunningly pierced, for the chamber was much better lighted than the hall which led to it. At the farther side of the great room there rose a dais with broad lapis-lazuli steps leading up to it, and on that dais there stood a massive chair with ornate arms and a high back which once doubtless supported a cloth-of-gold canopy. Conan grunted explosively and his eyes lit. The golden throne of Alkmeenon, named in immemorial legendry! He weighed it with a practised eye. It represented a fortune in itself, if he were but able to bear it away. Its richness fired his imagination concerning the treasure itself, and made him burn with eagerness. His fingers itched to plunge among the gems he had heard described by story-tellers in the market squares of Keshia, who repeated tales handed down from mouth to mouth through the centuries—jewels not to be duplicated in the world, rubies, emeralds, diamonds, bloodstones, opals, sapphires, the loot of the ancient world.

He had expected to find the oracle-effigy seated on the throne, but since it was not, it was probably placed in some other part of the palace, if, indeed, such a thing really existed. But since he had turned his face toward Keshan, so many myths had proved to be realities that he did not doubt that he would find some kind of image or god.

Behind the throne there was a narrow arched doorway which doubtless had been masked by hangings in the days of Alkmeenon's life. He glanced through it and saw that it let into an alcove, empty, and with a narrow corridor leading off from it at right angles. Turning away from it, he spied another arch to the left of the dais, and it, unlike the others, was furnished with a door. Nor was it any common door. The portal was of the same rich metal as the throne, and carved with many curious arabesques.

At his touch it swung open so readily that its hinges might recently have been oiled. Inside he halted, staring.

He was in a square chamber of no great dimensions, whose marble walls rose to an ornate ceiling, inlaid with gold. Gold friezes ran about the base and the top of the walls, and there was no door other than the one through which he had entered. But he noted these details mechanically. His whole attention was centered on the shape which lay on an ivory dais before him.

He had expected an image, probably carved with the skill of a forgotten art. But no art could mimic the perfection of the figure that lay before him.

It was no effigy of stone or metal or ivory. It was the actual body of a woman, and by what dark art the ancients had preserved that form unblemished for so many ages Conan could not even guess. The very garments she wore were intact—and Conan scowled at that, a vague uneasiness stirring at the back of his mind. The arts that preserved the body should not have affected the garments. Yet there they were—gold breast-plates set with concentric circles of small gems, gilded sandals, and a short silken skirt upheld by a jeweled girdle. Neither cloth nor metal showed any signs of decay.

Yelaya was coldly beautiful, even in death. Her body was like alabaster, slender yet voluptuous; a great crimson jewel gleamed against the darkly piled foam of her hair.

Conan stood frowning down at her, and then tapped the dais with his sword. Possibilities of a hollow containing the treasure occurred to him, but the dais rang solid.

He turned and paced the chamber in some indecision. Where should he search first, in the limited time at his disposal? The priest he had overheard babbling to a courtesan had said the treasure was hidden in the palace. But that included a space of considerable vastness. He wondered if he should hide himself until the priests had come and gone, and then renew the search. But there was a strong chance that they might take the jewels with them when they returned to Keshia. For he was convinced that Thutmekri had corrupted Gorulga.

Conan could predict Thutmekri's plans, from his knowledge of the man. He knew that it had been Thutmekri who had proposed the conquest of Punt to the kings of Zembabwei, which conquest was but one move toward their real goal—the capture of the Teeth of Gwahlur. Those wary kings would demand proof that the treasure really existed before they made any move. The jewels Thutmekri asked as a pledge would furnish that proof.

With positive evidence of the treasure's reality, the kings of Zembabwei would move. Punt would be invaded simultaneously from the east and the west, but the Zembabwans would see to it that the Keshani did most of the fighting, and then, when both Punt and Keshan were exhausted from the struggle, the Zembabwans would crush both races, loot Keshan and take the treasure by force, if they had to destroy every building and torture every living human in the kingdom.

But there was always another possibility: if Thutmekri could get his hands on the hoard, it would be characteristic of the man to cheat his employers, steal the jewels for himself and decamp, leaving the Zembabwan emissaries holding the sack.

Conan believed that this consulting of the oracle was but a ruse to persuade the king of Keshan to accede to Thutmekri's wishes—for he never for a moment doubted that Gorulga was as subtle and devious as all the rest mixed up in this grand swindle. Conan had not approached the high priest himself, because in the game of bribery he would have no chance against Thutmekri, and to attempt it would be to play directly into the Stygian's hands. Gorulga could denounce the Cimmerian to the people, establish a reputation for integrity, and rid Thutmekri of his rival at one stroke. He wondered how Thutmekri had corrupted the high priest, and just what could be offered as a bribe to a man who had the greatest treasure in the world under his fingers.

At any rate he was sure that the oracle would be made to say that the gods willed it that Keshan should follow Thutmekri's wishes, and he was sure, too, that it would drop a few pointed remarks concerning himself. After that Keshia would be too hot for the Cimmerian, nor had Conan had any intention of returning when he rode away in the night.

The oracle chamber held no clue for him. He went forth into the great throne room and laid his hands on the throne. It was heavy, but he could tilt it up. The floor beneath, a thick marble dais, was solid. Again he sought the alcove. His mind clung to a secret crypt near the oracle. Painstakingly he began to tap along the walls, and presently his taps rang hollow at a spot opposite the mouth of the narrow corridor. Looking more closely he saw that the crack between the marble panel at that point and the next was wider than usual. He inserted a dagger point and pried.

Silently the panel swung open, revealing a niche in the wall, but nothing else. He swore feelingly. The aperture was empty, and it did not look as if it had ever served as a crypt for treasure. Leaning into the niche he saw a system of tiny holes in the wall, about on a level with a man's mouth. He peered through, and grunted understandingly. That was the wall that formed the partition between the alcove and the oracle chamber. Those holes had not been visible in the chamber. Conan grinned. This explained the mystery of the oracle, but it was a bit cruder than he had expected. Gorulga would plant either himself or some trusted minion in that niche, to talk through the holes, and the credulous acolytes, black men all, would accept it as the veritable voice of Yelaya.

Remembering something, the Cimmerian drew forth the roll of parchment he had taken from the mummy and unrolled it carefully, as it seemed ready to fall to pieces with age. He scowled over the dim characters with which it was covered. In his roaming about the world the giant adventurer had picked up a wide smattering of knowledge, particularly including the speaking and reading of many alien tongues. Many a sheltered scholar would have been astonished at the Cimmerian's linguistic abilities, for he had experienced many adventures where knowledge of a strange language had meant the difference between life and death.

These characters were puzzling, at once familiar and unintelligible, and presently he discovered the reason. They were the characters of archaic Pelishtic, which possessed many points of difference from the modern script, with which he was familiar, and which, three centuries ago, had been modified by conquest by a nomad tribe. This older, purer script baffled him. He made out a recurrent phrase, however, which he recognized as a proper name: Bît-Yakin. He gathered that it was the name of the writer.

Scowling, his lips unconsciously moving as he struggled with the task, he blundered through the manuscript, finding much of it untranslatable and most of the rest of it obscure.

He gathered that the writer, the mysterious Bît-Yakin, had come from afar with his servants, and entered the valley of Alkmeenon. Much that followed was meaningless, interspersed as it was with unfamiliar phrases and characters. Such as he could translate seemed to indicate the passing of a very long period of time. The name of Yelaya was repeated frequently, and toward the last part of the manuscript it became apparent that Bît-Yakin knew that death was upon him. With a slight start Conan realized that the mummy in the cavern must be the remains of the writer of the manuscript, the mysterious Pelishti, Bît-Yakin. The man had died, as he had prophesied, and his servants, obviously, had placed him in that open crypt, high up on the cliffs, according to his instructions before his death.

It was strange that Bît-Yakin was not mentioned in any of the legends of Alkmeenon. Obviously he had come to the valley after it had been deserted by the original inhabitants—the manuscript indicated as much—but it seemed peculiar that the priests who came in the old days to consult the oracle had not seen the man or his servants. Conan felt sure that the mummy and this parchment was more than a hundred years old. Bît-Yakin had dwelt in the valley when the priests came of old to bow before dead Yelaya. Yet concerning him the legends were silent, telling only of a deserted city, haunted only by the dead.

Why had the man dwelt in this desolate spot, and to what unknown destination had his servants departed after disposing of their master's corpse?

Conan shrugged his shoulders and thrust the parchment back into his girdle—he started violently, the skin on the backs of his hands tingling. Startlingly, shockingly in the slumberous stillness, there had boomed the deep strident clangor of a great gong!

He wheeled, crouching like a great cat, sword in hand, glaring down the narrow corridor from which the sound had seemed to come. Had the priests of Keshia arrived? This was improbable, he knew; they would not have had time to reach the valley. But that gong was indisputable evidence of human presence.

Conan was basically a direct-actionist. Such subtlety as he possessed had been acquired through contact with the more devious races. When taken off guard by some unexpected occurrence, he reverted instinctively to type. So now, instead of hiding or slipping away in the opposite direction as the average man might have done, he ran straight down the corridor in the direction of the sound.

His sandals made no more sound than the pads of a panther would have made; his eyes were slits, his lips unconsciously asnarl. Panic had momentarily touched his soul at the shock of that unexpected reverberation, and the red rage of the primitive that is wakened by threat of peril, always lurked close to the surface of the Cimmerian.

He emerged presently from the winding corridor into a small open court. Something glinting in the sun caught his eye. It was the gong, a great gold disk, hanging from a gold arm extending from the crumbling wall. A brass mallet lay near, but there was no sound or sight of humanity. The surrounding arches gaped emptily. Conan crouched inside the doorway for what seemed a long time. There was no sound or movement throughout the great palace. His patience exhausted at last, he glided around the curve of the court, peering into the arches, ready to leap either way like a flash of light, or to strike right or left as a cobra strikes.

He reached the gong, stared into the arch nearest it. He saw only a dim chamber, littered with the debris of decay. Beneath the gong the polished marble flags showed no footprint, but there was a scent in the air—a faintly fetid odor he could not classify; his nostrils dilated like those of a wild beast as he sought in vain to identify it.

He turned toward the arch—with appalling suddenness the seemingly solid flags splintered and gave way under his feet. Even as he fell he spread wide his arms and caught the edges of the aperture that gaped beneath him. The edges crumbled off under his clutching fingers. Down into utter darkness he shot, into black icy water that gripped him and whirled him away with breathless speed.

2.

The Cimmerian at first made no attempt to fight the current that was sweeping him through lightless night.

He kept himself afloat, gripping between his teeth the sword, which he had not relinquished, even in his fall, and did not even seek to guess to what doom he was being borne. But suddenly a beam of light lanced the darkness ahead of him. He saw the surging, seething black surface of the water, in turmoil as if disturbed by some monster of the deep, and he saw the sheer stone walls of the channel curved up to a vault overhead. On each side ran a narrow ledge, just below the arching roof, but they were far out of his reach. At one point this roof had been broken, probably fallen in, and the light was streaming through the aperture. Beyond that shaft of light was utter blackness, and panic assailed the Cimmerian as he saw he would be swept on past that spot of light, and into the unknown blackness again.

Then he saw something else: bronze ladders extended from the ledges to the water's surface at regular intervals, and there was one just ahead of him. Instantly he struck out for it, fighting the current that would have held him to the middle of the stream. It dragged at him as with tangible, animate, slimy hands, but he buffeted the rushing surge with the strength of desperation and drew closer and closer inshore, fighting furiously for every inch. Now he was even with the ladder and with a fierce, gasping plunge he gripped the bottom rung and hung on, breathless.

A few seconds later he struggled up out of the seething water, trusting his weight dubiously to the corroded rungs. They sagged and bent, but they held, and he clambered up onto the narrow ledge which ran along the wall scarcely a man's length below the curving roof. The tall Cimmerian was forced to bend his head as he stood up. A heavy bronze door showed in the stone at a point even with the head of the ladder, but it did not give to Conan's efforts. He transferred his sword from his teeth to its scabbard, spitting blood—for the edge had cut his lips in that fierce fight with the river—and turned his attention to the broken roof.

He could reach his arms up through the crevice and grip the edge, and careful testing told him it would bear his weight. An instant later he had drawn himself up through the hole, and found himself in a wide chamber, in a state of extreme disrepair. Most of the roof had fallen in, as well as a great section of the floor, which was laid over the vault of a subterranean river. Broken arches opened into other chambers and corridors, and Conan believed he was still in the great palace. He wondered uneasily how many chambers in that palace had underground water directly under them, and when the ancient flags or tiles might give way again and precipitate him back into the current from which he had just crawled.

And he wondered just how much of an accident that fall had been. Had those rotten flags simply chanced to give way beneath his weight, or was there a more sinister explanation? One thing at least was obvious: he was not the only living thing in that palace. That gong had not sounded of its own accord, whether the noise had been meant to lure him to his death, or not. The silence of the palace became suddenly sinister, fraught with crawling menace.

Could it be someone on the same mission as himself? A sudden thought occurred to him, at the memory of the mysterious Bît-Yakin. Was it not possible that this man had found the Teeth of Gwahlur in his long residence in Alkmeenon—that his servants had taken them with them when they departed? The possibility that he might be following a will-o'-the wisp infuriated the Cimmerian.

Choosing a corridor which he believed led back toward the part of the palace he had first entered, he hurried along it, stepping gingerly as he thought of that black river that seethed and foamed somewhere below his feet.

His speculations recurrently revolved about the oracle chamber and its cryptic occupant. Somewhere in that vicinity must be the clue to the mystery of the treasure, if indeed it still remained in its immemorial hiding place.

The great palace lay silent as ever, disturbed only by the swift passing of his sandaled feet. The chambers and halls he traversed were crumbling into ruin, but as he advanced the ravages of decay became less apparent. He wondered briefly for what purpose the ladders had been suspended from the ledges over the subterranean river, but dismissed the matter with a shrug. He was little interested in speculating over unremunerative problems of antiquity.

He was not sure just where the oracle chamber lay, from where he was, but presently he emerged into a corridor which led back into the great throne room under one of the arches. He had reached a decision; it was useless for him to wander aimlessly about the palace, seeking the hoard. He would conceal himself somewhere here, wait until the Keshani priests came, and then, after they had gone through the farce of consulting the oracle, he would follow them to the hiding place of the gems, to which he was certain they would go. Perhaps they would take only a few of the jewels with them. He would content himself with the rest.

Drawn by a morbid fascination, he re-entered the oracle chamber and stared down again at the motionless figure of the princess who was worshipped as a goddess, entranced by her frigid beauty. What cryptic secret was locked in that marvelously molded form?

He started violently. The breath sucked through his teeth, the short hairs prickled at the back of his scalp. The body still lay as he had first seen it, silent, motionless, in breast-plates of jeweled gold, gilded sandals and silken skirt. But now there was a subtle difference. The lissom limbs were not rigid, a peach-bloom touched the cheeks, the lips were red—

With a panicky curse Conan ripped out his sword.

'Crom! She's alive!'

At his words the long dark lashes lifted; the eyes opened and gazed up at him inscrutably, dark, lustrous, mystical. He glared in frozen speechlessness.

She sat up with a supple ease, still holding his ensorcelled stare.

He licked his dry lips and found voice.

'You—are—are you Yelaya?' he stammered.

'I am Yelaya!' The voice was rich and musical, and he stared with new wonder. 'Do not fear. I will not harm you if you do my bidding.'

'How can a dead woman come to life after all these centuries?' he demanded, as if skeptical of what his senses told him. A curious gleam was beginning to smolder in his eyes.

She lifted her arms in a mystical gesture.

'I am a goddess. A thousand years ago there descended upon me the curse of the greater gods, the gods of darkness beyond the borders of light. The mortal in me died; the goddess in me could never die. Here I have lain for so many centuries, to awaken each night at sunset and hold my court as of yore, with specters drawn from the shadows of the past. Man, if you would not view that which will blast your soul for ever, get hence quickly! I command you! Go!' The voice became imperious, and her slender arm lifted and pointed.

Conan, his eyes burning slits, slowly sheathed his sword, but he did not obey her order. He stepped closer, as if impelled by a powerful fascination—without the slightest warning he grabbed her up in a bear-like grasp. She screamed a very ungoddess-like scream, and there was a sound of ripping silk, as with one ruthless wrench he tore off her skirt.

'Goddess! Ha!' His bark was full of angry contempt. He ignored the frantic writhings of his captive. 'I thought it was strange that a princess of Alkmeenon would speak with a Corinthian accent! As soon as I'd gathered my wits I knew I'd seen you somewhere. You're Muriela, Zargheba's Corinthian dancing girl. This crescent-shaped

birthmark on your hip proves it. I saw it once when
Zargheba was whipping you. Goddess! Bah!' He smacked
the betraying hip contemptuously and resoundingly with
his open hand, and the girl yelped piteously.

All her imperiousness had gone out of her. She was no
longer a mystical figure of antiquity, but a terrified and
humiliated dancing girl, such as can be bought at almost
any Shemitish market place. She lifted up her voice and
wept unashamedly. Her captor glared down at her with
angry triumph.

'Goddess! Ha! So you were one of the veiled women
Zargheba brought to Keshia with him. Did you think you
could fool me, you little idiot? A year ago I saw you in
Akbitana with that swine, Zargheba, and I don't forget
faces—or women's figures. I think I'll—'

Squirming about in his grasp she threw her slender
arms about his massive neck in an abandon of terror;
tears coursed down her cheeks, and her sobs quivered
with a note of hysteria.

'Oh, please don't hurt me! Don't! I had to do it!
Zargheba brought me here to act as the oracle!'

'Why, you sacrilegious little hussy!' rumbled Conan.
'Do you not fear the gods? Crom! is there no honesty
anywhere?'

'Oh, please!' she begged, quivering with abject fright.
'I couldn't disobey Zargheba. Oh, what shall I do? I shall
be cursed by these heathen gods!'

'What do you think the priests will do to you if they
find out you're an impostor?' he demanded.

At the thought her legs refused to support her, and she
collapsed in a shuddering heap, clasping Conan's knees
and mingling incoherent pleas for mercy and protection
with piteous protestations of her innocence of any malign
intention. It was a vivid change from her pose as the
ancient princess, but not surprising. The fear that had
nerved her then was now her undoing.

'Where is Zargheba?' he demanded. 'Stop yammering,
damn it, and answer me.'

'Outside the palace,' she whimpered, 'watching for the priests.'

'How many men with him?'

'None. We came alone.'

'Ha!' It was much like the satisfied grunt of a hunting lion. 'You must have left Keshia a few hours after I did. Did you climb the cliffs?'

She shook her head, too choked with tears to speak coherently. With an impatient imprecation he seized her slim shoulders and shook her until she gasped for breath.

'Will you quit that blubbering and answer me? How did you get into the valley?'

'Zargheba knew the secret way,' she gasped. 'The priest Gwarunga told him, and Thutmekri. On the south side of the valley there is a broad pool lying at the foot of the cliffs. There is a cave-mouth under the surface of the water that is not visible to the casual glance. We ducked under the water and entered it. The cave slopes up out of the water swiftly and leads through the cliffs. The opening on the side of the valley is masked by heavy thickets.'

'I climbed the cliffs on the east side,' he muttered. 'Well, what then?'

'We came to the palace and Zargheba hid me among the trees while he went to look for the chamber of the oracle. I do not think he fully trusted Gwarunga. While he was gone I thought I heard a gong sound, but I was not sure. Presently Zargheba came and took me into the palace and brought me to this chamber, where the goddess Yelaya lay upon the dais. He stripped the body and clothed me in the garments and ornaments. Then he went forth to hide the body and watch for the priests. I have been afraid. When you entered I wanted to leap up and beg you to take me away from this place, but I feared Zargheba. When you discovered I was alive, I thought I could frighten you away.'

'What were you to say as the oracle?' he asked.

'I was to bid the priests to take the Teeth of Gwahlur and give some of them to Thutmekri as a pledge, as he desired, and place the rest in the palace at Keshia. I was to tell them that an awful doom threatened Keshan if they did not agree to Thutmekri's proposals. And, oh, yes, I was to tell them that you were to be skinned alive immediately.'

'Thutmekri wanted the treasure where he—or the Zembabwans—could lay hand on it easily,' muttered Conan, disregarding the remark concerning himself. 'I'll carve his liver yet—Gorulga is a party to this swindle, of course?'

'No. He believes in his gods, and is incorruptible. He knows nothing about this. He will obey the oracle. It was all Thutmekri's plan. Knowing the Keshani would consult the oracle, he had Zargheba bring me with the embassy from Zembabwei, closely veiled and secluded.'

'Well, I'm damned!' muttered Conan. 'A priest who honestly believes in his oracle, and can not be bribed. Crom! I wonder if it was Zargheba who banged that gong. Did he know I was here? Could he have known about that rotten flogging? Where is he now, girl?'

'Hiding in a thicket of lotus trees, near the ancient avenue that leads from the south wall of the cliffs to the palace,' she answered. Then she renewed her importunities. 'Oh, Conan, have pity on me! I am afraid of this evil, ancient place. I know I have heard stealthy footfalls padding about me—oh, Conan, take me away with you! Zargheba will kill me when I have served his purpose here—I know it! The priests, too, will kill me if they discover my deceit.

'He is a devil—he bought me from a slave-trader who stole me out of a caravan bound through southern Koth, and has made me the tool of his intrigues ever since. Take me away from him! You can not be as cruel as he. Don't leave me to be slain here! Please! Please!'

She was on her knees, clutching at Conan hysterically, her beautiful tear-stained face upturned to him, her dark silken hair flowing in disorder over her white shoulders. Conan picked her up and set her on his knee.

'Listen to me. I'll protect you from Zargheba. The priests shall not know of your perfidy. But you've got to do as I tell you.'

She faltered promises of explicit obedience, clasping his corded neck as if seeking security from the contact.

'Good. When the priests come, you'll act the part of Yelaya, as Zargheba planned—it'll be dark, and in the torchlight they'll never know the difference. But you'll say this to them: "It is the will of the gods that the Stygian and his Shemitish dogs be driven from Keshan. They are thieves and traitors who plot to rob the gods. Let the Teeth of Gwahlur be placed in the care of the general Conan. Let him lead the armies of Keshan. He is beloved of the gods."'

She shivered, with an expression of desperation, but acquiesced.

'But Zargheba?' she cried. 'He'll kill me!'

'Don't worry about Zargheba,' he grunted. 'I'll take care of that dog. You do as I say. Here, put up your hair again. It's fallen all over your shoulders. And the gem's fallen out of it.'

He replaced the great glowing gem himself, nodding approval.

'It's worth a roomful of slaves, itself alone. Here, put your skirt back on. It's torn down the side, but the priests will never notice it. Wipe your face. A goddess doesn't cry like a whipped schoolgirl. By Crom, you *do* look like Yelaya, face, hair, figure and all! If you act the goddess with the priests as well as you did with me, you'll fool them easily.'

'I'll try,' she shivered.

'Good; I'm going to find Zargheba.'

At that she became panicky again.

'No! Don't leave me alone! This place is haunted!'

'There's nothing here to harm you,' he assured her impatiently. 'Nothing but Zargheba, and I'm going to look after him. I'll be back shortly. I'll be watching from close by in case anything goes wrong during the ceremony; but if you play your part properly, nothing will go wrong.'

And turning, he hastened out of the oracle chamber; behind him Muriela squeaked wretchedly at his going.

Twilight had fallen. The great rooms and halls were shadowy and indistinct; copper friezes glinted dully through the dusk. Conan strode like a silent phantom through the great halls, with a sensation of being stared at from the shadowed recesses by invisible ghosts of the past. No wonder the girl was nervous amid such surroundings.

He glided down the marble steps like a slinking panther, sword in hand. Silence reigned over the valley, and above the rim of the cliffs, stars were blinking out. If the priests of Keshia had entered the valley there was not a sound, not a movement in the greenery to betray them. He made out the ancient broken-paved avenue, wandering away to the south, lost amid clustering masses of fronds and thick-leaved bushes. He followed it warily, hugging the edge of the paving where the shrubs massed their shadows thickly, until he saw ahead of him, dimly in the dusk, the clump of lotus-trees, the strange growth peculiar to the black lands of Kush. There, according to the girl, Zargheba should be lurking. Conan became stealth personified. A velvet-footed shadow, he melted into the thickets.

He approached the lotus grove by a circuitous movement, and scarcely the rustle of a leaf proclaimed his passing. At the edge of the trees he halted suddenly, crouched like a suspicious panther among the deep shrubs. Ahead of him, among the dense leaves, showed a pallid oval, dim in the uncertain light. It might have been one of the great white blossoms which shone thickly among the branches. But Conan knew that it was a man's face. And it was turned toward him. He shrank quickly deeper into the shadows. Had Zargheba seen him? The man was looking directly toward him. Seconds passed. That dim face had not moved. Conan could make out the dark tuft below that was the short black beard.

And suddenly Conan was aware of something unnatural. Zargheba, he knew, was not a tall man. Standing erect, his head would scarcely top the Cimmerian's shoulder; yet that face was on a level with Conan's own. Was the man standing on something? Conan bent and peered toward the ground below the spot where the face showed, but his vision was blocked by undergrowth and the thick boles of the trees. But he saw something else, and he stiffened. Through a slot in the underbrush he glimpsed the stem of the tree under which, apparently, Zargheba was standing. The face was directly in line with that tree. He should have seen below that face, not the tree-trunk, but Zargheba's body—but there was no body there.

Suddenly tenser than a tiger who stalks his prey, Conan glided deeper into the thicket, and a moment later drew aside a leafy branch and glared at the face that had not moved. Nor would it ever move again, of its own volition. He looked on Zargheba's severed head, suspended from the branch of the tree by its own long black hair.

3.

Conan wheeled supplely, sweeping the shadows with a fiercely questing stare. There was no sign of the murdered man's body; only yonder the tall lush grass was trampled and broken down and the sward was dabbled darkly and wetly. Conan stood scarcely breathing as he strained his ears into the silence. The trees and bushes with their great pallid blossoms stood dark, still, and sinister, etched against the deepening dusk.

Primitive fears whispered at the back of Conan's mind. Was this the work of the priests of Keshan? If so, where were they? Was it Zargheba, after all, who had struck the gong? Again there rose the memory of Bît-Yakin and his mysterious servants. Bît-Yakin was dead, shriveled to a hulk of wrinkled leather and bound in his hollowed crypt to greet the rising sun for ever. But the servants of

Bît-Yakin were unaccounted for. *There was no proof they had ever left the valley.*

Conan thought of the girl, Muriela, alone and unguarded in that great shadowy palace. He wheeled and ran back down the shadowed avenue, and he ran as a suspicious panther runs, poised even in full stride to whirl right or left and strike death blows.

The palace loomed through the trees, and he saw something else—the glow of fire reflecting redly from the polished marble. He melted into the bushes that lined the broken street, glided through the dense growth and reached the edge of the open space before the portico. Voices reached him; torches bobbed and their flare shone on glossy ebon shoulders. The priests of Keshan had come.

They had not advanced up the wide, overgrown avenue as Zargheba had expected them to do. Obviously there was more than one secret way into the valley of Alkmeenon.

They were filing up the broad marble steps, holding their torches high. He saw Gorulga at the head of the parade, a profile chiseled out of copper, etched in the torch glare. The rest were acolytes, giant black men from whose skins the torches struck highlights. At the end of the procession there stalked a huge Negro with an unusually wicked cast of countenance, at the sight of whom Conan scowled. That was Gwarunga, whom Muriela had named as the man who had revealed the secret of the pool-entrance to Zargheba. Conan wondered how deeply the man was in the intrigues of the Stygian.

He hurried toward the portico, circling the open space to keep in the fringing shadows. They left no one to guard the entrance. The torches streamed steadily down the long dark hall. Before they reached the double-valved door at the other end, Conan had mounted the outer steps and was in the hall behind them. Slinking swiftly along the column-lined wall, he reached the great door as they crossed the huge throne room, their torches driving back the shadows. They did not look back. In single file, their ostrich plumes nodding, their leopardskin tunics contrasting curiously with the marble and arabesqued metal of the ancient palace, they moved across the wide room and halted momentarily at the golden door to the left of the throne-dais.

Gorulga's voice boomed eerily and hollowly in the great empty space, framed in sonorous phrases unintelligible to the lurking listener; then the high priest thrust open the golden door and entered, bowing repeatedly from his waist, and behind him the torches sank and rose, showering flakes of flame, as the worshippers imitated their master. The gold door closed behind them, shutting out sound and sight, and Conan darted across the throne-chamber and into the alcove behind the throne. He made less sound than a wind blowing across the chamber.

Tiny beams of light streamed through the apertures in the wall, as he pried open the secret panel. Gliding into the niche, he peered through. Muriela sat upright on the dais, her arms folded, her head leaning back against the wall, within a few inches of his eyes. The delicate perfume of her foamy hair was in his nostrils. He could not see her face, of course, but her attitude was as if she gazed tranquilly into some far gulf of space, over and beyond the shaven heads of the black giants who knelt before her. Conan grinned with appreciation. 'The little slut's an actress,' he told himself. He knew she was shriveling with terror, but she showed no sign. In the uncertain flare of the torches she looked exactly like the goddess he had seen lying on that same dais, if one could imagine that goddess imbued with vibrant life.

Gorulga was booming forth some kind of a chant in an accent unfamiliar to Conan, and which was probably some invocation in the ancient tongue of Alkmeenon, handed down from generation to generation of high priests. It seemed interminable. Conan grew restless. The longer the thing lasted, the more terrific would be the strain on Muriela. If she snapped—he hitched his sword and dagger forward. He could not see the little trollop tortured and slain by black men.

But the chant—deep, low-pitched and indescribably ominous—came to a conclusion at last, and a shouted acclaim from the acolytes marked its period. Lifting his head and raising his arms toward the silent form on the dais, Gorulga cried in the deep, rich resonance that was the natural attribute of the Keshani priests: 'O great goddess, dweller with the great one of darkness, let thy heart be melted, thy lips opened for the ears of thy slave whose head is in the dust beneath they feet! Speak, great goddess of the holy valley! Thou knowest the paths before us; the darkness that vexes us is as the light of the midday sun to thee. Shed the radiance of thy wisdom on the paths of thy servants! Tell us, O mouthpiece of the gods: what is their will concerning Thutmekri the Stygian?'

The high-piled burnished mass of hair that caught the torchlight in dull bronze gleams quivered slightly. A gusty sigh rose from the blacks, half in awe, half in fear. Muriela's voice came plainly to Conan's ears in the breathless silence, and it seemed cold, detached, impersonal, though he winced at the Corinthian accent.

'It is the will of the gods that the Stygian and his Shemitish dogs be driven from Keshan!' She was repeating his exact words. 'They are thieves and traitors who plot to rob the gods. Let the Teeth of Gwahlur be placed in the care of the general Conan. Let him lead the armies of Keshan. He is beloved of the gods!'

There was a quiver in her voice as she ended, and Conan began to sweat, believing she was on the point of an hysterical collapse. But the blacks did not notice, any more than they identified the Corinthian accent, of which they knew nothing. They smote their palms softly together and a murmur of wonder and awe rose from them. Gorulga's eyes glittered fanatically in the torchlight.

'Yelaya has spoken!' he cried in an exalted voice. 'It is the will of the gods! Long ago, in the days of our ancestors, they were made taboo and hidden at the command of the gods, who wrenched them from the awful jaws of Gwahlur the king of darkness, in the birth of the world. At the command of the gods the Teeth of Gwahlur were hidden; at their command they shall be brought forth again. O star-born goddess, give us your leave to go to the secret hiding-place of the Teeth to secure them for him whom the gods love!'

'You have my leave to go!' answered the false goddess, with an imperious gesture of dismissal that set Conan grinning again, and the priests backed out, ostrich plumes and torches rising and falling with the rhythm of their genuflexions.

The gold door closed and with a moan, the goddess fell back limply on the dais. 'Conan!' she whimpered faintly. 'Conan!'

'Shhh!' he hissed through the apertures, and turning, glided from the niche and closed the panel. A glimpse past the jamb of the carven door showed him the torches receding across the great throne room, but he was at the same time aware of a radiance that did not emanate from the torches. He was startled, but the solution presented itself instantly. An early moon has risen and its light slanted through the pierced dome which by some curious workmanship intensified the light. The shining dome of Alkmeenon was no fable, then. Perhaps its interior was of the curious whitely flaming crystal found only in the hills of the black countries. The light flooded the throne room and seeped into the chambers immediately adjoining.

But as Conan made toward the door that led into the throne room, he was brought around suddenly by a noise that seemed to emanate from the passage that led off the alcove. He crouched at the mouth, staring into it, remembering the clangor of the gong that had echoed from it to lure him into a snare. The light from the dome filtered only a little way into that narrow corridor, and showed him only empty space. Yet he could have sworn that he had heard the furtive pad of a foot somewhere down it.

While he hesitated, he was electrified by a woman's strangled cry from behind him. Bounding through the door behind the throne, he saw an unexpected spectacle, in the crystal light.

The torches of the priests had vanished from the great hall outside—but one priest was still in the palace: Gwarunga. His wicked features were convulsed with fury, and he grasped the terrified Muriela by the throat, choking her efforts to scream and plead, shaking her brutally.

'Traitress!' Between his thick red lips his voice hissed like a cobra. 'What game are you playing? Did not Zargheba tell you what to say? Aye, Thutmekri told me! Are you betraying your master, or is he betraying his friends through you? Slut! I'll twist off your false head—but first I'll—'

A widening of his captive's lovely eyes as she stared over his shoulder warned the huge black. He released her and wheeled, just as Conan's sword lashed down. The impact of the stroke knocked him headlong backward to the marble floor, where he lay twitching, blood oozing from a ragged gash in his scalp.

Conan started toward him to finish the job—for he knew that the black's sudden movement had caused the blade to strike flat—but Muriela threw her arms convulsively about him.

'I've done as you ordered!' she gasped hysterically. 'Take me away! Oh, please take me away!'

'We can't go yet,' he grunted. 'I want to follow the priests and see where they get the jewels. There may be more loot hidden there. But you can go with me. Where's that gem you wore in your hair?'

'It must have fallen out on the dais,' she stammered, feeling for it. 'I was so frightened—when the priests left I ran out to find you, and this big brute had stayed behind, and he grabbed me—'

'Well, go get it while I dispose of this carcass,' he commanded. 'Go on! That gem is worth a fortune itself.'

She hesitated, as if loth to return to that cryptic chamber; then, as he grasped Gwarunga's girdle and dragged him into the alcove, she turned and entered the oracle room.

Conan dumped the senseless black on the floor, and lifted his sword. The Cimmerian had lived too long in the wild places of the world to have any illusions about mercy. The only safe enemy was a headless enemy. But before he could strike, a startling scream checked the lifted blade. It came from the oracle chamber.

'Conan! Conan! *She's come back!*' The shriek ended in a gurgle and a scraping shuffle.

With an oath Conan dashed out of the alcove, across the throne dais and into the oracle chamber, almost before the sound had ceased. There he halted, glaring bewilderedly. To all appearances Muriela lay placidly on the dais, eyes closed as if in slumber.

'What in thunder are you doing?' he demanded acidly. 'Is this any time to be playing jokes—'

His voice trailed away. His gaze ran along the ivory thigh molded in the close-fitting silk skirt. That skirt should gape from girdle to hem. He knew, because it had been his own hand that tore it, as he ruthlessly stripped the garment from the dancer's writhing body. But the skirt showed no rent. A single stride brought him to the dais and he laid his hand on the ivory body—snatched it away as if it had encountered hot iron instead of the cold immobility of death.

'Crom!' he muttered, his eyes suddenly slits of balefire. 'It's not Muriela! It's Yelaya!'

He understood now that frantic scream that had burst from Muriela's lips when she entered the chamber. The goddess had returned. The body had been stripped by Zargheba to furnish the accouterments for the pretender.

Yet now it was clad in silk and jewels as Conan had first seen it. A peculiar prickling made itself manifest among the short hairs at the base of Conan's scalp.

'Muriela!' he shouted suddenly. '*Muriela!* Where the devil are you?'

The walls threw back his voice mockingly. There was no entrance that he could see except the golden door, and none could have entered or departed through that without his knowledge. This much was indisputable: Yelaya had been replaced on the dais within the few minutes that had elapsed since Muriela had first left the chamber to be seized by Gwarunga; his ears were still tingling with the echoes of Muriela's scream, yet the Corinthian girl had vanished as if into thin air. There was but one explanation, if he rejected the darker speculation that suggested the supernatural—somewhere in the chamber there was a secret door. And even as the thought crossed his mind, he saw it.

In what had seemed a curtain of solid marble, a thin perpendicular crack showed and in the crack hung a wisp of silk. In an instant he was bending over it. That shred was from Muriela's torn skirt. The implication was unmistakable. It had been caught in the closing door and torn off as she was borne through the opening by whatever grim beings were her captors. The bit of clothing had prevented the door from fitting perfectly into its frame.

Thrusting his dagger-point into the crack, Conan exerted leverage with a corded forearm. The blade bent, but it was of unbreakable Akbitanan steel. The marble door opened. Conan's sword was lifted as he peered into the aperture beyond, but he saw no shape of menace. Light filtering into the oracle chamber revealed a short flight of steps cut out of marble. Pulling the door back to is fullest extent, he drove his dagger into a crack in the floor, propping it open. Then he went down the steps without hesitation. He saw nothing, heard nothing. A dozen steps down, the stair ended in a narrow corridor which ran straight away into gloom.

He halted suddenly, posed like a statue at the foot
of the stair, staring at the paintings which frescoed the
walls, half visible in the dim light which filtered down
from above. The art was unmistakably Pelishti; he had
seen frescoes of identical characteristics on the walls of
Asgalun. But the scenes depicted had no connection
with anything Pelishti, except for one human figure, frequently recurrent: a lean, white-bearded old man whose
racial characteristics were unmistakable. They seemed to
represent various sections of the palace above. Several
scenes showed a chamber he recognized as the oracle
chamber with the figure of Yelaya stretched upon the
ivory dais and huge black men kneeling before it. And
there behind the wall, in the niche, lurked the ancient
Pelishti. And there were other figures, too—figures that
moved through the deserted palace, did the bidding of
the Pelishti, and dragged unnamable things out of the
subterranean river. In the few seconds Conan stood
frozen, hitherto unintelligible phrases in the parchment
manuscript blazed in his brain with chilling clarity. The
loose bits of the pattern clicked into place. The mystery
of Bît-Yakin was a mystery no longer, nor the riddle of
Bît-Yakin's servants.

Conan turned and peered into the darkness, an icy
finger crawling along his spine. Then he went along
the corridor, cat-footed, and without hesitation, moving
deeper and deeper into the darkness as he drew farther
away from the stair. The air hung heavy with the odor he
had scented in the court of the gong.

Now in utter blackness he heard a sound ahead of
him—the shuffle of bare feet, or the swish of loose
garments against stone, he could not tell which. But an
instant later his outstretched hand encountered a barrier
which he identified as a massive door of carved metal.
He pushed against it fruitlessly, and his sword-point
sought vainly for a crack. It fitted into the sill and
jambs as if molded there. He exerted all his strength,
his feet straining against the floor, the veins knotting in

his temples. It was useless; a charge of elephants would scarcely have shaken that titanic portal.

As he leaned there he caught a sound on the other side that his ears instantly identified—it was the creak of rusty iron, like a lever scraping in its slot. Instinctively action followed recognition so spontaneously that sound, impulse and action were practically simultaneous. And as his prodigious bound carried him backward, there was the rush of a great bulk from above, and a thunderous crash filled the tunnel with deafening vibrations. Bits of flying splinters struck him—a huge block of stone, he knew from the sound, dropped on the spot he had just quitted. An instant's slower thought or action and it would have crushed him like an ant.

Conan fell back. Somewhere on the other side of that metal door Muriela was a captive, if she still lived. But he could not pass that door, and if he remained in the tunnel another block might fall, and he might not be so lucky. It would do the girl no good for him to be crushed into a purple pulp. He could not continue his search in that direction. He must get above ground and look for some other avenue of approach.

He turned and hurried toward the stair, sighing as he emerged into comparative radiance. And as he set foot on the first step, the light was blotted out, and above him the marble door rushed shut with a resounding reverberation.

Something like panic seized the Cimmerian then, trapped in that black tunnel, and he wheeled on the stair, lifting his sword and glaring murderously into the darkness behind him, expecting a rush of ghoulish assailants. But there was no sound or movement down the tunnel. Did the men beyond the door—if they *were* men—believe that he had been disposed of by the fall of the stone from the roof, which had undoubtedly been released by some sort of machinery?

Then why had the door been shut above him? Abandoning speculation, Conan groped his way up the steps, his skin crawling in anticipation of a knife in his back at every stride, yearning to drown his semi-panic in a barbarous burst of bloodletting.

He thrust against the door at the top, and cursed soulfully to find that it did not give to his efforts. Then as he lifted his sword with his right hand to hew at the marble, his groping left encountered a metal bolt that evidently slipped into place at the closing of the door. In an instant he had drawn this bolt, and then the door gave to his shove. He bounded into the chamber like a slit-eyed, snarling incarnation of fury, ferociously desirous to come to grips with whatever enemy was hounding him.

The dagger was gone from the door. The chamber was empty, and so was the dais. Yelaya had again vanished.

'By Crom!' muttered the Cimmerian. 'Is she alive, after all?'

He strode out into the throne room, baffled, and then, struck by a sudden thought, stepped behind the throne and peered into the alcove. There was blood on the smooth marble where he had cast down the senseless body of Gwarunga—that was all. The black man had vanished as completely as Yelaya.

4.

Baffled wrath confused the brain of Conan the Cimmerian. He knew no more how to go about searching for Muriela than he had known how to go about searching for the Teeth of Gwahlur. Only one thought occurred to him—to follow the priests. Perhaps at the hiding-place of the treasure some clue would be revealed to him. It was a slim chance, but better than wandering about aimlessly.

As he hurried through the great shadowy hall that led to the portico he half expected the lurking shadows to come to life behind him with rending fangs and talons. But only the beat of his own rapid heart accompanied him into the moonlight that dappled the shimmering marble.

At the foot of the wide steps he cast about in the bright moonlight for some sign to show him the direction he must go. And he found it—petals scattered on the sward told where an arm or garment had brushed against a blossom-laden branch. Grass had been pressed down under heavy feet. Conan, who had tracked wolves in his native hills, found no insurmountable difficulty in following the trail of the Keshani priests.

It led away from the palace, through masses of exotic-scented shrubbery where great pale blossoms spread their shimmering petals, through verdant, tangled bushes that showered blooms at the touch, until he came at last to a great mass of rock that jutted like a titan's castle out from the cliffs at a point closest to the palace, which, however, was almost hidden from view by vine-interlaced trees. Evidently that babbling priest in Keshia had been mistaken when he said the Teeth were hidden in the palace. This trail had led him away from the place where Muriela had disappeared, but a belief was growing in Conan that each part of the valley was connected with that palace by subterranean passages.

Crouching in the deep velvet-black shadows of the bushes, he scrutinized the great jut of rock which stood out in bold relief in the moonlight. It was covered with strange, grotesque carvings, depicting men and animals, and half-bestial creatures that might have been gods or devils. The style of art differed so strikingly from that of the rest of the valley, that Conan wondered if it did not represent a different era and race, and was itself a relic of an age lost and forgotten at whatever immeasurably distant date the people of Alkmeenon had found and entered the haunted valley.

A great door stood open in the sheer curtain of the cliff, and a gigantic dragon's head was carved about it so that the open door was like the dragon's gaping mouth. The door itself was of carved bronze and looked to weigh

several tons. There was no lock that he could see, but
a series of bolts showing along the edge of the massive
portal, as it stood open, told him that there was some
system of locking and unlocking—a system doubtless
known only to the priests of Keshan.

The trail showed that Gorulga and his henchmen had
gone through that door. But Conan hesitated. To wait
until they emerged would probably mean to see the
door locked in his face, and he might not be able to
solve the mystery of its unlocking. On the other hand,
if he followed them in, they might emerge and lock
him in the cavern.

Throwing caution to the winds, he glided through the
great portal. Somewhere in the cavern were the priests,
the Teeth of Gwahlur, and perhaps a clue to the fate
of Muriela. Personal risks had never yet deterred him
from any purpose.

Moonlight illumined, for a few yards, the wide tunnel
in which he found himself. Somewhere ahead of him
he saw a faint glow and heard the echo of a weird
chanting. The priests were not so far ahead of him
as he had thought. The tunnel debouched into a wide
room before the moonlight played out, an empty cavern
of no great dimensions, but with a lofty, vaulted roof,
glowing with a phosphorescent encrustation, which, as
Conan knew, was a common phenomenon in that part
of the world. It made a ghostly half-light, in which he
was able to see a bestial image squatting on a shrine,
and the black mouths of six or seven tunnels leading off
from the chamber. Down the widest of these—the one
directly behind the squat image which looked toward the
outer opening—he caught the gleam of torches wavering,
whereas the phosphorescent glow was fixed, and heard
the chanting increase in volume.

Down it he went recklessly, and was presently peering
into a larger cavern than the one he had just left. There
was no phosphorus here, but the light of the torches
fell on a larger altar and a more obscene and repulsive

god squatting toad-like upon it. Before this repugnant
deity Gorulga and his ten acolytes knelt and beat their
heads upon the ground, while chanting monotonously.
Conan realized why their progress had been so slow.
Evidently approaching the secret crypt of the Teeth was
a complicated and elaborate ritual.

He was fidgeting in nervous impatience before the
chanting and bowing were over, but presently they rose
and passed into the tunnel which opened behind the idol.
Their torches bobbed away into the nighted vault, and he
followed swiftly. Not much danger of being discovered.
He glided along the shadows like a creature of the night,
and the black priests were completely engrossed in their
ceremonial mummery. Apparently they had not even
noticed the absence of Gwarunga.

Emerging into a cavern of huge proportions, about
whose upward curving walls gallery-like ledges marched
in tiers, they began their worship anew before an altar
which was larger, and a god which was more disgusting,
than any encountered thus far.

Conan crouched in the black mouth of the tunnel,
staring at the walls reflecting the lurid glow of the torches.
He saw a carven stone stair winding up from tier to tier of
the galleries; the roof was lost in darkness.

He started violently and the chanting broke off as
the kneeling blacks flung up their heads. An inhuman
voice boomed out high above them. They froze on their
knees, their faces turned upward with a ghastly blue hue
in the sudden glare of a weird light that burst blindingly
up near the lofty roof and then burned with a throbbing
glow. That glare lighted a gallery and a cry went up from
the high priest, echoed shudderingly by his acolytes. In
the flash there had been briefly disclosed to them a slim
white figure standing upright in a sheen of silk and a
glint of jewel-crusted gold. Then the blaze smoldered
to a throbbing, pulsing luminosity in which nothing
was distinct, and that slim shape was but a shimmering
blur of ivory.

'*Yelaya!*' screamed Gorulga, his brown features ashen. 'Why have you followed us? What is your pleasure?'

That weird unhuman voice rolled down from the roof, reechoing under that arching vault that magnified and altered it beyond recognition.

'Woe to the unbelievers! Woe to the false children of Keshia! Doom to them which deny their deity!'

A cry of horror went up from the priests. Gorulga looked like a shocked vulture in the glare of the torches.

'I do not understand!' he stammered. 'We are faithful. In the chamber of the oracle you told us—'

'Do not heed what you heard in the chamber of the oracle!' rolled that terrible voice, multiplied until it was as though a myriad voices thundered and muttered the same warning. 'Beware of false prophets and false gods! A demon in my guise spoke to you in the palace, giving false prophecy. Now harken and obey, for only I am the true goddess, and I give you one chance to save yourselves from doom!

'Take the Teeth of Gwahlur from the crypt where they were placed so long ago. Alkmeenon is no longer holy, because it has been desecrated by blasphemers. Give the Teeth of Gwahlur into the hands of Thutmekri, the Stygian, to place in the sanctuary of Dagon and Derketo. Only this can save Keshan from the doom the demons of the night have plotted. Take the Teeth of Gwahlur and go; return instantly to Keshia; there give the jewels to Thutmekri, and seize the foreign devil Conan and flay him alive in the great square.'

There was no hesitation in obeying. Chattering with fear the priests scrambled up and ran for the door that opened behind the bestial god. Gorulga led the flight. They jammed briefly in the doorway, yelping as wildly waving torches touched squirming black bodies; they plunged through, and the patter of their speeding feet dwindled down the tunnel.

Conan did not follow. He was consumed with a furious desire to learn the truth of this fantastic affair. Was that indeed Yelaya, as the cold sweat on the backs of his hands told him, or was it that little hussy Muriela, turned traitress after all? If it was—

Before the last torch had vanished down the black tunnel he was bounding vengefully up the stone stair. The blue glow was dying down, but he could still make out that the ivory figure stood motionless on the gallery. His blood ran cold as he approached it, but he did not hesitate. He came on with his sword lifted, and towered like a threat of death over the inscrutable shape.

'Yelaya!' he snarled. 'Dead as she's been for a thousand years! *Ha!*'

From the dark mouth of a tunnel behind him a dark form lunged. But the sudden, deadly rush of unshod feet had reached the Cimmerian's quick ears. He whirled like a cat and dodged the blow aimed murderously at his back. As the gleaming steel in the dark hand hissed past him, he struck back with the fury of a roused python, and the long straight blade impaled his assailant and stood out a foot and a half between his shoulders.

'So!' Conan tore his sword free as the victim sagged to the floor, gasping and gurgling. The man writhed briefly and stiffened. In the dying light Conan saw a black body and ebon countenance, hideous in the blue glare. He had killed Gwarunga.

Conan turned from the corpse to the goddess. Thongs about her knees and breast held her upright against a stone pillar, and her thick hair, fastened to the column, held her head up. At a few yards' distance these bonds were not visible in the uncertain light.

'He must have come to after I descended into the tunnel,' muttered Conan. 'He must have suspected I was down there. So he pulled out the dagger'—Conan stooped and wrenched the identical weapon from the stiffening fingers, glanced at it and replaced it in his own girdle—'and shut the door. Then he took Yelaya to befool his brother idiots. That was he shouting a while ago. You couldn't recognize his voice, under this echoing roof. And that bursting blue flame—I thought it looked familiar. It's a trick of the Stygian priests. Thutmekri must have given some of it to Gwarunga.'

The man could easily have reached the cavern ahead of his companions. Evidently familiar with the plan of the caverns by hearsay or by maps handed down in the priest-craft, he had entered the cave after the others, carrying the goddess, followed a circuitous route through the tunnels and chambers, and ensconced himself and his burden on the balcony while Gorulga and the other acolytes were engaged in their endless rituals.

The blue glare had faded, but now Conan was aware of another glow, emanating from the mouth of one of the corridors that opened on the ledge. Somewhere down that corridor there was another field of phosphorus, for he recognized the faint steady radiance. The corridor led in the direction the priests had taken, and he decided to follow it, rather than descend into the darkness of the great cavern below. Doubtless it connected with another gallery in some other chamber, which might be the destination of the priests. He hurried down it, the illumination growing stronger as he advanced, until he could make out the floor and the walls of the tunnel. Ahead of him and below he could hear the priests chanting again.

Abruptly a doorway in the left-hand wall was limned in the phosphorous glow, and to his ears came the sound of soft, hysterical sobbing. He wheeled, and glared through the door.

He was looking again into a chamber hewn out of solid rock, not a natural cavern like the others. The domed roof shone with the phosphorous light, and the walls were almost covered with arabesques of beaten gold.

Near the farther wall on a granite throne, staring for ever toward the arched doorway, sat the monstrous and obscene Pteor, the god of the Pelishti, wrought in brass, with his exaggerated attributes reflecting the grossness of his cult. And in his lap sprawled a limp white figure.

'Well, I'll be damned!' muttered Conan. He glanced suspiciously about the chamber, seeing no other entrance or evidence of occupation, and then advanced noiselessly and looked down at the girl whose slim shoulders shook with sobs of abject misery, her face sunk in her arms. From thick bands of gold on the idol's arms slim gold chains ran to smaller bands on her wrists. He laid a hand on her naked shoulder and she started convulsively, shrieked, and twisted her tear-stained face toward him.

'*Conan!*' She made a spasmodic effort to go into the usual clinch, but the chains hindered her. He cut through the soft gold as close to her wrists as he could, grunting: 'You'll have to wear these bracelets until I can find a chisel or a file. Let go of me, damn it! You actresses are too damned emotional. What happened to you, anyway?'

'When I went back into the oracle chamber,' she whimpered, 'I saw the goddess lying on the dais as I'd first seen her. I called out to you and started to run to the door—then something grabbed me from behind. It clapped a hand over my mouth and carried me through a panel in the wall, and down some steps and along a dark hall. I didn't see what it was that had hold of me until we passed through a big metal door and came into a tunnel whose roof was alight, like this chamber.

'Oh, I nearly fainted when I saw! They are not humans! They are gray, hairy devils that walk like men and speak a gibberish no human could understand. They stood there and seemed to be waiting, and once I thought I heard somebody trying the door. Then one of the *things* pulled a metal level in the wall, and something crashed on the other side of the door.

'Then they carried me on and on through winding tunnels and up stone stairways into this chamber, where they chained me on the knees of this abominable idol, and then they went away. Oh, Conan, what are they?'

'Servants of Bît-Yakin,' he grunted. 'I found a manuscript that told me a number of things, and then stumbled upon some frescoes that told me the rest. Bît-Yakin was

a Pelishti who wandered into the valley with his servants
after the people of Alkmeenon had deserted it. He found
the body of Princess Yelaya, and discovered that the
priests returned from time to time to make offerings to
her, for even then she was worshipped as a goddess.

'He made an oracle of her, and he was the voice of the
oracle, speaking from a niche he cut in the wall behind
the ivory dais. The priests never suspected, never saw
him or his servants, for they always hid themselves when
the men came. Bît-Yakin lived and died here without
ever being discovered by the priests. Crom knows how
long he dwelt here, but it must have been for centuries.
The wise men of the Pelishti know how to increase the
span of their lives for hundreds of years. I've seen some
of them myself. Why he lived here alone, and why he
played the part of oracle no ordinary human can guess,
but I believe the oracle part was to keep the city inviolate
and sacred, so he could remain undisturbed. He ate the
food the priests brought as an offering to Yelaya, and his
servants ate other things—I've always known there was a
subterranean river flowing away from the lake where the
people of the Puntish highlands throw their dead. That
river runs under this palace. They have ladders hung
over the water where they can hang and fish for the
corpses that come floating through. Bît-Yakin recorded
everything on parchment and painted walls.

'But he died at last, and his servants mummified
him according to instructions he gave them before his
death, and stuck him in a cave in the cliffs. The rest is
easy to guess. His servants, who were even more nearly
immortal than he, kept on dwelling here, but the next
time a high priest came to consult the oracle, not having a
master to restrain them, they tore him to pieces. So since
then—until Gorulga—nobody came to talk to the oracle.

'It's obvious they've been renewing the garments and
ornaments of the goddess, as they'd seen Bît-Yakin do.
Doubtless there's a sealed chamber somewhere where the
silks are kept from decay. They clothed the goddess and

brought her back to the oracle room after Zargheba had stolen her. And, oh, by the way, they took off Zargheba's head and hung it up in a thicket.'

She shivered, yet at the same time breathed a sigh of relief.

'He'll never whip me again.'

'Not this side of Hell,' agreed Conan. 'But come on. Gwarunga ruined my chances with his stolen goddess. I'm going to follow the priests and take my chance of stealing the loot from them after they get it. And you stay close to me. I can't spend all my time looking for you.'

'But the servants of Bît-Yakin!' she whispered fearfully.

'We'll have to take our chance,' he grunted. 'I don't know what's in their minds, but so far they haven't shown any disposition to come out and fight in the open. Come on.'

Taking her wrist he led her out of the chamber and down the corridor. As they advanced they heard the chanting of the priests, and mingling with the sound the low sullen rushing of waters. The light grew stronger above them as they emerged on a high-pitched gallery of a great cavern and looked down on a scene weird and fantastic.

Above them gleamed the phosphorescent roof; a hundred feet below them stretched the smooth floor of the cavern. On the far side this floor was cut by a deep, narrow stream brimming its rocky channel. Rushing out of impenetrable gloom, it swirled across the cavern and was lost again in darkness. The visible surface reflected the radiance above; the dark seething waters glinted as if flecked with living jewels, frosty blue, lurid red, shimmering green, an ever-changing iridescence.

Conan and his companion stood upon one of the gallery-like ledges that banded the curve of the lofty wall, and from this ledge a natural bridge of stone soared in a breath-taking arch over the vast gulf of the cavern to join a much smaller ledge on the opposite side, across the river. Ten feet below it another, broader arch spanned the cave. At either end a carved stair joined the extremities of these flying arches.

Conan's gaze, following the curve of the arch that swept away from the ledge on which they stood, caught a glint of light that was not the lurid phosphorus of the cavern. On that small ledge opposite them there was an opening in the cave wall through which stars were glinting.

But his full attention was drawn to the scene beneath them. The priests had reached their destination. There in a sweeping angle of the cavern wall stood a stone altar, but there was no idol upon it. Whether there was one behind it, Conan could not ascertain, because some trick of the light, or the sweep of the wall, left the space behind the altar in total darkness.

The priests had stuck their torches into holes in the stone floor, forming a semicircle of fire in front of the altar at a distance of several yards. Then the priests themselves formed a semicircle inside the crescent of torches, and Gorulga, after lifting his arms aloft in invocation, bent to the altar and laid hands on it. It lifted and tilted backward on its hinder edge, like the lid of a chest, revealing a small crypt.

Extending a long arm into the recess, Gorulga brought up a small brass chest. Lowering the altar back into place, he set the chest on it, and threw back the lid. To the eager watchers on the high gallery it seemed as if the action had released a blaze of living fire which throbbed and quivered about the opened chest. Conan's heart leaped and his hand caught at his hilt. The Teeth of Gwahlur at last! The treasure that would make its possessor the richest man in the world! His breath came fast between his clenched teeth.

Then he was suddenly aware that a new element had entered into the light of the torches and of the phosphorescent roof, rendering both void. Darkness stole around the altar, except for that glowing spot of evil radiance cast by the Teeth of Gwahlur, and that grew and grew. The blacks froze into basaltic statues, their shadows streaming grotesquely and gigantically out behind them.

The altar was laved in the glow now, and the astounded features of Gorulga stood out in sharp relief. Then the mysterious space behind the altar swam into the widening illumination. And slowly with the crawling light, figures became visible, like shapes growing out of the night and silence.

At first they seemed like gray stone statues, those motionless shapes, hairy, man-like, yet hideously human; but their eyes were alive, cold sparks of gray icy fire. And as the weird glow lit their bestial countenances, Gorulga screamed and fell backward, throwing up his long arms in a gesture of frenzied horror.

But a longer arm shot across the altar and a misshapen hand locked on his throat. Screaming and fighting, the high priest was dragged back across the altar; a hammer-like fist smashed down, and Gorulga's cries were stilled. Limp and broken he sagged across the altar, his brains oozing from his crushed skull. And then the servants of Bît-Yakin surged like a bursting flood from Hell on the black priests who stood like horror-blasted images.

Then there was slaughter, grim and appalling.

Conan saw black bodies tossed like chaff in the inhuman hands of the slayers, against whose horrible strength and agility the daggers and swords of the priests were ineffective. He saw men lifted bodily and their heads cracked open against the stone altar. He saw a flaming torch, grasped in a monstrous hand, thrust inexorably down the gullet of an agonized wretch who writhed in vain against the arms that pinioned him. He saw a man torn in two pieces, as one might tear a chicken, and the bloody fragments hurled clear across the cavern. The massacre was as short and devastating as the rush of a hurricane. In a burst of red abysmal ferocity it was over, except for one wretch who fled screaming back the way the priests had come, pursued by a swarm of blood-dabbled shapes of horror which reached out their red-smeared

hands for him. Fugitive and pursuers vanished down the
black tunnel, and the screams of the human came back
dwindling and confused by the distance.

Muriela was on her knees clutching Conan's legs; her
face pressed against his knee and her eyes tightly shut.
She was a quaking, quivering mold of abject terror. But
Conan was galvanized. A quick glance across at the
aperture where the stars shone, a glance down at the chest
that still blazed open on the blood-smeared altar, and he
saw and seized the desperate gamble.

'I'm going after that chest!' he grated. 'Stay here!'

'Oh, Mitra, no!' In an agony of fright she fell to
the floor and caught at his sandals. 'Don't! Don't! Don't
leave me!'

'Lie still and keep your mouth shut!' he snapped,
disengaging himself from her frantic clasp.

He disregarded the tortuous stair. He dropped from
ledge to ledge with reckless haste. There was no sign
of the monsters as his feet hit the floor. A few of the
torches still flared in their sockets, the phosphorescent
glow throbbed and quivered, and the river flowed with an
almost articulate muttering, scintillant with undreamed
radiances. The glow that had heralded the appearance
of the servants had vanished with them. Only the light
of the jewels in the brass chest shimmered and quivered.

He snatched the chest, noting its contents in one lustful
glance—strange, curiously shapen stones that burned
with an icy, non-terrestrial fire. He slammed the lid,
thrust the chest under his arm, and ran back up the
steps. He had no desire to encounter the hellish servants of Bît-Yakin. His glimpse of them in action had
dispelled any illusion concerning their fighting ability.
Why they had waited so long before striking at the
invaders he was unable to say. What human could guess
the motives or thoughts of these monstrosities? That
they were possessed of craft and intelligence equal to
humanity had been demonstrated. And there on the
cavern floor lay crimson proof of their bestial ferocity.

The Corinthian girl still cowered on the gallery where he had left her. He caught her wrist and yanked her to her feet, grunting: 'I guess it's time to go!'

Too bemused with terror to be fully aware of what was going on, the girl suffered herself to be led across the dizzy span. It was not until they were poised over the rushing water that she looked down, voiced a startled yelp and would have fallen but for Conan's massive arm about her. Growling an objurgation in her ear, he snatched her up under his free arm and swept her, in a flutter of limply waving arms and legs, across the arch and into the aperture that opened at the other end. Without bothering to set her on her feet, he hurried through the short tunnel into which this aperture opened. An instant later they emerged upon a narrow ledge on the outer side of the cliffs that circled the valley. Less than a hundred feet below them the jungle waved in the starlight.

Looking down, Conan vented a gusty sigh of relief. He believed that he could negotiate the descent, even though burdened with the jewels and the girl; although he doubted if even he, unburdened, could have ascended at that spot. He set the chest, still smeared with Gorulga's blood and clotted with his brains, on the ledge, and was about to remove his girdle in order to tie the box to his back, when he was galvanized by a sound behind him, a sound sinister and unmistakable.

'Stay here!' he snapped at the bewildered Corinthian girl. 'Don't move!' And drawing his sword, he glided into the tunnel, glaring back into the cavern.

Half-way across the upper span he saw a gray deformed shape. One of the servants of Bît-Yakin was on his trail. There was no doubt that the brute had seen them and was following them. Conan did not hesitate. It might be easier to defend the mouth of the tunnel—but this fight must be finished quickly, before the other servants could return.

He ran out on the span, straight toward the oncoming monster. It was no ape, neither was it a man. It was some

shambling horror spawned in the mysterious, nameless
jungles of the south, where strange life teemed in the
reeking rot without the dominance of man, and drums
thundered in temples that had never known the tread of a
human foot. How the ancient Pelishti had gained lordship
over them—and with it eternal exile from humanity—was
a foul riddle about which Conan did not care to speculate,
even if he had had opportunity.

Man and monster; they met at the highest arch of the
span, where, a hundred feet below, rushed the furious
black water. As the monstrous shape with its leprous gray
body and the features of a carven, unhuman idol loomed
over him, Conan struck as a wounded tiger strikes, with
every ounce of thew and fury behind the blow. That
stroke would have sheared a human body asunder; but
the bones of the servant of Bît-Yakin were like tempered
steel. Yet even tempered steel could not wholly have
withstood that furious stroke. Ribs and shoulder-bone
parted and blood spouted from the great gash.

There was no time for a second stroke. Before the
Cimmerian could lift his blade again or spring clear,
the sweep of a giant arm knocked him from the span
as a fly is flicked from a wall. As he plunged downward
the rush of the river was like a knell in his ears, but
his twisting body fell half-way across the lower arch.
He wavered there precariously for one blood-chilling
instant, then his clutching fingers hooked over the farther
edge, and he scrambled to safety, his sword still in
his other hand.

As he sprang up, he saw the monster, spurting blood
hideously, rush toward the cliff-end of the bridge, obviously intending to descend the stair that connected the
arches and renew the feud. At the very ledge the brute
paused in mid-flight—and Conan saw it too—Muriela,
with the jewel chest under her arm, stood staring wildly
in the mouth of the tunnel.

With a triumphant bellow the monster scooped her up
under one arm, snatched the jewel chest with the other

hand as she dropped it, and turning, lumbered back across the bridge. Conan cursed with passion and ran for the other side also. He doubted if he could climb the stair to the higher arch in time to catch the brute before it could plunge into the labyrinths of tunnels on the other side.

But the monster was slowing, like clockwork running down. Blood gushed from that terrible gash in his breast, and he lurched drunkenly from side to side. Suddenly he stumbled, reeled and toppled sidewise—pitched head-long from the arch and hurtled downward. Girl and jewel chest fell from his nerveless hands and Muriela's scream rang terribly above the snarl of the water below.

Conan was almost under the spot from which the creature had fallen. The monster struck the lower arch glancingly and shot off, but the writhing figure of the girl struck and clung, and the chest hit the edge of the span near her. One falling object struck on one side of Conan and one on the other. Either was within arm's length; for the fraction of a split second the chest teetered on the edge of the bridge, and Muriela clung by one arm, her face turned desperately toward Conan, her eyes dilated with the fear of death and her lips parted in a haunting cry of despair.

Conan did not hesitate, nor did he even glance toward the chest that held the wealth of an epoch. With a quickness that would have shamed the spring of a hungry jaguar, he swooped, grasped the girl's arm just as her fingers slipped from the smooth stone, and snatched her up on the span with one explosive heave. The chest toppled on over and struck the water ninety feet below, where the body of the servant of Bît-Yakin had already vanished. A splash, a jetting flash of foam marked where the Teeth of Gwahlur disappeared for ever from the sight of man.

Conan scarcely wasted a downward glance. He darted across the span and ran up the cliff stair like a cat, carrying the limp girl as if she had been an infant. A hideous ululation caused him to glance over his shoulder as he reached the higher arch, to see the other servants streaming back into the cavern below, blood dripping from their bared fangs. They raced up the stair that wound up from tier to tier, roaring vengefully; but he slung the girl unceremoniously over his shoulder, dashed through the tunnel and went down the cliffs like an ape himself, dropping and springing from hold to hold with breakneck recklessness. When the fierce countenances looked over the ledge of the aperture, it was to see the Cimmerian and the girl disappearing into the forest that surrounded the cliffs.

'Well,' said Conan, setting the girl on her feet within the sheltering screen of branches, 'we can take our time now. I don't think those brutes will follow us outside the valley. Anyway, I've got a horse tied at a water-hole close by, if the lions haven't eaten him. Crom's devils! What are you crying about *now?*'

She covered her tear-stained face with her hands, and her slim shoulders shook with sobs.

'I lost the jewels for you,' she wailed miserably. 'It was my fault. If I'd obeyed you and stayed out on the ledge, that brute would never have seen me. You should have caught the gems and let me drown!'

'Yes, I suppose I should,' he agreed. 'But forget it. Never worry about what's past. And stop crying, will you? That's better. Come on.'

'You mean you're going to keep me? Take me with you?' she asked hopefully.

'What else do you suppose I'd do with you?' He ran an approving glance over her figure and grinned at the torn skirt which revealed a generous expanse of tempting ivory-tinted curves. 'I can use an actress like you. There's no use going back to Keshia. There's nothing in Keshan now that I want. We'll go to Punt. The people of Punt worship an ivory woman, and they wash gold out of the rivers in wicker baskets. I'll tell them that Keshan is intriguing with Thutmekri to enslave them—which is true—and that the gods have sent me to protect them—for about a houseful of gold. If I can manage to smuggle you into their temple to exchange places with their ivory goddess, we'll skin them out of their jaw teeth before we get through with them!'

BRAN MAK MORN

Worms of the Earth

'STRIKE in the nails, soldiers, and let our guest see the reality of our good Roman justice!'

The speaker wrapped his purple cloak closer about his powerful frame and settled back into his official chair, much as he might have settled back in his seat at the Circus Maximus to enjoy the clash of gladiatorial swords. Realization of power colored his every move. Whetted pride was necessary to Roman satisfaction, and Titus Sulla was justly proud; for he was military governor of Eboracum and answerable only to the Emperor of Rome. He was a strongly built man of medium height, with the hawklike features of the pure-bred Roman. Now a mocking smile curved his full lips, increasing the arrogance of his haughty aspect. Distinctly military in appearance, he wore the golden-scaled corselet and chased breastplate of his rank, with the short stabbing-sword at his belt, and he held on his knee the silvered helmet with its plumed crest. Behind him stood a clump of impassive soldiers with shield and spear—blond titans from the Rhineland.

Before him was taking place the scene which apparently gave him so much real gratification—a scene common enough wherever stretched the far-flung boundaries of Rome. A rude cross lay flat upon the barren earth and on it was bound a man—half-naked, wild of aspect with his corded limbs, glaring eyes and shock of tangled hair.

His executioners were Roman soldiers, and with heavy hammers they prepared to pin the victim's hands and feet to the wood with iron spikes.

Only a small group of men watched this ghastly scene, in the dread place of execution beyond the city walls: the governor and his watchful guards; a few young Roman officers; the man to whom Sulla had referred as 'guest' and who stood like a bronze image, unspeaking. Beside the gleaming splendor of the Roman, the quiet garb of this man seemed drab, almost somber.

He was dark, but he did not resemble the Latins around him. There was about him none of the warm, almost Oriental sensuality of the Mediterranean which colored their features. The blond barbarians behind Sulla's chair were less unlike the man in facial outline than were the Romans. Not his were the full curving lips, nor the rich waving locks suggestive of the Greek. Nor was his dark complexion the rich olive of the south; rather it was the bleak darkness of the north. The whole aspect of the man vaguely suggested the shadowed mists, the gloom, the cold and icy winds of the naked northern lands. Even his black eyes were savagely cold, like black fires burning through fathoms of ice.

His height was only medium but there was something about him which transcended mere physical bulk—a certain fierce innate vitality, comparable only to that of a wolf or a panther. In every line of his supple, compact body, as well as in his coarse straight hair and thin lips, this was evident—in the hawklike set of the head on the corded neck, in the broad square shoulders, in the deep chest, the lean loins, the narrow feet. Built with the savage economy of a panther, he was an image of dynamic potentialities, pent in with iron self-control.

At his feet crouched one like him in complexion —but there the resemblance ended. This other was a stunted giant, with gnarly limbs, thick body, a low sloping brow and an expression of dull ferocity, now clearly mixed with fear. If the man on the cross resembled, in a tribal way, the man Titus Sulla called guest, he far more resembled the stunted crouching giant.

'Well, Partha Mac Othna,' said the governor with studied effrontery, 'when you return to your tribe, you will have a tale to tell of the justice of Rome, who rules the south.'

'I will have a tale,' answered the other in a voice which betrayed no emotion, just as his dark face, schooled to immobility, showed no evidence of the maelstrom in his soul.

'Justice to all under the rule of Rome,' said Sulla. '*Pax Romana*! Reward for virtue, punishment for wrong!' He laughed inwardly at his own black hypocrisy, then continued: 'You see, emissary of Pictland, how swiftly Rome punishes the transgressor.'

'I see,' answered the Pict in a voice which strongly curbed anger made deep with menace, 'that the subject of a foreign king is dealt with as though he were a Roman slave.'

'He has been tried and condemned in an unbiased court,' retorted Sulla.

'Aye! and the accuser was a Roman, the witnesses Roman, the judge Roman! He committed murder? In a moment of fury he struck down a Roman merchant who cheated, tricked and robbed him, and to injury added insult—aye, and a blow! Is his king but a dog, that Rome crucifies his subjects at will, condemned by Roman courts? Is his king too weak or foolish to do justice, were he informed and formal charges brought against the offender?'

'Well,' said Sulla cynically, 'you may inform Bran Mak Morn yourself. Rome, my friend, makes no account of her actions to barbarian kings. When savages come among us, let them act with discretion or suffer the consequences.'

The Pict shut his iron jaws with a snap that told Sulla further badgering would elicit no reply. The Roman made a gesture to the executioners. One of them seized a spike and placing it against the thick wrist of the victim smote heavily. The iron point sank deep through the flesh, crunching against the bones. The lips of the man on the cross writhed, though no moan escaped him. As a trapped wolf fights against his cage, the bound victim instinctively wrenched and struggled. The veins swelled in his temples, sweat beaded his low forehead, the muscles in arms and legs writhed and knotted. The hammers fell in inexorable strokes, driving the cruel points deeper and deeper, through wrists and ankles; blood flowed in a black river over the hands that held the spikes, staining the wood of the cross, and the splintering of bones was distinctly heard. Yet the sufferer made no outcry, though his blackened lips writhed back until the gums were visible, and his shaggy head jerked involuntarily from side to side.

The man called Partha Mac Othna stood like an iron image, eyes burning from an inscrutable face, his whole body as hard as iron from the tension of his control. At his feet crouched his misshapen servant, hiding his face from the grim sight, his arms locked about his master's knees. Those arms gripped like steel and under his breadth the fellow mumbled ceaselessly as if in invocation.

The last stroke fell; the cords were cut from arm and leg, so that the man would hang supported by the nails alone. He had ceased his struggling that only twisted the spikes in his agonizing wounds. His bright black eyes, unglazed, had not left the face of the man called Partha Mac Othna; in them lingered a desperate shadow of hope. Now the soldiers lifted the cross and set the end of it in the hole prepared, stamped the dirt about it to hold it erect.

The Pict hung in mid-air, suspended by the nails in his flesh, but still no sound escaped his lips. His eyes still hung on the somber face of the emissary, but the shadow of hope was fading.

'He'll live for days!' said Sulla cheerfully. 'These Picts are harder than cats to kill! I'll keep a guard of ten soldiers watching day and night to see that no one takes him down before he dies. Ho, there, Valerius, in honor of our esteemed neighbor, King Bran Mak Morn, give him a cup of wine!'

With a laugh the young officer came forward, holding a brimming wine-cup, and rising on his toes, lifted it to the parched lips of the sufferer. In the black eyes flared a red wave of unquenchable hatred; writhing his head aside to avoid even touching the cup, he spat full into the young Roman's eyes. With a curse Valerius dashed the cup to the ground, and before any could halt him, wrenched out his sword and sheathed it in the man's body.

Sulla rose with an imperious exclamation of anger; the man called Partha Mac Othna had started violently, but he bit his lip and said nothing. Valerius seemed somewhat surprised at himself as he sullenly cleaned his sword. The act had been instinctive, following the insult to Roman pride, the one thing unbearable.

'Give up your sword, young sir!' exclaimed Sulla. 'Centurion Publius, place him under arrest. A few days in a cell with stale bread and water will teach you to curb your patrician pride, in matters dealing with the will of the empire. What, you young fool, do you not realize that you could not have made the dog a more kindly gift? Who would not rather desire a quick death on the sword than the slow agony on the cross? Take him away. And you, centurion, see that guards remain at the cross so that the body is not cut down until the ravens pick bare the bones. Partha Mac Othna, I go to a banquet at the house of Demetrius—will you not accompany me?'

The emissary shook his head, his eyes fixed on the limp form which sagged on the black-stained cross. He made no reply. Sulla smiled sardonically, then rose and strode away, followed by his secretary who bore the gilded chair ceremoniously, and by the stolid soldiers, with whom walked Valerius, head sunken.

The man called Partha Mac Othna flung a wide

fold of his cloak about his shoulder, halted a moment
to gaze at the grim cross with its burden, darkly etched
against the crimson sky, where the clouds of night were
gathering. Then he stalked away, followed by his silent
servant.

2

In an inner chamber of Eboracum, the man called Partha
Mac Othna paced tigerishly to and fro. His sandaled feet
made no sound on the marble tiles.

'Grom!' he turned to the gnarled servant, 'well I know
why you held my knees so tightly—why you muttered
aid of the Moon-Woman—you feared I would lose my
self-control and make a mad attempt to succor the poor
wretch. By the gods, I believe that was what the dog
Roman wished—his iron-cased watchdogs watched me
narrowly, I know, and his baiting was harder to bear
than ordinarily.

'God black and white, dark and light!' he shook his
clenched fists above his head in the black gust of his
passion. 'That I should stand by and see a man of mine
butchered on a Roman cross—without justice and with
no more trial than that farce! Black gods of R'lyeh, even
you would I invoke to the ruin and destruction of those
butchers! I swear by the Nameless Ones, men shall die
howling for that deed, and Rome shall cry out as a woman
in the dark who treads upon an adder!'

'He knew you, master,' said Grom.

The other dropped his head and covered his eyes with
a gesture of savage pain.

'His eyes will haunt me when I lie dying. Aye, he
knew me, and almost until the last, I read in his eyes
the hope that I might aid him. Gods and devils, is Rome
to butcher my people beneath my very eyes? Then I am
not king but dog!'

'Not so loud, in the name of all the gods!' exclaimed

Grom in affright. 'Did these Romans suspect you were Bran Mak Morn, they would nail you on a cross beside that other.'

'They will know it ere long,' grimly answered the king. 'Too long I have lingered here in the guise of an emissary, spying upon my enemies. They have thought to play with me, these Romans, masking their contempt and scorn only under polished satire. Rome is courteous to barbarian ambassadors, they give us fine houses to live in, offer us slaves, pander to our lusts with women and gold and wine and games, but all the while they laugh at us; their very courtesy is an insult, and sometimes—as today—their contempt discards all veneer. Bah! I've seen through their baitings—have remained imperturbably serene and swallowed their studied insults. But this—by the fiends of Hell, this is beyond human endurance! My people look to me; if I fail them—if I fail even one—even the lowest of my people, who will aid them? To whom shall they turn? By the gods, I'll answer the gibes of these Roman dogs with black shaft and trenchant steel!'

'And the chief with the plumes?' Grom meant the governor, and his gutturals thrummed with the blood-lust. 'He dies?' He flicked out a length of steel.

Bran scowled. 'Easier said than done. He dies—but how may I reach him? By day his German guards keep at his back; by night they stand at door and window. He has many enemies, Romans as well as barbarians. Many a Briton would gladly slit his throat.'

Grom seized Bran's garment, stammering as fierce eagerness broke the bonds of his inarticulate nature.

'Let me go, master! My life is worth nothing. I will cut him down in the midst of his warriors!'

Bran smiled fiercely and clapped his hand on the stunted giant's shoulder with a force that would have felled a lesser man.

'Nay, old war-dog, I have too much need of thee! You shall not throw your life away uselessly. Sulla would

read the intent in your eyes, besides, and the javelins of
his Teutons would be through you ere you could reach
him. Not by the dagger in the dark will we strike this
Roman, not by the venom in the cup nor the shaft
from the ambush.'

The king turned and paced the floor a moment, his
head bent in thought. Slowly his eyes grew murky with
a thought so fearful he did not speak it aloud to the
waiting warrior.

'I have become somewhat familiar with the maze of
Roman politics during my stay in this accursed waste of
mud and marble,' said he. 'During a war on the Wall,
Titus Sulla, as governor of this province, is supposed
to hasten thither with his centuries. But this Sulla does
not do; he is no coward, but the bravest avoid certain
things—to each man, however bold, his own particular
fear. So he sends in his place Caius Camillus, who in
times of peace patrols the fens of the west, lest the Britons
break over the border. And Sulla takes his place in the
Tower of Trajan. Ha!'

He whirled and gripped Grom with steely fingers.

'Grom, take the red stallion and ride north! Let no
grass grow under the stallion's hoofs! Ride to Cormac na
Connacht and tell him to sweep the frontier with sword
and torch! Let his wild Gaels feast their fill of slaughter.
After a time I will be with him. But for a time I have
affairs in the west.'

Grom's black eyes gleamed and he made a passionate
gesture with his crooked hand—an instinctive move of
savagery.

Bran drew a heavy bronze seal from beneath his tunic.

'This is my safe-conduct as an emissary to Roman
courts,' he said grimly. 'It will open all gates between
this house and Baal-dor. If any official questions you too
closely—here!'

Lifting the lid of an iron-bound chest, Bran took out
a small, heavy leather bag which he gave into the hands
of the warrior.

'When all keys fail at a gate,' he said, 'try a golden key. Go now!'

There was no ceremonious farewell between the barbarian king and his barbarian vassal. Grom flung up his arm in a gesture of salute; then turning, he hurried out.

Bran stepped to a barred window and gazed out into the moonlit streets.

'Wait until the moon sets,' he muttered grimly. 'Then I'll take the road to—Hell! But before I go I have a debt to pay.'

The stealthy clink of a hoof on the flags reached him.

'With the safe-conduct and gold, not even Rome can hold a Pictish reaver,' muttered the king. 'Now I'll sleep until the moon sets.'

With a snarl at the marble friezework and fluted columns, as symbols of Rome, he flung himself down on a couch, from which he had long since impatiently torn the cushions and silk stuffs, as too soft for his hard body. Hate and the black passion for vengeance seethed in him, yet he went instantly to sleep. The first lesson he had learned in his bitter hard life was to snatch sleep any time he could, like a wolf that snatches sleep on the hunting trail. Generally his slumber was as light and dreamless as a panther's, but tonight it was otherwise.

He sank into fleecy gray fathoms of slumber and in a timeless, misty realm of shadows he met the tall, lean, white-bearded figure of old Gonar, the priest of the Moon, High counsellor to the king. And Bran stood aghast, for Gonar's face was white as driven snow and he shook with ague. Well might Bran stand appalled, for in all the years of his life he had never before seen Gonar the Wise show any sign of fear.

'What now, old one?' asked the king. 'Goes all well in Baal-dor?'

'All is well in Baal-dor where my body lies sleeping,' answered old Gonar. 'Across the void I have come to battle with you for your soul. King, are you mad, this thought you have in your brain?'

'Gonar,' answered Bran somberly, 'this day I stood still and watched a man of mine die on the cross of Rome. What his name or his rank, I do not know. I do not care. He might have been a faithful unknown warrior of mine, he might have been an outlaw. I only know that he was mine; the first scents he knew were the scents of the heather; the first light he saw was the sunrise on the Pictish hills. He belonged to me, not to Rome. If punishment was just, then none but me should have dealt it. If it were to be tried, none but me should have been his judge. The same blood flowed in our veins; the same fire maddened our brains; in infancy we listened to the same old tales, and in youth we sang the same old songs. He was bound to my heart-strings, as every man and every woman and every child of Pictland is bound. It was mine to protect him! Now it is mine to avenge him.'

'But in the name of the gods, Bran,' expostulated the wizard, 'take your vengeance in another way! Return to the heather—mass your warriors—join with Cormac and his Gaels, and spread a sea of blood and flame the length of the great Wall!'

'All that I will do,' grimly answered Bran. 'But now— *now*—I will have a vengeance such as no Roman ever dreamed of! Ha, what do they know of the mysteries of this ancient isle, which sheltered strange life long before Rome rose from the marshes of the Tiber?'

'Bran, there are weapons too foul to use, even against Rome!'

Bran barked short and sharp as a jackal.

'Ha! There are no weapons I would not use against Rome! My back is at the wall. By the blood of the fiends, has Rome fought me fair? Bah! I am a barbarian king with a wolfskin mantle and an iron crown, fighting with my handful of bows and broken pikes against the queen of the world. What have I? The heather hills, the wattle huts, the spears of my shock-headed tribesmen!

And I fight Rome—with her armored legions, her broad fertile plains and rich seas—her mountains and her rivers and her gleaming cities—her wealth, her steel, her gold, her mastery and her wrath. By steel and fire I will fight her—and by subtlety and treachery—by the thorn in the foot, the adder in the path, the venom in the cup, the dagger in the dark; aye,' his voice sank somberly, 'and by the worms of the earth!'

'But it is madness!' cried Gonar. 'You will perish in the attempt you plan—you will go down to Hell and you will not return! What of your people then?'

'If I cannot serve them I had better die,' growled the king.

'But you cannot reach the beings you seek,' cried Gonar. 'For untold centuries they have dwelt apart. There is no door by which you can come to them. Long ago they severed the bonds that bound them to the world we know.'

'Long ago,' answered Bran somberly, 'you told me that nothing in the universe was separated from the stream of Life—a saying the truth of which I have often seen evident. No race, no form of life but is close-knit somehow, by some manner, to the rest of Life and the world. Somewhere there is a thin link connecting *those* I seek to the world I know. Somewhere there is a Door. And somewhere among the bleak fens of the west I will find it.'

Stark horror flooded Gonar's eyes and he gave back crying, 'Wo! Wo! Wo! to Pictdom! Wo to the unborn kingdom! Wo, black wo to the sons of men!'

Bran awoke to a shadowed room and the starlight on the window-bars. The moon had sunk from sight, though its glow was still faint above the housetops. Memory of his dream shook him and he swore beneath his breath.

Rising, he flung off cloak and mantle, donning a light shirt of black mesh-mail, and girding a sword and dirk. Going again to the iron-bound chest he lifted several compact bags and emptied the clinking contents into the leathern pouch at his girdle. Then wrapping his wide cloak about him, he silently left the house. No servants there were to spy on him—he had impatiently refused the offer of slaves which it was Rome's policy to furnish her barbarian emissaries. Gnarled Grom had attended to all Bran's simple needs.

The stables fronted on the courtyard. A moment's groping in the dark and he placed his hand over the great stallion's nose, checking the nicker of recognition. Working without a light he swiftly bridled and saddled the great brute, and went through the courtyard into a shadowy side-street, leading him. The moon was setting, the border of floating shadows widening along the western wall. Silence lay on the marble palaces and mud hovels of Eboracum under the cold stars.

Bran touched the pouch at his girdle, which was heavy with minted gold that bore the stamp of Rome. He had come to Eboracum posing as an emissary of Pictdom, to act the spy. But being a barbarian, he had not been able to play his part in aloof formality and sedate dignity. He retained a crowded memory of wild feasts where wine flowed in fountains; of white-bosomed Roman women, who, sated with civilized lovers, looked with something more than favor on a virile barbarian; of gladiatorial games; and of other games where dice clicked and spun and tall stacks of gold changed hands. He had drunk deeply and gambled recklessly, after the manner of barbarians, and he had had a remarkable run of luck, due possibly to the indifference with which he won or lost. Gold to the Pict was so much dust, flowing through his fingers. In his land there was no need of it. But he had learned its power in the boundaries of civilization.

Almost under the shadow of the northwestern wall he saw ahead of him loom the great watch tower which was connected with and reared above the outer wall. One corner of the castle-like fortress, farthest from the wall, served as a dungeon. Bran left his horse standing in a dark alley, with the reins hanging on the ground, and stole like a prowling wolf into the shadows of the fortress.

The young officer Valerius was awakened from a light, unquiet sleep by a stealthy sound at the barred window. He sat up, cursing softly under his breath as the faint starlight which etched the window-bars fell across the bare stone floor and reminded him of his disgrace. Well, in a few days, he ruminated, he'd be well out of it; Sulla would not be too harsh on a man with such high connections; then let any man or woman gibe at him! Damn that insolent Pict! But wait, he thought suddenly, remembering: what of the sound which had roused him?

'Hssst!' it was a voice from the window.

Why so much secrecy? It could hardly be a foe—yet, why should it be a friend? Valerius rose and crossed his cell, coming close to the window. Outside all was dim in the starlight and he made out but a shadowy form close to the window.

'Who are you?' he leaned close against the bars, straining his eyes into the gloom.

His answer was a snarl of wolfish laughter, a long flicker of steel in the starlight. Valerius reeled away from the window and crashed to the floor, clutching his throat, gurgling horribly as he tried to scream. Blood gushed through his fingers, forming about his twitching body a pool that reflected the dim starlight dully and redly.

Outside Bran glided away like a shadow, without pausing to peer into the cell. In another minute the guards would round the corner on their regular routine. Even now he heard the measured tramp of their iron-clad feet. Before they came in sight he had vanished and they clumped stolidly by the cell windows with no intimation of the corpse that lay on the floor within.

Bran rode to the small gate in the western wall, unchallenged by the sleepy watch. What fear of foreign invasion in Eboracum?—and certain well-organized thieves and

women-stealers made it profitable for the watchmen not
to be too vigilant. But the single guardsman at the western
gate—his fellows lay drunk in a nearby brothel—lifted his
spear and bawled for Bran to halt and give an account of
himself. Silently the Pict reined closer. Masked in the
dark cloak, he seemed dim and indistinct to the Roman,
who was only aware of the glitter of his cold eyes in the
gloom. But Bran held up his hand against the starlight
and the soldier caught the gleam of gold; in the other hand
he saw a long sheen of steel. The soldier understood, and
he did not hesitate between the choice of a golden bribe
or a battle to the death with this unknown rider who
was apparently a barbarian of some sort. With a grunt
he lowered his spear and swung the gate open. Bran
rode through, casting a handful of coins to the Roman.
They fell about his feet in a golden shower, clinking
against the flags. He bent in greedy haste to retrieve
them and Bran Mak Morn rode westward like a flying
ghost in the night.

3

Into the dim fens of the west came Bran Mak Morn. A
cold wind breathed across the gloomy waste and against
the gray sky a few herons flapped heavily. The long
reeds and marsh grass waved in broken undulations
and out across the desolation of the wastes a few still
meres reflected the dull light. Here and there rose curiously regular hillocks above the general levels, and gaunt
against the somber sky Bran saw a marching line of
upright monoliths—menhirs, reared by what nameless
hands?

A faint blue line to the west lay the foothills that
beyond the horizon grew to the wild mountains of Wales
where dwelt still wild Celtic tribes—fierce blue-eyed men
that knew not the yoke of Rome. A row of well-garrisoned
watch towers held them in check. Even now, far away

across the moors, Bran glimpsed the unassailable keep men called the Tower of Trajan.

These barren wastes seemed the dreary accomplishment of desolation, yet human life was not utterly lacking. Bran met the silent men of the fen, reticent, dark of eye and hair, speaking a strange mixed tongue whose long-blended elements had forgotten their pristine separate sources. Bran recognized a certain kinship in these people to himself, but he looked on them with the scorn of a pure-blooded patrician for men of mixed strains.

Not that the common people of Caledonia were altogether pure-blooded; they got their stocky bodies and massive limbs from a primitive Teutonic race which had found its way into the northern tip of the isle even before the Celtic conquest of Britain was completed, and had been absorbed by the Picts. But the chiefs of Bran's folk had kept their blood from foreign taint since the beginnings of time, and he himself was a pure-bred Pict of the Old Race. But these fenmen, overrun repeatedly by British, Gaelic and Roman conquerors, had assimilated blood of each, and in the process almost forgotten their original language and lineage.

For Bran came of a race that was very old, which had spread over western Europe in one vast Dark Empire, before the coming of the Aryans, when the ancestors of the Celts, the Hellenes and the Germans were one primal people, before the days of tribal splitting-off and westward drift.

Only in Caledonia, Bran brooded, had his people resisted the flood of Aryan conquest. He had heard of a Pictish people called Basques, who in the crags of the Pyrenees called themselves an unconquered race; but he knew that they had paid tribute for centuries to the ancestors of the Gaels, before these Celtic conquerors abandoned their mountain realm and set sail for Ireland. Only the Picts of Caledonia had remained free, and they had been scattered into small feuding tribes—he was the first acknowledged king in five hundred years—the beginning of a new dynasty—no, a revival of an ancient dynasty under a new name. In the very teeth of Rome he dreamed of empire.

He wandered through the fens, seeking a Door. Of his quest he said nothing to the dark-eyed fenmen. They told him news that drifted from mouth to mouth—a tale of war in the north, the skirl of war pipes along the winding Wall, of gathering-fires in the heather, of flame and smoke and rapine and the glutting of Gaelic swords in the crimson sea of slaughter. The eagles of the legions were moving northward and the ancient road resounded to the measured tramp of the ironclad feet. And Bran, in the fens of the west, laughed, well pleased.

In Eboracum, Titus Sulla gave secret word to seek out the Pictish emissary with the Gaelic name who had been under suspicion, and who had vanished the night young Valerius was found dead in his cell with his throat ripped out. Sulla felt that this sudden bursting flame of war on the Wall was connected closely with his execution of a condemned Pictish criminal, and he set his spy system to work, though he felt sure that Partha Mac Othna was by this time far beyond his reach. He prepared to march from Eboracum, but he did not accompany the considerable force of legionaries which he sent north. Sulla was a brave man, but each man has his own dread, and Sulla's was Cormac na Connacht, the black-haired prince of the Gaels, who had sworn to cut out the governor's heart and eat it raw. So Sulla rode with his ever-present bodyguard, westward, where lay the Tower of Trajan with its warlike commander, Caius Camillus, who enjoyed nothing more than taking his superior's place when the red waves of war washed at the foot of the Wall. Devious politics, but the legate of Rome seldom visited this far isle, and what with his wealth and intrigues, Titus Sulla was the highest power in Britain.

And Bran, knowing all this, patiently waited his coming, in the deserted hut in which he had taken up his abode.

One gray evening he strode on foot across the moors, a stark figure, blackly etched against the dim crimson fire of the sunset. He felt the incredible antiquity of the slumbering land, as he walked like the last man on the day after the end of the world! Yet at last he saw a token of human life—a drab hut of wattle and mud, set in the reedy breast of the fen.

A woman greeted him from the open door and Bran's somber eyes narrowed with a dark suspicion. The woman was not old, yet the evil wisdom of ages was in her eyes; her garments were ragged and scanty, her black locks tangled and unkempt, lending her an aspect of wildness well in keeping with her grim surroundings. Her red lips laughed but there was no mirth in her laughter, only a hint of mockery, and under the lips her teeth showed sharp and pointed like fangs.

'Enter, master,' said she, 'if you do not fear to share the roof of the witch-woman of Dagon-moor!'

Bran entered silently and sat him down on a broken bench while the woman busied herself with the scanty meal cooking over an open fire on the squalid hearth. He studied her lithe, almost serpentine motions, the ears which were almost pointed, the yellow eyes which slanted curiously.

'What do you seek in the fens, my lord?' she asked, turning toward him with a supple twist of her whole body.

'I seek a Door,' he answered, chin resting on his fist. 'I have a song to sing to the worms of the earth!'

She started upright, a jar falling from her hands to shatter on the hearth.

'This is an ill saying, even spoken in chance,' she stammered.

'I speak not by chance but by intent,' he answered.

She shook her head. 'I know not what you mean.'

'Well you know,' he returned. 'Aye, you know well! My race is very old—they reigned in Britain before the nations of the Celts and the Hellenes were born out of the womb of peoples. But my people were not first in

Britain. By the mottles on your skin, by the slanting of your eyes, by the taint in your veins, I speak with full knowledge and meaning.'

Awhile she stood silent, her lips smiling but her face inscrutable.

'Man, are you mad?' she asked, 'that in your madness you come seeking that from which strong men fled screaming in old times?'

'I seek a vengeance,' he answered, 'that can be accomplished only by Them I seek.'

She shook her head.

'You have listened to a bird singing; you have dreamed empty dreams.'

'I have heard a viper hiss,' he growled, 'and I do not dream. Enough of this weaving of words. I came seeking a link between two worlds; I have found it.'

'I need lie to you no more, man of the North,' answered the woman. 'They you seek will dwell beneath the sleeping hills. They have drawn *apart*, farther and farther from the world you know.'

'But they still steal forth in the night to grip women straying on the moors,' said he, his gaze on her slanted eyes. She laughed wickedly.

'What would you of me?'

'That you bring me to Them.'

She flung back her head with a scornful laugh. His left hand locked like iron in the breast of her scanty garment and his right closed on his hilt. She laughed in his face.

'Strike and be damned, my northern wolf! Do you think that such life as mine is so sweet that I would cling to it as a babe to the breast?'

His hand fell away.

'You are right. Threats are foolish. I will buy your aid.'

'How?' the laughing voice hummed with mockery.

Bran opened his pouch and poured into his cupped palm a stream of gold.

'More wealth than the men of the fen ever dreamed of.'

Again she laughed. 'What is this rusty metal to me? Save it for some white-breasted Roman woman who will play the traitor for you!'

'Name me a price!' he urged. 'The head of an enemy—'

'By the blood in my veins, with its heritage of ancient hate, who is mine enemy but thee?' she laughed, and springing, struck catlike. But her dagger splintered on the mail beneath his cloak, and he flung her off with a loathsome flirt of his wrist which tossed her sprawling across her grass-strewn bunk. Lying there, she laughed up at him.

'I will name you a price, my wolf, and it may be in days to come you will curse the armor that broke Atla's dagger!' She rose and came close to him, her disquietingly long hands fastened fiercely into his cloak. 'I will tell you, Black Bran, king of Caledon! Oh, I knew you when you came into my hut with your black hair and your cold eyes! I will lead you to the doors of Hell if you wish—and the price shall be the kisses of a king!

'What of my blasted and bitter life, I, whom mortal men loathe and fear? I have not known the love of men, the clasp of a strong arm, the sting of human kisses, I, Atla, the were-woman of the moors! What have I known but the lone winds of the fens, the dreary fire of cold sunsets, the whispering of the marsh grasses?—the faces that blink up at me in the waters of the meres, the foot-pad of night—things in the gloom, the glimmer of red eyes, the grisly murmur of nameless beings in the night!

'I am half human, at least! Have I not known sorrow and yearning and crying wistfulness, and the drear ache of loneliness? Give to me, king—give me your fierce kisses and your hurtful barbarian's embrace. Then in the long drear years to come I shall not utterly eat out my heart in vain envy of the white-bosomed women of men; for I shall have a memory few of them can boast—the kisses of a king! One night of love, O king, and I will guide you to the gates of Hell!'

Bran eyed her somberly; he reached forth and gripped her arm in his iron fingers. An involuntary shudder shook him at the feel of her sleek skin. He nodded slowly and, drawing her close to him, forced his head down to meet her lifted lips.

4

The cold gray mists of dawn wrapped King Bran like a clammy cloak. He turned to the woman whose slanted eyes gleamed in the gray gloom.

'Make good your part of the contract,' he said roughly. 'I sought a link between worlds, and in you I found it. I seek the one thing sacred to Them. It shall be the Key opening the Door that lies unseen between me and Them. Tell me how I can reach it.'

'I will,' the red lips smiled terribly. 'Go to the mound men call Dagon's Barrow. Draw aside the stone that blocks the entrance and go under the dome of the mound. The floor of the chamber is made of seven great stones, six grouped about the seventh. Lift out the center stone— and you will see!'

'Will I find the Black Stone?' he asked.

'Dagon's Barrow is the Door to the Black Stone,' she answered, 'if you dare follow the Road.'

'Will the symbol be well guarded?' He unconsciously loosened his blade in its sheath. The red lips curled mockingly.

'If you meet any on the Road, you will die as no mortal man has died for long centuries. The Stone is not guarded, as men guard their treasures. Why should They guard what man has never sought? Perhaps They will be near, perhaps not. It is a chance you must take, if you wish the Stone. Beware, king of Pictdom! Remember it was your folk who, so long ago, cut the thread that bound Them to human life. They were almost human then—they overspread the land and knew the sunlight.

Now they have drawn *apart*. They know not the sunlight and they shun the light of the moon. Even the starlight they hate. Far, far apart have they drawn, who might have been men in time, but for the spears of your ancestors.'

The sky was overcast with misty gray, through which the sun shone coldly yellow when Bran came to Dagon's Barrow, a round hillock overgrown with rank grass of a curious fungoid appearance. On the eastern side of the mound showed the entrance of a crudely built stone tunnel which evidently penetrated the barrow. One great stone blocked the entrance to the tomb. Bran laid hold of the sharp edges and exerted all his strength. It held fast. He drew his sword and worked the blade between the blocking stone and the sill. Using the sword as a lever, he worked carefully, and managed to loosen the great stone and wrench it out. A foul charnel-house scent flowed out of the aperture, and the dim sunlight seemed less to illuminate the cavern-like opening than to be fouled by the rank darkness which clung there.

Sword in hand, ready for he knew not what, Bran groped his way into the tunnel, which was long and narrow, built up of heavy joined stones, and was too low for him to stand erect. Either his eyes became somewhat accustomed to the gloom, or the darkness was, after all, somewhat lightened by the sunlight filtering in through the entrance. At any rate, he came into a round, low chamber and was able to make out its general dome-like outline. Here, no doubt, in old times, had reposed the bones of him for whom the stones of the tomb had been joined and the earth heaped high above them; but now of those bones no vestige remained on the stone floor. And bending close and straining his eyes, Bran made out the strange, startlingly regular pattern of that floor: six well-cut slabs clustered about a seventh, six-sided stone.

He drove his sword-point into a crack and pried carefully. The edge of the central stone tilted slightly upward. A little work and he lifted it out and leaned it against the curving wall. Straining his eyes downward he saw only the gaping blackness of a dark well, with small, worn steps that led downward and out of sight. He did not hesitate. Though the skin between his shoulders crawled curiously, he swung himself into the abyss and felt the clinging blackness swallow him.

Groping downward, he felt his feet slip and stumble on steps too small for human feet. With one hand pressed hard against the side of the well he steadied himself, fearing a fall into unknown and unlighted depths. The steps were cut into solid rock, yet they were greatly worn away. The farther he progressed, the less like steps they became, mere bumps of worn stone. Then the direction of the shaft changed sharply. It still led down, but at a shallow slant down which he could walk, elbows braced against the hollowed sides, head bent low beneath the curved roof. The steps had ceased altogether and the stone felt slimy to the touch, like a serpent's lair. What beings, Bran wondered, had slithered up and down this slanting shaft, for how many centuries?

The tunnel narrowed until Bran found it rather difficult to shove through. He lay on his back and pushed himself along with his hands, feet first. Still he knew he was sinking deeper and deeper into the very guts of the earth; how far below the surface he was, he dared not contemplate. Then ahead a faint witch-fire gleam tinged the abysmal blackness. He grinned savagely and without mirth. If They he sought came suddenly upon him, how could he fight in that narrow shaft? But he had put the thought of personal fear behind him when he began this hellish quest. He crawled on, thoughtless of all else but his goal.

And he came at last into a vast space where he could stand upright. He could not see the roof of the place, but he got an impression of dizzying vastness. The blackness pressed in on all sides, and behind him he could see the entrance to the shaft from which he had just emerged—a black well in the darkness. But in front of him a strange grisly radiance glowed about a grim altar built of human skulls. The source of that light he could not determine, but on the altar lay a sullen, night-black object—the Black Stone!

Bran wasted no time in giving thanks that the guardians of the grim relic were nowhere near. He caught up the Stone, and gripping it under his left arm, crawled into the shaft. When a man turns his back on peril, its clammy menace looms more grisly than when he advances upon it. So Bran, crawling back up the nighted shaft with his grisly prize, felt the darkness turn on him and slink behind him, grinning with dripping fangs. Clammy sweat beaded his flesh and he hastened to the best of his ability, ears strained for some stealthy sound to betray that fell shapes were at his heels. Strong shudders shook him, despite himself, and the short hair on his neck prickled as if a cold wind blew at his back.

When he reached the first of the tiny steps he felt as if he had attained to the outer boundaries of the mortal world. Up them he went, stumbling and slipping, and with a deep gasp of relief, came out into the tomb, whose spectral grayness seemed like the blaze of noon in comparison to the stygian depths he had just traversed. He replaced the central stone and strode into the light of the outer day, and never was the cold yellow light of the sun more grateful, as it dispelled the shadows of black-winged nightmares of fear and madness that seemed to have ridden him up out of the black deeps. He shoved the great blocking stone back into place, and picking up the cloak he had left at the mouth of the tomb, he wrapped it about the Black Stone and hurried away, a strong revulsion and loathing shaking his soul and lending wings to his strides.

A gray silence brooded over the land. It was desolate as the blind side of the moon; yet Bran felt the potentialities of life—under his feet, in the brown earth—sleeping, but how soon to waken, and in what horrific fashion?

He came through the tall, masking reeds to the still deep mere called Dagon's Mere. No slightest ripple ruffled the cold blue water to give evidence of the grisly monster legend said dwelt beneath. Bran closely scanned the breathless landscape. He saw no hint of life, human or unhuman. He sought the instincts of his savage soul to know if any unseen eyes fixed their lethal gaze upon him, and found no response. He was alone as if he were the last man on earth.

Swiftly he unwrapped the Black Stone, and as it lay in his hands like a solid, sullen block of darkness, he did not seek to learn the secret of its material nor scan the cryptic characters carved thereon. Weighing it in his hands and calculating the distance, he flung it far out, so that it fell almost exactly in the middle of the lake. A sullen splash and the waters closed over it. There was a moment of shimmering flashes on the bosom of the lake; then the blue surface stretched placid and unrippled again.

5

The were-woman turned swiftly as Bran approached her door. Her slant-eyes widened.

'You! And alive! And sane!'

'I have been into Hell and I have returned,' he growled. 'What is more, I have that which I sought.'

'The Black Stone?' she cried. 'You really dared steal it? Where is it?'

'No matter; but last night my stallion screamed in his stall and I heard something crunch beneath his thundering hoofs which was not the wall of the stable—and there was blood on his hoofs when I came to see, and blood on the floor of the stall. And I have heard stealthy sounds in the night, and noises beneath my dirt floor, as if worms burrowed deep in the earth. They know I have stolen their Stone. Have you betrayed me?'

She shook her head.

'I keep your secret; they do not need my word to know you. The father they have retreated from the world of men, the greater have grown their powers in other uncanny ways. Some dawn your hut will stand empty, and if men dare investigate they will find nothing—except crumbling bits of earth on the dirt floor.'

Bran smiled terribly.

'I have not planned and toiled thus far to fall prey to the talons of vermin. If They strike me down in the night, They will never know what became of their idol—or whatever it be to Them. I would speak with Them.'

'Dare you come with me and meet Them in the night?' she asked.

'Thunder of all gods!' he snarled. 'Who are you to ask me if I dare? Lead me to Them and let me bargain for a vengeance this night. The hour of retribution draws nigh. This day I saw silvered helmets and bright shields gleam across the fens—the new commander has arrived at the Tower of Trajan and Caius Camillus has marched to the Wall.'

That night the king went across the dark desolation of the moors with the silent were-woman. The night was thick and still as if the land lay in ancient slumber. The stars blinked vaguely, mere points of red struggling through the unbreathing gloom. Their gleam was dimmer than the glitter in the eyes of the woman who glided beside the king. Strange thoughts shook Bran, vague, titanic, primeval. Tonight ancestral linkings with these slumbering fens stirred in his soul and troubled him with the fantasmal, eon-veiled shapes of monstrous dreams. The vast age of his race was borne upon him; where now he walked an outlaw and an alien, dark-eyed kings in whose mold he was cast had reigned in old times. The Celtic and Roman invaders were as strangers to this ancient isle beside his people. Yet his race likewise had been invaders, and there was an older race than his—a race whose beginnings lay lost and hidden back beyond the dark oblivion of antiquity.

Ahead of them loomed a low range of hills, which
formed the easternmost extremity of those straying chains
which far away climbed at last to the mountains of Wales.
The woman led the way up what might have been a
sheep-path, and halted before a wide, black, gaping cave.

'A door to those you seek, O king!' her laughter rang
hateful in the gloom. 'Dare ye enter?'

His fingers closed in her tangled locks and he shook
her viciously.

'Ask me but once more if I dare,' he grated, 'and your
head and shoulders part company! Lead on.'

Her laughter was like sweet deadly venom. They passed into the cave and Bran struck flint and steel. The
flicker of the tinder showed him a wide, dusty cavern, on
the roof of which hung clusters of bats. Lighting a torch,
he lifted it and scanned the shadowy recesses, seeing
nothing but dust and emptiness.

'Where are They?' he growled.

She beckoned him to the back of the cave and leaned
against the rough wall, as if casually. But the king's keen
eyes caught the motion of her hand pressing hard against a
projecting ledge. He recoiled as a round black well gaped
suddenly at his feet. Again her laughter slashed him like
a keen silver knife. He held the torch to the opening and
again saw small worn steps leading down.

'They do not need those steps,' said Atla. 'Once they
did, before your people drove them into the darkness. But
you will need them.'

She thrust the torch into a niche above the well; it shed
a faint red light into the darkness below. She gestured into
the well and Bran loosened his sword and stepped into the
shaft. As he went down into the mystery of the darkness,
the light was blotted out above him, and he thought for
an instant Atla had covered the opening again. Then he
realized that she was descending after him.

The descent was not a long one. Abruptly Bran felt
his feet on a solid floor. Atla swung down beside him

and stood in the dim circle of light. Bran could not see the limits of the place into which he had come.

'Many caves in these hills,' said Atla, her voice sounding small and strangely brittle in the vastness, 'are but doors to greater caves which lie beneath, even as a man's words and deeds are but small indications of the dark caverns of murky thought lying behind and beneath.'

And now Bran was aware of movement in the gloom. The darkness was filled with stealthy noises not like those made by any human foot. Abruptly sparks began to flash and float in the blackness, like flickering fireflies. Closer they came until they girdled him in a wide half-moon. And beyond the ring gleamed other sparks, a solid sea of them, fading away in the gloom until the farthest were mere tiny pinpoints of light. And Bran knew they were the slanted eyes of the beings who had come upon him in such numbers that his brain reeled at the contemplation—and at the vastness of the cavern.

Now that he faced his ancient foes, Bran knew no fear. He felt the waves of terrible menace emanating from them, the grisly hate, the inhuman threat to body, mind and soul. More than a member of a less ancient race, he realized the horror of his position, but he did not fear, though he confronted the ultimate Horror of the dreams and legends of his race. His blood raced fiercely, but it was with the hot excitement of the hazard, not the drive of terror.

'They know you have the Stone, O king,' said Atla, and though he knew she feared, though he felt her physical efforts to control her trembling limbs, there was no quiver of fright in her voice. 'You are in deadly peril; they know your breed of old—oh, they remember the days when their ancestors were men! I cannot save you; both of us will die as no human has died for ten centuries. Speak to them, if you will; they can understand your speech, though you may not understand theirs. But it will avail not—you are human—and a Pict.'

Bran laughed, and the closing ring of fire shrank back at the savagery in his laughter. Drawing his sword with a soul-chilling rasp of steel, he set his back against what he hoped was a solid stone wall. Facing the glittering eyes with his sword gripped in his right hand and his dirk in his left, he laughed as a blood-hungry wolf snarls.

'Aye,' he growled, 'I am a Pict, a son of those warriors who drove your brutish ancestors before them like chaff before the storm!—who flooded the land with your blood and heaped high your skulls for a sacrifice to the Moon-Woman! You who fled of old before my race, dare ye now snarl at your master? Roll on me like a flood, now, if ye dare! Before your viper fangs drink my life I will reap your multitudes like ripened barley—of your severed heads will I build a tower and of your mangled corpses will I rear up a wall! Dogs of the dark, vermin of Hell, worms of the earth, rush in and try my steel! When Death finds me in this dark cavern, your living will howl for the scores of your dead and your Black Stone will be lost to you forever—for only I know where it is hidden, and not all the tortures of all the Hells can wring the secret from my lips!'

Then followed a tense silence; Bran faced the firelit darkness, tensed like a wolf at bay, waiting the charge; at his side the woman cowered, her eyes ablaze. Then from the silent ring that hovered beyond the dim torchlight rose a vague abhorrent murmur. Bran, prepared as he was for anything, started. Gods, was *that* the speech of creatures which had once been called men?

Atla straightened, listening intently. From her lips came the same hideous soft sibilances, and Bran, though he had already known the grisly secret of her being, knew that never again could he touch her save with soul-shaken loathing.

She turned to him, a strange smile curving her red lips dimly in the ghostly light.

'They fear you, O king! By the black secrets of R'lyeh, who are you that Hell itself quails before you? Not your steel, but the stark ferocity of your soul has driven unused fear into their strange minds. They will buy back the Black Stone at any price.'

'Good.' Bran sheathed his weapons. 'They shall promise not to molest you because of your aid of me. And,' his voice hummed like the purr of a hunting tiger, 'They shall deliver into my hands Titus Sulla, governor of Eboracum, now commanding the Tower of Trajan. This They can do—how, I know not. But I know that in the old days, when my people warred with these Children of the Night, babes disappeared from guarded huts and none saw the stealers come or go. Do They understand?'

Again rose the low frightful sounds, and Bran, who feared not their wrath, shuddered at their voices.

'They understand,' said Atla 'Bring the Black Stone to Dagon's Ring tomorrow night when the earth is veiled with the blackness that foreruns the dawn. Lay the Stone on the altar. There They will bring Titus Sulla to you. Trust Them; They have not interfered in human affairs for many centuries, but They will keep their word.'

Bran nodded and, turning, climbed up the stairs with Atla close behind him. At the top he turned and looked down once more. As far as he could see floated a glittering ocean of slanted yellow eyes upturned. But the owners of those eyes kept carefully beyond the dim circle of torchlight and of their bodies he could see nothing. Their low hissing speech floated up to him, and he shuddered as his imagination visualized, not a throng of biped creatures, but a swarming, swaying myriad of serpents, gazing up at him with their glittering, unwinking eyes.

He swung into the upper cave and Atla thrust the blocking stone back in place. It fitted into the entrance of the well with uncanny precision; Bran was unable to discern any crack in the apparently solid floor of the cavern. Atla made a motion to extinguish the torch, but the king stayed her.

'Keep it so until we are out of the cave,' he grunted. 'We might tread on an adder in the dark.'

Atla's sweetly hateful laughter rose maddeningly in the flickering gloom.

6

It was not long before sunset when Bran came again to the reed-grown marge of Dagon's Mere. Casting cloak and sword-belt on the ground, he stripped himself of his short leathern breeches. Then gripping his naked dirk in his teeth, he went into the water with the smooth ease of a diving seal. Swimming strongly, he gained the center of the small lake, and turning, drove himself downward.

The mere was deeper than he had thought. It seemed he would never reach the bottom, and when he did, his groping hands failed to find what he sought. A roaring in his ears warned him, and he swam to the surface.

Gulping deep of the refreshing air, he dived again, and again his quest was fruitless. A third time he sought the depth, and this time his groping hands met a familiar object in the silt of the bottom. Grasping it, he swam up to the surface.

The Stone was not particularly bulky, but it was heavy. He swam leisurely, and suddenly was aware of a curious stir in the waters about him which was not caused by his own exertions. Thrusting his face below the surface, he tried to pierce the blue depths with his eyes and thought to see a dim, gigantic shadow hovering there.

He swam faster, not frightened, but wary. His feet struck the shallows and he waded up on the shelving shore. Looking back he saw the waters swirl and subside. He shook his head, swearing. He had discounted the ancient legend which made Dagon's Mere the lair of a nameless water-monster, but now he had a feeling as if his escape had been narrow. The time-worn myths of the ancient land were taking form and coming to life before his eyes. What primeval shape lurked below the surface of that treacherous mere, Bran could not guess, but he felt that the fenmen had good reason for shunning the spot, after all.

Bran donned his garments, mounted the black stallion and rode across the fens in the desolate crimson of the sunset's afterglow, with the Black Stone wrapped in his cloak. He rode, not to his hut, but to the west, in the direction of the Tower of Trajan and the Ring of Dagon. As he covered the miles that lay between, the red stars winked out. Midnight passed him in the moonless night and still Bran rode on. His heart was hot for his meeting with Titus Sulla. Atla had gloated over the anticipation of watching the Roman writhe under torture, but no such thought was in the Pict's mind. The governor should have his chance with weapons—with Bran's own sword he should face the Pictish king's dirk, and live or die according to his prowess. And though Sulla was famed throughout the provinces as a swordsman, Bran felt no doubt as to the outcome.

Dagon's Ring lay some distance from the Tower—a sullen circle of tall, gaunt stones planted upright, with a rough-hewn stone altar in the center. The Romans looked on these menhirs with aversion; they thought the Druids had reared them; but the Celts supposed Bran's people, the Picts, had planted them—and Bran well knew what hands reared those grim monoliths in lost ages, though for what reasons, he but dimly guessed.

The king did not ride straight to the Ring. He was consumed with curiosity as to how his grim allies intended carrying out their promise. That They could snatch Titus Sulla from the very midst of his men, he felt sure, and he believed he knew how They would do it. He felt the gnawings of a strange misgiving, as if he had tampered with powers of unknown breadth and depth, and had loosed forces which he could not control. Each time he remembered that reptilian murmur, those slanted eyes of the night before, a cold breath passed over him. They had been abhorrent enough when his people drove Them into the caverns under the hills, ages ago; what had

long centuries of retrogression made of Them? In their
nighted, subterranean life, had They retained any of the
attributes of humanity at all?

Some instinct prompted him to ride towards the
Tower. He knew he was near; but for thick darkness he
could have plainly seen its stark outline tusking the
horizon. Even now he should be able to make it out
dimly. An obscure, shuddery premonition shook him,
and he spurred the stallion into swift canter.

And suddenly Bran staggered in his saddle as from
a physical impact, so stunning was the surprise of what
met his gaze. The impregnable Tower of Trajan was no
more! Bran's astounded gaze rested on a gigantic pile
of ruins—of shattered stone and crumbled granite, from
which jutted the jagged and splintered ends of broken
beams. At one corner of the tumbled heap one tower
rose out of the waste of crumpled masonry, and it leaned
drunkenly as if its foundations had been half cut away.

Bran dismounted and walked forward, dazed by bewilderment. The moat was filled in places by fallen stones
and brown pieces of mortared wall. He crossed over and
came among the ruins. Where, he knew, only a few hours
before the flags had resounded to the martial tramp of
iron-clad feet, and the walls had echoed to the clang of
shields and the blast of the loud-throated trumpets, a
horrific silence reigned.

Almost under Bran's feet, a broken shape writhed and
groaned. The king bent down to the legionary, who lay
in a sticky red pool of his own blood. A single glance
showed the Pict that the man, horribly crushed and
shattered, was dying.

Lifting the bloody head, Bran placed his flask to the
pulped lips, and the Roman instinctively drank deep,
gulping through splintered teeth. In the dim starlight
Bran saw his glazed eyes roll.

'The walls fell,' muttered the dying man. 'They crashed down like the skies falling on the day of doom. Ah

Jove, the skies rained shards of granite and hailstones of marble!'

'I have felt no earthquake shock,' Bran scowled, puzzled.

'It was no earthquake,' muttered the Roman. 'Before last dawn it began, the faint dim scratching and clawing far below the earth. We of the guard heard it—like rats burrowing, or like worms hollowing out the earth. Titus laughed at us, but all day long we heard it. Then at midnight the Tower quivered and seemed to settle—as if the foundations were being dug away—'

A shudder shook Bran Mak Morn. The worms of the earth! Thousands of vermin digging like moles far below the castle, burrowing away the foundations—gods, the land must be honeycombed with tunnels and caverns—these creatures were even less human than he had thought—what ghastly shapes of darkness had he invoked to his aid?

'What of Titus Sulla?' he asked, again holding the flask to the legionary's lips; in that moment the dying Roman seemed to him almost like a brother.

'Even as the Tower shuddered we heard a fearful scream from the governor's chamber,' muttered the soldier. 'We rushed there—as we broke down the door we heard his shrieks—they seemed to recede—*into the bowels of the earth!* We rushed in; the chamber was empty. His blood-stained sword lay on the floor; in the stone flags of the floor a black hole gaped. Then—the—towers—reeled—the—roof broke;—through—a—storm—of—crashing—walls—I—crawled.'

A strong convulsion shook the broken figure.

'Lay me down,' whispered the Roman. 'I die.'

He had ceased to breathe before Bran could comply. The Pict rose, mechanically cleansing his hands. He hastened from the spot, and as he galloped over the darkened fens, the weight of the accursed Black Stone under his cloak was as the weight of a foul nightmare on a mortal breast.

As he approached the Ring, he saw an eery glow within, so that the gaunt stones stood etched like the ribs of a skeleton in which a witch-fire burns. The stallion snorted and reared as Bran tied him to one of the menhirs. Carrying the Stone he strode into the grisly circle and saw Atla standing beside the altar, one hand on her hips, her sinuous body swaying in a serpentine manner. The altar glowed all over with ghastly light, and Bran knew someone, probably Alta, had rubbed it with phosphorous from some dank swamp or quagmire.

He strode forward and, whipping his cloak from about the Stone, flung the accursed thing onto the altar.

'I have fulfilled my part of the contract,' he growled.

'And They theirs,' she retorted. 'Look!—They come!'

He wheeled, his hand instinctively dropping to his sword. Outside the Ring the great stallion screamed savagely and reared against his tether. The night wind moaned through the waving grass and an abhorrent soft hissing mingled with it. Between the menhirs flowed a dark tide of shadows, unstable and chaotic. The Ring filled with glittering eyes which hovered beyond the dim, illusive circle of illumination cast by the phosphorescent altar. Somewhere in the darkness a human voice tittered and gibbered idiotically. Bran stiffened, the shadows of a horror clawing at his soul.

He strained his eyes, trying to make out the shapes of those who ringed him. But he glimpsed only billowing masses of shadow which heaved and writhed and squirmed with almost fluid consistency.

'Let them make good their bargain!' he exclaimed angrily.

'Then see, O king!' cried Atla in a voice of piercing mockery.

There was a stir, a seething in the writhing shadows, and from the darkness crept, like a four-legged animal, a human shape that fell down and groveled at Bran's feet and writhed and mowed, and lifting a death's-head,

howled like a dying dog. In the ghastly light, Bran,
soul-shaken, saw the blank glassy eyes, the bloodless
features, the loose, writhing, froth-covered lips of sheer
lunacy—gods, was this Titus Sulla, the proud lord of life
and death in Eboracum's proud city?

Bran bared his sword.

'I had thought to give this stroke in vengeance,' he said
somberly. 'I give it in mercy—*Vale Caesar!*'

The steel flashed in the eery light and Sulla's head
rolled to the foot of the glowing altar, where it lay staring
up at the shadowed sky.

'They harmed him not!' Atla's hateful laugh slashed the
sick silence. 'It was what he saw and came to know that
broke his brain! Like all his heavy-footed race, he knew
nothing of the secrets of this ancient land. This night he
has been dragged through the deepest pits of Hell, where
even you might have blenched!'

'Well for the Romans that they know not the secrets
of this accursed land!' Bran roared, maddened, 'with its
monster-haunted meres, its foul witch-women, and its
lost caverns and subterranean realms where spawn in the
darkness shapes of Hell!'

'Are they more foul than a mortal who seeks their
aid?' cried Alta with a shriek of fearful mirth. 'Give them
their Black Stone!'

A cataclysmic loathing shook Bran's soul with red fury.

'Aye, take your cursed Stone!' he roared, snatching
it from the altar and dashing it among the shadows with
such savagery that bones snapped under its impact. A
hurried babble of grisly tongues rose and the shadows
heaved in turmoil. One segment of the mass detached
itself for an instant, and Bran cried out in fierce revulsion,
though he caught only a fleeting glimpse of the thing, had
only a brief impression of a broad, strangely flattened
head, pendulous writhing lips that bared curved, pointed
fangs, and a hideously misshapen, dwarfish body that
seemed *mottled*—all set off by those unwinking reptilian
eyes. Gods!—the myths had prepared him for horror in

human aspect, horror induced by bestial visage and stunted deformity—but this was the horror of nightmare and the night.

'Go back to Hell and take your idol with you!' he yelled, brandishing his clenched fists to the skies, as the thick shadows receded, flowing back and away from him like the foul waters of some black flood. 'Your ancestors were men, though strange and monstrous—but gods, ye have become in ghastly fact what my people called ye in scorn!

'Worms of the earth, back into your holes and burrows! Ye foul the air and leave on the clean earth the slime of the serpents ye have become! Gonar was right—there are shapes too foul to use even against Rome!'

He sprang from the Ring as a man flees the touch of a coiling snake, and tore the stallion free. At his elbow Atla was shrieking with fearful laughter, all human attributes dropped from her like a cloak in the night.

'King of Pictland!' she cried. 'King of fools! Do you blench at so small a thing? Stay and let me show you real fruits of the pits! Ha! ha! ha! Run, fool, run! But you are stained with the taint—you have called them forth and they will remember! And in their own time they will come to you again!'

He yelled a wordless curse and struck her savagely in the mouth with his open hand. She staggered, blood starting from her lips, but her fiendish laughter only rose higher.

Bran leaped into the saddle, wild for the clean heather and the cold blue hills of the north where he could plunge his sword into clean slaughter and his sickened soul into the red maelstrom of battle, and forget the horror which lurked below the fens of the west. He gave the frantic stallion the rein, and rode through the night like a hunted ghost, until the hellish laughter of the howling were-woman died out in the darkness behind.

CORMAC OF CONNACHT

Kings of the Night

> The Caesar lolled on his ivory throne—
> His iron legions came
> To break a king in a land unknown,
> And a race without a name.
>
> *The Song of Bran*

THE dagger flashed downward. A sharp cry broke in a
gasp. The form on the rough altar twitched convulsively
and lay still. The jagged flint edge sawed at the crimsoned
breast, and thin bony fingers, ghastly dyed, tore out the
still twitching heart. Under matted white brows, sharp
eyes gleamed with a ferocious intensity.

Besides the slayer, four men stood about the crude pile
of stones that formed the altar of the God of Shadows. One
was of medium height, lithely built, scantily clad, whose
black hair was confined by a narrow iron band in the
center of which gleamed a single red jewel. Of the others,
two were dark like the first. But where he was lithe,
they were stocky and misshapen, with knotted limbs, and
tangled hair falling over sloping brows. His face denoted
intelligence and implacable will; theirs merely a beast-life
ferocity. The fourth man had little in common with the
rest. Nearly a head taller, though his hair was black
as theirs, his skin was comparatively light and he was
gray-eyed. He eyed the proceedings with little favor.

And, in truth, Cormac of Connacht was little at ease.
The Druids of his own isle of Erin had strange dark rites of

worship, but nothing like this. Dark trees shut in this grim
scene, lit by a single torch. Through the branches moaned
an eery night-wind. Cormac was alone among men of a
strange race and he had just seen the heart of a man
ripped from his still pulsing body. Now the ancient priest,
who looked scarcely human, was glaring at the throbbing
thing. Cormac shuddered, glancing at him who wore the
jewel. Did Bran Mak Morn, king of the Picts, believe that
this white-bearded old butcher could foretell events by
scanning a bleeding human heart? The dark eyes of the
king were inscrutable. There were strange depths to the
man that Cormac could not fathom, nor any other man.

'The portents are good!' exclaimed the priest wildly,
speaking more to the two chieftains than to Bran. 'Here
from the pulsing heart of a captive Roman I read—defeat
for the arms of Rome! Triumph for the sons of the
heather!'

The two savages murmured beneath their breath,
their fierce eyes smoldering.

'Go and prepare your clans for battle,' said the
king, and they lumbered away with the apelike gait
assumed by such stunted giants. Paying no more heed
to the priest who was examining the ghastly ruin on the
altar, Bran beckoned to Cormac. The Gael followed him
with alacrity. Once out of that grim grove, under the
starlight, he breathed more freely. They stood on an
eminence, looking out over long swelling undulations of
gently waving heather. Near at hand a few fires twinkled,
their fewness giving scant evidence of the hordes of
tribesmen who lay close by. Beyond these were more fires
and beyond these still more, which last marked the camp
of Cormac's own men, hard-riding, hard-fighting Gaels,
who were of that band which was just beginning to get a
foothold on the western coast of Caledonia—the nucleus
of what was later to become the kingdom of Dalriadia.
To the left of these, other fires gleamed.

And far away to the south were more fires—mere
pinpoints of light. But even at the distance the Pictish

king and his Celtic ally could see that these fires were laid out in regular order.

'The fires of the legions,' muttered Bran. 'The fires that have lit a path around the world. The men who light those fires have trampled the races under their iron heels. And now—we of the heather have our backs at the wall. What will fall on the morrow?'

'Victory for us, says the priest,' answered Cormac.

Bran made an impatient gesture. 'Moonlight on the ocean. Wind in the fir tops. Do you think that I put faith in such mummery? Or that I enjoyed the butchery of a captive legionary? I must hearten my people; it was for Gron and Bocah that I let old Gonar read the portents. The warriors will fight better.'

'And Gonar?'

Bran laughed. 'Gonar is too old to believe—anything. He was high priest of the shadows a score of years before I was born. He claims direct descent from that Gonar who was a wizard in the days of Brule, the Spear-slayer who was the first of my line. No man knows how old he is—sometimes I think he is the original Gonar himself!'

'At least,' said a mocking voice, and Cormac started as a dim shape appeared at his side, 'at least I have learned that in order to keep the faith and trust of the people, a wise man must appear to be a fool. I know secrets that would blast even your brain, Bran, should I speak them. But in order that the people may believe in me, I must descend to such things as they think proper magic—and prance and yell and rattle snakeskins, and dabble about in human blood and chicken livers.'

Cormac looked at the ancient with new interest. The semi-madness of his appearance had vanished. He was no longer the charlatan, the spell-mumbling shaman. The starlight lent him a dignity which seemed to increase his very height, so that he stood like a white-bearded patriarch.

'Bran, your doubt lies there.' The lean arm pointed to the fourth ring of fires.

'Aye,' the king nodded gloomily. 'Cormac—you know as well as I. Tomorrow's battle hinges upon the circle of the fires. With the chariots of the Britons and your own Western horsemen, our success would be certain, but—surely the devil himself is in the heart of every Northman! And now that their chief, Rognar, is dead, they swear that they will be led only by a king of their own race! Else they will break their vow and go over to the Romans. Without them we are doomed, for we can not change our former plan.'

'Take heart, Bran,' said Gonar. 'Touch the jewel in your iron crown. Mayhap it will bring you aid.'

Bran laughed bitterly. 'Now you talk as the people think. I am no fool to twist with empty words. What of the gem? It is a strange one, truth, and has brought me luck ere now. But I need now, no jewels, but the allegiance of three hundred fickle Northmen who are the only warriors among us who may stand the charge of the legions on foot.'

'But the jewel, Bran, the jewel!' persisted Gonar.

'Well, the jewel!' cried Bran impatiently. 'It is older than this world. It was old when Atlantis and Lemuria sank into the sea. It was given to Brule, the Spear-slayer, first of my line, by the Atlantean Kull, king of Valusia, in the days when the world was young. But shall that profit us now?'

'Who knows?' asked the wizard obliquely. 'Time and space exist not. There was no past, and there shall be no future. NOW is all. All things that ever were, are, or ever will be, transpire *now*. Man is forever at the center of what we call time and space. I have gone into yesterday and tomorrow and both were as real as today—which is like the dreams of ghosts! But let me sleep and talk with Gonar. Mayhap he shall aid us.'

'What means he?' asked Cormac, with a slight twitching of his shoulders, as the priest strode away in the shadows.

'He has ever said that the first Gonar comes to him
in his dreams and talks with him,' answered Bran. 'I have
seen him perform deeds that seemed beyond human ken. I
know not. I am but an unknown king with an iron crown,
trying to lift a race of savages out of the slime into which
they have sunk. Let us look to the camps.'

As they walked Cormac wondered. By what strange
freak of fate had such a man risen among the race of
savages, survivors of a darker, grimmer age? Surely he
was an atavism, an original type of the days when the
Picts ruled all Europe, before their primitive empire fell
before the bronze swords of the Gauls. Cormac knew how
Bran, rising by his own efforts from the negligent position
of the son of a Wolf clan chief, had to an extent united
the tribes of the heather and now claimed kingship over
all Caledon. But his rule was loose and much remained
before the Pictish clans would forget their feuds and
present a solid front to foreign foes. On the battle of the
morrow, the first pitched battle between the Picts under
their king and the Romans, hinged the future of the rising
Pictish kingdom.

Bran and his ally walked through the Pictish camp
where the swart warriors lay sprawled about their small
fires, sleeping or gnawing half-cooked food. Cormac was
impressed by their silence. A thousand men camped
here, yet the only sounds were occasional low guttural
intonations. This silence of the Stone Age rested in the
souls of these men.

They were all short—most of them crooked of
limb. Giant dwarfs; Bran Mak Morn was a tall man
among them. Only the older men were bearded and
they scantily, but their black hair fell about their eyes
so that they peered fiercely from under the tangle. They
were barefoot and clad scantily in wolfskins. Their arms
consisted of short barbed swords of iron, heavy black
bows, arrows tipped with flint, iron and copper, and
stone-headed mallets. Defensive armor they had none,

save for a crude shield of hide-covered wood; many had
worked bits of metal into their tangled manes as a slight
protection against sword-cuts. Some few, sons of long
lines of chiefs, were smooth-limbed and lithe like Bran,
but in the eyes of all gleamed the unquenchable savagery
of the primeval.

These men are fully savages, thought Cormac, *worse
than the Gauls, Britons and Germans. Can the old legends
be true—that they reigned in a day when strange cities rose
where now the sea rolls? And that they survived the flood that
washed those gleaming empires under, sinking again into that
savagery from which they once had risen?*

Close to the encampment of the tribesmen were the
fires of a group of Britons—members of fierce tribes
who lived south of the Roman Wall but who dwelt in
the hills and forests to the west and defied the power
of Rome. Powerfully built men they were, with blazing
blue eyes and shocks of tousled yellow hair, such men as
had thronged the Ceanntish beaches when Caesar brought
the Eagles into the Isles. These men, like the Picts, wore
no armor, and were clad scantily in coarse-worked cloth
and deerskin sandals. They bore small round bucklets of
hard wood, braced with bronze, to be worn on the left
arm, and long heavy bronze swords with blunt points.
Some had bows, though the Britons were indifferent
archers. Their bows were shorter that the Picts' and
effective only at close range. But ranged close by their
fires were the weapons that had made the name Briton
a word of terror to Pict, Roman and Norse raider alike.
Within the circle of firelight stood fifty bronze chariots
with long cruel blades curving out from the sides. One
of these blades could dismember half a dozen men at
once. Tethered close by under the vigilant eyes of their
guards grazed the chariot horses—big, rangy steeds,
swift and powerful.

'Would that we had more of them,' mused Bran.
'With a thousand chariots and my bowmen I could drive
the legions into the sea.'

'The free British tribes must eventually fall before Rome,' said Cormac. 'It would seem they would rush to join you in your war.'

Bran made a helpless gesture. 'The fickleness of the Celt. They cannot forget old feuds. Our ancient men have told us how they would not even unite against Caesar when the Romans first came. They will not make head against a common foe together. These men came to me because of some dispute with their chief, but I cannot depend on them when they are not actually fighting.'

Cormac nodded. 'I know; Caesar conquered Gaul by playing one tribe against another. My own people shift and change with the waxing and waning of the tides. But of all Celts, the Cymry are the most changeable, the least stable. Not many centuries ago my own Gaelic ancestors wrested Erin from the Cymric Danaans, because though they outnumbered us, they opposed us as separate tribes, rather than as a nation.'

'And so these Cymric Britons face Rome,' said Bran. 'These will aid us on the morrow. Further I cannot say. But how shall I expect loyalty from alien tribes, who am not sure of my own people? Thousands lurk in the hills, holding aloof. I am king in name only. Let me win tomorrow and they will flock to my standard; if I lose, they will scatter like birds before a cold wind.'

A chorus of rough welcome greeted the two leaders as they entered the camp of Cormac's Gaels. Five hundred in number they were, tall rangy men, black-haired and gray-eyes mainly, with the bearing of men who lived by war alone. While there was nothing like close discipline among them, there was an air of more system and practical order than existed in the lines of the Picts and Britons. These men were of the last Celtic race to invade the Isles and their barbaric civilization was of much higher order than that of their Cymric kin. The ancestors of the Gaels had learned the arts of war on the vast plains of Scythia and at the courts of the Pharaohs where they had fought as mercenaries of Egypt, and much of what they learned they brought into Ireland with them. Excelling in metal work, they were armed, not with clumsy bronze swords, but with high-grade weapons of iron.

They were clad in well-woven kilts and leathern sandals. Each wore a light shirt of chain mail and a vizorless helmet, but this was all of their defensive armor. Celts, Gaelic or Brythonic, were prone to judge a man's valor by the amount of armor he wore. The Britons who faced Caesar deemed the Romans cowards because they cased themselves in metal, and many centuries later the Irish clans thought the same of the mail-clad Northman knights of Strongbow.

Cormac's warriors were horsemen. They neither knew nor esteemed the use of the bow. They bore the inevitable round, metal-braced buckler, dirks, long straight swords and light single-handed axes. Their tethered horses grazed not far away—big boned animals, not so ponderous as those raised by the Britons, but swifter.

Bran's eyes lighted as the two strode through the camp. 'These men are keen-beaked birds of war! See how they whet their axes and jest of the morrow! Would that the raiders in yon camp were as staunch as your men, Cormac! Then would I greet the legions with a laugh when they come up from the south tomorrow.'

They were entering the circle of the Northmen fires. Three hundred men sat about gambling, whetting their weapons and drinking deep of the heather ale furnished them by their Pictish allies. These gazed upon Bran and Cormac with no great friendliness. It was striking to note the difference between them and the Picts and Celts—the difference in their cold eyes, their strong moody faces, their very bearing. Here was ferocity, and savagery, but not of the wild, upbursting fury of the Celt. Here was fierceness backed by grim determination and stolid stubbornness. The charge of the British clans was terrible, overwhelming. But they had no patience; let them be balked of immediate victory and they were likely to lose heart and scatter or fall to bickering among themselves.

There was the patience of the cold blue North in these seafarers—a lasting determination that would keep them steadfast to the bitter end, once their face was set toward a definite goal.

As to personal stature, they were giants; massive yet rangy. That they did not share the ideas of the Celts regarding armor was shown by the fact that they were clad in heavy scale mail shirts that reached below mid-thigh, heavy horned helmets and hardened hide leggings, reinforced, as were their shoes, with plates of iron. Their shields were huge oval affairs of hard wood, hide and brass. As to weapons, they had long iron-headed spears, heavy iron axes, and daggers. Some had long wide-bladed swords.

Cormac scarcely felt at ease with the cold magnetic eyes of these flaxen-haired men fixed upon him. He and they were hereditary foes, even though they did chance to be fighting on the same side at present—but were they?

A man came forward, a tall gaunt warrior on whose scarred, wolfish face the flickering firelight reflected deep shadows. With his wolfskin mantle flung carelessly about his wide shoulders, and the great horns on his helmet added to his height, he stood there in the swaying shadows, like some half-human thing, a brooding shape of the dark barbarism that was soon to engulf the world.

Well, Wulfhere,' said the Pictish king, 'you have drunk the mead of council and have spoken about the fires— what is your decision?'

The Northman's eyes flashed in the gloom. 'Give us a king of our own race to follow if you wish us to fight for you.'

Bran flung out his hands. 'Ask me to drag down the stars to gem your helmets! Will not your comrades follow you?'

'Not against the legions,' answered Wulfhere sullenly. 'A king led us on the Viking path—a king must lead us against the Romans. And Rognar is dead.'

'I am a king,' said Bran. 'Will you fight for me if I stand at the tip of your fight wedge?'

'A king of our own race,' said Wulfhere doggedly. 'We are all picked men of the North. We fight for none but a king, and a king must lead us—against the legions.'

Cormac sensed a subtle threat in this repeated phrase.

'Here is a prince of Erin,' said Bran. 'Will you fight for the Westerner?'

'We fight under no Celt, West or East,' growled the Viking, and a low rumble of approval rose from the onlookers. 'It is enough to fight by their side.'

The hot Gaelic blood rose in Cormac's brain and he pushed past Bran, his hand on his sword. 'How mean you that, pirate?'

Before Wulfhere could reply Bran interposed: 'Have done! Will you fools throw away the battle before it is fought, by your madness? What of your oath, Wulfhere?'

'We swore it under Rognar; when he died from a Roman arrow we were absolved of it. We will follow only a king—against the legions.'

'But your comrades will follow you—against the heather people!' snapped Bran.

'Aye,' the Northman's eyes met his brazenly. 'Send us a king or we join the Romans tomorrow.'

Bran snarled. In his rage he dominated the scene, dwarfing the huge men who towered over him.

'Traitors! Liars! I hold your lives in my hand! Aye, draw your swords if you will—Cormac, keep your blade in its sheath. These wolves will not bite a king! Wulfhere —I spared your lives when I could have taken them.

'You came to raid the countries of the South, sweeping down from the northern sea in your galleys. You ravaged the coasts and the smoke of burning villages hung like a cloud over the shores of Caledon. I trapped you all when you were pillaging and burning—with the blood of my people on your hands. I burned your longships and ambushed you when you followed. With thrice your number of bowmen who burned for your lives hidden in the heathered hills about you, I spared you when we could have shot you down like trapped wolves. Because I spared you, you swore to come and fight for me.

'And shall we die because the Picts fight Rome?' rumbled a bearded raider.

'Your lives are forfeit to me; you came to ravage the South. I did not promise to send you all back to your homes in the North unharmed and loaded with loot. Your vow was to fight one battle against Rome under my standard. Then I will aid your survivors to build ships and you may go where you will, with a goodly share of the plunder we take from the legions. Rognar had kept his oath. But Rognar died in a skirmish with Roman scouts and now you, Wulfhere the Dissension-breeder, you stir up your comrades to dishonor themselves by that which a Northman hates—the breaking of the sword word.'

'We break no oath,' snarled the Viking, and the king sensed the basic Germanic stubbornness, far harder to combat than the fickleness of the fiery Celts. 'Give us a king, neither Pict, Gael nor Briton, and we will die for you. If not—then we will fight tomorrow for the greatest of all kings—the emperor of Rome!'

For a moment Cormac thought that the Pictish king, in his black rage, would draw and strike the Northman dead. The concentrated fury that blazed in Bran's dark eyes caused Wulfhere to recoil and drop a hand to his belt.

'Fool!' said Mak Morn in a low voice that vibrated with passion. 'I could sweep you from the earth before the Romans are near enough to hear your death howls. Choose—fight for me on the morrow—or die tonight under a black cloud of arrows, a red storm of swords, a dark wave of chariots!'

At the mention of the chariots, the only arm of war that had ever broken the Norse shield-wall, Wulfhere changed expression, but he held his ground.

'War be it,' he said doggedly. 'Or a king to lead us!'

The Northmen responded with a short deep roar and a clash of swords on shields. Bran, eyes blazing, was about to speak again when a white shape glided silently into the ring of firelight.

'Soft words, soft words,' said old Gonar tranquilly. 'King, say no more. Wulfhere, you and your fellows will fight for us if you have a king to lead you?'

'We have sworn.'

'Then be at ease,' quoth the wizard; 'for ere battle joins on the morrow I will send you such a king as no man on earth has followed for a hundred thousand years! A king neither Pict, Gael nor Briton, but one to whom the emperor of Rome is as but a village headman!'

While they stood undecided, Gonar took the arms of Cormac and Bran. 'Come. And you, Northmen, remember your vow, and my promise which I have never broken. Sleep now, nor think to steal away in the darkness to the Roman camp, for if you escaped our shafts you would not escape either my curse or the suspicions of the legionaries.'

So the three walked away and Cormac, looking back, saw Wulfhere standing by the fire, fingering his golden beard, with a look of puzzled anger on his lean face.

The three walked silently through the waving heather under the faraway stars while the weird night wind whispered ghostly secrets about them.

'Ages ago,' said the wizard suddenly, 'in the days when the world was young, great lands rose where now the ocean roars. On these lands thronged mighty nations and kingdoms. Greatest of all these was Valusia—Land of Enchantment. Rome is as a village compared to the splendor of the cities of Valusia. And the greatest king was Kull, who came from the land of Atlantis to wrest the crown of Valusia from a degenerate dynasty. The Picts who dwelt in the isles which now form the mountain peaks of a strange land upon the Western Ocean, were allies of Valusia, and the greatest of all the Pictish war-chiefs was Brule the Spear-slayer, first of the line men call Mak Morn.

'Kull gave to Brule the jewel which you now wear in your iron crown, oh king, after a strange battle in a dim land, and down the long ages it has come to us, ever a sign of the Mak Morn, a symbol of former greatness. When at last the sea rose and swallowed Valusia, Atlantis, and Lemuria, only the Picts survived and they were scattered and few. Yet they began again the slow climb upward, and though many of the arts of civilization were lost in the great flood, yet they progressed. The art of metal-working was lost, so they excelled in the working of flint. And they ruled all the new lands flung up by the sea and now called Europe, until down from the north came younger tribes who had scarce risen from the ape when Valusia reigned in her glory, and who, dwelling in the icy lands about the Pole, knew naught of the lost splendor of the Seven Empires and little of the flood that had swept away half a world.

'And still they have come—Aryans, Celts, Germans, swarming down from the great cradle of their race which lies near the Pole. So again was the growth of the Pictish nation checked and the race hurled into savagery. Erased from the earth, on the fringe of the world with our backs to the wall we fight. Here in Caledon is the last stand of a once mighty race. And we change. Our people have mixed with the savages of an elder age which we drove into the North when we came into the Isles, and now, save for their chieftains, such as thou, Bran, a Pict is strange and abhorrent to look upon.'

'True, true,' said the king impatiently, 'but what has that to do—'

'Kull, king of Valusia,' said the wizard imperturbably, 'was a barbarian in his age as thou art in thine, though he ruled a mighty empire by the weight of his sword. Gonar, friend of Brule, your first ancestor, has been dead a hundred thousand years as we reckon time. Yet I talked with him a scant hour agone.'

'You talked with his ghost—'

'Or he with mine? Did I go back a hundred thousand years, or did he come forward? If he came to me out of the past, it is not I who talked with a dead man, but he who talked with a man unborn. Past, present and future are one to a wise man. I talked to Gonar while he was alive; likewise was I alive. In a timeless, spaceless land we met and he told me many things.'

The land was growing light with the birth of dawn. The heather waved and bent in long rows before the dawn wind as bowing in worship of the rising sun.

'The jewel in your crown is a magnet that draws down the eons,' said Gonar. 'The sun is rising—and who comes out of the sunrise?'

Cormac and the king started. The sun was just lifting a red orb above the eastern hills. And full in the glow, etched boldly against the golden rim, a man suddenly appeared. They had not seen him come. Against the golden birth of day he loomed colossal; a gigantic god from the dawn of creation. Now as he strode toward them the waking hosts saw him and sent up a sudden shout of wonder.

'Who—or what—is it?' exclaimed Bran.

'Let us go to meet him, Bran,' answered the wizard. 'He is the king Gonar has sent to save the people of Brule.'

2

I have reached these lands but newly
From an ultimate dim Thule;
        From a wild weird clime that lieth sublime
        Out of Space—out of Time.

                                                              Poe

The army fell silent as Bran, Cormac and Gonar went toward the stranger who approached in long swinging strides. As they neared him the illusion of monstrous size vanished, but they saw he was a man of great stature. At first Cormac thought him to be a Northman but a second glance told him that nowhere before had he seen such a man. He was built much like the Vikings, at once massive and lithe—tigerish. But his features were not as theirs, and his square-cut, lionlike mane of hair was as black as Bran's own. Under heavy brows glittered eyes gray as steel and cold as ice. His bronzed face, strong and inscrutable, was clean-shaven, and the broad forehead betokened a high intelligence just as the firm jaw and thin lips showed will-power and courage. But more than all, the bearing of him, the unconscious lionlike stateliness, marked him as a natural king, a ruler of men.

Sandals of curious make were on his feet and he wore a pliant coat of strangely meshed mail which came almost to his knees. A broad belt with a great golden buckle encircled his waist, supporting a long straight sword in a heavy leather scabbard. His hair was confined by a wide, heavy golden band about his head.

Such was the man who paused before the silent group. He seemed slightly puzzled, slightly amused. Recognition flickered in his eyes. He spoke in a strange archaic Pictish which Cormac scarcely understood. His voice was deep and resonant.

'Ha, Brule, Gonar did not tell me I would dream of you!'

For the first time in his life Cormac saw the Pictish king completely thrown off his balance. He gasped, speechless. The stranger continued:

'And wearing the gem I gave you, in a circlet on your head! Last night you wore it in a ring on your finger.'

'Last night?' gasped Bran.

'Last night or a hundred thousand years ago—all one!' murmured Gonar in evident enjoyment of the situation.

'I am not Brule,' said Bran. 'Are you made to thus speak of a man dead a hundred thousand years? He was first of my line.'

The stranger laughed unexpectedly. 'Well, now I know I am dreaming! This will be a tale to tell Brule when I waken on the morrow! That I went into the future and saw men claiming descent from the Spear-slayer who is, as yet, not even married. No, you are not Brule, I see now, though you have his eyes and his bearing. But he is taller and broader in the shoulders. Yet you have his jewel—oh, well—anything can happen in a dream, so I will not quarrel with you. For a time I thought I had been transported to some other land in my sleep, and was in reality awake in a strange country, for this is the clearest dream I ever dreamed. Who are you?'

'I am Bran Mak Morn, king of the Caledonian Picts. And this ancient is Gonar, a wizard, of the line of Gonar. And this warrior is Cormac na Connacht, a prince of the isle of Erin.'

The stranger slowly shook his lionlike head. 'These words sound strangely to me, save Gonar—and that one is not Gonar, though he too is old. What land is this?'

'Caledon, or Alba, as the Gaels call it.'

'And who are those squat apelike warriors who watch us yonder, all agape?'

'They are the Picts who own my rule.'

'How strangely distorted folk are in dreams!' muttered the stranger. 'And who are those shock-headed men about the chariots?'

'They are Britons—Cymry from south of the Wall.'

'What Wall?'

'The Wall built by Rome to keep the people of the heather out of Briton.'

'Britain?' the tone was curious. 'I never heard of that land—and what is Rome?'

'What!' cried Bran. 'You never heard of Rome, the empire that rules the world?'

'No empire rules the world,' answered the other haughtily. 'The mightiest kingdom on earth is that wherein I reign.'

'And who are you?'

'Kull of Atlantis, king of Valusia!'

Cormac felt a coldness trickle down his spine. The cold gray eyes were unswerving—but this was incredible—monstrous—unnatural.

'Valusia!' cried Bran. 'Why, man, the sea waves have rolled above the spires of Valusia for untold centuries!'

Kull laughed outright. 'What a mad nightmare this is! When Gonar put on me the spell of deep sleep last night—or this night!—in the secret room of the inner palace, he told me I would dream strange things, but this is more fantastic that I reckoned. And the strangest thing is, I know I am dreaming!'

Gonar interposed as Bran would have spoken. 'Question not the acts of the gods,' muttered the wizard. 'You are king because in the past you have seen and seized opportunities. The gods or the first Gonar have sent you this man. Let me deal with him.'

Brand nodded, and while the silent army gaped in speechless wonder, just within earshot, Gonar spoke: 'Oh great king, you dream, but is not all life a dream? How reckon you but that your former life is but a dream from which you have just awakened? Now we dream-folk have our wars and our peace, and just now a great host comes up form the south to destroy the people of Brule. Will you aid us?'

Kull grinned with pure zest. 'Aye! I have fought battles in dreams ere now, have slain and been slain and was amazed when I woke from my visions. And at times, as now, dreaming I have known I dreamed. See, I pinch myself and feel it, but I know I dream for I have felt the pain of fierce wounds, in dreams. Yes, people of my dream, I will fight for you against the other dream-folk. Where are they?'

'And that you enjoy the dream more,' said the wizard subtly, 'forget that it is a dream and pretend that by the magic of the first Gonar, and the quality of the jewel you gave Brule, that now gleams on the crown of the Morni, you have in truth been transported forward into another,

wilder age where the people of Brule fight for their life
against a stronger foe.'

For a moment the man who called himself king of
Valusia seemed startled; a strange look of doubt, almost
of fear, clouded his eyes. Then he laughed.

'Good! Lead on, wizard.'

But now Bran took charge. He had recovered himself
and was at ease. Whether he thought, like Cormac, that
this was all a gigantic hoax arranged by Gonar, he
showed no sign.

'King Kull, see you those men yonder who lean on
their long-shafted axes as they gaze upon you?'

'The tall men with the golden hair and beards?'

'Aye—our success in the coming battle hinges on them.
They swear to go over to the enemy if we give them not
a king to lead them—their own having been slain. Will
you lead them to battle?'

Kull's eyes glowed with appreciation. 'They are men
such as my own Red Slayers, my picked regiment. I will
lead them.'

'Come then.'

The small group made their way down the slope,
through throngs of warriors who pushed forward eagerly
to get a better view of the stranger, then pressed back as
he approached. An undercurrent of tense whispering ran
through the horde.

The Northmen stood apart in a compact group. Their
cold eyes took in Kull and he gave back their stares, taking
in every detail of their appearance.

'Wulfhere,' said Bran, 'we have brought you a king. I
hold you to your oath.'

'Let him speak to us,' said the Viking harshly.

'He cannot speak your tongue,' answered Bran, knowing that the Northmen knew nothing of the legends of
his race.

'He is a great king of the South—'

'He comes out of the past,' broke in the wizard calmly.
'He was the greatest of all kings, long ago.'

'A dead man!' The Vikings moved uneasily and the rest of the horde pressed forward, drinking in every word. But Wulfhere scowled: 'Shall a ghost lead living men? You bring us a man you say is dead. We will not follow a corpse.'

'Wulfhere,' said Bran in still passion, 'you are a liar and a traitor. You set us this task, thinking it impossible. You yearn to fight under the Eagles of Rome. We have brought you a king neither Pict, Gael nor Briton and you deny your vow!'

'Let him fight me, then!' howled Wulfhere in uncontrollable wrath, swinging his ax about his head in a glittering arc. 'If your dead man overcomes me—then my people will follow you. If I overcome him, you shall let us depart in peace to the camp of the legions!'

'Good!' said the wizard. 'Do you agree, wolves of the North?'

A fierce yell and a brandishing of swords was the answer. Bran turned to Kull, who had stood silent, understanding nothing of what was said. But the Atlantean's eyes gleamed. Cormac felt that those cold eyes had looked on too many such scenes not to understand something of what had passed.

'This warrior says you must fight him for the leadership,' said Bran, and Kull, eyes glittering with growling battle-joy, nodded: 'I guessed as much. Give us space.'

'A shield and a helmet!' shouted Bran, but Kull shook his head.

'I need none,' he growled. 'Back and give us room to swing our steel!'

Men pressed back on each side, forming a solid ring about the two men, who now approached each other warily. Kull had drawn his sword and the great blade shimmered like a live thing in his hand. Wulfhere, scarred by a hundred savage fights, flung aside his wolfskin mantle and came in cautiously, fierce eyes peering over the top of his out-thrust shield, ax half lifted in his right hand.

Suddenly when the warriors were still many feet apart Kull sprang. His attack brought a gasp from men used to deeds of prowess; for like a leaping tiger he shot through the air and his sword crashed on the quickly lifted shield. Sparks flew and Wulfhere's ax hacked in, but Kull was under its sweep and as it swished viciously above his head he thrust upward and sprang out again, catlike. His motions had been too quick for the eye to follow. The upper edge of Wulfhere's shield showed a deep cut, and there was a long rent in his mail shirt where Kull's sword had barely missed the flesh beneath.

Cormac, trembling with the terrible thrill of the fight, wondered at this sword that could thus slice through scale-mail. And the blow that gashed the shield should have shattered the blade. Yet not a notch showed in the Valusian steel! Surely this blade was forged by another people in another age!

Now the two giants leaped again to the attack and like double strokes of lightning their weapons crashed. Wulfhere's shield fell from his arm in two pieces as the Atlantean's sword sheared clear through it, and Kull staggered as the Northman's ax, driven with all the force of his great body, descended on the golden circlet about his head. That blow should have sheared through the gold like butter to split the skull beneath, but the ax rebounded, showing a great notch in the edge. The next instant the Northman was overwhelmed by a whirlwind of steel—a storm of strokes delivered with such swiftness and power that he was borne back as on the crest of a wave, unable to launch an attack of his own. With all his tried skill he sought to parry the singing steel with his ax. But he could only avert his doom for a few seconds; could only for an instant turn the whistling blade that hewed off bits of his mail, so close fell the blows. One of the horns flew from his helmet; then the ax-head itself fell away, and the same blow that severed the handle, bit through the Viking's helmet into the scalp beneath. Wulfhere was dashed to his knees, a trickle of blood starting down his face.

Kull checked his second stroke, and tossing his sword to Cormac, faced the dazed Northman weaponless. The Atlantean's eyes were blazing with ferocious joy and he roared something in a strange tongue. Wulfhere gathered his legs under him and bounded up, snarling like a wolf, a dagger flashing into his hand. The watching horde gave tongue in a yell that ripped the skies as the two bodies clashed. Kull's clutching hand missed the Northman's wrist but the desperately lunging dagger snapped on the Atlantean's mail, and dropping the useless hilt, Wulfhere locked his arms about his foe in a bear-like grip that would have crushed the ribs of a lesser man. Kull grinned tigerishly and returned the grapple, and for a moment the two swayed on their feet. Slowly the black-haired warrior bent his foe backward until it seemed his spine would snap. With a howl that had nothing of the human in it, Wulfhere clawed frantically at Kull's face, trying to tear out his eyes, then turned his head and snapped his fang-like teeth into the Atlantean's arm. A yell went up as a trickle of blood started: 'He bleeds! He bleeds! He is no ghost, after all, but a mortal man!'

Angered, Kull shifted his grip, shoving the frothing Wulfhere away from him, and smote him terrifically under the ear with his right hand. The Viking landed on his back a dozen feet away. Then, howling like a wild man, he leaped up with a stone in his hand and flung it. Only Kull's incredible quickness saved his face; as it was, the rough edge of the missile tore his cheek and inflamed him to madness. With a lionlike roar he bounded upon his foe, enveloped him in an irresistible blast of sheer fury, whirled him high above his head as if he were a child and cast him a dozen feet away. Wulfhere pitched on his head and lay still—broken and dead.

Dazed silence reigned for an instant; then from the Gaels went up a thundering roar, and the Britons and Picts took it up, howling like wolves, until the echoes of the shouts and the clangor of sword on shield reached the ears of the marching legionaries, miles to the south.

'Men of the gray North,' shouted Bran, 'will you hold by your oath, *now?*'

The fierce souls of the Northmen were in their eyes as their spokesman answered. Primitive, superstitious, steeped in tribal lore of fighting gods and mythical heroes, they did not doubt that the black-haired fighting man was some supernatural being sent by the fierce gods of battle.

'Aye! Such a man as this we have never seen! Dead man, ghost, or devil, we will follow him, whether the trail lead to Rome or Valhalla!'

Kull understood the meaning, if not the words. Taking his sword for Cormac with a word of thanks, he turned to the waiting Northmen and silently held the blade toward them high above his head, in both hands, before he returned it to its scabbard. Without understanding, they appreciated the action. Bloodstained and disheveled, he was an impressive picture of stately, magnificent barbarism.

'Come,' said Bran, touching the Atlantean's arm; 'a host is marching on us and we have much to do. There is scant time to arrange our forces before they will be upon us. Come to the top of yonder slope.'

There the Pict pointed. They were looking down into a valley which ran north and south, widening from a narrow gorge in the north until it debouched upon a plain to the south. The whole valley was less than a mile in length.

'Up this valley will our foes come,' said the Pict, 'because they have wagons loaded with supplies and on all sides of this vale the ground is too rough for such travel. Here we plan an ambush.'

'I would have thought you would have had your men lying in wait long before now,' said Kull. 'What of the scouts the enemy is sure to send out?'

'The savages I lead would never have waited in ambush so long,' said Bran with a touch of bitterness. 'I could not post them until I was sure of the Northmen. Even so I had not dared to post them ere now—even yet they may take panic from the drifting of a cloud or the blowing of a leaf, and scatter like birds before a cold wind. King Kull—the fate of the Pictish nation is at stake. I am called king of the Picts, but my rule as yet is but a hollow mockery. The hills are full of wild clans who refuse to fight for me. Of the thousand bowmen now at my command, more than half are of my own clan.

'Some eighteen hundred Romans are marching against us. It is not a real invasion, but much hinges upon it. It is the beginning of an attempt to extend their boundaries. They plan to build a fortress a day's march to the north of this valley. If they do, they will build other forts, drawing bands of steel about the heart of the free people. If I win this battle and wipe out this army, I will win a double victory. Then the tribes will flock to me and the next invasion will meet a solid wall of resistance. If I lose, the clans will scatter, fleeing into the north until they can no longer flee, fighting as separate clans rather than as one strong nation.

'I have a thousand archers, five hundred horsemen, fifty chariots with their drivers and swordsmen—one hundred fifty men in all—and, thanks to you, three hundred heavily armed Northern pirates. How would you arrange your battle lines?'

'Well,' said Kull, 'I would have barricaded the north end of the valley—no! That would suggest a trap. But I would block it with a band of desperate men, like those you have given me to lead. Three hundred could hold the gorge for a time against any number. Then, when the enemy was engaged with these men to the narrow part of the valley, I would have my archers shoot down into them until their ranks are broken, from both sides of the vale. Then, having my horsemen concealed behind the other, I would charge with both simultaneously and sweep the foe into a red ruin.'

Brian's eyes glowed. 'Exactly, king of Valusia. Such was my exact plan—'

'But what of the scouts?'

'My warriors are like panthers; they hide under the noses of the Romans. Those who ride into the valley will see only what we wish them to see. Those who ride over the ridge will not come back to report. An arrow is swift and silent.

'You see that the pivot of the whole thing depends on the men that hold the gorge. They must be men who can fight on foot and resist the charges of the heavy legionaries long enough for the trap to close. Outside these Northmen I had no such force of men. My naked warriors with their short swords could never stand such a charge for an instant. Nor is the armor of the Celts made for such work; moreover, they are not foot-fighters, and I need them elsewhere.

'So you see why I had such desperate need of the Northmen. Now will you stand in the gorge with them and hold back the Romans until I can spring the trap? Remember, most of you will die.'

Kull smiled. 'I have taken chances all my life, though Tu, chief councillor, would say my life belongs to Valusia and I have no right to so risk it—' His voice trailed off and a strange look fitted across his face. 'By Valka,' said he, laughing uncertainly, 'sometimes I forget this is a dream! All seems so real. But it is—of course it is! Well, then, if I die I will but awaken as I have done in times past. Lead on, king of Caledon!'

Cormac, going to his warriors, wondered. Surely it was all a hoax; yet—he heard the arguments of the warriors all about him as they armed themselves and prepared to take their posts. The black-haired king was Neid himself, the Celtic war-god; he was an antediluvian king brought out of the past by Gonar; he was a mythical fighting man out of Valhalla. He was no man at all but a ghost! No, he was mortal, for he had bled. But the gods themselves bled, though they did not die. So the controversies raged. At least, thought Cormac, if it was all a hoax to inspire the warriors with the feeling of supernatural aid, it had succeeded. The belief that Kull was more than a mortal man had fired Celt, Pict, and Viking alike into a sort of inspired madness. And Cormac asked himself—what did he himself believe? This man was surely one from some far land—yet in his every look and action there was a vague hint of a greater difference than mere distance of space—a hint of alien Time, of misty abysses and gigantic gulfs of eons lying between the black-haired stranger and the men with whom he walked and talked. Clouds of bewilderment mazed Cormac's brain and he laughed in whimsical self-mockery.

3

And the two wild peoples of the north
   Stood fronting in the gloam,
And heard and knew each in his mind
A third great sound upon the wind,
The living walls that hedge mankind,
   The walking walls of Rome.

Chesterton

The sun slanted westward. Silence lay like an invisible mist over the valley. Cormac gathered the reins in his hand and glanced up at the ridges on both sides. The waving heather which grew rank on those steep slopes gave no evidence of the hundreds of savage warriors who lurked there. Here in the narrow gorge which widened gradually southward was the only sign of life. Between the steep walls three hundred Northmen were massed solidly in their wedge-shaped shield-wall, blocking the pass. At the tip, like the point of a spear, stood the man who called himself Kull, king of Valusia. He wore no helmet, only the great, strangely worked headband of hard gold, but he bore on his left arm the great shield borne by the dead Rognar; and in his right hand he held the heavy iron mace wielded by the sea-king. The

Vikings eyed him in wonder and savage admiration. They could not understand his language, or he theirs. But no further orders were necessary. At Bran's directions they had bunched themselves in the gorge, and their only order was—hold the pass!

Bran Mak Morn stood just in front of Kull. So they faced each other, he whose kingdom was yet unborn, and he whose kingdom had been lost in the mists of Time for unguessed ages. Kings of darkness, thought Cormac, nameless kings of the night, whose realms are gulfs and shadows.

The hand of the Pictish king went out. 'King Kull, you are more than king—you are a man. Both of us may fall within the next hour—but if we live, ask what you will of me.'

Kull smiled, returning the firm grip. 'You too are a man after my own heart, king of the shadows. Surely you are more than a figment of my sleeping imagination. Mayhap we will meet in waking life some day.'

Bram shook his head in puzzlement, swung into the saddle and rode away, climbing the eastern slope and vanishing over the ridge. Cormac hesitated: 'Strange man, are you in truth of flesh and blood, or are you a ghost?'

'When we dream, we are all flesh and blood—so long as we are dreaming,' Kull answered:'This is the strangest nightmare I have ever known—but you, who will soon fade into sheer nothingness as I awaken, seem as real to me *now*, as Brule, or Kananu, or Tu, or Kelkor.'

Cormac shook his head as Bran had done, and with a last salute, which Kull returned with barbaric stateliness, he turned and trotted away. At the top of the western ridge he paused. Away to the south a light cloud of dust rose and the head of the marching column was in sight. Already he believed he could feel the earth vibrate slightly to the measured tread of a thousand mailed feet beating in perfect unison. He dismounted, and one of his chieftains, Domnail, took his steed and let it down the slope away from the valley, where trees grew thickly. Only an occasional vague movement among them gave evidence of the five hundred men who stood there, each at his horse's head with a ready hand to check a chance nicker.

Oh, thought Cormac, *the gods themselves made this valley for Bran's ambush!* The floor of the valley was treeless and the inner slopes were bare save for the waist-high heather. But at the foot of each ridge on the side facing away from the vale, where the soil long washed from the rocky slopes had accumulated, there grew enough trees to hide five hundred horsemen or fifty chariots.

At the northern end of the valley stood Kull and his three hundred Vikings, in open view, flanked on each side by fifty Pictish bowmen. Hidden on the western side of the western ridge were the Gaels. Along the top of the slopes, concealed in the tall heather, lay a hundred Picts with their shafts on string. The rest of the Picts were hidden on the eastern slopes beyond which lay the Britons with their chariots in full readiness. Neither they nor the Gaels to the west could see what went on in the vale, but signals had been arranged.

Now the long column was entering the wide mouth of the valley and their scouts, light-armed men on swift horses, were spreading out between the slopes. They galloped almost within bowshot of the silent host that blocked the pass, then halted. Some whirled and raced back to the main force, while the others deployed and cantered up the slopes, seeking to see what lay beyond. This was the crucial moment. If they got any hint of the ambush, all was lost. Cormac, shrinking down into the heather, marveled at the ability of the Picts to efface themselves from view so completely. He saw a horseman pass within three feet of where he knew a bowman lay, yet the Roman saw nothing.

The scouts topped the ridges, gazed about; then most of them turned and trotted back down the slopes. Cormac wondered at their desultory manner of scouting. He had never fought Romans before, knew nothing of their arrogant self-confidence, of their incredible shrewdness in some ways, their incredible stupidity in others. These men were over-confident; feeling radiating from their officers. It had been years since a force of Caledonians had stood before the legions. And most of these men were but newly come to Britain; part of a legion which had been quartered in Egypt. They despised their foes and suspected nothing.

But stay—three riders on the opposite ridge had turned and vanished on the other side. And now one, sitting his steed at the crest of the western ridge, not a hundred yards from where Cormac lay, looked long and narrowly down into the mass of trees at the foot of the slope. Cormac saw suspicion grow on his brown, hawklike face. He half turned as though to call to his comrades, then instead reined his steed down the slope, leaning forward in his saddle. Cormac's heart pounded. Each moment he expected to see the man wheel and gallop back to raise the alarm. He resisted a mad impulse to leap up and charge the Roman on foot. Surely the man could feel the tenseness in the air—the hundreds of fierce eyes upon him. Now he was halfway down the slope, out of sight of the men in the valley. And now the twang of an unseen bow broke the painful stillness. With a strangled gasp the Roman flung his hands high, and as the steed reared, he pitched headlong, transfixed by a long black arrow that had flashed from the heather. A stocky dwarf sprang out of nowhere, seemingly, and seized the bridle, quieting the snorting horse and leading it down the slope. At the fall of the Roman, short crooked men rose like a sudden flight of birds from the grass and Cormac saw the flash of a knife. Then with unreal suddenness all had subsided. Slayers and slain were unseen and only the still waving heather marked the grim deed.

The Gael looked back into the valley. The three who had ridden over the eastern ridge had not come back and Cormac knew they never would. Evidently the other scouts had borne word that only a small band of warriors was ready to dispute the passage of the legionaries. Now the head of the column was almost below him and he thrilled at the sight of these men who were doomed, swinging along with their superb arrogance. And the sight of their splendid armor, their hawklike faces and perfect discipline awed him as much as it is possible for a Gael to be awed.

Twelve hundred men in heavy armor who marched as one so that the ground shook to their tread! Most of them were of middle height, with powerful chests and shoulders and bronzed faces—hard-bitten veterans of a hundred campaigns. Cormac noted their javelins, short keen swords and heavy shields; their gleaming armor and crested helmets, the eagles on the standards. These were the men beneath whose tread the world had shaken and empires crumbled! Not all were Latins; there were Romanized Britons among them, and one century or hundred was composed of huge yellow-haired men—Gauls and Germans, who fought for Rome as fiercely as did the native-born, and hated their wilder kinsmen more savagely.

On each side was a swarm of calvary, outriders, and the column was flanked by archers and slingers. A number of lumbering wagons carried the supplies of the army. Cormac saw the commander riding in his place—a tall man with a lean, imperious face, evident even at that distance. Marcus Sulius—the Gael knew him by repute.

A deep-throated roar rose from the legionaries as they approached their foes. Evidently they intended to slice their way through and continue without a pause, for the column moved implacably on. Whom the gods destroy they first make mad—Cormac had never heard the phrase but it came to him that the great Sulius was a fool. Roman arrogance! Marcus was used to lashing the cringing peoples of a decadent East; little he guessed of the iron in these western races.

A group of cavalry detached itself and raced into the mouth of the gorge, but it was only a gesture. With loud jeering shouts they wheeled three spears length

away and cast their javelins, which rattled harmlessly on
the overlapping shields of the silent Northmen. But their
leader dared too much; swinging in, he leaned from his
saddle and thrust at Kull's face. The great shield turned
the lance and Kull struck back as a snake strikes; the
ponderous mace crushed helmet and head like an eggshell,
and the very steed went to its knees from the shock of
that terrible blow. From the Northmen went up a short
fierce roar, and the Picts beside them howled exultantly
and loosed their arrows among the retreating horsemen.
First blood for the people of the heather! The oncoming
Romans shouted vengefully and quickened their pace as
the frightened horse raced by, a ghastly travesty of a
man, foot caught in the stirrup, trailing beneath the
pounding hoofs.

Now the first line of the legionaries, compressed
because of the narrowness of the gorge, crashed against
the solid wall of shields—crashed and recoiled upon itself.
The shield-wall had not shaken an inch. This was the first
time the Roman legions had met with that unbreakable
formation—that oldest of all Aryan battle lines—the
ancestor of the Spartan regiment—the Theban phalanx
—the Macedonian formation—the English square.

Shield crashed on shield and the short Roman sword
sought for an opening in that iron wall. Viking spears,
bristling in solid ranks above, thrust and reddened;
heavy axes chopped down, shearing through iron, flesh
and bone. Cormac saw Kull, looming above the stocky
Romans in the forefront of the fray, dealing blows,
like thunderbolts. A burly centurion rushed in, shield
held high, stabbing upward. The iron mace crashed
terribly, shivering the sword, rending the shield apart,
shattering the helmet, crushing the skull down between
the shoulders—in a single blow.

The front line of the Romans bent like a steel bar about
the wedge, as the legionaries sought to struggle through
the gorge on each side and surround their opposers. But
the pass was too narrow; crouching close against the

steep walls the Picts drove their black arrows in a hail of
death. At this range the heavy shafts tore through shield
and corselet, transfixing the armored men. The front line
of battle rolled back, red and broken, and the Northmen
trod their few dead under foot to close the gaps their fall
had made. Stretched the full width of their front lay a thin
line of shattered forms—the red spray of the tide which
had broken upon them in vain.

Cormac had leaped to his feet, waving his arms.
Domnail and his men broke cover at the signal and came
galloping up the slope, lining the ridge. Cormac mounted
the horse brought him and glanced impatiently across the
narrow vale. No sign of life appeared on the eastern ridge.
Where was Bran—and the Britons?

Down in the valley, the legions, angered at the unexpected opposition of the paltry force in front of them, but
not suspicious, were forming in more compact body. The
wagons which had halted were lumbering on again and the
whole column was once more in motion as if it intended
to crash through by sheer weight. With the Gaulish
century in the forefront, the legionaries, were advancing
again in the attack. This time, with the full force of twelve
hundred men behind, the charge would batter down the
resistance of Kull's warriors like a heavy ram; would
stamp them down, sweep over their red ruins. Cormac's
men trembled in impatience. Suddenly Marcus Sulius
turned and gazed westward, where the line of horsemen
was etched against the sky. Even at that distance Cormac
saw his face pale. The Roman at last realized the metal
of the men he faced, and that he had walked into a trap.
Surely in that moment there flashed a chaotic picture
through his brain—defeat—disgrace—red ruin!

It was too late to retreat—too late to form into a
defensive square with the wagons for barricade. There
was but one possible way out, and Marcus, crafty general
in spite of his recent blunder, took it. Cormac heard his
voice cut like a clarion through the din, and though he
did not understand the words, he knew that the Roman

was shouting for his men to smite that knot of Northmen
like a blast—to hack their way through and out of the trap
before it could close!

Now the legionaries, aware of their desperate plight,
flung themselves headlong and terribly on their foes. The
shield-wall rocked, but it gave not an inch. The wild faces
of the Gauls and the hard brown Italian faces glared over
locked shields into the blazing eyes of the North. Shields
touching, they smote and slew and died in a red storm
of slaughter, where crimsoned axes rose and fell and
dripping spears broke on notched swords.

Where in God's name was Bran with his chariots?
A few minutes more would spell the doom of every
man who held that pass. Already they were falling fast,
though they locked their ranks closer and held like iron.
Those wild men of the North were dying in their tracks;
and looming among their gold heads the black lion-mane
of Kull shone like a symbol of slaughter, and his reddened
mace showered a ghastly rain as it splashed brains and
blood like water.

Something snapped in Cormac's brain.

'These men will die while we wait for Bran's signal!'
he shouted. 'On! Follow me into Hell, sons of Gael!'

A wild roar answered him, and loosing rein he shot
down the slope with five hundred yelling riders plunging
headlong after him. And even at that moment a storm
of arrows swept the valley from either side like a dark
cloud and the terrible clamor of the Picts split the skies.
And over the eastern ridge, like a sudden burst of rolling
thunder on Judgment Day, rushed the war-chariots.
Headlong down the slope they roared, foam flying from
the horses' distended nostrils, frantic feet scarcely seem-
ing to touch the ground, making naught of the tall
heather. In the foremost chariot, with his dark eyes
blazing, crouched Bran Mak Morn, and in all of them
the naked Britons were screaming and lashing as if
possessed by demons. Behind the flying chariots came
the Picts, howling like wolves and loosing their arrows

as they ran. The heather belched them forth from all sides in a dark wave.

So much Cormac saw in chaotic glimpses during the wild ride down the slopes. A wave of cavalry swept between him and the main line of the column. Three long leaps ahead of his men, the Gaelic prince met the spears of the Roman riders. The first lance turned on his buckler, and rising in his stirrups he smote downward, cleaving his man from shoulders to breastbone. The next Roman flung a javelin that killed Domnail, but at that instant Cormac's steed crashed into his, breast to breast, and the lighter horse rolled headlong under the shock, flinging his rider beneath the pounding hoofs.

Then the whole blast of the Gaelic charge smote the Roman cavalry, shattering it, crashing and rolling it down and under. Over its red ruins Cormac's yelling demons struck the heavy Roman infantry, and the whole line reeled at the shock. Swords and axes flashed up and down and the force of their rush carried them deep into the massed ranks. Here, checked, they swayed and strove. Javelins thrust, swords flashed upward bringing down horse and rider, and greatly outnumbered, leaguered on every side, the Gaels had perished among their foe, but at that moment, from the other side the crashing chariots smote the Roman ranks. In one long line they struck almost simultaneously, and at the moment of impact the charioteers wheeled their horses sidelong and raced parallel down the ranks, shearing men down like the mowing of wheat. Hundreds died on those curving blades in that moment, and leaping from the chariots, screaming like blood-mad wildcats, the British swordsmen flung themselves upon the spears of the legionaries, hacking madly with their two-handed swords. Crouching, the Picts drove their arrows pointblank and then sprang in to slash and thrust. Maddened with the sight of victory, these wild peoples were like wounded tigers, feeling no wounds, and dying on their feet with their last gasp a snarl of fury.

But the battle was not over yet. Dazed, shattered, their formation broken and nearly half their number down already, the Romans fought back with desperate fury. Hemmed in on all sides they slashed and smote singly, or in small clumps, fought back to back, archers, slingers, horsemen and heavy legionaries mingled into a chaotic mass. The confusion was complete, but not the victory. Those bottled in the gorge still hurled themselves upon the red axes that barred their way, while the massed and serried battle thundered behind them. From one side Cormac's Gaels raged and slashed; from the other chariots swept back and forth, retiring and returning like iron whirlwinds. There was no retreat, for the Picts had flung a cordon across the way they had come, and having cut the throats of the camp followers and possessed themselves of the wagons, they sent their shafts in a storm of death into the rear of the shattered column. Those long black arrows pierced armor and bone, nailing men together. Yet the slaughter was not all on one side. Picts died beneath the lightning thrust of javelin and shortsword, Gaels pinned beneath their falling horses were hewed to pieces, and chariots, cut loose from their horses, were deluged with the blood of the charioteers.

And at the narrow head of the valley still the battle surged and eddied. Great gods—thought Cormac, glancing between lightning-like blows—do these men still hold the gorge? Aye! They held it! A tenth of their original number, dying on their feet, they still held back the frantic charges of the dwindling legionaries.

Over all the field went up the roar and the clash of arms, and birds of prey, swift-flying out of the sunset, circled above. Cormac, striving to reach Marcus Sulius through the press, saw the Roman's horse sink under him, and the rider rise alone in a waste of foes. He saw the Roman sword flash thrice, dealing a death at each blow; then form the thickest of the fray bounded a terrible figure. It was Bran Mak Morn, stained from head to foot. He cast away his broken sword as he ran, drawing a dirk. The

Roman struck, but the Pictish king was under the thrust, and gripping the swordwrist, he drove the dirk again and again through the gleaming armor.

A mighty roar went up as Marcus died, and Cormac, with a shout, rallied the remnants of his force about him and, striking in the spurs, burst through the shattered lines and rode full speed for the other end of the valley.

But as he approached he saw that he was too late. As they had lived, so had they died, those fierce sea-wolves, with their faces to the foe and their broken weapons red in their hands. In a grim and silent band they lay, even in death preserving some of the shield-wall formation. Among them, in front of them and all about them lay high-heaped the bodies of those who had sought to break them, in vain. *They had not given back a foot!* To the last man, they had died in their tracks. Nor were there any left to stride over their torn shapes; those Romans who had escaped the Viking axes had been struck down by the shafts of the Picts and swords of the Gael from behind.

Yet this part of the battle was not over. High up on the steep western slope Cormac saw the ending of that drama. A group of Gauls in the armor of Rome pressed upon a single man—a black-haired giant on whose head gleamed a golden crown. There was iron in these men, as well as in the man who had held them to their fate. They were doomed—their comrades were being slaughtered behind them—but before their turn came they would at least have the life of the black-haired chief who had led the golden-haired men of the North.

Pressing upon him from three sides they had forced him slowly back up the steep gorge wall, and the crumpled bodies that stretched along his retreat showed how fiercely every foot of the way had been contested. Here on this steep it was task enough to keep one's footing alone; yet these men at once climbed and fought. Kull's shield and the huge mace were gone, and the great sword in his right hand was dyed crimson. His mail, wrought with a forgotten art, now hung in shreds, and blood streamed from a hundred wounds on limbs, head and body. But his eyes still blazed with the battle-joy and his wearied arm still drove the mighty blade in strokes of death.

But Cormac saw that the end would come before they could reach him. Now at the very crest of the steep, a hedge of points menaced the strange king's life, and even his iron strength was ebbing. Now he split the skull of a huge warrior and the backstrode shore through the neck-cords of another; reeling under a very rain of swords he struck again and his victim dropped at his feet, cleft to the breastbone. Then, even as a dozen swords rose above the staggering Atlantean for the death stroke, a strange thing happened. The sun was sinking into the western sea; all the heather swam red like an ocean of blood. Etched in the dying sun, as he had first appeared, Kull stood, and then, like a mist lifting, a mighty vista opened behind the reeling king. Cormac's astounded eyes caught a fleeting gigantic glimpse of other climes and spheres—as if mirrored in summer clouds he saw, instead of the heather hills stretching away to the sea, a dim and mighty land of blue mountains and gleaming quiet lakes—the golden, purple and sapphirean spires and towering walls of a mighty city such as the earth has not known for many a drifting age.

Then like the fading of a mirage it was gone, but the Gauls on the high slope had dropped their weapons and stared like men dazed—*For the man called Kull had vanished and there was no trace of his going!*

As if in a daze Cormac turned his steed and rode back across the trampled field. His horse's hoofs splashed in lakes of blood and against the helmets of dead men. Across the valley the shout of victory was thundering. Yet all seemed shadowy and strange. A shape was striding across the torn corpses and Cormac was dully aware that it was Bran. The Gael swung from his horse and fronted the king. Bran was weaponless and gory; blood trickled from gashes on brow, breast and limb; what armor he had worn was clean hacked away and a cut had shorn halfway through his iron crown. But the red jewel still gleamed unblemished like a star of slaughter.

'It is in my mind to slay you,' said the Gael heavily and like a man speaking in a daze, 'for the blood of brave men is on your head. Had you given the signal to charge sooner, some would have lived.'

Bran folded his arms; his eyes were haunted. 'Strike if you will; I am sick of slaughter. It is a cold mead, this kinging it. A king must gamble with men's lives and naked swords. The lives of all my people were at stake; I sacrificed the Northmen—yes; and my heart is sore within me, for they were men! But had I given the order when you would have desired, all might have gone awry. The Romans were not yet massed in the narrow mouth of the gorge, and might have had time and space to form their ranks again and beat us off. I waited until the last moment—and the rovers died. A king belongs to his people, and cannot let either his own feelings or the lives of men influence him. Now my people are saved; but my heart is cold in my breast.'

Cormac wearily dropped his sword-point to the ground. 'You are a born king of men, Bran,' said the Gaelic prince.

Bran's eyes rove the field. A mist of blood hovered over all, where the victorious barbarians were looting the dead, while those Romans who had escaped slaughter by throwing down their swords, and now stood under guard, looked on with hot smoldering eyes.

'My kingdom—my people—are saved,' said Bran wearily. 'They will come from the heather by the thousands and when Rome moves against us again, she will meet a solid nation. But I am weary. What of Kull?'

'My eyes and brain were mazed with battle,' answered Cormac. 'I thought to see him vanish like a ghost into the sunset. I will seek his body.'

'Seek not for him,' said Bran. 'Out of the sunrise he came—into the sunset he has gone. Out of the mists of the ages he came to us, and back into the mists of the eons has he returned—to his own kingdom.'

Cormac turned away; night was gathering. Gonar stood like a white specter before him. 'To his own kingdom,' echoed the wizard. 'Time and Space are naught. Kull has returned to his own kingdom—his own crown—his own age.'

'Then he was a ghost?'

'Did you not feel the grip of his solid hand? Did you not hear his voice—see him eat and drink, laugh and slay and bleed?'

Still Cormac stood like one in a trance.

'Then if it be possible for a man to pass from one age into one yet unborn, or come forth from a century dead and forgotten, whichever you will, with his flesh-and-bloody body and his arms—then he is as mortal as he was in his own day. Is Kull dead, then?'

'He died a hundred thousand years ago, as men reckon time,' answered the wizard, 'but in his own age. He died not from the swords of the Gauls at this age. Have we not heard in legends how the king of Valusia traveled into a strange, timeless land of the misty future ages, and there fought in a great battle? Why, so he did! A hundred thousand years ago, or today!

'And a hundred thousand years ago—or a moment agone!—Kull, king of Valusia, roused himself on the silken couch in his secret chamber and laughing, spoke to the first Gonar, saying: "Ha, wizard, I have in truth dreamed strangely, for I went into a far clime and a far time in my visions, and fought for the king of a strange shadow-people!" And the great sorcerer smiled and pointed silently at the red, notched sword, and the torn mail and the many wounds that the king carried. And Kull, fully woken from his 'vision' and feeling the sting and the weakness of these yet bleeding wounds, fell silent and mazed, and all life and time and space seemed like a dream of ghosts to him, and he wondered thereat all the rest of his life. For the wisdom of the Eternities is denied even unto princes and Kull could no more understand what Gonar told him than you can understand my words.'

'And then Kull lived despite his many wounds,' said Cormac, 'and has returned to the mists of silence and the centuries. Well—he thought us a dream; we thought him a ghost. And sure, life is but a web spun of ghosts and dreams and illusion, and it is in my mind that the kingdom which has this day been born of swords and slaughter in this howling valley is a thing no more solid than the foam of the bright sea.'

TURLOGH O'BRIEN

The Gods of Bal-Sagoth

1. Steel in the Storm

LIGHTNING dazzled the eyes of Turlogh O'Brien and his foot slipped in a smear of blood as he staggered on the reeling deck. The clashing of steel rivaled the bellowing of the thunder, and screams of death cut through the roar of waves and wind. The incessant lightning flicker gleamed on the corpses sprawling redly, the gigantic horned figures that roared and smote like huge demons of the midnight storm, the great beaked prow looming above.

The play was quick and desperate; in the momentary illumination a ferocious bearded face shone before Turlogh, and his swift ax licked out, splitting it to the chin. In the brief, utter blackness that followed the flash, an unseen stroke swept Turlogh's helmet from his head and he struck back blindly, feeling his ax sink into flesh, and hearing a man howl. Again the fires of the raging skies sprang, showing the Gael the ring of savage faces, the hedge of gleaming steel that hemmed him in.

Back against the mainmast, Turlogh parried and smote; then through the madness of the fray a great voice thundered, and in a flashing instant the Gael caught a glimpse of a giant form—a strangely familiar face. Then the world crashed into fire-shot blackness.

Consciousness returned slowly. Turlogh was first aware of a swaying, rocking motion of his whole body which he could not check. Then a dull throbbing in his head racked him and he sought to raise his hands to it. Then it was he realized he was bound hand and foot—not an altogether new experience. Clearing sight showed him that he was tied to the mast of the dragon ship whose warriors had struck him down. Why they had spared him, he could not understand, because if they knew him at all, they knew him to be an outlaw—an outcast from his clan, who would pay no ransom to save him from the very pits of Hell.

The wind had fallen greatly but a heavy sea was flowing, which tossed the long ship like a chip from gulf-like trough to foaming crest. A round silver moon, peering through broken clouds, lighted the tossing billows. The Gael, raised on the wild west coast of Ireland, knew that the serpent ship was crippled. He could tell it by the way she labored, plowing deep into the spume, heeling to the lift of the surge. Well, the tempest which had been raging on these southern waters had been enough to damage even such staunch craft as these vikings built.

The same gale had caught the French vessel on which Turlogh had been a passenger, driving her off her course and far southward. Days and nights had been a blind, howling chaos in which the ship had been hurled, flying like a wounded bird before the storm. And in the very rack of the tempest a beaked prow had loomed in the scud above the lower, broader craft, and the grappling irons had sunk in. Surely these Norsemen were wolves and the bloodlust that burned in their hearts was not human. In the terror and roar of the storm they leaped howling to the onslaught, and while the raging heavens hurled their full wrath upon them, and each shock of the frenzied waves threatened to engulf both vessels, these sea-wolves glutted their fury to the utmost—true sons of the sea, whose wildest rages found echo in their own bosoms. It had been a slaughter rather than a fight—the Celt had been the only fighting man aboard the doomed ship—and now he remembered the strange familiarity of the face he had glimpsed just before he was struck down. Who—?

'Good hail, my bold Dalcassian, it's long since we met!'

Turlogh stared at the man who stood before him, feet braced to the lifting of the deck. He was of huge stature, a good half head taller than Turlogh who stood well above six feet. His legs were like columns, his arms like oak and iron. His beard was of crisp gold, matching the massive armlets he wore. A shirt of scale-mail added to his war-like appearance as the horned helmet seemed to increase his height. But there was no wrath in the calm gray eyes which gazed tranquilly into the smoldering blue eyes of the Gael.

'Athelstane, the Saxon!'

'Aye—it's been a long day since you gave me this,' the giant indicated a thin white scar on his temple. 'We seem fated to meet on nights of fury—we first crossed steel the night you burned Thorfel's skalli. Then I fell before your ax and you saved me from Brogar's Picts—alone of all the folk who followed Thorfel. Tonight it was I who struck you down.' He touched the great two-handed sword strapped to his shoulders and Turlogh cursed.

'Nay, revile me not,' said Athelstane with a pained expression, 'I could have slain you in the press—I struck with the flat, but knowing you Irish have cursed hard skulls, I struck with both hands. You have been senseless for hours. Lodbrog would have slain you with the rest of the merchant ship's crew but I claimed your life. But the Vikings would only agree to spare you on condition that you be bound to the mast. They know you of old.'

'Where are we?'

'Ask me not. The storm blew us far out of our course. We were sailing to harry the coasts of Spain. When chance threw us in with your vessel, of course we seized the opportunity, but there was scant spoil. Now we are racing with the sea-flow, unknowing. The steer sweep

is crippled and the whole ship lamed. We may be riding
the very rim of the world for aught I know. Swear to join
us and I will loose you.'

'Swear to join the hosts of Hell!' snarled Turlogh.
'Rather will I go down with the ship and sleep forever
under the green waters, bound to this mast. My only
regret is that I can not send more sea-wolves to join the
hundred-odd I have already sent to Purgatory!'

'Well, well,' said Athelstane tolerantly, 'a man must
eat—here—I will loose your hands at least—now, set your
teeth into this joint of meat.'

Turlogh bent his head to the great joint and tore
at it ravenously. The Saxon watched him a moment,
then turned away. A strange man, reflected Turlogh,
this renegade Saxon who hunted with the wolf-pack of
the North—a savage warrior in battle, but with fibers of
kindliness in his make-up which set him apart from the
men with whom he consorted.

The ship reeled on blindly in the night, and
Athelstane, returning with a great horn of foaming ale,
remarked on the fact that the clouds were gathering again,
obscuring the seething face of the sea. He left the Gael's
hands unbound but Turlogh was held fast to the mast by
cords about legs and body. The rovers paid no heed to the
prisoner; they were too much occupied in keeping their
crippled ship from going down under their feet.

At last Turlogh believed he could catch at times
a deep roaring above the wash of the waves. This grew
in volume, and even as the duller-eared Norsemen heard
it, the ship leaped like a spurred horse, straining in
every timber. As by magic the clouds, lightening for
dawn, rolled away on each side, showing a wild waste
of tossing gray waters, and a long line of breakers dead
ahead. Beyond the frothing madness of the reefs loomed
land, apparently an island. The roaring increased to
deafening proportions, as the long ship, caught in the tide
rip, raced headlong to her doom. Turlogh saw Lodbrog
rushing about, his long beard flowing in the wind as

he brandished his fists and bellowed futile commands.
Athelstane came running across the deck.

'Little chance for any of us,' he growled as he cut the
Gael's bonds, 'but you shall have as much as the rest—'

Turlogh sprang free. 'Where is my ax?'

'There in that weapon-rack. But Thor's blood, man,'
marvelled the big Saxon, 'you won't burden yourself
now—'

Turlogh had snatched the ax and confidence flowed
like wine through his veins at the familiar feel of the slim,
graceful shaft. His ax was as much a part of him as his
right hand; if he must die he wished to die with it in his
grip. He hastily slung it to his girdle. All armor had been
stripped from him when he had been captured.

'There are sharks in these waters,' said Athelstane,
preparing to doff his scale-mail. 'If we have to swim—'

The ship struck with a crash that snapped her masts
and shivered her prow like glass. Her dragon beak shot
high in the air and men tumbled like tenpins from her
slanted deck. A moment she poised, shuddering like a
live thing, then slid from the hidden reef and went down
in a blinding smother of spray.

Turlogh had left the deck in a long dive that carried
him clear. Now he rose in the turmoil, fought the waves
for a mad moment, then caught a piece of wreckage that
the breakers flung up. As he clambered across this, a
shape bumped against him and went down again. Turlogh
plunged his arm deep, caught a sword-belt and heaved
the man up and on his makeshift raft. For in that instant
he had recognized the Saxon, Athelstane, still burdened
with the armor he had not had time to remove. The man
seemed dazed. He lay limp, limbs trailing.

Turlogh remembered that ride through the breakers
as a chaotic nightmare. The tide tore them through,
plunging their frail craft into the depths, then flinging
them into the skies. There was naught to do but hold
on and trust to luck. And Turlogh held on, gripping the
Saxon with one hand and their raft with the other, while it

seemed his fingers would crack with the strain. Again and
again they were almost swamped; then by some miracle
they were through, riding in water comparatively calm
and Turlogh saw a lean fin cutting the surface a yard
away. It swirled in and Turlogh unslung his ax and
struck. Red dyed the waters instantly and a rush of
sinuous shapes made the craft rock. While the sharks tore
their brother, Turlogh, paddling with his hands, urged
the rude raft ashore until he could feel the bottom. He
waded to the beach, half carrying the Saxon; then, iron
though he was, Turlogh O'Brien sank down, exhausted
and soon slept soundly.

2. Gods from the Abyss

Turlogh did not sleep long. When he awoke the sun
was just risen above the sea-rim. The Gael rose, feeling
as refreshed as if he had slept the whole night through,
and looked about him. The broad white beach sloped
gently from the water to a waving expanse of gigantic
trees. There seemed no underbrush, but so close together
were the huge boles, his sight could not pierce into the
jungle. Athelstane was standing some distance away on
a spit of sand that ran out into the sea. The huge
Saxon leaned on his great sword and gazed out toward
the reefs.

Here and there on the beach lay the stiff figures that
had been washed ashore. A sudden snarl of satisfaction
broke from Turlogh's lips. Here at his very feet was a
gift from the gods; a dead Viking lay there, fully armed
in the helmet and mail shirt he had not had time to doff
when the ship foundered, and Turlogh saw they were
his own. Even the round light bucklet strapped to the
Norseman's back was his. Turlogh did pause to wonder
how all his accouterments had come into the possession
of one man, but stripped the dead and donned the plain
round helmet and the shirt of black chain mail. Thus

armed he went up the beach toward Athelstane, his eyes gleaming unpleasantly.

The Saxon turned as he approached. 'Hail to you, Gael,' he greeted, 'We be all of Lodbrog's ship-people left alive. The hungry green sea drank them all. By Thor, I owe my life to you! What with the weight of my mail, and the crack my skull got on the rail, I had most certainly been food for the shark but for you. It all seems like a dream now.'

'You saved my life,' snarled Turlogh, 'I saved yours. Now the debt is paid, the accounts are squared, so up with your sword and let us make an end.'

Athelstane stared. 'You wish to fight me? Why— what—?'

'I hate your breed as I hate Satan!' roared the Gael, a tinge of madness in his blazing eyes. 'Your wolves have ravaged my people for five hundred years! The smoking ruins of the Southland, the seas of spilled blood call for vengeance! The screams of a thousand ravished girls are ringing in my ears, night and day! Would that the North had but a single breast for my ax to cleave!'

'But I am no Norseman,' rumbled the giant in worriment.

'The more shame to you, renegade,' raved the maddened Gael. 'Defend yourself lest I cut you down in cold blood!'

'This is not my linking,' protested Athelstane, lifting his mighty blade, his gray eyes serious but unafraid. 'Men speak truly who say there is madness in you.'

Words ceased as the men prepared to go into deadly action. The Gael approached his foe, crouching panther-like, eyes ablaze. The Saxon waited the onslaught, feet braced wide apart, sword held high in both hands. It was Turlogh's ax and shield against Athelstane's two-handed sword; in a contest one stroke might end either way. Like two great jungle beasts they played their deadly, wary game then—

Even as Turlogh's muscles tensed for the deathleap, a fearful sound split the silence! Both men started and recoiled. From the depths of the forest behind them rose a ghastly and inhuman scream. Shrill, yet of great volume, it rose higher and higher until it ceased at the highest pitch, like a triumph of a demon, like the cry of some grisly ogre gloating over its human prey.

'Thor's blood!' gasped the Saxon, letting his sword-point fall. 'What was that?'

Turlogh shook his head. Even his iron nerve was slightly shaken. 'Some fiend of the forest. This is a strange land in a strange sea. Mayhap Satan himself reigns here and it is the gate to Hell.'

Athelstane looked uncertain. He was more pagan than Christian and his devils were heathen devils. But they were none the less grim for that.

'Well,' said he, 'let us drop our quarrel until we see what it may be. Two blades are better than one, whether for man or devil—'

A wild shriek cut him short. This time it was a human voice, blood-chilling in its horror and despair. Simultaneously came the swift patter of feet and the lumbering rush of some heavy body among the trees. The warriors wheeled toward the sound, and out of the deep shadows a half-naked woman came flying like a white leaf blown on the wind. Her loose hair streamed like a flame of gold behind her, her white limbs flashed in the morning sun, her eyes blazed with frenzied terror. And behind her—

Even Turlogh's hair stood up. The thing that pursued the fleeing girl was neither man nor beast. In form it was like a bird, but such a bird as the rest of the world had not seen for many an age. Some twelve feet high it towered, and its evil head with the wicked red eyes and cruel curved beak was as big as a horse's head. The long arched neck was thicker than a man's thigh and the huge taloned feet could have gripped the fleeing woman as an eagle grips a sparrow.

This much Turlogh saw in one glance as he sprang between the monster and its prey who sank down with a cry on the beach. It loomed above him like a mountain of death and the evil beak darted down, denting the shield he raised and staggering him with the impact. At the same instant he struck, but the keen ax sank harmlessly into a cushioning mass of spiky feathers. Again the beak flashed at him and his sidelong leap saved his life by a hair's breadth. And then Athelstane ran in, and bracing his feet wide, swung his great sword with both hands and all his strength. The mighty blade sheared through one of the tree-like legs below the knee, and with an abhorrent screech, the monster sank on its side, flapping its short heavy wings widely. Turlogh drove the backspike of his ax between the glaring red eyes and the gigantic bird kicked convulsively and lay still.

'Thor's blood!' Athelstane's gray eyes were blazing with battle lust. 'Truly we've come to the rim of the world—'

'Watch the forest lest another come forth,' snapped Turlogh, turning to the woman who had scrambled to her feet and stood panting, eyes wide with wonder. She was a splendid young animal, tall, clean-limbed, slim and shapely. Her only garment was a sheer bit of silk hung carelessly about her hips. But though the scantiness of her dress suggested the savage, her skin was snowy white, her loose hair of purest gold and her eyes gray. Now she spoke hastily, stammeringly, in the tongue of the Norse, as if she had not so spoken in years.

'You—who are you men? When come you? What do you on the Isle of the Gods?'

'Thor's blood!' rumbled the Saxon; 'she's of our own kind!'

'Not mine!' snapped Turlogh, unable even in that moment to forget his hate for the people of the North.

The girl looked curiously at the two. 'The world must have changed greatly since I left it,' she said, evidently in full control of herself once more, 'else how is it that wolf and wild bull hunt together? By your black hair, you are a Gael, and you, big man, have a slur in your speech that can be naught but Saxon.'

'We are two outcasts,' answered Turlogh. 'You see these dead men lining the strand? They were the crew of the dragon ship which bore us here, storm-driven. This man, Athelstane, once of Wessex, was a swordsman on that ship and I was a captive. I am Turlogh Dubh, once a chief of Clan na O'Brien. Who are you and what land is this?'

'This is the oldest land in the world,' answered the girl, 'Rome, Egypt, Cathay are as but infants beside it. I am Brunhild, daughter of Rane Thorfin's son, of the Orkneys, and until a few days ago, queen of this ancient kingdom.'

Turlogh looked uncertaintly at Athelstane. This sounded like sorcery.

'After what we have just seen,' rumbled the giant, 'I am ready to believe anything. But are you in truth Rane Thorfin's son's stolen child?'

'Aye!' cried the girl, 'I am that one! I was stolen when Tostig the Mad raided the Orkneys and burned Rane's steading in the absence of its master—'

'And then Tostig vanished from the face of the earth—or the sea!' interrupted Athelstane, 'He was in truth a madman. I sailed with him for a ship-harrying many years ago when I was but a youth.'

'And his madness cast me on this island,' answered Brunhild; 'for after he had harried the shores of England, the fire in his brain drove him out into unknown seas—south and south and ever south until even the fierce wolves he led murmured. Then a storm drove us on yonder reef, though at another part, rending the dragon ship even as yours was rended last night. Tostig and all his strong men perished in the waves, but I clung to pieces of wreckage and a whim of the gods cast me ashore, half dead. I was fifteen years old. That was ten years ago.

'I found a strange terrible people dwelling here, a brown-skinned folk who knew many dark secrets of magic. They found me lying senseless on the beach and because I was the first white human they had ever seen, their priests divined that I was a goddess given them by the sea, whom they worship. So they put me in the temple with the rest of their curious gods and did reverence to me. And their high-priest, old Gothan—cursed be his name!—taught me many strange and fearful things. Soon I learned their language and much of their priests' inner mysteries. And as I grew into womanhood the desire for power stirred in me; for the people of the North are made to rule the folk of the world, and it is not for the daughter of a sea-king to sit meekly in a temple and accept the offerings of fruit and flowers and human sacrifices!'

She stopped for a moment, eyes blazing. Truly, she looked a worthy daughter of the fierce race she claimed.

'Well,' she continued, 'there was one who loved me— Kotar, a young chief. With him I plotted and at last I rose and flung off the yoke of old Gothan. That was a wild season of plot and counter-plot, intrigue, rebellion and red carnage! Men and women died like flies and the street of Bal-Sagoth ran red—but in the end we triumphed, Kotar and I! The dynasty of Angar came to an end on a night of blood and fury and I reigned supreme on the Isle of the Gods, queen and goddess!'

She had drawn herself up to her full height, her beautiful face alight with fierce pride, her bosom heaving. Turlogh was at once fascinated and repelled. He had seen rulers rise and fall, and between the lines of her brief narrative he read the bloodshed and carnage, the cruelty and the treachery—sensing the basic ruthlessness of this girl-woman.

'But if you were queen,' he asked, 'how is it that we find you hunted through the forests of your domain by this monster, like a runaway serving wench?'

Brunhild bit her lip and an angry flush mounted to her cheeks. 'What is it that brings down every woman, whatever her station? I trusted a man—Kotar, my lover, with whom I shared my rule. He betrayed me; after I had raised him to the highest power in the kingdom, next to my own, I found he secretly made love to another girl. I killed them both!'

Turlogh smiled coldly: 'You are a true Brunhild! And then what?'

'Kotar was loved by the people. Old Gothan stirred them up. I made my greatest mistake when I let that old one live. Yet I dared not slay him. Well, Gothan rose against me, as I had risen against him, and the warriors rebelled, slaying those who stood faithful to me. Me they took captive but dared not kill; for after all, I was a goddess, they believed. So before dawn, fearing the people would change their minds again and restore me to power, Gothan had me taken to the lagoon which separates this part of the island from the other. The priests rowed me across the lagoon and left me, naked and helpless, to my fate.'

'And that fate was—this?' Athelstane touched the huge carcass with his foot.

Brunhild shuddered. 'Many ages ago there were many of these monsters on the isles, the legends say. They warred on the people of Bal-Sagoth and devoured them by hundreds. But at last all were exterminated on the main part of the isle and on this side of the lagoon all died but this one, who had abided here for centuries. In the old times hosts of men came against him, but he was greatest of all the devil-birds and he slew all who fought him. So the priests made a god of him and left this part of the island to him. None comes here except those brought as sacrifices—as I was. He could not cross to the main island, because the lagoon swarms with great sharks which would rend even him to pieces.

'For a while I eluded him, stealing among the trees, but at last he spied me out—and you know the rest. I owe my life to you. Now what will you do with me?'

Athelstane looked at Turlogh and Turlogh shrugged. 'What can we do, save starve in the forest?'

'I will tell you!' the girl cried in a ringing voice, her eyes blazing anew to the swift working of her keen brain. 'There is an old legend among this people—that men of iron will come out of the sea and the city of Bal-Sagoth will fall! You, with your mail and helmets, will seem as iron men to these folk who know nothing of armor! You have slain Groth-golka the bird-god—you have come out of the sea as did I—the people will look on you as gods. Come with me and aid me to win back my kingdom! You shall be my right-hand men and I will heap honors on you! Fine garments, gorgeous palaces, fairest girls shall be yours!'

Her promises slid from Turlogh's mind without leaving an imprint, but the mad splendor of the proposal intrigued him. Strongly he desired to look on this strange city of which Brunhild spoke, and the thought of two warriors and one girl pitted against a whole nation for a crown stirred the utmost depths of his knight-errant Celtic soul.

'It is well,' said he. 'And what of you, Athelstane?'

'My belly is empty,' growled the giant. 'Lead me to where there is food and I'll hew my way to it, through a horde of priests and warriors.'

'Lead us to this city!' said Turlogh to Brunhild.

'Hail!' she cried flinging her white arms high in wild exultation. 'Now let Gothan and Ska and Gelka tremble! With ye at my side I'll win back the crown they tore from me, and this time I'll not spare my enemy! I'll hurl old Gothan from the highest battlement, though the bellowing of his demons shake the very bowels of the earth! And we shall see if the god Gol-goroth shall stand against the sword that cut Groth-golka's leg from under him. Now hew the head from this carcass that the people may know you have overcome the bird-god. Now follow me, for the sun mounts the sky and I would sleep in my own palace tonight!'

The three passed into the shadows of the mighty forest. The interlocking branches, hundreds of feet above their heads, made dim and strange such sunlight as filtered through. No life was seen except for an occasional gayly hued bird or a huge ape. These beasts, Brunhild said, were survivors of another age, harmless except when attacked. Presently the growth changed somewhat, the trees thinned and became smaller and fruit of many kinds was seen among the branches. Brunhild told the warriors which to pluck and eat as they walked along. Turlogh was quite satisfied with the fruit, but Athelstane, though he ate enormously, did so with scant relish. Fruit was light sustenance to a man used to such solid stuff as formed his regular diet. Even among the gluttonous Danes the Saxon's capacity for beef and ale was admired.

'Look!' cried Brunhild sharply, halting and pointing. 'The spires of Bal-Sagoth!'

Through the trees the warriors caught a glimmer, white and shimmery, and apparently far away. There was an illusory impression of towering battlements, high in the air, with fleecy clouds hovering about them. The sight woke strange dreams in the mystic deeps of the Gael's soul, and even Athelstane was silent as if he too were struck by the pagan beauty and mystery of the scene.

So they progressed through the forest, now losing sight of the distant city as tree tops obstructed the view, now seeing it again. And at last they came out on the low shelving banks of a broad blue lagoon and the full beauty of the landscape burst upon their eyes. From the opposite shores the country sloped upward in long gentle undulations which broke like great slow waves at the foot of a range of blue hills a few miles away. These wild swells were covered with deep grass and many groves of trees, while miles away on either hand there was seen curving away into the distance the strip of thick forest which Brunhild said belted the whole island. And among those blue dreaming hills brooded the age-old city of Bal-Sagoth, its white walls and sapphire towers clean-cut against the morning sky. The suggestion of great distance had been an illusion.

'Is that not a kingdom worth fighting for?' cried Brunhild, her voice vibrant. 'Swift now—let us bind this dry wood together for a raft. We could not live an instant swimming in that shark-haunted water.'

At that instant a figure leaped up from the tall grass on the other shore—a naked, brown skinned man who stared for a moment, agape. Then as Athelstane shouted and held up the grim head of Groth-golka the fellow gave a startled cry and raced away like an antelope.

'A slave Gothan left to see if I tried to swim the lagoon,' said Brunhild with angry satisfaction. 'Let him run to the city and tell them—but let us make haste and cross the lagoon before Gothan can arrive and dispute our passage.'

Turlogh and Athelstane were already busy. A number of dead trees lay about and these they stripped of their branches and bound together with long vines. In a short time they had built a raft, crude and clumsy, but capable of bearing them across the lagoon. Brunhild gave a frank sigh of relief when they stepped on the other shore.

'Let us go straight to the city,' said she. 'The slave has reached it ere now and they will be watching us from the walls. A bold course is our only one. Thor's hammer, but I'd like to see Gothan's face when the slave tells him Brunhild is returning with two strange warriors and the head of him to whom she was given as sacrifice!'

'Why did you not kill Gothan when you had the power?' asked Athelstane.

She shook her head, her eyes clouding with something akin to fear: 'Easier said than done. Half the people hate Gothan, half love him, and all fear him. The most ancient men of the city say that he was old when they were babes. The people believe him to be more god than priest, and I myself have seen him do terrible and mysterious things, beyond the power of a common man.

'Nay, when I was but a puppet in his hands, I came only to the outer fringe of his mysteries, yet I have looked on sight that froze my blood, I have seen strange shadows flit along the midnight walls, and groping along black subterranean corridors in the dead of night I have heard unhallowed sounds and have felt the presence of hideous beings. And once I heard the grisly slavering bellowings of the nameless Thing Gothan has chained deep in the bowels of the hills on which rests the city of Bal-Sagoth.'

Brunhild shuddered.

'There are many gods in Bal-Sagoth, but the greatest of all is Gol-goroth, the god of darkness who sits forever in the Temple of Shadows. When I overthrew the power of Gothan, I forbade men to worship Gol-goroth, and made the priest hail, as one true deity, A-ala, the daughter of the sea—myself. I had strong men take heavy hammers and smite the image of Gol-goroth, but their blows only shattered the hammers and gave strange hurts to the men who wielded them. Gol-goroth was indestructible and showed no mar. So I desisted and shut the doors of the Temple of Shadows which were opened only when I was overthrown and Gothan, who had been skulking in the secret places of the city, came again into his own. Then Gol-goroth reigned again in his full terror and the idols of A-ala were overthrown in the Temple of the Sea, and the priests of A-ala died howling on the red-stained altar before the black god. But now we shall see!'

'Surely you are a very Valkyrie,' muttered Athelstane. 'But three against a nation is great odds—especially such a people as this, who must assuredly be all witches and sorcerers.'

'Bah!' cried Brunhild contemptuously, 'there are many sorcerers, it is true, but though the people are strange to us, they are mere fools in their own way, as are all nations. When Gothan led me captive down the streets they spat on me. Now watch them turn on Ska, the new King Gothan has given them, when it seems my star rises again! But now we approach the city gates—be bold but wary!'

They had ascended the long swelling slopes and were not far from the walls which rose immensely upward.

Surely, thought Turlogh, heathen gods built this city. The walls seemed of marble and with their fretted battlements and slim watch-towers, dwarfed the memory of such cities as Rome, Damascus, and Byzantium. A broad wide winding road led up from the lower levels to the plateau before the gates and as they came up this road, the three adventurers felt hundreds of hidden eyes fixed on them with fierce intensity. The walls seemed deserted; it might have been a dead city. But the impact of those staring eyes was felt.

Now they stood before the massive gates, which to the amazed eyes of the warriors seemed to be of chased silver.

'Here is an emperor's ransom!' muttered Athelstane, eyes ablaze. 'Thor's blood, if we had but a stout band of reavers and a ship to carry away the plunder!'

'Smite on the gate and then step back, lest something fall upon you,' said Brunhild, and the thunder of Turlogh's ax on the portals woke the echoes in the sleeping hills.

The three then fell back a few paces and suddenly the mighty gates swung inward and a strange concourse of people stood revealed. The two white warriors looked on a pageant of barbaric grandeur. A throng of tall, slim, brown-skinned men stood in the gates. Their only garments were loin-cloths of silk, the fine work of which contrasted strangely with the near-nudity of the wearers. Tall waving plumes of many colors decked their heads, and armlets and leglets of gold and silver, crusted with gleaming gems, completed their ornamentation. Armor they wore none, but each carried a light shield on his left arm, made of hard wood, highly polished, and braced with silver. Their weapons were slim-bladed spears, light hatchets and slender daggers, all bladed with fine steel. Evidently these warriors depended more on speed and skill than on brute force.

At the front of this band stood three men who instantly commanded attention. One was a lean hawk-face warrior,

almost as tall as Athelstane, who wore about his neck
a great golden chain from which was suspended a curious symbol in jade. One of the other men was young,
evil-eyed; an impressive riot of colors in the mantle of
parrot-feathers which swung from his shoulders. The
third man had nothing to set him apart from the rest
save his own strange personality. He wore no mantle, bore no weapons. His only garment was a plain
loin-cloth. He was very old; he alone of all the throng
was bearded, and his beard was as white as the long
hair which fell about his shoulders. He was very tall
and very lean, and his great dark eyes blazed as from
a hidden fire. Turlogh knew without being told that
this man was Gothan, priest of the Black God. The
ancient exuded a very aura of age and mystery. His
great eyes were like windows of some forgotten temple,
behind which passed like ghosts his dark and terrible
thoughts. Turlogh sensed that Gothan had delved too
deep in forbidden secrets to remain altogether human.
He had passed through doors that had cut him off from
the dreams, desires and emotions of ordinary mortals.
Looking into those unwinking orbs Turlogh felt his skin
crawl, as if he had looked into the eyes of a great
serpent.

Now a glance upward showed that the walls were
thronged with silent dark-eyed folk. The stage was set; all
was in readiness for the swift, red drama. Turlogh felt his
pulse quicken with fierce exhilaration and Athelstane's
eyes began to glow with ferocious light.

Brunhild stepped forward boldly, head high, her splendid figure vibrant. The white warriors naturally could
not understand what passed between her and the others,
except as they read from gestures and expressions, but
later Brunhild narrated the conversation almost word
for word.

'Well, people of Bal-Sagoth,' said she, spacing her
word slowly, 'what words have you for your goddess
whom you mocked and reviled?'

'What will you have, false one?' exclaimed the tall man, Ska, the king set up by Gothan; 'you who mocked at the customs of our ancestors, defied the laws of Bal-Sagoth, which are older than the world, murdered your lover and defiled the shrine of Gol-goroth? You were doomed by law, king and god and placed in the grim forest beyond the lagoon—'

'And I, who am likewise a goddess and greater than any god,' answered Brunhild mockingly, 'am returned from the realm of horror with the head of Groth-golka!'

At a word from her, Athelstane held up the great beaked head, and a low whispering ran about the battlements, tense with fear and bewilderment.

'Who are these men?' Ska bent a worried front on the two warriors.

'*They are iron men who have come out of the sea!*' answered Brunhild in a clear voice that carried far; the beings who have come in response to the old prophesy, to overthrow the city of Bal-Sagoth, whose people are traitors and whose priests are false!'

At these words the fearful murmur broke out afresh all up and down the line of the walls, till Gothan lifted his vulture-head and the people fell silent and shrank before the icy stare of his terrible eyes.

Ska glared bewilderedly, his ambition struggling with his superstitious fears.

Turlogh, looking closely at Gothan, believed that he read beneath the inscrutable mask of the old priest's face. For all his inhuman wisdom, Gothan had his limitations. This sudden return of one he thought well disposed of, and the appearance of the white-skinned giants accompanying her, had caught Gothan off his guard, Turlogh believed, rightly. There had been no time to properly prepare for their reception. The people had already began to murmur in the streets against the severity of Ska's brief rule. They had always believed in Brunhild's divinity; now that she returned with two tall men of her own hue, bearing the grim trophy that marked the conquest of another of their gods, the people were wavering. Any small thing might turn the tide either way.

'People of Bal-Sagoth!' shouted Brunhild suddenly, springing back and flinging her arms high, gazing full into the faces that looked down at her, 'I bid you avert your doom before it is too late! You cast me out and spat on me; you turned to darker gods than I! Yet all this will I forgive if you return and do obeisance to me! Once you reviled me—you called me bloody and cruel! True, I was a hardy mistress—but has Ska been an easy master? You said I lashed the people with whips of rawhide—has Ska stroked you with parrot feathers?

'A virgin died on my alter at the full tide of each moon—but youths and maidens die at the waxing and the waning, the rising and the settling of each moon, before Gol-goroth, on whose altar a fresh human heart forever throbs! Ska is but a shadow! Your real lord is Gothan, who sits above the city like a vulture! Once you were a mighty people; your galleys filled the seas. Now you are a remnant and that is dwindling fast! Fools! You will all die on the altar of Gol-goroth ere Gothan is done and he will stalk alone among the silent ruins of Bal-Sagoth!

'Look at him!' her voice rose to a scream as she lashed herself to an inspired frenzy, and even Turlogh, to whom the words were meaningless shivered. 'Look at him where he stands there like an evil spirit out of the past! He is not even human! I tell you, he is a foul ghost, whose beard is dabbled with the blood of a million butcheries—an incarnate fiend out of the mist of the ages come to destroy the people of Bal-Sagoth!

'Choose now! Rise up against the ancient devil and his blasphemous gods, receive your rightful queen and deity again and you shall regain some of your former greatness. Refuse, and the ancient prophesy shall be fulfilled and the sun will set on the silent and crumbled ruins of Bal-Sagoth!'

Fired by her dynamic words, a young warrior with the insignia of a chief sprang to the parapet and shouted: 'Hail to A-ala! Down with the bloody gods!'

Among the multitude many took up the shout and steel clashed as a score of fights started. The crowd on the battlements and in the street surged and eddied, while Ska glared, bewildered. Brunhild, forcing back her companions who quivered with eagerness for action of some kind, shouted: 'Hold! Let no man strike a blow yet! People of Bal-Sagoth, it has been a tradition since the beginning of time that a king must fight for his crown! Let Ska cross steel with one of these warriors! If Ska wins, I will kneel before him and let him strike off my head! If Ska loses, then you shall accept me as your rightful queen and goddess!'

A great roar of approval went up from the walls as the people ceased their brawls, glad enough to shift responsibility to their rulers.

'Will you fight, Ska?' asked Brunhild, turning to the king mockingly. 'Or will you give me your head without further argument?'

'Slut!' howled Ska, driven to madness, 'I will take the skulls of these fools for drinking cups, and then I will rend you between two bent trees!'

Gothan laid a hand on his arm and whispered in his ear, but Ska had reached the point where he was deaf to all but his fury. His achieved ambition, he had found, had faded to the mere part of a puppet dancing on Gothan's string; now even the hollow bauble of his kingship was slipping from him and this wench mocked him to his face before his people. Ska went, to all practical effects, stark mad.

Brunhild turned to her two allies. 'One of you must fight Ska.'

'Let me be the one!' urged Turlogh, eyes dancing with eager battle-lust. 'He has the look of a man quick as a wildcat, and Athelstane, while a very bull for strength, is a thought slow for such work—'

'Slow!' broke in Athelstane reproachfully. 'Why, Turlogh, for a man my weight—'

'Enough,' Brunhild interrupted. 'He must choose for himself.'

She spoke to Ska, who glared red-eyed for an instant, then indicated Athelstane, who grinned joyfully, cast aside the bird's head and unslung his sword. Turlogh swore and stepped back. The king had decided that he would have a better chance against this huge buffalo of a man who looked slow, than against the black-haired tigerish warrior, whose cat-like quickness was evident.

'This Ska is without armor,' rumbled the Saxon. 'Let me likewise doff my mail and helmet so that we fight on equal terms—'

'No!' cried Brunhild. 'Your armor is your only chance! I tell you, this false king fights like the play of summer lightning! You will be hard put to your own as it is. Keep on your armor, I say!'

'Well, well,' grumbled Athelstane, 'I will—I will. Though I say it is scarcely fair. But let him come on and make an end of it.'

The huge Saxon strode ponderously toward his foe, who warily crouched and circled away. Athelstane held his great sword in both hands before him, pointed upward, the hilt somewhat below the level of his chin, in position to strike a blow to right or left, or parry a sudden attack.

Ska had flung away his light shield, his fighting-sense telling him that it would be useless before the stroke of that heavy blade. In his right hand he held his slim spear as a man holds a throwing-dart, in his left a light, keen-edged hatchet. He meant to make a fast, shifty fight of it, and his tactics were good. But Ska, having never encountered armor before, made his fatal mistake in supposing it to be apparel or ornament through which his weapons would pierce.

Now he sprang in, thrusting at Athelstane's face with his spear. The Saxon parried with ease and instantly cut tremendously at Ska's legs. The king bounded high, clearing the whistling blade, and in midair he hacked down at Athelstane's bent head. The light hatchet shivered to bits on the Viking's helmet and Ska sprang back out of reach with a blood-lusting howl.

And now it was Athelstane who rushed with unexpected quickness, like a charging bull, and before that terrible onslaught Ska, bewildered by the breaking of his hatchet, was caught off his guard—flat-footed. He caught a fleeting glimpse of the giant looming over him like an overwhelming wave and he sprang in, instead of out, stabbing ferociously. That mistake was his last. The thrusting spear glanced harmlessly from the Saxon's mail, and in that instant the great sword sang down in a stroke the king could not evade. The force of that stroke tossed him as a man is tossed by a plunging bull. A dozen feet away fell Ska, king of Bal-Sagoth, to lie shattered and dead in a ghastly welter of blood and entrails. The throng gaped, struck silent by the prowess of that deed.

'Hew off his head!' cried Brunhild, her eyes flaming as he clenched her hands so that the nails bit into her palms. 'Impale that carrion's head on your sword-point so that we may carry it through the city gates with us as token of victory!'

But Athelstane shook his head, cleansing his blade: 'Nay, he was a brave man and I will not mutilate his corpse. It is no great feat I have done, for he was naked and I full-armed. Else it is in my mind, the brawl had gone differently.'

Turlogh glanced at the people on the walls. They had recovered from their astonishment and now a vast roar went up: 'A-ala! Hail to the true goddess!' And the warriors in the gateway dropped to their knees and bowed their foreheads in the dust before Brunhild, who stood proudly erect, bosom heaving with fierce triumph. Truly, thought Turlogh, she is more than a queen—she is a shield woman, a Valkyrie, as Athelstane said.

Now she stepped aside and tearing the golden chain with its jade symbol from the dead neck of Ska, held it on high and shouted: 'People of Bal-Sagoth, you have seen how your false king died before this golden-bearded giant, who being of iron, shows no single cut! Choose now—do you receive me of your own free will?'

'Aye, we do!' the multitude answered in a great shout. 'Return to your people, oh mighty and all-powerful queen!'

Brunhild smiled sardonically. 'Come,' said she to the warriors; 'they are lashing themselves into a very frenzy of love and loyalty, having already forgotten their treachery. The memory of the mob is short!'

Aye, thought Turlogh, as at Brunhild's side he and the mighty Saxon passed through the mighty gates between files of prostrate chieftains; aye, the memory of the mob is very short. But a few days have passed since they were yelling as wildly for Ska the liberator—scant hours had passed since Ska sat enthroned, master of life and death, and the people bowed before his feet. Now—Turlogh glanced at the mangled corpse which lay deserted and forgotten before the silver gates. The shadow of a circling vulture fell across it. The clamor of the multitude filled Turlogh's ears and he smiled a bitter smile.

The great gates closed behind the three adventurers and Turlogh saw a broad white street stretching away in front of him. Other lesser streets radiated from this one. The two warriors caught a jumbled and chaotic impression of great white stone buildings shouldering each other; of sky-lifting towers and broad stair-fronted palaces. Turlogh knew there must be an ordered system by which the city was laid out, but to him all seemed a waste of stone and metal and polished wood, without rime or reason. His baffled eyes sought the street again.

Far up the street extended a mass of humanity, from which rose a rhythmic thunder of sound. Thousands of naked, gayly plumed men and women knelt there, bending forward to touch the marble flags with their foreheads, then swaying back with an upward flinging of their arms, all moving in perfect unison like the bending and rising of tall grass before the wind. And in time to their bowing they lifted a monotoned chant that sank and swelled in a frenzy of ecstasy. So her wayward people welcomed back the goddess A-ala.

Just within the gates Brunhild stopped and there came to her the young chief who had first raised the shout of revolt upon the walls. He knelt and kissed her bare feet, saying: 'Oh great queen and goddess, thou knowest Zomar was ever faithful to thee! Thou knowest how I fought for thee and barely escaped the altar of Gol-goroth for thy sake!'

'Thou hast indeed been faithful, Zomar,' answered Brunhild in the stilted language required for such occasions, 'nor shall thy fidelity go unrewarded. Henceforth thou art commander of my own bodyguard.' Then in a lower voice she added: 'Gather a band from your own retainers and from those who have espoused my cause all along, and bring them to the palace. I do not trust the people any more than I have to!'

Suddenly Athelstane, not understanding the conversation, broke in: 'Where is the old one with the beard?'

Turlogh started and glanced around. He had almost forgotten the wizard. He had not seen him go—yet he was gone! Brunhild laughed ruefully.

'He's stolen away to breed more trouble in the shadows. He and Gelka vanished when Ska fell. He has secret ways of coming and going and none may stay him. Forget him for the time being; heed ye well—we shall have plenty of him anon!'

Now the chiefs brought a finely carved and highly ornamented palanquin carried by two strong slaves, and Brunhild stepped into this, saying to her companions: 'They are fearful of touching you, but ask if you would be carried. I think it better that you walk, one on each side of me.'

'Thor's blood!' rumbled Athelstane, shouldering the huge sword he had never sheathed, 'I'm no infant! I'll split the skull of the man who seeks to carry me!'

And so up the long white street went Brunhild, daughter of Rane Thorfin's son in the Orkneys, goddess of the sea, queen of age-old Bal-Sagoth. Borne by two great slaves she went, with a white giant striding on each side with bared steel, and the concourse of chiefs following, while the multitude gave way to right and left, leaving a wide lane down which she passed. Golden trumpets sounded a fanfare of triumph, drums thundered, chants of worship echoed to the ringing skies. Surely in this riot of glory, this barbaric pageant of splendor, the proud soul of the North-born girl drank deep and grew drunken with imperial pride.

Athelstane's eyes glowed with simple delight at this flame of pagan magnificence, but to the black haired fighting-man of the West, it seemed that even in the loudest clamor of triumph, the trumpet, the drum and shouting faded away into the forgotten dust and silence of eternity. Kingdoms and empires pass away like mist from the sea, thought Turlogh; the people shout and triumph and even in the revelry of Belshazzar's feast, the Medes break the gates of Babylon. Even now the shadow of doom is over this city and the slow tides of oblivion lap the feet of this unheeding race. So in a strange mood Turlogh O'Brien strode beside the palanquin, and it seemed to him that he and Athelstane walked in a dead city, through throngs of dim ghosts, cheering a ghost queen.

3. The Fall of the Gods

Night had fallen on the ancient city of Bal-Sagoth. Turlogh, Athelstane and Brunhild sat alone in a room of the inner palace. The queen half reclined on a silken couch, while the men sat on mahogany chairs, engaged in the viands that slave-girls had served on golden dishes.

The walls of this room, as of all the palace, were of marble, with golden scrollwork. The ceiling was of lapis-lazuli and the floor of silver-inlaid marble tiles. Heavy velvet hangings decorated the walls and silken cushions; richly made divans and mahogany chairs and tables littered the room in careless profusion.

'I would give much for a horn of ale, but this wine is not sour to the palate,' said Athelstane, emptying a golden flagon with relish. 'Brunhild, you have deceived us. You let us understand it would take hard fighting to win back your crown—yet I have struck but one blow and my sword is thirsty as Turlogh's ax which has not drunk at all. We hammered on the gates and the people fell down and worshipped with no more ado. And until a while ago, we but stood by your throne in the great palace room, while you spoke to the throngs that came and knocked their heads on the floor before you—by Thor, never have I heard such clattering and jabbering! My ears ring till now—what were they saying? And where is that old conjurer Gothan?'

'Your steel will drink deep yet, Saxon,' answered the girl grimly, resting her chin on her hands and eyeing the warriors with deep moody eyes. Had you gambled with cities and crowns as I have done you would know that seizing a throne may be easier than keeping it. Our sudden appearance with the birdgod's head, your killing of Ska, swept the people off their feet. As for the rest—I held audience in the palace as you saw, even if you did not understand and the people who came in bowing droves were assuring me of their unswerving loyalty—ha! I graciously pardoned them all, but I am no fool. When they have time to think, they will begin to grumble again. Gothan is lurking in the shadows somewhere, plotting evil to us all, you may be sure. This city is honey-combed with secret corridors and subterranean passages of which only the priests know. Even I, who have traversed some of them when I was Gothan's puppet, know not where to look for the secret

doors, since Gothan always led me through them blind-
folded.

'Just now, I think I hold the upper hand. The people
look on you with more awe than they regard me. They
think your armor and helmets are part of your bodies and
that you are invulnerable. Did you not move them timidly
touching your mail as we passed through the crowd, and
the amazement on their faces as they felt the iron of it?'

'For a people so wise in some ways they are very
foolish in others,' said Turlogh. 'Who are they and
whence came they?'

'They are so old,' answered Brunhild, 'that their most
ancient legends give no hint of their origin. Ages ago
they were a part of a great empire which spread out over
the many isles of this sea. But some of the islands sank
and vanished with their cities and people. Then the red-
skinned savages assailed them and isle after isle fell before
them. At last only this island was left unconquered, and
the people have become weaker and forgotten many
ancient arts. For lack of ports to sail to, the galleys rotted
by the wharves which themselves crumbled into decay.
Not in the memory of man has any son of Bal-Sagoth
sailed the seas. At irregular intervals the red people
descend upon the Isle of the Gods, traversing the seas
in their long war-canoes which bear grinning skulls on
the prows. Not far away as a Viking would reckon a
sea-voyage, but out of sight over the sea rim lie the islands
inhabited by these red men who centuries ago slaughtered
the folk who dwelt there. We have always beaten them
off; they can not scale the walls, but still they come and
the fear of their raid is always hovering over the isle.

'But it is not them I fear; it is Gothan, who is at this
moment either slipping like a loathly serpent through his
black tunnels or else brewing abominations in one of his
hidden chambers. In the caves deep in the hills to which
his tunnels lead, he works fearful and unholy magic. His
subjects are beasts—serpents, spiders, and great apes;
and men—red captives and wretches of his own race.

Deep in his grisly caverns he makes beasts of men and half-men of beasts, mingling bestial with human in ghastly creation. No man dares guess at the horrors that have spawned in the darkness, or what shapes of terror and blasphemy have come into being during the ages Gothan has wrought his abominations; for he is not as other men, and has discovered the secret of life everlasting. He has at least brought into foul life one creature that even he fears, the gibbering, mowing, nameless Thing he keeps chained in the farthest cavern that no human foot, save his, has trod. He would loose it against me if he dared . . .

'But it grows late and I would sleep. I will sleep in the room next to this, which has no other opening than this door. Not even a slave-girl will I keep with me, for I trust none of these people fully. You shall keep this room, and though the outer door is bolted, one had better watch while the other sleeps. Zomar and his guardsmen patrol the corridors outside, but I shall feel safer with two men of my own blood between me and the rest of the city.'

She rose, and with a strangely lingering glance at Turlogh, entered her chamber and closed the door behind her.

Athelstane stretched and yawned. 'Well, Turlogh,' said he lazily, 'men's fortunes are unstable as the sea. Last night I was the picked swordsman of a band of reavers and you a captive. This dawn we were lost outcasts springing at each other's throats. Now we are sword brothers and right-hand men to a queen. And you, I think, are destined to become a king.'

'How so?'

'Why, have you not noticed the Orkney girl's eyes on you? Faith there's more than friendship in her glances that rest on those black locks and that brown face of yours. I tell you—'

'Enough,' Turlogh's voice was harsh as an old wound stung him. 'Women in power are white-fanged wolves. It was the spite of a woman that—' He stopped.

'Well, well,' returned Athelstane tolerantly, 'there are more good women than bad ones. I know—it was the intrigues of a woman that made you an outcast. Well, we should be good comrades. I am an outlaw, too. If I should show my face in Wessex I would soon be looking down on the countryside from a stout oak limb.'

'What drove you out on the Viking path? So far have the Saxons forgotten the ocean-ways that King Alfred was obliged to hire Frisian rovers to build and man his fleet when he fought the Danes.'

Athelstane shrugged his mighty shoulders and began whetting his dirk.

'I had a yearning for the sea even when I was a shock-headed child in Wessex. I was still a youth when I killed a young eorl and fled the vengeance of his people. I found refuge in the Orkneys and the ways of the Vikings were more to my liking than the ways of my own blood. But I came back to fight against Canute, and when England submitted to his rule, he gave me command of his house-carles. That made the Danes jealous because of the honor given a Saxon who had fought against them, and the Saxons remembered I had left Wessex under a cloud once and murmured that I was overly-well favored by the conquerors. Well, there was a Saxon thane and the Danish jarl who one night at feast assailed me with fiery words and I forgot myself and slew them both.

'So England—was—again—barred—to—me. I—took —the—viking—path—again—'

Athelstane's words trailed off. His hands slid limply from his lap and the whetstone and dirk dropped to the floor. His head fell forward on his broad chest and his eyes closed.

'Too much wine,' muttered Turlogh. 'But let him slumber; I'll keep watch.'

Yet even as he spoke, the Gael was aware of a strange lassitude stealing over him. He lay back in the broad chair. His eyes felt heavy and sleep veiled his brain despite himself. And as he lay there, a strange nightmare vision came to him. One of the heavy hangings on the wall opposite the door swayed violently and from behind it slunk a fearful shape that crept slavering across the room. Turlogh watched it apathetically, aware that he was dreaming and at the same time wondering at the strangeness of the dream. The thing was grotesquely like a crooked gnarled man in shape, but its face was bestial. It bared yellow fangs as it lurched silently toward him, and from under penthouse brows small reddened eyes gleamed demoniacally. Yet there was something of the human in his countenance; it was neither ape nor man, but an unnatural creature horribly compounded of both.

Now the foul apparition halted before him, and as the gnarled fingers clutched his throat, Turlogh was suddenly and fearfully aware that this was no dream but a fiendish reality. With a burst of desperate effort he broke the unseen chains that held him and hurled himself from the chair. The grasping fingers missed his throat, but quick as he was, he could not elude the swift lunge of those hairy arms, and the next moment he was tumbling about the floor in a death grip with the monster, whose sinews felt like pliant steel.

That fearful battle was fought in silence save for the hissing of hand-drawn breath. Turlogh's left forearm was thrust under the apish chin, holding back the grisly fangs from his throat, about which the monster's fingers had locked. Athelstane still slept in his chair, head fallen forward. Turlogh tried to call to him, but those throttling hands had shut off his voice, were fast choking out his life. The room swam in a red haze before his distended eyes. His right hand, clenched into an iron mallet, battered desperately at the fearful face bent toward his; the beast-like teeth shattered under his blows and the blood splattered, but still the red eyes gloated and the taloned fingers sank deeper and deeper until a ringing in Turlogh's ears knelled his soul's departure.

Even as he sank into a semi-unconsciousness, his falling hand struck something his numbed fighting-brain recognized as the dirk Athelstane had dropped on the floor. Blindly, with a dying gesture, Turlogh struck and felt the fingers loosen suddenly. Feeling the return of life and power, he heaved up and over, with his assailant beneath him, and he drove the dirk home until the dumb horror lay still with wide staring eyes.

The Gael staggered to his feet, dizzy and panting trembling in every limb. He drew in great gulps of air and his giddiness slowly cleared. Blood trickled plentifully from the wounds in his throat. He noted with amazement that the Saxon still slumbered. And suddenly he began to feel again the tides of unnatural weariness and lassitude that had rendered him helpless before. Picking up his ax, he shook off the feeling with difficulty and stepped toward the curtain from behind which the ape-man had come. Like an invisible wave a subtle power emanating from those hangings struck him, and with weighted limbs he forced his way across the room. Now he stood before the curtain and felt the power of a terrific evil will beating upon his own, menacing his very soul, threatening to enslave him, brain and body. Twice he raised his hand and twice it dropped limply to his side. Now for the third time he made a mighty effort and tore the hangings bodily from the wall. For a flashing instant he caught a glimpse of a bizarre, half-naked figure in a mantle of parrot-feathers and a head-gear of waving plumes. Then as he felt the full hypnotic blast of those blazing eyes, he closed his own eyes and struck blind. He felt his ax sink deep; then he opened his eyes and gazed at the silent figure which lay at his feet, cleft head in a widening crimson pool.

And now Athelstane suddenly heaved erect, eyes flaring bewilderedly, sword out. 'What—?' he stammered, glaring wildly, 'Turlogh, what in Thor's name's happened? Thor's blood! That is a priest there, but what is this dead thing?'

'One of the devils of this foul city,' answered Turlogh
wrenching his ax free, 'I think Gothan has failed again.
This one stood behind the hangings and bewitched us
unawares. He put the spell of sleep on us.'

'Aye, I slept,' the Saxon nodded dazedly. 'But how
came they here—'

'There must be a secret door behind those hangings,
though I cannot find it—'

'Hark!' From the room where the queen slept there
came a vague scuffling sound, that in its very faintness
seemed fraught with grisly potentialities.

'Brunhild!' Turlogh shouted. A strange gurgle answered him. He thrust against the door. It was locked. As he
heaved up his ax to hew it open, Athelstane brushed him
aside and hurled his full weight against it. The panels
crashed and through their ruins Athelstane plunged into
the room. A roar burst from his lips. Over the Saxon's
shoulder Turlogh saw a vision of delirium. Brunhild,
queen of Bal-Sagoth, writhed helpless in midair, gripped
by the black shadow of a nightmare. Then as the great
black shape turned cold flaming eyes on them Turlogh
saw it was a living creature. It stood, man-like, upon two
tree-like legs, but its outline and face were not of a man,
beast or devil. This, Turlogh felt, was the horror that
even Gothan had hesitated to loose upon his foes; the
archfiend that the demoniac priest had brought into life
in his hidden caves of horror. What ghastly knowledge
had been necessary, what hideous blending of human
and bestial things with nameless shapes from outer voids
of darkness?

Held like a babe in arms Brunhild writhed, eyes flaring
with horror, and as the Thing took a misshapen hand
from her white throat to defend itself, a scream of heart-
shaking fright burst from her pale lips. Athelstane, first in
the room, was ahead of the Gael. The black shape loomed
over the giant Saxon, dwarfing and overshadowing him,
but Athelstane, gripping the hilt with both hands, lunged
upward. The great sword sank over half its length into the

black body and came out crimson as the monster reeled back. A hellish pandemonium of sound burst forth, and the echoes of that hideous yell thundered through the palace and deafened the hearers. Turlogh was springing in, ax high, when the fiend dropped the girl and fled reeling across the room, vanishing in a dark opening that now gaped in the wall. Athelstane, clean berserk, plunged after it.

Turlogh made to follow, but Brunhild, reeling up, threw her white arms around him in a grip even he could hardly break. 'No!' she screamed, eyes ablaze with terror, 'do not follow them into that fearful corridor! It must lead to Hell itself! The Saxon will never return! Let you not share his fate!'

'Loose me, woman!' roared Turlogh in a frenzy, striving to disengage himself without hurting her. 'My comrade may be fighting for his life!'

'Wait till I summon the guard!' she cried, but Turlogh flung her from him, and as he sprang through the secret doorway, Brunhild smote on the jade gong until the palace echoed. A loud pounding began in the corridor and Zomar's voice shouted: 'Oh, queen, are you in peril? Shall we burst the door?'

'Hasten!' she screamed, as she rushed to the outer door and flung it open.

Turlogh, leaping recklessly into the corridor, raced along in darkness for a few moments, hearing ahead of him the agonized bellowing of the wounded monster and the deep fierce shouts of the Viking. Then these noises faded away in the distance as he came into the narrow passageway faintly lighted with torches stuck into niches. Face down on the floor lay a brown man, clad in gray feathers, his skull crushed like an egg-shell.

How long Turlogh O'Brien followed the dizzy windings of the shadowy corridor he never knew. Other smaller passages led off to each side but he kept to the main corridor. At last he passed under an arched doorway and came out into a strange vasty room.

Somber massive columns upheld a shadowy ceiling so high it seemed like a brooding cloud arched against a midnight sky. Turlogh saw that he was in a temple. Behind a black red-stained stone altar loomed a mighty form, sinister and abhorent. The god Gol-goroth! Surely it must be he. But Turlogh spared only a single glance for the colossal figure that brooded there in the shadows. Before him was a strange tableau. Athelstane leaned on his great sword and gazed at the two shapes which sprawled in a red welter at his feet. Whatever foul magic had brought the Black Thing into life, it had taken but a thrust of English steel to hurl it back into a limbo from whence it came. The monster lay half across its last victim—a gaunt white bearded man whose eyes were starkly evil, even in death.

'Gothan!' ejaculated the startled Gael.

'Aye, the priest—I was close behind the troll or whatever it is, all the way along the corridor, but for all its size it fled like a deer. Once one in a feather mantle tried to halt it, and it smashed his skull and paused not an instant. At last we burst into this temple, I close upon the monster's heels with my sword raised for the death-cut. But Thor's blood. When it saw the old one standing by that altar, it gave one fearful howl and tore him to pieces and died itself, all in an instant, before I could reach it and strike.'

Turlogh gazed at the huge formless thing. Looking directly at it, he could form no estimate of its nature. He got only a chaotic impression of great size and inhuman evil. Now it lay like a vast shadow blotched out on the marble floor. Surely black wings beating from moonless gulfs had hovered over its birth, and the grisly souls of nameless demons had gone into its being.

And now Brunhild rushed from the dark corridor with Zomar and the guardsmen. And from outer doors and secret nooks came others silently—warriors, and priests in feathered mantles, until a great throng stood in the Temple of Darkness.

A fierce cry broke from the queen as she saw what had happened. Her eyes blazed terribly and she was gripped by a strange madness.

'At last!' she screamed, spurning the corpse of her arch-foe with her heel, 'at last I am true mistress of Bal-Sagoth! The secrets of the hidden ways are mine now, and old Gothan's beard is dabbled in his own blood!'

She flung her arms high in fearful triumph, and ran toward the grim idol, screaming exultant insults like a mad-woman. And at that instant the temple rocked! The colossal image swayed outward, and then pitched suddenly forward as a tall tower falls. Turlogh shouted and leaped forward, but even as he did, with a thunder like the bursting of a word, the god Gol-goroth crashed down upon the doomed woman, who stood frozen. The mighty image splintered into a thousand great fragments, blotting from the sight of men forever Brunhild, daughter of Rane Thorfin's son, queen of Bal-Sagoth. From under the ruins there oozed a wide crimson stream.

Warriors and priests stood frozen, deafened by the crash of that fall, stunned by the weird catastrophe. An icy hand touched Turlogh's spine. Had that vast bulk been thrust over by the hand of a dead man? As it had rushed downward it had seemed to the Gael that the inhuman features had for an instant taken on the likeness of the dead Gothan!

Now as all stood speechless, the acolyte Gelka saw and seized his opportunity.

'Gol-goroth has spoken!' he screamed. 'He has crushed the false goddess! She was but a wicked mortal! And these strangers, too, are mortal! See—he bleeds!'

The priest's finger stabbed at the dried blood on Turlogh's throat and a wild roar went up from the throng. Dazed and bewildered by the swiftness and magnitude of the late events, they were like crazed wolves, ready to wipe out doubts and fear in a burst of bloodshed. Gelka bounded at Turlogh, hatchet flashing, and a knife in the hand of a satellite licked into Zomar's back. Turlogh had not understood the shout, but he realized the air was tense with danger for Athelstane and himself. He met the leaping Gelka with a stroke that sheared through the waving plumes and the skull beneath, then half a dozen lances broke on his buckler and a rush of bodies swept him back against a great pillar. Then Athelstane, slow of thought, who had stood gaping for the flashing second it had taken this to transpire, awoke in a blast of awesome fury. With a deafening roar he swung his heavy sword in a mighty arc. The whistling blade whipped off a head, sheared through a torso and sank deep into a spinal column. The three corpses fell across each other and even in the madness of the strife, men cried out at the marvel of that single stroke.

But like a brown, blind tide of fury the maddened people of Bal-Sagoth rolled on their foes. The guardsmen of the dead queen, trapped in the press, died to a man without a chance to strike a blow. But the overthrow of the two white warriors was no such easy task. Back to back they smashed and smote; Athelstane's sword was a thunderbolt of death; Turlogh's ax was lightning. Hedged closed by a sea of snarling brown faces and flashing steel they hacked their way slowly toward a doorway. The very mass of the attackers hindered the warriors of Bal-Sagoth, for they had no space to guide their strokes, while the weapons of the seafarers kept a bloody ring clear in front of them.

Heaping a ghastly row of corpses as they went, the comrades slowly cut their way through the snarling press. The Temple of Darkness, witness of many a bloody deed, was flooded with gore spilled like a red sacrifice to her broken gods. The heavy weapons of the white fighters wrought fearful havoc among their naked, lighter-limbed foes, while their armor guarded their own lives. But their arms, legs and faces were cut and gashed by the frantically flying steel and it seemed the sheer numbers of their foes would overwhelm them ere they could reach the door.

Then they had reached it, and made desperate play until the brown warriors, no longer able to come upon them from all sides, drew back for a breathing-space, leaving a torn red heap before the threshold. And in that instant the two sprang back into the corridor and seizing the great brazen door, slammed it in the very faces of the warriors who leaped howling to prevent it. Athelstane, bracing his mighty legs, held it against their combined efforts until Turlogh had time to find and slip the bolt.

'Thor!' gasped the Saxon, shaking the blood in a red shower from his face. 'This is close play! What now, Turlogh?'

'Down the corridor, quick!' snapped the Gael, 'before they come on us from this way and trap us like rats against this door. By Satan, the whole city must be roused! Hark to that roaring!'

In truth, as they raced down the shadowed corridor, it seemed to them that all Bal-Sagoth had burst into rebellion and civil war. From all sides came the clashing of steel, the shouts of men, and the screams of women, overshadowed by a hideous howling. A lurid glow became apparent down the corridor and even then as Turlogh, in the lead, rounded a corner and came out into an open courtyard, a vague figure leaped at him and a heavy weapon fell with unexpected force on his shield, almost felling him. But even as he staggered he struck back and the upper-spike on his ax sank under the heart of his attacker who fell at his feet. In the glare that illumined all, Turlogh saw his victim differed from the brown warriors he had been fighting. This man was naked, powerfully muscled and of a copperish red rather than brown. The heavy animal-like jaw, the slanting low forehead showed none of the intelligence and refinement of the brown people, but only a brute ferocity. A heavy war-club, rudely carved, lay beside him.

'By Thor!' exclaimed Athelstane, 'the city burns!'

Turlogh looked up. They were standing on a sort of raised courtyard from which broad steps led down into the streets and from this vantage-point they had a plain view of the terrific end of Bal-Sagoth. Flames leaped madly higher and higher, paling the moon, and in the red glare pigmy figures ran to and fro, falling and dying like puppets dancing to the tune of the Black Gods. Through the roar of the flames and the crashing of falling walls cut screams of death and shrieks of ghastly triumph. The city was swarming with naked, copper-skinned devils who burned and ravished and butchered in one red carnival of madness.

The red men of the isles! By the thousands they had descended on the Isle of the Gods in the night, and whether stealth or treachery let them through the walls, the comrades never knew, but now they ravened through the corpse-strewn streets, glutting their blood-lust in holocaust and massacre wholesale. Not all the gashed forms that lay in the crimson-running streets were brown; the people of the doomed city fought with desperate courage, but outnumbered and caught off guard, their courage was futile. The red men were like blood-hungry tigers.

'What ho, Turlogh!' shouted Athelstane, beard a-bristle, eyes ablaze as the madness of the scene fired a like passion in his own fierce soul, 'the world ends! Let us into the thick of it and glut our steel before we die! Who shall we strike for—the red or the brown?'

'Steady!' snapped the Gael. 'Either people would cut out throats. We must hack our way through to the gates, and the Devil take them all. We have no friends here. This way—down these stairs. Across the roofs in yonder direction I see the arch of a gate.'

The comrades sprang down the stairs, gained the narrow street below and ran swiftly in the way Turlogh indicated. About them washed a red inundation of slaughter. A thick smoke veiled all now, and in the murk chaotic groups merged, writhed and scattered, littering the shattered flags with gory shapes. It was like a nightmare in which demoniac figures leaped and capered, looming suddenly in the fire-shot mist, vanishing as suddenly. The flames from each side of the streets shouldered each other, singeing the hair of the warriors as they ran. Roofs fell in with an awesome thunder and walls crashing into ruin filled the air with flying death. Men struck blindly from the smoke and the seafarers cut them down and never knew whether their skins were brown or red.

Now a new note rose in the cataclysmic horror. Blinded by the smoke, confused by the winding streets, the red men were trapped in the snare of their own making. Fire is impartial; it can burn the lighter as well as the intended victim; and a falling wall is blind. The red men abandoned their prey and ran howling to and fro like beasts, seeking escape; many, finding this futile, turned back in a last unreasoning storm of madness as a blinded tiger turns, and made their last moments of life a crimson burst of slaughter.

Turlogh, with the unerring sense of direction that comes to men who live the life of the wolf, ran toward the point where he knew an outer gate to be; yet in the windings of the streets and the screen of smoke, doubt assailed him. From the flame-shot murk in front of him a fearful scream rang out. A naked girl reeled blindly into view and fell at Turlogh's feet, blood gushing from her mutilated breast. A howling, red-stained devil, close on her heels, jerked back her head and cut her throat, a fraction of a second before Turlogh's ax ripped the head from its shoulders and spun it grinning into the street. And at that second a sudden wind shifted the writhing smoke and the comrades saw the open gateway ahead of them, aswarm with red warriors. A fierce shout, a blasting rush, a mad instant of volcanic ferocity that littered the gateway with corpses, and they were through and racing down the slopes toward the distant forest and the beach beyond. Before then the sky was reddening for dawn; behind them rose the soul-shaking tumult of the doomed city.

Like hunted things they fled, seeking brief shelter among the many groves from time to time, to avoid groups of savages who ran toward the city. The whole island seemed to be swarming with them; the chiefs must have drawn on all the isles within hundreds of miles for a raid of such magnitude. And at last the comrades reached the strip of forest, and breathed deeply as they came to the beach and found it abandoned save for a number of long skull-decorated war canoes.

Athelstane sat down and gasped for breath. 'Thor's blood! What now? What may we do but hide in these woods until those red devils hunt us out?'

'Help me launch this boat,' snapped Turlogh. 'We'll take our chance on the open main—'

'Ho!' Athelstane leaped erect, pointing, 'Thor's blood, a ship!'

The sun was just up, gleaming like a great golden coin on the sea-rim. And limned in the sun swam a tall, high-pooped craft. The comrades leaped into the nearest canoe, shoved off and rowed like mad, shouting and waving their oars to attract the attention of the crew. Powerful muscles drove the long slim craft along at an incredible clip, and it was not long before the ship stood about and allowed them to come alongside. Dark-faced men, clad in mail, looked over the rail.

'Spaniards,' muttered Athelstane. 'If they recognize me, I had better stayed on the island!'

But he clambered up the chain without hesitation, and the two wanderers fronted the lean somber-faced man whose armor was that of a knight of Asturias. He spoke to them in Spanish and Turlogh answered him, for the Gael, like many of his race, was a natural linguist and had wandered far and spoken many tongues. In a few words the Dalcassian told their story and explained the great pillar of smoke which now rolled upward in the morning air from the isle.

'Tell him there is a king's ransom for the taking,' put in Athelstane. 'Tell of the silver gates, Turlogh.'

But when the Gael spoke of the vast loot in the doomed city, the commander shook his head.

'Good sir, we have not time to secure it, nor men to waste in the taking. Those red fiends you describe would hardly give up anything—though useless to them—without a fierce battle and neither my time nor my force is mine. I am Don Roderigo del Cortez of Castile and this ship, the *Gray Friar*, is one of a fleet that sailed to harry the Moorish Corsairs. Some days agone we were separated from the rest of the fleet in a sea skirmish and the tempest blew us far off our course. We are even now beating back to rejoin the fleet if we can find it; if not, to harry the infidel as well as we may. We serve God and the king and we cannot halt from mere dross as you suggest. But you are welcome aboard this ship and we have need of such fighting men as you appear to be. You will not regret it, should you wish to join us and strike a blow for Christendom, against the Moslems.'

In the narrow-bridged nose and deep dark eyes, as in the lean ascetic face, Turlogh read the fanatic, the stainless cavalier, the knight errant. He spoke to Athelstane: 'This man is mad, but there are good blows to be struck and strange lands to see; anyway, we have no other choice.'

'One place is as good as another to masterless men and wanderers,' quoth the huge Saxon. 'Tell him we will follow him to Hell and singe the tail of the Devil if there be any chance of loot.'

4. Empire

Turlogh and Athelstane leaned on the rail, gazing back at the swiftly receding Island of the Gods, from which rose a pillar of smoke, laden with the ghosts of a thousand centuries and the shadows and mysteries of a forgotten empire, and Athelstane cursed as only a Saxon can.

'A king's ransom—and after all that blood-letting—no loot!'

Turlogh shook his head. 'We have seen an ancient kingdom fall—we have seen the last remnant of the world's oldest empire sink into flames and the abyss of oblivion, and barbarism rear its brute head above the ruins. So pass the glory and the splendor and the imperial purple—in red flames and yellow smoke.'

'But not one bit of plunder—' persisted the Viking.

Again Turlogh shook his head. 'I brought away with me the rarest gem upon the island—something for which men and women have died and the gutters run with blood.'

He drew from his girdle a small object—a curiously carved symbol of jade.

'The emblem of kingship!' exclaimed Athelstane.

'Aye—as Brunhild struggled with me to keep me from following you into the corridor, this thing caught in my mail and was torn from the golden chain that held it.'

'He who bears it is king of Bal-Sagoth,' ruminated the mighty Saxon. 'As I predicted, Turlogh, you are a king!'

Turlogh laughed with bitter mirth and pointed to the great billowing column of smoke which floated in the sky away on the sea-rim.

'Aye—a kingdom of the dead—an empire of ghosts and smoke. I am Ard-Righ of a phantom city—I am King Turlogh of Bal-Sagoth and my kingdom is fading in the morning sky. And therein it is like all other empires in the world—dreams and ghosts and smoke.'

CORMAC FITZGEOFFREY

Hawks of Outremer

1. A Man Returns

'**H**ALT!' the bearded man-at-arms swung his pike about,
growling like a surly mastiff. It paid to be wary on the
road to Antioch. The stars blinked redly through the
thick night and their light was not sufficient for the
fellow to make out what sort of man it was who loomed
so gigantically before him.

An iron-clad hand shot out suddenly and closed
on the soldier's mailed shoulder in a grasp that numbed
his whole arm. From beneath the helmet the guardsman
saw the blaze of ferocious blue eyes that seemed lambent,
even in the dark.

'Saints preserve us!' gasped the frightened man-at-
arms, 'Cormac Fitzgeoffrey! Avaunt! Back to Hell with
ye, like a good knight! I swear to you, sir – '

'Swear me no oaths,' growled the knight. 'What is
this talk?'

'Are you not an incorporeal spirit?' mouthed the
soldier. 'Were you not slain by the Moorish corsairs on
your homeward voyage?'

'By the accursed gods!' snarled Fitzgeoffrey. 'Does
this hand feel like smoke?'

He sank his mailed fingers into the soldier's arm and
grinned bleakly at the resultant howl.

'Enough of such mummery; tell me who is within
that tavern.'

'Only my master, Sir Rupert de Vaile, of Rouen.'

'Good enough,' grunted the other. 'He is one of the few men I count friends, in the East or elsewhere.'

The big warrior strode to the tavern door and entered, treading lightly as a cat despite his heavy armor. The man-at-arms rubbed his arm and stared after him curiously, noting, in the dim light, that Fitzgeoffrey bore a shield with the horrific emblem of his family – a white grinning skull. The guardsman knew him of old – a turbulent character, a savage fighter and the only man among the Crusaders who had been esteemed stronger than Richard the Lion-hearted. But Fitzgeoffrey had taken ship for his native isle even before Richard had departed from the Holy Land. The Third Crusade had ended in failure and disgrace; most of the Frankish knights had followed their kings homeward. What was this grim Irish killer doing on the road to Antioch?

Sir Rupert de Vaile, once of Rouen, now a lord of the fast-fading Outremer, turned as the great form bulked in the doorway. Cormac Fitzgeoffrey was a fraction of an inch above six feet, but with his mighty shoulders and two hundred pounds of iron muscle, he seemed shorter. The Norman stared in surprized recognition, and sprang to his feet. His fine face shone with sincere pleasure.

'Cormac, by the saints! Why, man, we heard that you were dead!'

Cormac returned the hearty grip, while his thin lips curved slightly in what would have been, in another man, a broad grin of greeting. Sir Rupert was a tall man, and well knit, but he seemed almost slight beside the huge Irish warrior who combined bulk with a sort of dynamic aggressiveness that was apparent in his every movement.

Fitzgeoffrey was clean-shaven and the various scars that showed on his dark, grim face, lent his already formidable features a truly sinister aspect. When he took off his plain vizorless helmet and thrust back his mail coif, his square-cut, black hair that topped his low broad forehead contrasted strongly with his cold blue eyes. A true son of the most indomitable and savage race that ever trod the blood-stained fields of battle, Cormac Fitzgeoffrey looked to be what he was – a ruthless fighter, born to the game of war, to whom the ways of violence and bloodshed were as natural as the ways of peace are to the average man.

Son of a woman of the O'Briens and a renegade Norman knight, Geoffrey the Bastard, in whose veins, it is said, coursed the blood of William the Conqueror, Cormac had seldom known an hour of peace or ease in all his thirty years of violent life. He was born in a feud-torn and blood-drenched land, and raised in a heritage of hate and savagery. The ancient culture of Erin had long crumbled before the repeated onslaughts of Norsemen and Danes. Harried on all sides by cruel foes, the rising civilization of the Celts had faded before the fierce necessity of incessant conflict, and the merciless struggle for survival had made the Gaels as savage as the heathens who assailed them.

Now, in Cormac's time, war upon red war swept the crimson isle, where clan fought clan, and the Norman adventurers tore at one another's throats, or resisted the attacks of the Irish, playing tribe against tribe, while from Norway and the Orkneys the still half-pagan Vikings ravaged all impartially.

A vague realization of all this flashed through Sir Rupert's mind as he stood staring at his friend.

'We heard you were slain in a sea-fight off Sicily,' he repeated.

Cormac shrugged his shoulders. 'Many died then, it is true, and I was struck senseless by a stone from a ballista. Doubtless that is how the rumor started. But you see me, as much alive as ever.'

'Sit down, old friend.' Sir Rupert thrust forward one of the rude benches which formed part of the tavern's furniture. 'What is forward in the West?'

Cormac took the wine goblet proferred him by a dark-skinned servitor, and drank deeply.

'Little of note,' said he. 'In France the king counts his pence and squabbles with his nobles. Richard – if he lives – languishes somewhere in Germany, 'tis thought. In England Shane – that is to say, John – oppresses the people and betrays the barons. And in Ireland – Hell!' He laughed shortly and without mirth. 'What shall I say of Ireland but the same old tale? Gael and foreigner cut each other's throat and plot together against the king. John De Coursey, since Hugh de Lacy supplanted him as governor, has raged like a madman, burning and pillaging, while Donal O'Brien lurks in the west to destroy what remains. Yet, by Satan, I think this land is but little better.'

'Yet there is peace of a sort now,' murmured Sir Rupert.

'Aye – peace while the jackal Saladin gathers his powers,' grunted Cormac. 'Think you he will rest idle while Acre, Antioch and Tripoli remain in Christian hands? He but waits an excuse to seize the remnants of Outremer.'

Sir Rupert shook his head, his eyes shadowed.

'It is a naked land and a bloody one. Were it not akin to blasphemy I could curse the day I followed my King eastward. Betimes I dream of the orchards of Normandy, the deep cool forests and the dreaming vineyards. Methinks my happiest hours were when a page of twelve years – '

'At twelve,' grunted Fitzgeoffrey, 'I was running wild with shock-head kerns on the naked fens – I wore wolfskins, weighed near to fourteen stone, and had killed three men.'

Sir Rupert looked curiously at his friend. Separated from Cormac's native land by a width of sea and the breadth of Britain, the Norman knew but little of the affairs in that far isle. But he knew vaguely that Cormac's life had not ben an easy one. Hated by the Irish and despised by the Normans, he had paid back contempt and ill-treatment with savage hate and ruthless vengeance. It was known that he owned a shadow of allegiance only to the great house of Fitzgerald, who, as much Welsh as Norman, had even then begun to take up Irish customs and Irish quarrels.

'You wear another sword than that you wore when I saw you last.'

'They break in my hands,' said Cormac. 'Three Turkish sabers went into the forging of the sword I wielded at Joppa – yet it shattered like glass in that sea-fight off Sicily. I took this from the body of a Norse sea-king who led a raid into Munster. It was forged in Norway – see the pagan runes on the steel?'

He drew the sword and the great blade shimmered bluely, like a thing alive in the candle light. The servants crossed themselves and Sir Rupert shook his head.

'You should not have drawn it here – they say blood follows such a sword.'

'Bloodshed follows my trail anyway,' growled Cormac. 'This blade has already drunk Fitzgeoffrey blood – with this that Norse sea-king slew my brother, Shane.'

'And you wear such a sword?' exclaimed Sir Rupert in horror. 'No good will come of that evil blade, Cormac!'

'Why not? asked the big warrior impatiently. 'It's a good blade – I wiped out the stain of my brother's blood when I slew his slayer. By Satan, but that sea-king was a grand sight in his coat of mail with silvered scales. His silvered helmet was strong too – ax, helmet and skull shattered together.'

'You had another brother, did you not?'

'Aye – Donal. Eochaidh O'Donnell ate his heart out after the battle at Coolmanagh. There was a feud between us at the time, so it may be Eochaidh merely saved me the trouble – but for all that I burned the O'Donnell in his own castle.'

'How came you to first ride on the Crusade?' asked Sir Rupert curiously. 'Were you stirred with a desire to cleanse your soul by smiting the Paynim?'

'Ireland was too hot for me,' answered the Norman-Gael candidly. 'Lord Shamus MacGearailt – James Fitzgerald – wished to make peace with the English king and I feared he would buy favor by delivering me into the hands of the king's governor. As there was feud between my family and most of the Irish clans, there was nowhere for me to go. I was about to seek my fortune in Scotland when young Eamonn Fitzgerald was stung by the hornet of Crusade and I accompanied him.'

'But you gained favor with Richard – tell me the tale.'

'Soon told. It was on the plains of Azotus when we came to grips with the Turks. Aye, you were there! I was fighting alone in the thick of the fray and helmets and turbans were cracking like eggs all around when I noted a strong knight in the forefront of our battle. He cut deeper and deeper into the close-ranked lines of the heathen and his heavy mace scattered brains like water. But so dented was his shield and so stained with blood his armor, I could not tell who he might be.

'But suddenly his horse went down and in an instant he was hemmed in on all sides by the howling fiends who bore him down by sheer weight of numbers. So hacking a way to his side I dismounted – '

'Dismounted?' exclaimed Sir Rupert in amazement.

Cormac's head jerked up in irritation at the interruption. 'Why not?' he snapped. 'I am no French she-knight to fear wading in the muck – anyway, I fight better on foot. Well, I cleared a space with a sweep or so of my sword, and the fallen knight, the press being lightened, came up roaring like a bull and swinging his blood-clotted mace with such fury he nearly brained *me* as well as the Turks. A charge of English knights swept the heathen away and when he lifted his vizor I saw I had succored Richard of England.

'Who are you and who is your master?' said he.

'I am Cormac Fitzgeoffrey and I have no master,'
said I. 'I followed young Eamonn Fitzgerald to Holy
Land and since he fell before the walls of Acre, I seek
my fortune alone.'

'What think ye of me as a master?' asked he, while
the battle raged half a bow-shot about us.

'You fight reasonably well for a man with Saxon
blood in his veins,' I answered, 'but I own allegiance to
no English king.'

'He swore like a trooper. "By the bones of the
saints," said he, "that had cost another man his head.
You saved my life, but for this insolence, no prince
shall knight you!"

'Keep your knighthoods and be damned,' said I. 'I
am a chief in Ireland – but we waste words; yonder are
pagan heads to be smashed.'

'Later he bade me to his royal presence and waxed
merry with me; a rare drinker he is, though a fool withal.
But I distrust kings – I attached myself to the train of
a brave and gallant young knight of France – the Sieur
Gerard de Gissclin, full of insane ideals of chivalry, but
a noble youth.

'When peace was made between the hosts, I heard
hints of a renewal of strife between the Fitzgeralds and
the Le Boteliers, and Lord Shamus having been slain
by Nial Mac Art, and I being in favor with the king
anyway, I took leave of Sieur Gerard and betook myself
back to Erin. Well – we swept Ormond with torch and
sword and hanged old Sir William Le Botelier to his
own barbican. Then, the Geraldines having no particular
need of my sword at the moment, I bethought myself
once more of Sieur Gerard to whom I owed my life
and which debt I have not yet had opportunity to
pay. How, Sir Rupert, dwells he still in his castle
of Ali-El-Yar?'

Sir Rupert's face went suddenly white, and he
leaned back as if shrinking from something. Cormac's
head jerked up and his dark face grew more forbidding

and fraught with somber potentialities. He seized the Norman's arm in an unconsciously savage grip.

'Speak, man,' he rasped. 'What ails you?'

'Sieur Gerard,' half-whispered Sir Rupert. 'Had you not heard? Ali-El-Yar lies in smoldering ruins and Gerard is dead.'

Cormac snarled like a made dog, his terrible eyes blazing with a fearful light. He shook Sir Rupert in the intensity of his passion.

'Who did the deed? He shall die, were he Emperor of Byzantium!'

'I knot not!' Sir Rupert gasped, his mind half stunned by the blast of the Gael's primitive fury. 'There be foul rumours – Sieur Gerard loved a girl in a sheihk's harem, it is said. A horde of wild riders from the desert assailed his castle and a rider broke through to ask aid of the baron Conrad Von Gonler. But Conrad refused – '

'Aye!' snarled Cormac, with a savage gesture. 'He hated Gerard because long ago the youngster had the best of him at sword-play on shipboard before old Frederick Barbarossa's eyes. And what then?'

'Ali-El-Yar fell with all its people. Their stripped and mutilated bodies lay among the coals, but no sign was found of Gerard. Whether he died before or after the attack of the castle is not known, but dead he must be, since no demand for ransom has been made.'

'Thus Saladin keeps the peace!'

Sir Rupert, who knew Cormac's unreasoning hatred for the great Kurdish sultan, shook his head. 'This was no work of his – there is incessant bickering along the border – Christian as much at fault as Moslem. It could not be otherwise with Frankish barons holding castles in the very heart of Muhammadan country. There are many private feuds and there are wild desert and mountain tribes who owe no lordship even to Saladin, and wage their own wars. Many suppose that the sheihk Nureddin El Ghoor destroyed Ali-El-Yar and put Sieur Gerard to death.'

Cormac caught up his helmet.

'Wait!' exclaimed Sir Rupert, rising. 'What would you do?'

Cormac laughed savagely. 'What would I do? I have eaten the bread of the de Gissclins. Am I a jackal to sneak home and leave my patron to the kites? Out on it!'

'But wait, Sir Rupert urged. 'What will your life be worth if you ride on Nureddin's trail alone? I will return to Antioch and gather my retainers; we will avenge your friend together.'

'Nureddin is a half-independent chief and I am a masterless wanderer,' rumbled the Norman-Gael, 'but you are Seneschal of Antioch. If you ride over the border with your men-at-arms, the swine Saladin will take advantage to break the truce and sweep the remnants of the Christian kingdoms into the sea. They are but weak shells, as it is, shadows of the glories of Baldwin and Bohemund. No – the Fitzgeoffreys wreak their own vengeance. I ride alone.'

He jammed his helmet into place and with a gruff 'Farewell!' he turned and strode into the night, roaring for his horse. A trembling servant brought the great black stallion, which reared and snorted with a flash of wicked teeth. Cormac seized the reins and savagely jerked down the rearing steed, swinging into the saddle before the pawing front hoofs touched the earth.

'Hate and the glutting of vengeance!' he yelled savagely, as the great stallion whirled away, and Sir Rupert, staring bewilderedly after him, heard the swiftly receding clash of the brazen-shod hoofs. Cormac Fitzgeoffrey was riding east.

2. The Cast of an Ax

White dawn surged out of the Orient to break in rose-red billows on the hills of Outremer. The rich tints softened the rugged outlines, deepened the blue wastes of the sleeping desert.

The castle of the baron Conrad Von Gonler frowned out over a wild and savage waste. Once a stronghold of the Seljuk Turks, its metamorphosis into the manor of a Frankish lord had abated none of the eastern menace of its appearance. The walls had been strengthened and a barbican built in place of the usual wide gates. Otherwise the keep had not been altered.

Now in the dawn a grim, dark figure rode up to the deep, waterless moat which encircled the stronghold, and smote with iron-clad fist on hollow-ringing shield until the echoes reverberated among the hills. A sleepy man-at-arms thrust his head and his pike over the wall the barbican and bellowed a challenge.

The lone rider threw back his helmeted head, disclosing a face dark with a passion that an all-night's ride had not cooled in the least.

'You keep rare watch here,' roared Cormac Fitzgeoffrey. 'Is it because you're so hand-in-glove with the Paynim that you fear no attack? Where is that ale-guzzling swine you call your liege?'

'The baron is at wine,' the fellow answered sullenly, in broken English.

'So early?' marveled Cormac.

'Nay,' the other gave a surly grin, 'he has feasted all night.'

'Wine-bibber! Glutton!' raged Cormac. 'Tell him I have business with him.'

'And what shall I say your business is, Lord Fitzgeoffrey?' asked the carl, impressed.

'Tell him I bring a passport to Hell!' yelled Cormac, gnashing his teeth, and the scared soldier vanished like a puppet on a string.

The Norman-Gael sat his horse impatiently, shield slung on his shoulders, lance in its stirrup socket, and to his surprise, suddenly the barbican door swung wide and out of it strutted a fantastic figure. Baron Conrad Von

Gonler was short and fat; broad of shoulder and portly of belly, though still a young man. His long arms and wide shoulders had gained him a reputation as a deadly broadsword man, but just now he looked little of the fighter. Germany and Austria sent many noble knights to Holy Land. Baron Von Gonler was not one of them.

His only arm was a gold-chased dagger in a richly brocaded sheath. He wore no armor, and his costume, flaming with gay silk and heavy with gold, was a bizarre mingling of European gauds and Oriental finery. In one hand, on each finger of which sparkled a great jewel, he held a golden wine goblet. A band of drunken revellers reeled out behind him – minnesingers, dwarfs, dancing girls, wine-companions, vacuous-faced, blinking like owls in the daylight. All the boot-kissers and hangers-on that swarm after a rich and degenerate lord trooped with their master – scum of both races. The luxury of the East had worked quick ruin on Baron Von Gonler.

'Well,' shouted the baron, 'who is it wishes to interrupt my drinking?'

'Any but a drunkard would know Cormac Fitzgeoffrey,' snarled the horseman, his lip writhing back from his strong teeth in contempt. 'We have an account to settle.'

That name and Cormac's tone had been enough to sober any drunken knight of the Outremer. But Von Gonler was not only drunk; he was a degenerate fool. The baron took a long drink while his drunken crew stared curiously at the savage figure on the other side of the dry moat, whispering to one another.

'Once you were a man, Von Gonler,' said Cormac in a tone of concentrated venom; 'now you have become a groveling debauchee. Well, that's your own affair. The matter I have in mind is another – why did you refuse aid to the Sieur de Gissclin?'

The German's puffy, arrogant face took on new hauteur. He pursed his thick lips haughtily, while his bleared eyes blinked over his bulbous nose like an owl. He was an image of pompous stupidity that made Cormac grind his teeth.

'What was the Frenchman to me?' the baron retorted brutally. 'It was his own fault – out of a thousand girls he might have taken, the young fool tried to steal one a sheihk wanted himself. He, the purity of honor! Bah!'

He added a coarse jest and the creatures with him screamed with mirth, leaping and flinging themselves into obscene postures. Cormac's sudden and lion-like roar of fury gave them pause.

'Conrad Von Gonler!' thundered the maddened Gael, 'I name you liar, traitor and coward – dastard, poltroon and villain! Arm yourself and ride out here on the plain. And haste – I can not waste much time on you – I must kill you quick and ride on lest another vermin escape me.'

The baron laughed cynically. 'Why should I fight you? You are not even a knight. You wear no knightly emblem on your shield.'

'Evasions of a coward,' raged Fitzgeoffrey. 'I am a chief in Ireland and I have cleft the skulls of men whose boots you are not worthy to touch. Will you arm yourself and ride out, or are you become the swinish coward I deem you?'

Von Gonler laughed in scornful anger.

'I need not risk my hide fighting you. I will not fight you, but I will have my men-at-arms fill your hide with crossbow bolts if you tarry longer.'

'Von Gonler,' Cormac's voice was deep and terrible in its brooding menace, 'will you fight, or die in cold blood?'

The German burst into a sudden brainless shout of laughter.

'Listen to him!' he roared. 'He threatens me – he on the other side of the moat, with the drawbridge lifted – I here in the midst of my henchmen!'

He smote his fat thigh and roared with his fool's laughter, while the debased men and women who served his pleasures laughed with him and insulted the grim Irish warrior with shrill anathema and indecent gestures. And suddenly Cormac, with a bitter curse, rose in his stirrups, snatched his battle-ax from his saddle-bow, and hurled it with all his mighty strength.

The men-at-arms on the towers cried out and the dancing girls screamed. Von Gonler had thought himself to be out of reach – but there is no such thing as being out of reach of Norman-Irish vengeance. The heavy ax hissed as it clove the air and dashed out Baron Conrad's brains.

The fat, gross body buckled to the earth like a mass of melted tallow, one fat, white hand still gripping the empty wine goblet. The gay silks and cloth-of-gold were dabbled in a deeper red than ever was sold in the bazar, and the jesters and dancers scattered like birds, screaming at the sight of that blasted head and the crimson ruin that had been a human face.

Cormac Fitzgeoffrey made a fierce, triumphant gesture and voiced a deep-chested yell of such ferocious exultation that men blenched to hear. Then wheeling his black steed suddenly, he raced away before the dazed soldiers could get their wits together to send a shower of arrows after him.

He did not gallop far. The great steed was weary from a hard night's travel. Cormac soon swung in behind a jutting crag, and reining his horse up a steep incline, halted and looked back the way he had come. He was out of sight of the keep, but he heard no sounds of pursuit. A wait of some half-hour convinced him that no attempt had been made to follow him. It was dangerous and foolhardy to ride out of a safe castle into these hills. Cormac might well have been one of an ambushing force.

At any rate, whatever his enemies' thoughts were on the subject, it was evident that he need expect no present attempt at retaliation, and he grunted with angry satisfaction. He never shunned a fight, but just now he had other business on hand.

Cormac rode eastward.

3. The Road to El Ghor

The way to El Ghor was rough indeed. Cormac wound his way between huge jagged boulders, across deep ravines and up treacherous steeps. The sun slowly climbed toward the zenith and the heat waves began to dance and shimmer. The sun beat fiercely on Cormac's helmeted head, and glancing back from the bare rocks, dazzled his narrowed eyes. But the big warrior gave no heed; in his own land he learned to defy sleet and snow and bitter cold; following the standard of Coeur de Lion, before the shimmering walls of Acre, on the dusty plains of Azotus, and before Joppa, he had become inured to the blaze of the Oriental sun, to the glare of naked sands, to the slashing dust winds.

At noon he halted long enough to allow the black stallion an hour's rest in the shade of a giant boulder. A tiny spring bubbled there, known to him of old, and it slaked the thirst of the man and the horse. The stallion cropped eagerly at the scrawny fringe of grass about the spring and Cormac ate of the dried meats he carried in a small pouch. Here he had watered his steed in the old days, when he rode with Gerard. Ali-El-Yar lay to the west; in the night he had swung around it in a wide circle as he rode to the castle of Von Gonler. He had had no wish to gaze on the moldering ruins. The nearest Moslem chief of any importance was Nureddin El Ghor, who with his brother-at-arms, Kosru Malik, the Seljuk, held the castle of El Ghor, in the hills to the east.

Cormac rode on stolidly through the savage heat. As mid-afternoon neared he rode up out of a deep, wide defile and came onto the higher levels of the hills. Up this defile he had ridden aforetime to raid the wild tribes to the east, and on the small plateaus at the head of the defile stood a gibbet where Sieur Gerard de Gissclin had onced hanged a red-handed Turkoman chief as a warning to those tribes.

Now, as Fitzgcoffrey rode up on the plateau, he saw the old tree again bore fruit. His keen eyes made out a human form suspended in midair, apparently by the wrists. A tall warrior in the peaked helmet and light mail shirt of a Moslem stood beneath, tentatively prodding at the victim with a spear, making the body sway and spin on the rope. A bay Turkoman horse stood near. Cormac's cold eyes narrowed. The man on the rope – his naked body glistened too white in the sun for a Turk. The Norman-Gael touched spurs to the black stallion and swept across the plateau at a headlong run.

At the sudden thunder of hoofs the Muhammadan started and whirled. Dropping the spear with which he had been tormenting the captive, he mounted swiftly, stringing a short heavy bow as he did so. This done, and his left forearm thrust through the straps of a small round buckler, he trotted out to meet the onset of the Frank.

Cormac was approaching at a thundering charge, eyes glaring over the edge of his grim shield. He knew that this Turk would never meet him as a Frankish knight would have met him – breast to breast. The Moslem would avoid his ponderous rushes, and circling him on his nimbler steed, drive in shaft after shaft until one found its mark. But he rushed on as recklessly as if he had never before encountered Saracen tactics.

Now the Turk bent his bow and the arrow glanced from Cormac's shield. They were barely within javelin cast of each other, but even as the Moslem laid another shaft to string, doom smote him. Cormac, without checking his headlong gait, suddenly rose in his stirrups and gripping his long lance in the middle, cast it like a javelin. The unexpectedness of the move caught the Seljuk off guard and he made the mistake of throwing up his shield instead of dodging. The lance-head tore through the light buckler and crashed full on his mail-clad breast. The point bent on his hauberk without piercing the links, but the terrific impact dashed the Turk from his saddle and as he rose, dazed and groping for his simitar, the great black stallion was already looming horrific over him, and under those frenzied hoofs he went down, torn and shattered.

Without a second glance at his victims Cormac rode under the gibbet and rising in the saddle, stared into the face of he who swung therefrom.

'By Satan,' muttered the big warrior, ' 'tis Micaul na Blaos – Michael de Blois, one of Gerard's squires. What devil's work is this?'

Drawing his sword he cut the rope and the youth slid into his arms. Young Michael's lips were parched and swollen, his eyes dull with suffering. He was naked except for short leathern breeks, and the sun had dealt cruelly with his fair skin. Blood from a slight scalp wound caked his yellow hair, and there were shallow cuts on his limnbs – marks left by his tormentor's spear.

Cormac laid the young Frenchman in the shade cast by the motionless stallion and trickled water through the parched lips from his canteen. As soon as he could speak, Michael croaked: 'Now I know in truth that I am dead, for there is but one knight ever rode in Outremer who could cast a long lance like a javelin – and Cormac Fitzgeoffrey has been dead for many months. But I be dead, where is Gerard – and Yulala?'

'Rest and be at ease,' growled Cormac. 'You live – and so do I.'

He loomed the cords that had cut deep into the flesh of Michael's wrists and set himself to gently rub and massage the numb arms. Slowly the delirium faded from the youth's eyes. Like Cormac, he too came of a race that was tough as spring steel; an hour's rest and plenty of water, and his intense vitality asserted itself.

'How long have you hung from this gibbet?' asked Cormac.

'Since dawn.' Michael's eyes were grim as he rubbed his lacerated wrists. 'Nureddin and Kosru Malik said that since Sieur Gerard once hanged one of their race here, it was fitting that one of Gerard's men should grace this gibbet.'

'Tell me how Gerard died,' growled the Irish warrior. 'Men hint at foul tales – '

Michael's fine eyes filled with tears. 'Ah, Cormac, I who loved him, brought about his death. Listen – there is more to this than meets the casual eye. I think that Nureddin and his comrade-at-arms have been stung by the hornet of empire. It is in my mind that they, with various dog-knights among the Franks, dream of a mongrel kingdom among these hills, which shall hold allegiance neither to Saladin nor any king of the West.

'They begin to broaden their holdings by treachery. The nearest Christian hold was that of Ali-El-Yar, of course. Sieur Gerard was a true knight, peace be upon his fair soul, and he must be removed. All this I learned later – would to God I had known it beforehand! Among Nureddin's slaves is a Persian girl named Yulala, and with this innocent tool of their evil wishes, the twain sought to ensnare my lord – to slay at once his body and his good name. And God help me, through me they succeeded where otherwise they had failed.

'For my lord Gerard was honorable beyond all men. When in peace, and at Nureddin's invitation, he visited El Ghor, he paid no heed to Yulala's blandishments. For according to the commands of her masters, which she dared not disobey, the girl allowed Gerard to look on her, unveiled, and as if by chance, and she pretended affection for him. But Gerard gave her no heed. But I – I fell victim to her charms.'

Cormac snorted in disgust. Michael clutched his arm.

'Cormac,' he cried, 'bethink you – all men are not iron like you! I swear I loved Yulala from the moment I first set eyes on her – and she loved me! I contrived to see her again – to steal into El Ghor itself – '

'Whence men got the tale that it was Gerard who was carrying on an affair with Nureddin's slave,' snarled Fitzgeoffrey.

Michael hid his face in his hands. 'Mine the fault,' he groaned. 'Then one night a mute brought a note signed by Yulala – apparently – begging me to come with Sieur Gerard and his men-at-arms and save her from a frightful fate – our love had been discovered, the note read, and they were about to torture her. I was wild with rage and fear. I went to Gerard and told him all, and he, white soul of honor, vowed to aid me. He could not break the truce and bring Saladin's wrath upon the Christian's cities, but he donned his mail and rode forth alone with me. We would see if there was any way whereby we might steal Yulala away, secretly; if not, my lord would go boldly to Nureddin and ask the girl as a gift, or offer to pay a great ransom for her. I would marry her.

'Well, when we reached the place outside the wall of El Ghor, where I was wont to meet Yulala, we found we were trapped. Nureddin, Kosru Malik and their warriors rose suddenly about us on all sides. Nureddin first spoke to Gerard, telling him of the trap he had set and baited, hoping to entice my lord into his power alone. And the Moslem laughed to think that the chance love of a squire had drawn Gerard into the trap where the carefully wrought plan had failed. As for the missive – Nureddin wrote that himself, believing, in his craftiness, that Sieur Gerard would do just as indeed he did.

'Nureddin and the Turk offered to allow Gerard to join them in their plan of empire. They told him plainly that his castle and lands were the price a certain powerful nobleman asked in return for his alliance, and they offered alliance with Gerard instead of this noble. Sieur Gerard merely answered that so long as life remained in him, he would keep faith with his king and his creed, and at the word the Moslems rolled on us like a wave.

'Ah, Cormac, Cormac, had you but been there with our men-at-arms! Gerard bore himself right manfully as was his wont – back to back we fought and I swear to you that we trod a knee-deep carpet of the dead before Gerard fell and they dragged me down. "Christ and the Cross!" were his last words, as the Turkish spears and swords pierced him through and through. And his fair body – naked and gashed, and thrown to the kites and the jackals!'

Michael sobbed convulsively, beating his fists together in his agony. Cormac rumbled deep in his chest like a savage bull. Blue lights burned and flickered in his eyes.

'And you?' he asked harshly.

'Me they flung into a dungeon for torture,' answered Michael, 'but that night Yulala came to me. An old servitor who loved her, and who had dwelt in El Ghor before it fell to Nureddin, freed me and led us both through a secret passage that leads from the torture chamber, beyond the wall. We went into the hills on foot and without weapons and wandered there for days, hiding from the horsemen sent forth to hunt us down. Yesterday we were recaptured and brought back to El Ghor. An arrow had struck down the old slave who showed us the passageway, unknown to the present masters of the castle, and we refused to tell how we had escaped though Nureddin threatened us with torture. This dawn he brought me forth from the castle and hanged me to this gibbet, leaving that one to guard me. What he has done to Yulala, God alone knows.

'You knew that Ali-El-Yar had fallen?'

'Aye,' Michael nodded dully, 'Kosru Malik boasted of it. The lands of Gerard now fall heir to his enemy, the traitor knight who will come to Nureddin's aid when the Moslem strikes for a crown.'

'And who is this traitor?' asked Cormac softly.

'The baron Conrad Von Gonler, whom I swear to spit – '

Cormac smiled thinly and bleakly. 'Swear me no oaths. Von Gonler has been in Hell since dawn. I knew only that he refused to come to Gerard's aid. I could have slain him no deader had I known his whole infamy.'

Michael's eyes blazed. 'A de Gissclin to the rescue!' he shouted fiercely. 'I thank thee, old war-dog! One traitor is accounted for – what now? Shall Nureddin and the Turk live while two men wear de Gissclin steel?'

'Not if steel cuts and blood runs red,' snarled Cormac. Tell me of this secret way – nay, waste no time in words – *show* me this secret way. If you escaped thereby, why should we not enter the same way? Here – take the arms from that carrion while I catch his steed which I see browses on the moss among the rocks. Night is not far away; mayhap we can gain through to the interior of the castle – there – '

His big hands clenched into iron sledges and his terrible eyes blazed; in his whole bearing there was apparent a plain tale of fire and carnage, of spears piercing bosoms and swords splitting skulls.

4. The Faith of Cormac

When Cormac Fitzgeoffrey took up the trail to El Ghor again, one would have thought at a glance that a Turk rode with him. Michael de Blois rode the Bay Turkoman steed and wore the peaked Turkish helmet. He was girt with the curved simitar and carried the bow and quiver of arrows, but he did not wear the mail shirt; the hammering hoofs of the plunging stallion had battered and brayed it out of all usefulness.

The companions took a circuitous route into the hills to avoid outposts, and it was dusk before they looked down on the towers of El Ghor which stood, grim and sullen, girt on three sides by scowling hills. Westward a broad road wound down the steeps on which the castle stood. On all other sides ravine cut slopes straggled to the beetling walls. They had made such a wide circle that they now stood in the hills almost directly east of the keep, and Cormac, gazing westward over the turrets, spoke suddenly to his friend.

'Look – a cloud of dust far out on the plain – '

Michael shook his head: 'Your eyes are far keener than mine. The hills are so clouded with the blue shadows of twilight I can scarcely make out the blurred expanse that is the plain beyond, much less discern any movement upon it.'

'My life has often depended on my eyesight,' growled the Norman-Gael. 'Look closely – see that tongue of plainsland that cleaves far into the hills like a broad valley, to the north? A band of horsemen, riding hard, are just entering the defiles, if I may judge by the cloud of dust they raise. Doubltess a band of raiders returning to El Ghor. Well – they are in the hills now where going is rough and it will be hours before they get to the castle. Let us to our task – stars are blinking in the east.'

They tied their horses in a place hidden from sight of any watcher below down among the gullies. In the last dim light of dusk they saw the turbans of the sentries on the towers, but gliding among boulders and defiles, they kept well concealed. At last Michael turned into a deep ravine.

'This leads into the subterranean corridor,' said he. 'God grant it has not been discovered by Nureddin. He had his warriors searching for something of the sort, suspecting its existence when we refused to tell how we had escaped.'

They passed along the ravine, which grew narrower and deeper, for some distance, feeling their way; then Michael halted with a groan. Cormac, groping forward, felt iron bars, and as his eyes grew accustomed to the darkness, made out an opening like the mouth of a cave. Solid iron sills had been firmly bolted into the solid rock, and into these sills were set heavy bars, too close together to allow the most slender human to slip through.

'They have found the tunnel and closed it,' groaned Michael. 'Cormac, what are we to do?'

Cormac came close and laid hands tentatively on the bars. Night had fallen and it was so dark in the ravine even his cat-like eyes could hardly make out objects close at hand. The big Norman-Celt took a deep breath, and gripping a bar in each mighty hand, braced his iron legs and slowly exerted all his incredible strength. Michael, watching in amazement, sensed rather than saw the great muscles roll and swell under the pliant mail, the veins swell in the giant's forehead and sweat burst out. The bars groaned and creaked, and even as Michael remembered that this man was stronger than King Richard himself, the breath burst from Cormac's lips in an explosive grunt and simultaneously the bars gave way like reeds in his iron hands. One came away, literally torn from its sockets, and the others bent deeply. Cormac gasped and shook the sweat out of his eyes, tossing the bar aside.

'By the saints,' muttered Michael, 'are you man or devil, Cormac Fitzgeoffrey? That is a feat I deemed even beyond your power.'

'Enough words,' grunted the Norman. 'Let us make haste, if we can squeeze through. It's likely that we'll find a guard in this tunnel, but it's a chance we must take. Draw your steel and follow me.'

It was as dark as the maw of Hades in the tunnel. They groped their way forward, expecting every minute to blunder into a trap, and Michael, stealing close at the heels of his friend, cursed the pounding of his own heart and wondered at the ability of the giant to move stealthily and with no rattling of arms.

To the comrades it seemed that they groped forward in the darkness for an eternity, and just as Michael leaned forward to whisper that he believed they were inside the castle's outer walls, a faint glow was observed ahead. Stealing warily forward they came to a sharp turn in the corridor around which shone the light. Peering cautiously about the corner they saw that the light emanated from a flickering torch thrust into a niche in the wall, and beside this stood a tall Turk, yawning as he leaned on his spear. Two other Moslems lay sleeping on their cloaks near by. Evidently Nureddin did not lay too much trust in the bars with which he had blocked the entrance.

'The guard,' whispered Michael, and Cormac nodded, stepping back and drawing his companion with him. The Norman-Gael's wary eyes had made out a flight of stone steps beyond the warriors, with a heavy door at the top.

'These seem to be all the weapon-men in the tunnel,' muttered Cormac. 'Loose a shaft at the waking warrior – and do not miss.'

Michael fitted notch to string, and leaning close to the angle of the turn, aimed at the Turk's throat, just above the hauberk. He silently cursed the flickering, illusive light. Suddenly the drowsy warrior's head jerked up and he glared in their direction, suspicion flaring his eyes. Simultaneously came the twang of the loosed string and the Turk staggered and went down, gurgling horribly and clawing at the shaft that transfixed his bull neck.

The other two, awakened by their comrade's death throes and the sudden swift drum of feet on the ground, started up – and were cut down as they rubbed at sleep-filled eyes and groped for weapons.

'That was well done,' growled Cormac, shaking the red drops from his steel. 'There was no sound that should have carried through yonder door. Still, if it be bolted from within, our work is useless and we undone.'

But it was not bolted, as the presence of the warriors in the tunnel suggested. As Cormac gently opened the heavy iron door, a sudden pain-fraught whimper from the other side electrified them.

'Yulala!' gasped Michael whitening. ' 'Tis the torture chamber, and that is her voice! In God's name, Cormac – in!'

And the big Norman-Gael recklessly flung the door wide and leaped through like a charging tiger, with Michael at his heels. They halted short. It was the torture chamber, right enough, and on the floor and the walls stood or hung all the hellish appliances that the mind of man has invented for the torment of his brother. Three people were in the dungeon and two of these were bestial-faced men in leathern breeches, who looked up, startled, as the Franks entered. The third was a girl who lay bound to a sort of bench, naked as they day she was born. Coals glowed in braziers near by, and one of the mutes was in the very act of reaching for a pair of white-hot pinchers. He crouched now, glaring in amazement, his arm still outstretched.

From the white throat of the captive girl burst a piteous cry.

'Yulala!' Michael cried out fiercely and leaped forward, a red mist floating before his eyes. One of the beast-faced mutes was before him, lifting a short sword, but the young Frank, without checking his stride, brought down his simitar in a sweeping arc that drove the curved blade through scalp and skull. Wrenching his weapon free, he dropped to his knees beside the torture bench, a great sob tearing his throat.

'Yulala! Yulala! Oh girl, what have they done to you?'

'Michael, my beloved!' Her great dark eyes were like stars in the mist. 'I knew you would come. They have not tortured me – save for a whipping – they were just about to begin – '

The other mute had glided swiftly toward Cormac as a snake glides, knife in hand.

'Satan!' grunted the big warrior. 'I won't sully my steel with such blood – '

His left hand shot out and caught the mute's wrist and there was a crunch of splintering bones. The knife flew from the mute's fingers, which spread wide suddenly like an inflated glove. Blood burst from the finger tips and the creature's mouth gaped in silent agony. And at that instant Cormac's right hand closed on his throat and through the open lips burst a red deluge of blood as the Norman's iron fingers ground flesh and vertebrae to a crimson pulp.

Flinging aside the sagging corpse, Cormac turned to Michael, who had freed the girl and now was nearly crushing her in his arms as he gripped her close in a very passion of relief and joy. A heavy hand on his shoulder brought him back to a realization of their position.

Cormac had found a cloak and this he wrapped about the naked girl.

'Go, at once,' he said swiftly. 'It may not be long before others come to take the place of the guards in the tunnel. Here – you have no armor – take my shield – no, don't argue. You may need it to protect the girl from arrows if you – if we, are pursued. Haste now – '

'But you, Cormac?' Michael lingered, hesitant.

'I will make fast that outer door,' said the Norman, 'I can heap benches against it. Then I will follow you. But don't wait for me. This is a command, do you understand? Hasten through the tunnel and go to the horses. There, instantly mount the Turkoman horse and ride! I will follow by another route – aye, by a road none but I can ride! ride ye to Sir Rupert de Vaile, Seneschal of Antioch. He is our friend; hasten now.'

Cormac stood a moment in the doorway at the head of the stairs and watched Michael and the girl hurry down the steps, past the place where the silent sentries lay, and vanish about the turn in the tunnel. Then he turned back into the torture chamber and closed the door. He crossed the room, threw the bolt on the outer door and swung it wide. He gazed up a winding flight of stairs. Cormac's face was immobile. He had voluntarily sealed his doom.

The giant Norman-Celt was an opportunist. He knew that such chance as had led him into the heart of his foe's stronghold was not likely to favor him again. Life was uncertain in Outremer; if he waited another opportunity to strike at Nureddin and Kosru Malik, that opportunity might not come. This was his best opportunity for the vengeance for which his barbaric soul lusted.

That he would lose his own life in the consummating of that vengeance made no difference. Men were born to die in battle, according to his creed, and Cormac Fitzgeoffrey secretly leaned toward the belief of his Viking ancestors in a Valhalla for the souls loosed gloriously in the clash of swords. Michael, having found the girl, had instantly forgotten the original plan of vengeance. Cormac had no blame for him; life and love were sweet to the young. But the grim Irish warrior owed a debt to the murdered Gerard and was prepared to pay with his own life. This Cormac kept faith with the dead.

He wished that he could have bade Michael ride the black stallion, but he knew that the horse would allow none but himself to bestride it. Now it would fall into Moslems hands, he thought with a sigh. He went up the stairs.

5. The Lion of Islam

At the top of the stairs, Cormac came into a corridor and along this he strode swiftly but warily, the Norse sword shimmering bluely in his hand. Going at random he turned into another corridor and here came full on a Turkish warrior, who stopped short, agape, seeing a supernatural horror in this grim slayer who strode like a silent phantom of death through the castle. Before the Turk could regain his wits, the blue sword shore through his neck cords.

Cormac stood above his victim for a moment, listening intently. Somewhere ahead of him he heard a low hum of voices, and the attitude of this Turk, with shield and drawn simitar, had suggested that he stood guard before some chamber door. An irregular torch faintly illumined the wide corridor, and Cormac, groping in the semi-darkness for a door, found instead a wide portal masked by heavy silk curtains. Parting them cautiously, he gazed through into a great room thronged with armed men.

Warriors in mail and peaked helmets, and bearing wide-pointed, curved swords, lined the walls, and on silken cushions sat the chieftains – rulers of El Ghor and their satellites. Across the room sat Nureddin El Ghor, tall, lean, with a high-bridged, thin nose and keen dark eyes; his whole aspect distinctly hawk-like. His Semitic features contrasted with the Turks about him. His lean strong hand continually caressed the ivory hilt of a long, lean saber, and he wore a shirt of mesh-mail. A renegade chief from southern Arabia, this sheihk was a man of great ability; his dream of an independent kingdom in these hills was no mad hashish hallucination. Let him win the alliance of a few Seljuk chiefs, of a few Frankish renegades like Von Gonler, and with the hordes of Arabs, Turks and Kurds that would assuredly flock to his banner, Nureddin would be a menace both to Saladin and the Franks who still clung to the fringes of Outremer. Among the mailed Turks Cormac saw the sheepskin caps and wolfskins of wild chiefs from beyond the hills – Kurds and Turkomans. Already the Arab's fame was spreading, if such unstable warriors as these were rallying to him.

Near the curtain-hung doorway sat Kosru Malik, known to Cormac of old, a warrior typical of his race, strongly built, of medium height, with a dark cruel face. Even as he sat in council he wore a peaked helmet and a gilded mail hauberk and held across his knees a jeweled-hilted simitar. It seemed to Cormac that these men argued some matter just before setting out on some raid, as they were all fully armed. But he wasted no time on speculation. He tore the hangings aside with a mailed hand and strode into the room.

Amazement held the warriors frozen for an instant, and in that instant the giant Frank reached Kosru Malik's side. The Turk, his dark features paling, sprang to his feet like a steel spring released, raising his simitar, but even as he did so, Cormac braced his feet and smote with all his power. The Norse sword shivered the curved blade and, rending the gilded mail, severed the Turk's shoulder-bone and cleft his breast.

Cormac wrenched the heavy blade free from the split breast-bone and with one foot on Kosru Malik's body, faced his foes like a lion at bay. His helmeted head was lowered, his cold blue eyes flaming from under the heavy black brows, and his mighty right hand held ready the stained sword. Nureddin had leaped to his feet and stood trembling in rage and astonishment. This sudden apparition came as near to unmanning him as anything had ever done. His thin, hawk-like features lowered in a wrathful snarl, his beard bristled and with a quick motion he unsheathed his ivory-hilted saber. Then even as he stepped forward and his warriors surged in behind him, a startling interruption occurred.

Cormac, a fierce joy surging in him as he braced himself for the charge, saw, on the other side of the great room, a wide door swing open and a host of armed warriors appear, accompanied by sundry of Nureddin's men, who wore empty scabbards and uneasy faces.

The Arab and his warriors whirled to face the new-comers. These men, Cormac saw, were dusty as if from long riding, and his memory flashed to the horsemen he had seen riding into the hills at dusk. Before them strode a tall, slender man, whose fine face was traced with lines and weariness, but whose aspect was that of a ruler of men. His garb was simple in comparison with the resplendent armor and silken attendants. And Cormac swore in amazed recognition.

Yet his surprize was no greater than that of the men of El Ghor.

'What do you do in my castle, unannounced?' gasped Nureddin.

A giant in silvered mail raised his hand warningly and spoke sonorously: 'The Lion of Islam, Protector of the Faithful, Yusef ibn Eyyub, Salah-ud-din, Sultan of Sultans, needs no announcement to enter yours or any castle, Arab.'

Nureddin stood his ground, though his followers began salaaming madly; there was iron in this Arabian renegade.

'My lord,' said he stoutly, 'it is true I did not recognize you when you first came into the chamber; but El Ghor is mine, not by virtue of right or aid or grant from any sultan, but the might of my own arm. Therefore, I make you welcome but do not beg your mercy for my hasty words.'

Saladin merely smiled in a weary way. Half a century of intrigue and waring rested heavily on his shoulders. His brown eyes, strangely mild for so great a lord, rested on the silent Frankish giant who still stood with his mail-clad foot on what had been the chief Kosru Malik.

'And what is this?' asked the Sultan.

Nureddin scowled: 'A Nazarene outlaw has stolen into my keep and assassinated my comrade, the Seljuk. I beg your leave to dispose of him. I will give you his skull, set in silver – '

A gesture stopped him. Saladin stepped past his men and confronted the dark, brooding warrior.

'I thought I had recognized those shoulders and that dark face,' said the Sultan with a smile. 'So you have turned you face east again, Lord Cormac?'

'Enough!' the deep voice of the Norman-Irish giant filled the chamber. 'You have me in your trap; my life is forfeit. Waste not your time in taunts; send your jackals against me and make an end of it. I swear by my clan, many of them shall bite the dust before I die, and the dead will be more than the living!'

Nureddin's tall frame shook with passion; he gripped his hilt until the knuckles showed white. 'Is this to be borne, my Lord?' he exclaimed fiercely. 'Shall this Nazarene dog fling dirt into our faces – '

Saladin shook his head slowly, smiling as if at some secret jest: 'It may be his is no idle boast. At Acre, at Azotus, at Joppa I have seen the skull on his shield glitter like a star of death in the mist, and the Faithful fall before his sword like garnered grain.'

The great Kurd turned his head, leisurely surveying the ranks of silent warriors and the bewildered chieftains who avoided his level gaze.

'A notable concourse of chiefs, for these times of truce,' he murmured, half to himself. 'Would you ride forth in the night with all these warriors to fight genii in the desert, or to honor some ghostly sultan, Nureddin? Nay,

nay, Nureddin, thou hast tasted the cup of ambition, meseemeth – and thy life is forfeit!'

The unexpectedness of the accusation staggered Nureddin, and while he groped for reply, Saladin followed it up: 'It comes to me that you have plotted against me – aye, that it was your purpose to seduce various Moslem and Frankish lords from their allegiances, and set up a kingdom of your own. And for that reason you broke the truce and murdered a good knight, albeit a Caphar, and burned his castle. I have spies, Nureddin.'

The tall Arab glanced quickly about, as if ready to dispute the question with Saladin himself. But when he noted the number of the Kurd's warriors, and saw his own fierce ruffians shrinking away from him, awed, a smile of bitter contempt crossed his hawk-like features, and sheathing his blade, he folded his arms.

'God gives,' he said simply, with the fatalism of the Orient.

Saladin nodded in appreciation, but motioned back a chief who stepped forward to bind the sheikh. 'Here is one,' said the Sultan, 'to whom you owe a greater debt than to me, Nureddin. I have heard Cormac Fitzgeoffrey was brother-at-arms to the Sieur Gerard. You owe many debts of blood, oh Nureddin; pay one, therefore, by facing the lord Cormac with the sword.'

The Arab's eyes gleamed suddenly. 'And if I slay him shall I go free?'

'Who am I to judge?' asked Saladin. 'It shall be as Allah wills it. But if you fight the Frank you will die, Nureddin, even though you slay him; he comes of a breed that slays even in their death-throes. Yet it is better to die by the sword than by the cord, Nureddin.'

The sheikh's answer was to draw his ivory-hilted saber. Blue sparks flickered in Cormac's eyes and he rumbled deeply like a wounded lion. He hated Saladin as he hated all his race, with the savage and relentless hatred of the Norman-Celt. He had ascribed the Kurd's courtesy to King Richard and the Crusaders, to Oriental subtlety, refusing to believe that there could be ought but trickery and craftiness in a Saracen's mind. Now he saw in the Sultan's suggestion but the scheming of a crafty trickster to match two of his foes against each other, and a feline-gloating over his victims. Cormac grinned without mirth. He asked no more from life than to have his enemy at sword-points. But he felt no gratitude toward Saladin, only a smoldering hate.

The Sultan and the warriors gave back, leaving the rivals a clear space in the center of the great room. Nureddin came forward swiftly, having donned a plain round steel cap with a mail drop that fell about his shoulders.

'Death to you, Nazarene!' he yelled, and sprang in with the pantherish leap and headlong recklessness of an Arab's attack. Cormac had no shield. He parried the hacking saber with upflung blade and slashed back. Nureddin caught the heavy blade on his round buckler, which he turned slightly slantwise at the instant of impact, so that the stroke glanced off. He returned the blow with a thrust that rasped against Cormac's coif, and leaped a spear's length backward to avoid the whistling sweep of the Norse sword.

Again he leaped in, slashing, and Cormac caught the saber on his left forearm. Mail links parted beneath the keen edge, and blood spattered, but almost simultaneously the Norse sword crashed under the Arab's arm, bones cracked and Nureddin was flung his full length to the floor. Warriors gasped as they realized the full power of the Irishman's tigerish strokes.

Nureddin's rise from the floor was so quick that he almost seemed to rebound from his fall. To the onlookers it seemed that he was not hurt, but the Arab knew. His mail had held; the sword edge had not gashed his flesh, but the impact of that terrible blow had snapped a rib like a rotten twig, and the realization that he could not long avoid the Frank's rushes filled him with a wild beast determination to take his foe with him to Eternity.

Cormac was looming over Nureddin, sword high, but the Arab nerving himself to a dynamic burst of superhuman quickness, sprang up as a cobra leaps from its coil, and struck with desperate power. Full on Cormac's bent head the whistling saber clashed, and the Frank staggered as the keen edge bit through steel cap and coif links into his scalp. Blood jetted down his face, but he braced his feet and struck back with all the power of arm and shoulders behind the sword. Again Nureddin's buckler blocked the stroke, but this time the Arab had no time to turn the shield, and the heavy blade struck squarely. Nureddin went to his knees beneath the stroke, bearded face twisted in agony. With tenacious courage he reeled up again, shaking the shattered buckler from his numbed and broken arm, but even as he lifted the saber, the Norse sword crashed down, cleaving the Moslem helmet and splitting the skull to the teeth.

Cormac set a foot on his fallen foe and wrenched free his gory sword. His fierce eyes met the whimsical gaze of Saladin.

'Well, Saracen,' said the Irish warrior challengingly, 'I have killed your rebel for you.'

'And your enemy,' reminded Saladin.

'Aye,' Cormac grinned bleakly and ferociously. 'I thank you – though well I know it was no love of me or mine that prompted you to send the Arab against me. Well – make an end, Saracen.'

'Why do you hate me, Lord Cormac?' asked the Sultan curiously.

Cormac snarled. 'Why do I hate any of my foes? You are no more and no less than any other robber chief to me. You tricked Richard and the rest with courtly words and fine deeds, but you never deceived me, who well knew you sought to win by deceit where you could not gain by force of arms.'

Saladin shook his head, murmuring to himself. Cormac glared at him, tensing himself for a sudden leap that would carry the Kurd with him into the Dark. The

Norman Gael was a product of his age and his country; among the warring chiefs of blood-drenched Ireland, mercy was unknown and chivalry an outworn and forgotten myth. Kindness to a foe was a mark of weakness; courtesy to an enemy a form of craft, a preparation for treachery; to such teachings had Cormac grown up, in a land where a man took every advantage, gave no quarter and fought like a blood-mad devil if he expected to survive.

Now at a gesture from Saladin, those crowding the door gave back.

'Your way is open, Lord Cormac.'

The Gael glared, his eyes narrowing to slits: 'What game is this?' he growled. 'Shall I turn my back to your blades? Out on it!'

'All swords are in their sheaths. None shall harm you.'

Cormac's lion-like head swung from side to side as he glared at the Moslems.

'You honestly mean I am to go free, after breaking the truce and slaying your jackals?'

'The truce was already broken,' answered Saladin. 'I find in you no fault. You have repaid blood for blood, and kept your faith to the dead. You are rough and savage, but I would fain have men like you in mine own train. There is a fierce loyalty in you, and for this I honor you.'

Cormac sheathed his sword ungraciously. A grudging admiration for this weary-faced Moslem was born in him and it angered him. Dimly he realized at last that this attitude of fairness, justice and kindliness, even to foes, was not a crafty pose of Saladin's, not a manner of guile, but a natural nobility of the Kurd's nature. He saw suddenly embodied in the Sultan, the ideals of chivalry and high honor so much talked of – and so little practised – by the Frankish knights. Blondel had been right then, and Sieur Gerard, when they argued with Cormac that high-minded chivalry was no mere romantic dream of an outworn age, but had existed, and still existed and lived in the hearts of certain men. But Cormac was born and bred in a savage land where men lived the desperate existence of the wolves whose hides covered their nakedness. He suddenly realized his own innate barbarism and was ashamed. He shrugged his lion's shoulders.

'I have misjudged you, Moslem,' he growled. 'There is fairness in you.'

'I thank you, Lord Cormac,' smiled Saladin. 'Your road to the west is clear.'

And the Moslem warriors courteously salaamed as Cormac Fitzgeoffrey strode from the royal presence of the slender noble who was Protector of the Califs, Lion of Islam, Sultan of Sultans.

SOLOMON KANE

Wings in the night

1. The Horror on the Stake

SOLOMON Kane leaned on his strangely carved staff and gazed in scowling perplexity at the mystery which spread silently before him. Many a deserted village Kane had seen in the months that had passed since he turned his face east from the Slave Coast and lost himself in the mazes of jungle river, but never one like this.

It was not famine that had driven away the inhabitants, for yonder the wild rice still grew rank and unkempt in the untilled fields. There were no Arab slave-raiders in this nameless land—it must have been a tribal war that devastated the village, Kane decided, as he gazed sombrely at the scattered bones and grinning skulls that littered the space among the rank weeds and grasses. These bones were shattered and splintered, and Kane saw jackals and a hyena furtively slinking among the ruined huts. But why had the slayers left the spoils? There lay war spears, their shafts crumbling before the attacks of the white ants. There lay shields, moldering in the rains and sun. There lay the cooking pots, and about the neck-bones of a shattered skeleton glistened a necklace of gaudily painted pebbles and shells—surely rare loot for any savage conqueror.

He gazed at the huts, wondering why the thatch roofs of so many were torn and rent, as if by taloned things seeking entrance. Then something made his cold eyes narrow in startled unbelief. Just outside the moldering mound that was once the village wall towered a gigantic baobab tree, branchless for sixty feet, its mighty bole too large to be gripped and scaled. Yet in the topmost branches dangled a skeleton, apparently impaled on a broken limb.

The cold hand of mystery touched the shoulder of Solomon Kane. How came those pitiful remains in that tree? Had some monstrous ogre's inhuman hand flung them there?

Kane shrugged his broad shoulders and his hand unconsciously touched the black butts of his heavy pistols, the hilt of his long rapier, and the dirk in his belt. Kane felt no fear as an ordinary man would feel, confronted with the Unknown and Nameless. Years of wandering in strange lands and warring with strange creatures had melted away from brain, soul, and body all that was not steel and whalebone. He was tall and spare, almost gaunt, built with the savage economy of the wolf. Broad-shouldered, long-armed, with nerves of ice and thews of spring steel, he was no less the natural killer than the born swordsman.

The brambles and thorns of the jungle had dealt hardly with him; his garments hung in tatters, his featherless slouch hat was torn and his boots of Cordovan leather were scratched and worn. The sun had baked his chest and limbs to a deep bronze, but his ascetically lean face was impervious to its rays. His complexion was still of that strange, dark pallor which gave him an almost corpse-like appearance, belied only by his cold, light eyes.

And now Kane, sweeping the village once more with his searching gaze, pulled his belt into a more comfortable position, shifted to his left hand the cat-headed stave N'Longa had given him, and took up his way again.

To the west lay a strip of thin forest, sloping downward to a broad belt of savannas, a waving sea of grass waist-deep and deeper. Beyond that rose another narrow strip of woodlands, deepening rapidly into dense jungle.

Out of that jungle Kane had fled like a hunted wolf with
pointed-toothed men hot on his trail. Even now a vagrant
breeze brought faintly the throb of a savage drum which
whispered its obscene tale of hate and blood-hunger and
belly-lust across miles of jungle and grassland.

The memory of his flight and narrow escape was
vivid in Kane's mind, for only the day before had he
realized too late that he was in cannibal country, and all
that afternoon in the reeking stench of the thick jungle,
he had crept and run and hidden and doubled and twisted
on his track with the fierce hunters ever close behind him,
until night fell and he gained and crossed the grasslands
under cover of darkness.

Now in the late morning he had seen nothing, heard
nothing of his pursuers, yet he had no reason to believe
that they had abandoned the chase. They had been close
on his heels when he took to the savannas.

So Kane surveyed the land in front of him. To the
east, curving from north to south ran a straggling range of
hills, for the most part dry and barren, rising in the south
to a jagged black skyline that reminded Kane of the black
hills of Negari. Between him and these hills stretched a
broad expanse of gently rolling country, thickly treed, but
nowhere approaching the density of a jungle. Kane got
the impression of a vast upland plateau, bounded by the
curving hills to the east and by the savannas to the west.

Kane set out for the hills with his long, swinging,
tireless stride. Surely somewhere behind him the savage
demons were stealing after him, and he had no desire to
be driven to bay. A shot might send them flying in sudden
terror, but on the other hand, so low they were in the scale
of humanity, it might transmit no supernatural fear to
their dull brains. And not even Solomon Kane, whom Sir
Francis Drake had called Devon's king of swords, could
win in a pitched battle with a whole tribe.

The silent village with its burden of death and
mystery faded out behind him. Utter silence reigned
among these mysterious uplands where no birds sang and

only a silent macaw flitted among the great trees. The only sounds were Kane's catlike tread, and the whisper of the drum-haunted breeze.

And then Kane caught a glimpse among the trees that made his heart leap with a sudden, nameless horror, and a few moments later he stood before Horror itself, stark and grisly. In a wide clearing, on a rather bold incline stood a grim stake, and to this stake was bound a thing that had once been a man. Kane had rowed, chained to the bench of a Turkish galley, and he had toiled in Barbary vineyards; he had battled red Indians in the New Lands and had languished in the dungeons of Spain's Inquisition. He knew much of the fiendishness of man's inhumanity, but now he shuddered and grew sick. Yet it was not so much the ghastliness of the mutilations, horrible as they were, that shook Kane's soul, but the knowledge that the wretch still lived.

For as he drew near, the gory head that lolled on the butchered breast lifted and tossed from side to side, spattering blood from the stumps of ears, while a bestial, rattling whimper drooled from the shredded lips.

Kane spoke to the ghastly thing and it screamed unbearably, writhing in incredible contortions, while its head jerked up and down with the jerking of mangled nerves, and the empty, gaping eye-sockets seemed striving to see from their emptiness. And moaning low and brain-shatteringly it huddled its outraged self against the stake where it was bound and lifted its head in a grisly attitude of listening, as if it expected something out of the skies.

'Listen,' said Kane, in the dialect of the river tribes. 'Do not fear me—I will not harm you and nothing else shall harm you any more. I am going to loose you.'

Even as he spoke Kane was bitterly aware of the emptiness of his words. But his voice had filtered dimly into the crumbling, agony-shot brain of the man before him. From between splintered teeth fell words, faltering and uncertain, mixed and mingled with the slavering droolings of imbecility. He spoke a language akin to the

dialects Kane had learned from friendly river folk on his
wanderings, and Kane gathered that he had been bound
to the stake for a long time—many moons, he whimpered
in the delirium of approaching death; and all this time,
inhuman, evil things had worked their monstrous will
upon him. These things he mentioned by name, but
Kane could make nothing of it for he used an unfamiliar
term that sounded like akaana. But these things had not
bound him to the stake, for the torn wretch slavered the
name of Goru, who was a priest and who had drawn a
cord too tight about his legs—and Kane wondered that
the memory of this small pain should linger through
the red mazes of agony that the dying man should
whimper over it.

And to Kane's horror, the man spoke of his brother
who had aided in the binding of him, and he wept with
infantile sobs. Moisture formed in the empty sockets and
made tears of blood. And he muttered of a spear broken
long ago in some dim hunt, and while he muttered in his
delirium, Kane gently cut his bonds, and eased his broken
body to the grass. But even at the Englishman's careful
touch, the poor wretch writhed and howled like a dying
dog, while blood started anew from a score of ghastly
gashes, which, Kane noted, were more like the wounds
made by fang and talon than by knife or spear. But at
last it was done and the bloody, torn thing lay on the soft
grass with Kane's old slouch hat beneath its death's-head,
breathing in great, rattling gasps.

Kane poured water from his canteen between the
mangled lips, and bending close, said: 'Tell me more of
these devils, for by the God of my people, this deed shall
not go unavenged, though Satan himself bar my way.'

It is doubtful if the dying man heard. But he heard
something else. The macaw, with the curiosity of its
breed, swept from a near-by grove and passed so close its
great wings fanned Kane's hair. And at the sound of those
wings the butchered man heaved upright and screamed
in a voice that haunted Kane's dreams to the day of his

death: 'The wings! The wings! They come again! Ahhh,
mercy, the wings!'

And the blood burst in a torrent from his lips and
so he died.

Kane rose and wiped the cold sweat from his forehead. The upland forest shimmered in the noonday heat.
Silence lay over the land like an enchantment of dreams.
Kane's brooding eyes ranged to the black, malevolent
hills crouching in the distance and back to the far-away
savannas. An ancient curse lay over that mysterious land
and the shadow of it fell across the soul of Solomon Kane.

Tenderly he lifted the red ruin that had once pulsed
with life and youth and vitality, and carried it to the
edge of the glade, where arranging the cold limbs as best
he might, and shuddering once again at the unnamable
mutilations, he piled stones above it till even a prowling
jackal would find it hard to get at the flesh below.

And he had scarcely finished when something jerked
him back out of his somber broodings to a realization of
his own position. A slight sound—or his own wolf-like
instinct—made him whirl.

On the other side of the glade he caught a movement
among the tall grasses—the glimpse of a hideous face,
with an ivory ring in the flat nose, thick lips parted to
reveal teeth whose filed points were apparent even at that
distance, beady eyes and a low slanting forehead topped
by a mop of frizzly hair. Even as the face faded from
view Kane leaped back into the shelter of the ring of
trees which circled the glade, and ran like a deer-hound,
flitting from tree to tree and expecting at each moment to
hear the exultant clamor of the warriors and to see them
break cover at his back.

But soon he decided that they were content to hunt
him down as certain beasts track their prey, slowly and
inevitably. He hastened through the upland forest, taking
advantage of every bit of cover, and he saw no more of
his pursuers; yet he knew, as a hunted wolf knows, that

they hovered close behind him, waiting their moment to strike him down without risk to their own hides.

Kane smiled bleakly and without mirth. If it was to be a test of endurance, he would see how savage thews compared with his own spring-steel resilience. Let night come and he might yet give them the slip. If not—Kane knew in his heart that the savage essence of his very being which chafed at his flight, would make him soon turn at bay, though his pursuers outnumbered him a hundred to one.

The sun sank westward. Kane was hungry, for he had not eaten since early morning when he wolfed down the last of his dried meat. An occasional spring had given him water, and once he though he glimpsed the roof of a large hut far away through the trees. But he gave it a wide berth. It was hard to believe that this silent plateau was inhabited, but if it were, the natives were doubtless as ferocious as those hunting him.

Ahead of him the land grew rougher, with broken boulders and steep slopes as he neared the lower reaches of the brooding hills. And still no sight of his hunters except for faint glimpses caught by wary backward glances—a drifting shadow, the bending of the grass, the sudden straightening of a trodden twig, a rustle of leaves. Why should they be so cautious? Why did they not close in and have it over?

Night fell and Kane reached the first long slopes which led upward to the foot of the hills which now brooded black and menacing above him. They were his goal, where he hoped to shake off his persistent foes at last, yet a nameless aversion warned him away from them. They were pregnant with hidden evil, repellent as the coil of a great sleeping serpent, glimpsed in the tall grass.

Darkness fell heavily. The stars winked redly in the thick heat of the tropic night. And Kane, halting for a moment in an unusually dense grove, beyond which the trees thinned out on the slopes, heard a stealthy movement that was not the night wind—for no breath of air stirred the heavy leaves. And even as he turned, there was a rush in the dark, under the trees.

A shadow that merged with the shadows flung itself on Kane with a bestial mouthing and a rattle of iron, and the Englishman, parrying by the gleam of the stars on the weapon, felt his assailant duck into close quarters and meet him chest to chest. Lean wiry arms locked about him, pointed teeth gnashed at him as Kane returned the fierce grapple. His tattered shirt ripped beneath a jagged edge, and by blind chance Kane found and pinioned the hand that held the iron knife, and drew his own dirk, flesh crawling in anticipation of a spear in the back.

But even as the Englishman wondered why the others did not come to their comrade's aid, he threw all of his iron muscles into the single combat. Close-clinched they swayed and writhed in the darkness, each striving to drive his blade into the other's flesh, and as the superior strength of the Puritan began to assert itself, the cannibal howled like a rabid dog, tore and bit.

A convulsive spin-wheel of effort pivoted them out into the starlit glade where Kane saw the ivory nose-ring and the pointed teeth that snapped beast-like at his throat. And simultaneously he forced back and down the hand that gripped his knife-wrist, and drove the dirk deep into the savage wrists. The warrior screamed, and the raw acrid scent of blood flooded the night air. And in that instant Kane was stunned by a sudden savage rush and beat of mightly wings that dashed him to earth, and the cannibal was torn from his grip and vanished with a scream of mortal agony. Kane leaped to his feet, shaken to his foundation. The dwindling scream of the wretched savage sounded faintly and from above him.

Straining his eyes into the skies he thought he caught a glimpse of a shapeless and horrific Thing crossing the dim stars—in which the writhing limbs of a human mingled namelessly with great wings and a shawdowy shape—but so quickly it was gone, he could not be sure.

And now he wondered if it were not all a nightmare. But groping in the grove he found the ju-ju stave with which he had parried the short stabbing spear that lay beside it. And here, if more proof was needed, was his long dirk, still stained with blood.

Wings! Wings in the night! The skeleton in the village of torn roofs—the mutilated warrior whose wounds were not made with knife or spear and who died shrieking of wings. Surely those hills were the haunt of gigantic birds who made humanity their prey. Yet if birds, why had they not wholly devoured the torn man on the stake? And Kane knew in his heart that no true bird ever cast such a shadow as he had seen flit across the stars.

He shrugged his shoulders, bewildered. The night was silent. Where were the rest of the cannibals who had followed him from their distant jungle? Had the fate of their comrade frightened them into flight? Kane looked to his pistols. Cannibals or no, he went not up into those dark hills that night.

Now he must sleep, if all the devils of the Elder World were on his track. A deep roaring to the westward warned him that beasts of prey were aroam, and he walked rapidly down the rolling slopes until he came to a dense grove some distance from that in which he had fought the cannibal. He climbed high among the great branches until he found a thick crotch that would accommodate even his tall frame. The branches above would guard him from a sudden swoop of any winged thing, and if savages were lurking near, their clamber into the tree would warm him, for he slept lightly as a cat. As for serpents and leopards, they were chances he had taken a thousand times.

Solomon Kane slept and his dreams were vague, chaotic, haunted with a suggestion of prehuman evil and which at last merged into a vision vivid as a scene in waking life. Solomon dreamed he woke with a start, drawing a pistol—for so long had his life been that of the wolf, that reaching for a weapon was his natural reaction upon waking suddenly.

His dream was that a strange, shadowy thing had perched upon a great branch close by and gazed at him with greedy, luminous yellow eyes that seared into his brain. The dream-thing was tall and lean and strangely misshapen, so blended with the shadows that it seemed a shadow itself, tangible only in the yellow eyes. And Kane dreamed he waited, spellbound, while uncertainty came into those eyes and then the creature walked out on the limb as a man would walk, raised great shadowy wings, sprang into space and vanished.

Kane jerked upright, the mists of sleep fading. In the dim starlight, under the arching Gothic-like branches, the tree was empty save for himself. Then it had been a dream, after all—yet it had been so vivid, so fraught with inhuman foulness—even now a faint scent like that exuded by birds of prey seemed to linger in the air. Kane strained his ears. He heard the sighing of the night wind, the whisper of the leaves, the far-away roaring of a lion, but naught else. Again Solomon slept—while high above him a shadow wheeled against the stars, circling again and again as a vulture circles a dying wolf.

2. The Battle in the Sky

Dawn was spreading whitely over the eastern hills when Kane woke. The thought of his nightmare came to him and he wondered again at its vividness as he climbed down out of the tree. A nearby spring slaked his thirst and some fruit, rare in these highlands, eased his hunger.

Then he turned his face again to the hills. A finish fighter was Solomon Kane. Along that grim skyline dwelt some evil foe to the sons of men, and that mere fact was as much a challenge to the Puritan as had ever been a glove thrown in his face by some hot-headed gallant of Devon..

Refreshed by his night's sleep, he set out with his long easy stride, passing the grove that had witnessed the battle in the night, and coming into the region where the trees thinned at the foot of the slopes. Up these slopes he went, halting for a moment to gaze back over the way he had come. Now that he was above the plateau, he could easily make out a village in the distance—a cluster of mud-and-bamboo huts with one unusually large hut a short distance from the rest on a sort of low knoll.

And while he gazed, with a sudden rush of grisly wings the terror was upon him! Kane whirled, galvanized. All signs had pointed to the theory of a winged thing that hunted by night. He had not expected attack in broad daylight—but here a bat-like monster was swooping at him out of the very eye of the rising sun. Kane saw a spread of mighty wings, from which glared a horribly human face; then he drew and fired with unerring aim and the monster veered wildly in midair and came whirling and tumbling out of the sky to crash at his feet.

Kane leaned forward, pistol smoking in his hand, and gazed wide-eyed. Surely this thing was a demon out of the pits of hell, said the sombre mind of the Puritan; yet a leaden ball had slain it. Kane shrugged his shoulders, baffled; he had never seen aught to approach this, though all his life had fallen in strange ways.

The thing was like a man, inhumanly tall and inhumanly thin; the head was long, narrow, and hairless—the head of a predatory creature. The ears were small, close-set and queerly pointed. The eyes, set in death, were narrow, oblique and of a strange yellowish color. The nose was thin and hooked, like the beak of a bird of prey, the mouth a wide cruel gash, whose thin lips, writhed in a death snarl and flecked with foam, disclosed wolfish fangs.

The creature, which was naked and hairless, was not unlike a human being in other ways. The shoulders were broad and powerful, the neck long and lean. The arms were long and muscular, the thumb being set beside the

fingers after the manner of the great apes. Fingers and
thumbs were armed with heavy hooked talons. The chest
was curiously misshapen, the breast-bone jutting out like
the keel of a ship, the ribs curving back from it. The legs
were long and wiry with huge, hand-like, prehensile feet,
the great toe set opposite the rest like a man's thumb. The
claws on the toes were merely long nails.

But the most curious feature of this curious creature
was on its back. A pair of great wings, shaped much
like the wings of a moth but with a bony frame and of
leathery substance, grew from its shoulders, beginning
at a point just back and above where the arms joined
the shoulders, and extending half way to the narrow
hips. These wings, Kane reckoned, would measure some
eighteen feet from tip to tip.

He laid hold on the creature, involuntarily shuddering
at the slick, hard leather-like feel of the skin, and half-
lifted it. The weight was little more than half as much as
it would have been in a man the same height—some six
and a half feet. Evidently the bones were of a peculiar
bird-like structure and the flesh consisted almost entirely
of stringy muscles.

Kane stepped back, surveying the thing again. Then
his dream had been no dream after all—that foul thing
or another like it had in grisly reality lighted in the
tree beside him—a whir of mighty wings! A sudden
rush through the sky! Even as Kane whirled he realized he had committed the jungle–farer's unpardonable
crime—he had allowed his astonishment and curiosity
to throw him off guard. Already a winged fiend was at
his throat and there was no time to draw and fire his
other pistol. Kane saw, in a maze of thrashing wings, a
devilish, semi-human face—he felt those wings battering
at him—he felt cruel talons sink deep into his breast;
then he was dragged off his feet and felt empty space
beneath him.

The winged man had wrapped his limbs about the Englishman's legs, and the talons he had driven into Kane's

breast muscles held like fanged vises. The wolf-like fangs drove at Kane's throat, but the Puritan gripped the bony throat and thrust back the grisly head, while with his right hand he strove to draw his dirk. The birdman was mounting slowly and a fleeting glance showed Kane that they were already high above the trees. The Englishman did not hope to survive this battle in the sky, for even if he slew his foe, he would be dashed to death in the fall. But with the innate ferocity of the fighting man he set himself grimly to take his captor with him.

Holding those keen fangs at bay, Kane managed to draw his dirk, and he plunged it deep into the body of the monster. The bat-man veered wildly and a rasping, raucous screech burst from his half-throttled throat. He floundered wildly, beating frantically with his great wings, bowing his back and twisting his head fiercely in a vain effort to free it and sink home his deadly fangs. He sank the talons of one hand agonizingly deeper and deeper into Kane's breast muscles, while with the other he tore at his foe's head and body. But the Englishman, gashed and bleeding, with the silent and tenacious savagery of a bulldog, sank his fingers deeper into the lean neck and drove his dirk home again and again, while far below awed eyes watched the fiendish battle that was raging at that dizzy height.

They had drifted out over the plateau, and the fast-weakening wings of the batman barely supported their weight. They were sinking earthward swiftly, but Kane, blinded with blood and battle fury, knew nothing of this. With a great piece of his scalp hanging loose, his chest and shoulders cut and ripped, the world had become a blind, red thing in which he was aware of but one sensation—the bulldog urged to kill his foe.

Now the feeble and spasmodic beating of the dying monster's wings held them hovering for an instant above a thick grove of gigantic trees, while Kane felt the grip of claws and twining limbs grow weaker and the slashing of the talons become a futile flailing.

With a last burst of power he drove the reddened dirk straight through the breastbone and felt a convulsive tremor run through the creature's frame. The great wings fell limp—and victor and vanquished dropped headlong and plummet-like earthward.

Through a red wave Kane saw the waving branches rushing up to meet them—he felt them flail his face and tear at his clothing, as still locked in that death-clinch he rushed downward through leaves which eluded his vainly grasping hand; then his head crashed against a great limb, and an endless abyss of blackness engulfed him.

3. The People in the Shadow

Through colossal, black basaltic corridors of night, Solomon Kane fled for a thousand years. Gigantic winged demons, horrific in the utter darkness, swept over him with a rush of great bat-like pinions and in the blackness he fought with them as a cornered rat fights a vampire bat, while fleshless jaws drooled fearful blasphemies and horrid secrets in his ears, and the skulls of men rolled under his groping feet.

Solomon Kane came back suddenly from the land of delirium and his first sight of sanity was that of a fat, kindly native face bending over him. Kane saw he was in a roomy, clean and well-ventilated hut, while from a cooking pot bubbling outside wafted savoury scents. Kane realized he was ravenously hungry. And he was strangely weak. The hand he lifted to his bandaged head shook, and its bronze was dimmed.

The fat man and another, a tall, gaunt, grim faced warrior, bent over him, and the fat man said: 'He is awake, Kuroba, and of sound mind.' The gaunt man nodded and called something which was answered from without.

'What is this place?' asked Kane in a language he had learned that was similar to the dialect just used. 'How long have I lain here?'

'This is the last village of Bogonda.' The fat man pressed him back with hands as gentle as a woman's. 'We found you lying beneath the trees on the slopes, badly wounded and senseless. You have raved in delirium for many days. Now eat.'

A lithe young warrior entered with a wooden bowl full of steaming food and Kane ate ravenously.

'He is like a leopard, Kuroba,' said the flat man admiringly. 'Not one in a thousand would have lived with his wounds.'

'Aye,' returned the other. 'And he slew the akaana that rent him, Goru.'

Kane struggled to his elbows. 'Goru?' he cried fiercely. 'The priest who binds men to stakes for devils to eat?'

And he strove to rise so that he could strangle the fat man, but his weakness swept over him like a wave, the hut swam dizzily to his eyes and he sank back panting, where he soon fell into a sound, natural sleep.

Later he awoke and found a slim young girl, named Nayela, watching him. She fed him, and feeling much stronger, Kane asked questions which she answered shyly but intelligently.

This was Bogonda, ruled by Kuroba the chief and Goru the priest. None in Bogonda had ever seen or heard of a white man before. She counted the days Kane had lain helpless, and he was amazed. But such a battle as he had been through was enough to kill an ordinary man. He wondered that no bones had been broken, but the girl said the branches had broken his fall and he had landed on the body of the akaana. He asked for Goru, and the fat priest came to him, bringing Kane's weapons.

'Some we found with you where you lay,' said Goru, 'some by the body of the akaana you slew with the weapon which speaks in fire and smoke. You must be a god—yet the gods bleed not and you have just all but died. Who are you?'

'I am no god,' Kane answered, 'but a man like yourself. I come from a far land amid the sea, which land, mind

ye, is the fairest and noblest of all lands. My name is
Solomon Kane and I am a landless wanderer. From the
lips of a dying man I first heard your name. Yet your face
seemeth kindly.'

A shadow crossed the eyes of the shaman and he hung
his head.

'Rest and grow strong, oh man, or god or whatever
you be,' said he, 'and in time you will learn of the ancient
curse that rests upon this ancient land.'

And in the days that followed, while Kane recovered
and grew strong with the wild beast vitality that was his,
Goru and Kuroba sat and spoke to him at length, telling
him many curious things.

Their tribe was not aboriginal here, but had come
upon the plateau a hundred and fifty years before, giving
it the name of their former home. They had once been
a powerful tribe in Old Bogonda, on a great river far to
the south. But tribal wars broke their power, and at last
before a concerted uprising, the whole tribe gave way, and
Goru repeated legends of that great flight of a thousand
miles through jungle and swampland, harried at every
step by cruel foes.

At last, hacking their way through a country of ferocious cannibals, they found themselves safe from man's
attack—but prisoners in a trap from which neither they
nor their descendants could ever escape. They were in
the horror-country of Akaana, and Goru said his ancestors
came to understand the jeering laughter of the maneaters
who had hounded them to the very borders of the plateau.

The Bogondi found a fertile country with good water
and plenty of game. There were numbers of goats and a
species of wild pig that throve here in great abundance.
At first the people ate these pigs, but later they spared
them for a good reason. The grasslands between plateau
and jungle swarmed with antelopes, buffaloes and the
like, and there were many lions. Lions also roamed the
plateau, but Bogonda meant 'Lion-slayer' in their tongue
and it was not many moons before the remnants of the

great cats took to the lower levels. But it was not lions
they had to fear, as Goru's ancestors soon learned.

Finding that the cannibals would not come past the
savannas, they rested from their long trek and built two
villages—Upper and Lower Bogonda. Kane was in Upper
Bogonda; he had seen the ruins of the lower village. But
soon they found that they had strayed into a country of
nightmares with dripping fangs and talons. They heard
the beat of mighty wings at night, and saw horrific
shadows cross the stars and loom against the moon.
Children began to disappear and at last a young hunter
strayed off into the hills, where night overtook him. And
in the gray light of dawn a mangled, half-devoured corpse
fell from the skies into the village street and a whisper
of ogreish laughter from high above froze the horrified
onlookers. Then a little later the full horror of their
position burst upon the Bogondi.

At first the winged men were afraid of the newcomers.
They hid themselves and ventured from their caverns
only at night. Then they grew bolder. In the full daylight,
a warrior shot one with an arrow, but the fiends had
learned they could slay a human, and its death scream
brought a score of the devils dropping from the skies,
who tore the slayer to pieces in full sight of the tribe.

The Bogondi then prepared to leave that devil's country and a hundred warriors went up into the hills to find a
pass. They found steep walls, up which a man must climb
laboriously, and they found the cliffs honey combed with
caves where the winged men dwelt.

Then was fought the first pitched battle between men
and bat-men, and it resulted in a crushing victory for
the monsters. The bows and spears of the natives proved
futile before the swoops of the taloned fiends, and of all
that hundred that went up into the hills, not one survived;
for the akaanas hunted down those that fled and dragged
down the last one within bowshot of the upper village.

Then it was that the Bogondi, seeing they could not
hope to win through the hills, sought to fight their way

out again the way they had come. But a great horde of cannibals met them in the grasslands, and in a great battle that lasted nearly all day, hurled them back, broken and defeated. And Goru said while the battle raged, the skies were thronged with hideous shapes, circling above and laughing their fearful mirth to see men die wholesale.

So the survivors of those two battles, licking their wounds, bowed to the inevitable with the fatalistic philosophy of the savage. Some fifteen hundred men, women and children remained, and they built their huts, tilled the soil and lived stolidly in the shadow of the nightmare.

In those days there were many of the bird-people, and they might have wiped out the Bogondi utterly, had they wished. No one warrior could cope with an akaana, for he was stronger than a human, he struck as a hawk strikes, and if he missed, his wings carried him out of reach of a counterblow.

Here Kane interrupted to ask why the Bogondi did not make war on the demons with arrows. But Goru answered that it took a quick and accurate archer to strike an akaana in midair at all, and so tough were their hides that unless the arrow struck squarely it would not penetrate. Kane knew that the natives were very indifferent bowmen and that they pointed their shafts with chipped stone, bone, or hammered iron almost as soft as copper; he thought of Poitiers and Agincourt and wished grimly for a file of stout English archers—or a rank of musketeers.

But Goru said the akaanas did not seem to wish to destroy the Bogondi utterly. Their chief food consisted of the little pigs which then swarmed the plateau, and young goats. Sometimes they went out on the savannas for antelope, but they distrusted the open country and feared the lions. Nor did they haunt the jungles beyond, for the trees, grew too close for the spread of their wings. They kept to the hills and the plateau—and what lay beyond those hills none in Bogonda knew.

The akaanas allowed the Bogondi to inhabit the plateau much as men allow wild animals to thrive, or stock lakes with fish—for their own pleasure. The bat-people, said Goru, had a strange and grisly sense of humor which was tickled by the sufferings of a howling human. Those grim hills had echoed to cries that turned men's heart to ice.

But for many years, Goru said, once the Bogondi learned not to resist their masters, the akaanas were content to snatch up a baby from time to time, or devour a young girl strayed from the village or a youth whom night caught outside the walls. The bat-folk distrusted the village; they circled high above it but did not venture within. There the Bogondi were safe until late years.

Goru said that the akaanas were fast dying out; once there had been hope that the remnants of his race would outlast them—in which event, he said fatalistically, the cannibals would undoubtedly come up from the jungle and put the survivors in their cooking pots. Now he doubted if there were more than a hundred and fifty akaanas altogether. Kane asked him why did not the warriors then sally forth on a great hunt and destroy the devils utterly, and Goru smiled a bitter smile and repeated his remarks about the prowess of the bat-people in battle. Moreover, said he, the whole tribe of Bogonda numbered only about four hundred souls now, and the bat-people were their only protection against the cannibals to the west.

Goru said the tribe had thinned more in the past thirty years than in all the years previous. As the numbers of the akaanas dwindled, their hellish savagery increased. They seized more and more of the Bogondi to torture and devour in their grim black caves high up in the hills, and Goru spoke of sudden raids on hunting parties and toilers in the plantain fields, and of the nights made ghastly by horrible screams and gibberings from the dark hills, and blood-freezing laughter that was half-human; of dismembered limbs and gory grinning heads flung from the skies to fall in the shuddering village, and of grisly feasts among the stars.

Then came drouth, Gory said, and a great famine.

Many of the springs dried up and the crops of rice and
yams and plantains failed. The gnus, deer, and buffaloes
which had formed the main part of Bogonda's meat
diet withdrew to the jungle in quest of water, and the
lions, their hunger overcoming their fear of man, ranged
into the uplands. Many of the tribe died, and the rest
were driven by hunger to eat the pigs which were the
natural prey of the bat-people. This angered the akaanas
and thinned the pigs. Famine, Bogondi, and the lions
destroyed all the goats and half the pigs.

At last the famine was past, but the damage was done.
Of all the great droves which once swarmed the plateau,
only a remnant was left, and these were hard to catch.
The Bogondi had eaten the pigs, so the akaanas ate the
Bogondi. Life became a hell for the humans, and the
lower village, numbering now only some hundred and
fifty souls, rose in revolt. Driven to frenzy by repeated
outrages, they turned on their masters. An akaana lighting in the very streets to steal a child was set on and shot
to death with arrows. And the people of Lower Bogonda
drew into their huts and waited for their doom.

And in the night, said Goru, it came. The akaanas
had overcome their distrust of the huts. The full flock of
them swarmed down from the hills, and Upper Bogonda
awoke to hear the fearful cataclysm of screams and
blasphemies that marked the end of the other village.
All night Goru's people had lain sweating in terror, not
daring to move, harkening to the howling and gibbering
that rent the night. At last these sounds ceased, Goru
said, wiping the cold sweat from his brow, but sounds
of grisly and obscene feasting still haunted the night with
demon's mockery.

In the early dawn Goru's people saw the hell-flock
winging back to their hills, like demons flying back to
hell through the dawn. They flew slowly and heavily,
like gorged vultures. Later the people dared to steal
down to the accursed village, and what they found there
sent them shrieking away. And to that day, Goru said, no
man passed within three bow shots of that silent horror.

And Kane nodded in understanding, his cold eyes more sombre than ever.

For many days after that, Goru said the people waited in quaking fear. Finally in desperation of fear, which breeds unspeakable cruelty, the tribe cast lots and the loser was bound to a stake between the two villages, in hopes that the akaanas would recognize this as a token of submission so that the people of Bogonda might escape the fate of their kinsmen. The custom, said Goru, had been borrowed from the cannibals who in old times worshipped the akaanas and offered a human sacrifice at each moon. But chance had shown them that the akaanas could be killed, so they ceased to worship them—at least that was Goru's deduction, and he explained at much length that no mortal thing is worthy of real adoration, however evil or powerful it may be.

His own ancestors had made occasional sacrifices to placate the winged devils, but until lately it had not been a regular custom. Now it was necessary; the akaanas expected it, and each moon they chose from their waning numbers a strong young man or a girl whom they bound to the stake.

Kane watched Goru's face closely as he spoke of his sorrow for this unspeakable necessity, and the Englishman realized that the priest was sincere. Kane shuddered at the thought of a tribe of human beings thus passing slowly but surely into the maws of a race of monsters.

Kane spoke of the wretch he had seen, and Goru nodded, pain in his soft eyes. For a day and a night he had been hanging there, while the akaanas glutted their vile torture-lust on his quivering, agonized flesh. Thus far the sacrifices had kept doom from the village. The remaining pigs furnished sustenance for the dwindling akaanas, together with an occasional baby snatched up, and they were content to have their nameless sport with the single victim each moon.

A thought came to Kane.

'The cannibals never come up into the plateau?'

Goru shook his head; safe in their jungle, they never raided past the savannas.

'But they hunted me to the very foot of the hills.'

Again Goru shook his head. There was only one cannibal; they had found his footprints. Evidently a single warrior, bolder than the rest, had allowed his passion for the chase to overcome his fear of the grisly plateau and had paid the penalty. Kane's teeth came together with a vicious snap which ordinarily took the place of profanity with him. He was stung by the thought of fleeing so long from a single enemy. No wonder that enemy had followed so cautiously, waiting until dark to attack. But, asked Kane, why had the akaana seized the cannibal instead of himself—and why had he not been attacked by the bat-man who alighted in his tree that night?

The cannibal was bleeding, Goru answered. The scent called the bat-fiend to attack, for they scented raw blood as far as vultures. And they were very wary. They had never seen a man like Kane, who showed no fear. Surely they had decided to spy on him, take him off guard before they struck.

Who were these creatures? Kane asked. Goru shrugged his shoulders. They were there when his ancestors came, who had never heard of them before they saw them. There was no intercourse with the cannibals, so they could learn nothing from them. The akaanas lived in caves, naked like beasts; they knew nothing of fire and ate only fresh, raw meat. But they had a language of a sort and acknowledged a king among them. Many died in the great famine when the stronger ate the weaker. They were vanishing swiftly; of late years no females or young had been observed among them. When these males died at last, there would be no more akaanas; but Bogonda, observed Goru, was doomed already, unless—he looked strangely and wistfully at Kane. But the Puritan was deep in thought.

Among the swarm of native legends he had heard on his wanderings, one now stood out. Long, long ago, an old,

old ju-ju man had told him, winged devils came flying
out of the north and passed over his country, vanishing
in the maze of the jungle-haunted south. And the ju-ju
man related an old, old legend concerning these creatures—that once they had abode in myriad numbers far
on a great lake of bitter water many moons to the north,
and ages and ages ago a chieftain and his warriors fought
them with bows and arrows and slew many, driving the
rest into the south. The name of the chief was N'Yasunna
and he owned a great war canoe with many oars driving it
swiftly through the bitter water.

And now a cold wind blew suddenly on Solomon
Kane, as if from a Door opened suddenly on Outer gulfs
of Time and Space. For now he realized the truth of that
garbled myth, and the truth of an older, grimmer legend.
For what was the great bitter lake but the Mediterranean
Ocean and who was the chief N'Yasunna but the hero
Jason, who conquered the harpies and drove them—not
alone into the Strophades Isles but into Africa as well?
The old pagan tale was true then, Kane thought dizzily,
shrinking aghast from the strange realm of grisly possibilities this opened up. For if this myth of the harpies
were a reality, what of the other legends—the Hydra, the
centaurs, the chimera, Medusa, Pan, and the satyrs?

All those myths of antiquity—behind them did there
lie and lurk nightmare realities with slavering fangs and
talons steeped in shuddersome evil? Africa, the Dark
Continent, land of shadows and horror, of bewitchment
and sorcery, into which all evil things had been banished
before the growing light of the western world!

Kane came out of his reveries with a start. Goru was
tugging gently and timidly at his sleeve.

'Save us from the akaanas!' said Goru. 'If you be not a
god, there is the power of a god in you! You bear in your
hand the mighty ju-ju stave which has in times gone by
been the scepter of fallen empires and the staff of mighty
priests. And you have weapons which speak death in fire
and smoke—for our young men watched and saw you slay

two akaanas. We will make you king—god—what you will! More than a moon has passed since you came into Bogonda and the time for the sacrifice is gone by, but the bloody stake stands bare. The akaanas shun the village where you lie; they steal no more babes from us. We have thrown off their yoke because our trust is in you!'

Kane clasped his temples with his hands. 'You know not what you ask!' he cried. 'God knoweth it is in my deepest heart to rid the land of this evil, but I am no god. With my pistols I can slay a few of the fiends, but I have but a little powder left. Had I great store of powder and ball, and the musket I shattered in the vampire-haunted Hills of the Dead, then indeed would there be a rare hunting. But even if I slew all those fiends, what of the cannibals?'

'They too will fear you!' cried old Kuroba, while the girl Nayela and the lad, Loga, who was to have been the next sacrifice, gazed at him with their souls in their eyes. Kane dropped his chin on his fist and sighed.

'Yet will I stay here in Bogonda all the rest of my life if ye think I be protection to the people.'

So Solomon Kane stayed at the village of Bogonda of the Shadow. The people were a kindly folk, whose natural sprightliness and fun-loving spirits were subdued and saddened by long dwelling in the Shadow. But now they had taken new heart by the Englishman's coming, and it wrenched Kane's heart to note the pathetic trust they placed in him. Now they sang in the plaintain fields and danced about the fire, and gazed at him with adoring faith in their eyes. But Kane, cursing his own helplessness, knew how futile would be his fancied protection if the winged fiends swept suddenly out of the skies.

But he stayed in Bogonda. In his dreams the gulls wheeled above the cliffs of old Devon carved in the clean, blue, wind-whipped skies, and in the day the call of the unknown lands beyond Bogonda clawed at his heart with fierce yearning. But he abode in Bogonda and racked his

brains for a plan. He sat and gazed for hours at the ju-ju
stave, hoping in desperation that black magic would aid
him, where his mind failed. But N'Longa's ancient gift
gave him no aid. Once he had summoned the Slave Coast
shaman to him across leagues of intervening space—but
it was only when confronted with supernatural manifestations that N'Longa could come to him, and these harpies
were not supernatural.

The germ of an idea began to grow at the back of
Kane's mind, but he discarded it. It had to do with
a great trap—and how could the akaanas be trapped?
The roaring of lions played a grim accompaniment to his
brooding meditations. As man dwindled on the plateau,
the hunting beasts who feared only the spears of the
hunters were beginning to gather. Kane laughed bitterly.
It was not lions, that might be hunted down and slain
singly, that he had to deal with.

At some little distance from the village stood the great
hut of Goru, once a council hall. This hut was full of many
strange fetishes, which Goru said with a helpless wave of
his fat hands, were strong magic against evil spirits but
scant protection against winged hellions of gristle and
bone and flesh.

4. The Madness of Solomon

Kane woke suddenly from a dreamless sleep. A hideous
medley of screams burst horrific in his ears. Outside his
hut, people were dying in the night, horribly, as cattle die
in the shambles. He had slept, as always, with his weapons buckled on him. Now he bounded to the door, and
something fell mouthing and slavering at his feet to grasp
his knees in a convulsive grin and gibber incoherent pleas.
In the faint light of a smoldering fire near by, Kane
in horror recognized the face of the youth Loga, now

frightfully torn and drenched in blood, already freez-
ing into a death mask. The night was full of fearful
sounds, inhuman howlings mingled with the whisper
of mighty wings, the tearing of thatch and a ghastly
demon-laughter. Kane freed himself from the locked
dead arms and sprang to the dying fire. He could make
out only a confused and vague maze of fleeing forms
and darting shapes, the shift and blur of dark wings
against the stars.

He snatched up a brand and thrust it against the
thatch of his hut—and as the flame leaped up and showed
him the scene he stood frozen and aghast. Red, howling
doom had fallen on Bogonda. Winged monsters raced
screaming through her streets, wheeled above the heads
of the fleeing people, or tore apart the hut thatches to get
at the gibbering victims within.

With a choked cry the Englishman woke from his
trance of horror, drew and fired at a darting flame-eyed
shadow which fell at his feet with a shattered skull. And
Kane gave tongue to one deep, fierce roar and bounded
into the melee, all the berserk fury of his heathen Saxon
ancestors bursting into terrible being.

Dazed and bewildered by the sudden attack, cowed by
long years of submission, the Bogondi were incapable of
combined resistance and for the most part died like sheep.
Some maddened by desperation, fought back, but their
arrows went wild or glanced from the tough wings while
the devilish agility of the creatures made spear thrust
and ax stroke uncertain. Leaping from the ground they
avoided the blows of their victims and, sweeping down
upon their shoulders, dashed them to earth where fang
and talon did their crimson work.

Kane saw old Kuroba, gaunt and bloodstained, at bay
against a hut wall with his foot on the neck of a monster
who had not been quick enough. The grim-faced old chief
wielded a two-handed ax in great sweeping blows that for
the moment held back the screeching onset of half a dozen
of the devils. Kane was leaping to his aid when a low,

pitiful whimper checked him. The girl Nayela writhed
weakly, prone in the bloody dust, while on her back a
vulture-like thing crouched and tore. Her dulling eyes
sought the face of the Englishman in anguished appeal.

Kane ripped out a bitter oath and fired point blank.
The winged devil pitched backward with an abhorrent
screeching and a wild flutter of dying wings, and Kane
bent to the dying girl. She whimpered and kissed his
hands with uncertain lips as he cradled her head in his
arms. Her eyes set.

Kane lain the body gently down, looking for Kuroba.
He saw only a huddled cluster of grisly shapes that
sucked and tore at something between them. And Kane
went mad. With a scream that cut through the inferno he
bounded up, slaying even as he rose. Even in the act of
lunging up from bent knee he drew and trust, transfixing
a vulturelike throat. Then whipping out his rapier as the
thing floundered and twitched in its death struggle, the
raging Puritan charged forward seeking new victims.

On all sides of him the people of Bogonda were dying
hideously. They fought futilely or they fled and the
demons coursed them down as a hawk courses a hare.
They ran into the huts and the fiends rent the thatch
or burst the door, and what took place in those huts was
mercifully hidden from Kane's eyes.

And to the frantic Puritan's horror-distorted brain it
seemed that he alone was responsible. The Bogondi had
trusted him to save them. They had withheld the sacrifice
and defied their grim masters. Now they were paying the
horrible penalty and he was unable to save them. In the
agony-dimmed eyes turned toward him, Kane quaffed
the black dregs of the bitter cup. It was not anger or the
vindictiveness of fear. It was hurt and a stunned reproach.
He was their god and he had failed them.

Now he ravened through the massacre and the fiends
avoided him, turning to the easy victims. But Kane was
not to be denied. In a red haze that was not of the burning
hut, he saw a culminating horror; a harpy gripped a

writhing naked thing that had been a woman, and the
wolfish fangs gorged deep. As Kane sprang, thrusting,
the bat-man dropped his yammering, mowing prey and
soared aloft. But Kane dropped his rapier and with the
bound of a blood-mad panther caught the demon's throat
and locked his iron legs about its lower body.

Once again he found himself battling in midair, but
this time close above the hut roofs. Terror had entered
the cold brain of the harpy. He did not fight to hold and
slay; he wished only to be rid of this silent, clinging thing
that stabbed so savagely for his life. He floundered wildly,
screaming abhorrently and thrashing with his wings, then
as Kane's dirk bit deeper, dipped suddenly sidewise and
fell headlong.

The thatch of a hut broke their fall, and Kane and the
dying harpy crashed through to land on a writhing mass
on the hut floor. In the lurid flickering of the burning
hut outside that vaguely lighted the hut into which he
had fallen, Kane saw a deed of brain-shaking horror
being enacted—red-dripping fangs in a yawning gash of a
mouth, and a crimson travesty of a human form that still
writhed with agonized life. Then, in the maze of madness
that held him, his steel fingers closed on the fiend's throat
in a grip that no tearing of talons or hammering of wings
could loosen, until he felt the horrid life flow out from
under his fingers and the bony neck hung broken.

Outside, the red madness of slaughter continued. Kane
bounded up, his hand closing blindly on the haft of some
weapon, and as he leaped from the hut a harpy soared
from under his very feet. It was an ax that Kane had
snatched up, and he dealt a stroke that spattered the
demon's brains like water. He sprang forward, stumbling
over bodies and parts of bodies, blood streaming from a
dozen wounds, and then halted baffled and screaming
with rage.

The bat-people were taking to the air. No longer
would they face this strange madman who in his insanity
was more terrible than they. But they went not alone

into the upper regions. In their lustful talons they bore
writhing, screaming forms, and Kane, raging to and fro
with his dripping ax, found himself alone in a corpse-
choked village.

He threw back his head to shriek his hate at the fiends
above him and he felt warm, thick drops fall into his face,
while the shadowy skies were filled with screams of agony
and the laughter of monsters.

As the sounds of that ghastly feast in the skies filled the
night and the blood that rained from the stars fell into his
face, Kane's last vestige of reason snapped. He gibbered
to and fro, screaming chaotic blasphemies.

And was he not a symbol of Man, staggering among
the tooth-marked bones and severed grinning heads of
humans, brandishing a futile ax, and screaming incoherent hate at the grisly, winged shapes of Night that make
him their prey, chuckling in demoniac triumph above
him and dripping into his mad eyes the pitiful blood of
their human victims?

5. The Conqueror

A shuddering, white-faced dawn crept over the black
hills to shiver above the red shambles that had been
the village of Bogonda. The huts stood intact, except
for the one which had sunk to smoldering coals, but
the thatches of many were torn. Dismembered bones,
half or wholly stripped of flesh, lay in the streets, and
some were splintered as though they had been dropped
from a great height.

It was a realm of the dead where was but one sign of life.
Solomon Kane leaned on his blood-clotted ax and gazed
upon the scene with dull, mad eyes. He was grimmed and
clotted with half-dried blood from long gashes on chest,
face, and shoulders, but he paid no need to his hurts.

The people of Bogonda had not died alone. Seventeen
harpies lay among the bones. Six of these Kane had slain.

The rest had fallen before the frantic dying desperation of
the Bogondi. But it was poor toll to take in return. Of the
four hundred odd people of Upper Bogonda, not one had
lived to see the dawn. And the harpies were gone—back
to their caves in the black hills, gorged to repletion.

With slow, mechanical steps Kane went about gathering up his weapons. He found his sword, dirk, pistols,
and the ju-ju stave. He left the main village and went up
the slope to the great hut of Goru. And there he halted,
stung by a new horror. The ghastly humor of the harpies
had prompted a delicious jest. Above the hut door stared
the severed head of Goru. The fat cheeks were shrunken,
the lips lolled in an aspect of horrified idiocy, and the eyes
stared like a hurt child. And in those dead eyes Kane saw
wonder and reproach.

Kane looked at the shambles that had been Bogonda,
and he looked at the death mask of Goru. And he lifted
his clenched fists above his head, and with glaring eyes
raised and writhing lips flecked with froth, he cursed the
sky and the earth and the spheres above and below. He
cursed the cold stars, the blazing sun, the mocking moon,
and the whisper of the wind. He cursed all fates and
destinies, all that he had loved or hated, the silent cities
beneath the seas, the past ages and the future eons. In
one soul-shaking burst of blasphemy he cursed the gods
and devils who make mankind their sport, and he cursed
Man who lives blindly on and blindly offers his back to
the iron-hoofed feet of his gods.

Then as breath failed he halted, panting. From the
lower reaches sounded the deep roaring of a lion and
into the eyes of Solomon Kane came a crafty gleam. He
stood long, as one frozen, and out of his madness grew a
desperate plan. And he silently recanted his blasphemy,
for if the brazen-hoofed gods made Man for their sport
and plaything, they also gave him a brain that holds craft
and cruelty greater than any other living thing.

'There you shall bide,' said Solomon Kane to the
head of Goru. 'The sun will wither you and the cold

dews of night will shrivel you. But I will keep the kites
from you and your eyes shall see the fall of your slayers.
Aye, I could not save the people of Bogonda, but by the
God of my race, I can avenge them. Man is the sport and
sustenance of titanic beings of Night and Horror whose
giant wings hover ever above him. But even evil things
may come to an end—and watch ye, Goru.'

In the days that followed Kane labored mightily, beginning with the first gray light of dawn and toiling on past
sunset, into the white moonlight till he fell and slept the
sleep of utter exhaustion. He snatched food as he worked
and he gave his wounds absolutely no heed, scarcely being
aware that they healed of themselves. He went down into
the lower levels and cut bamboo, great stacks of long,
tough stalks. He cut thick branches of trees, and tough
vines to serve as ropes.

With this material he reinforced the walls and roof
of Goru's hut. He set the bamboos deep in the earth,
hard against the wall, and interwove and twined them,
binding them fast with the vines that were pliant and
tough as cords. The long branches he made fast along
the thatch, binding them close together. When he had
finished, an elephant could scarcely have burst through
the walls.

The lions had come into the plateau in great numbers
and the herds of little pigs dwindled fast. Those the lions
spared, Kane slew, and tossed to the jackals. This racked
Kane's heart, for he was a kindly man and this wholesale
slaughter, even of pigs who would fall prey to hunting
beats anyhow, grieved him. But it was part of his plan of
vengeance, and he steeled his heart.

The days stretched into weeks. Kane toiled by day and
by night, and between his stints he talked to the shriveled,
mummied head of Goru, whose eyes, strangely enough,
did not change in the blaze of the sun or the haunt of the
moon, but retained their life-like expression. When the
memory of those lunacy-haunted days had become only
a vague nightmare, Kane wondered if, as it had seemed

to him, Goru's dried lips had moved in answer, speaking strange and mysterious things.

Kane saw the akaanas wheeling against the sky at a distance, but they did not come near, even when he slept in the great hut, pistols at hand. They feared his power to deal death with smoke and thunder.

At first he noted that they flew sluggishly, gorged with the flesh they had eaten on that red night, and the bodies they had borne to their caves. But as the weeks passed they appeared leaner and leaner and ranged far afield in search of food. And Kane laughed, deeply and madly.

This plan of his would never have worked before, but now there were no humans to fill the bellies of the harpy-folk. And there were nor more pigs. In all the plateau there were no creatures for the bat-people to eat. Why they did not range east of the hills, Kane thought he knew. That must be a region of thick jungle like the country to the west. He saw them fly into the grassland for antelopes and he saw the lions take toll of them. After all, the akaanas were weak beings among the hunters, strong enough only to slay pig and deer—and humans.

At last they began to soar close to him at night, and he saw their greedy eyes glaring at him through the gloom. He judged the time was ripe. Huge buffaloes, too big and ferocious for the bat-people to slay, had strayed up into the plateau to ravage the deserted fields of the dead Bogondi. Kane cut one of these out of the herd and drove him, with shouts and volleys of stones, to the hut of Goru. It was a tedious, dangerous task, and time and again Kane barely escaped the surly bull's sudden charges, but persevered and at last shot the beast before the hut.

A strong west wind was blowing and Kane flung handfuls of blood into the air for the scent to waft to the harpies in the hills. He cut the bull to pieces and carried its quarters into the hut, then managed to drag the huge trunk itself inside. Then he retired into the thick trees nearby and waited.

He had not long to wait. The morning air filled suddenly with the beat of many winds, and a hideous flock

alighted before the hut of Goru. All of the beasts—or
men—seemed to be there, and Kane gazed in wonder
at the tall, strange creatures, so like to humanity and yet
so unlike—the veritable demons of priestly legend. They
folded their wings like cloaks about them as they walked
upright, and they talked to one another in a strident,
crackling voice that had nothing of the human in it.

No, Kane decided, these things were not men. They
were the materialization of some ghastly jest of Nature—
some travesty of the world's infancy when Creation was
an experiment. Perhaps they were the offspring of a
forbidden and obscene mating of man and beast; more
likely they were a freakish offshoot on the branch of
evolution—for Kane had long ago dimly sensed a truth
in the heretical theories of the ancient philosophers, that
Man is but a higher beast. And if Nature made many
strange beasts in the past ages, why should she not have
experimented with monstrous forms of mankind? Surely
Man as Kane knew him was not the first of his breed to
walk the earth, nor yet to be the last.

Now the harpies hesitated, with their natural distrust
for a building, and some soared to the roof and tore at
the thatch. But Kane had builded well. They returned to
earth and at last, driven beyond endurance by the smell of
raw blood and the sight of the flesh within, one of them
ventured inside. In an instant all were crowded into the
great hut, tearing ravenously at the meat, and when the
last one was within, Kane reached out a hand and jerked
a long vine which tripped the catch that held the door he
had built. It fell with a crash, and the bar he had fashioned
dropped into place. That door would hold against the
charge of a wild bull.

Kane came from his cover and scanned the sky. Some
hundred and forty harpies had entered the hut. He saw
no more winging through the skies and believed it safe
to suppose he had the whole flock trapped. Then with
a cruel, brooding smile, Kane struck flint and steel to
a pile of dead leaves next the wall. Within sounded an
uneasy mumbling as the creatures realized that they were

prisoners. A thin wisp of smoke curled upward and a flicker of red followed it; the whole heap burst into flame and the dry bamboo caught.

A few moments later the whole side of the wall was ablaze. The fiends inside scented the smoke and grew restless. Kane heard them crackling wildly and clawing at the walls. He grinned savagely, bleakly and without mirth. Now a veer of the wind drove the flames around the wall and up over the thatch—with a roar the whole hut caught and leaped into flame.

From within sounded a fearful pandemonium. Kane heard bodies crash against the walls, which shook to the impact but held. The horrid screams were music to his soul, and brandishing his arms, he answered them with screams of fearful, soul-shaking laughter. The cataclysm of horror rose unbearably, paling the tumult of the flames. Then it dwindled to a medley of strangled gibbering and gasps as the flames ate in and the smoke thickened. An intolerable scent of burning flesh pervaded the atmosphere, and had there been room in Kane's brain for aught else than insane triumph, he would have shuddered to realize that the scent was of that nauseating and indescribable odor that only human flesh emits when burning.

From the thick cloud of smoke, Kane saw a mowing, gibbering thing emerge through the shredding roof and flap slowly and agonizingly upward on fearfully burned wings. Calmly he aimed and fired, and the scorched and blinded thing tumbled back into the flaming mass just as the walls crushed in. To Kane it seemed that Goru's crumbling face, vanishing in the smoke, split suddenly in a wide grin and a sudden shout of exultant human laughter mingled eerily in the roar of the flames. But the smoke and insane brain plays queer tricks.

Kane stood with the ju-ju stave in one hand the smoking pistol in the other, above the smoldering ruins that hid forever from the sight of man the last of those terrible, semi-human monsters whom another hero had banished from Europe in an unknown age. Kane stood, and unconscious statue of triumph—cold-eyed, dominant, the supreme fighting man.

Smoke curled upward into the morning sky, and the roaring of foraging lions shook the plateau. Slowly, like light breaking through mists, sanity returned to him.

'The light of God's morning enters even into dark and lonesome lands,' said Solomon Kane sombrely. 'Evil rules in the waste lands of the earth, but even evil may come to an end. Dawn follows midnight and even in this lost land the shadows shrink. Strange are Thy ways, oh God of my people, and who am I to question Thy wisdom? My feet have fallen in evil ways but Thou hast brought me forth scatheless and hast made me a scourge for the Powers of Evil. Over the souls of men spread the condor wings of colossal monsters and all manner of evil things prey upon the heart and soul and body of Man. Yet it may be in some far day these shadows shall fade and the Prince of Darkness be chained forever in his hell. And till then mankind can but stand up stoutly to the monsters in his own heart and without, and with the aid of God he may yet triumph.'

And Solomon Kane looked up into the silent hills and felt the silent call of the hills and the unguessed distances beyond; and Solomon Kane shifted his belt, took his staff firmly in his hand and turned his face eastward.

KIRBY O'DONNELL

Swords of Shahrazar

KIRBY O'Donnell opened his chamber door and gazed out, his long keen-bladed *kindhjal* in his hand. Somewhere a cresset glowed fitfully, dimly lighting the broad hallway, flanked by thick columns. The spaces between these columns were black arched wells of darkness, where anything might be lurking.

Nothing moved within his range of vision. The great hall seemed deserted. But he knew that he had not merely dreamed that he heard the stealthy pad of bare feet outside his door, the stealthy sound of unseen hands trying the portal.

O'Donnell felt the peril that crawled unseen about him, the first white man ever to set foot in forgotten Shahrazar, the forbidden, age-old city brooding high among the Afghan mountains. He believed his disguise was perfect; as Ali el Ghazi, a wandering Kurd, he had entered Shahrazar, and as such he was a guest in the palace of its prince. But the furtive footfalls that had awakened him were a sinister portent.

He stepped out into the hall cautiously, closing the door behind him. A single step he took – it was the swish of a garment that warned him. He whirled, quick as a cat, and saw, all in a split second, a great black body, hurtling at him from the shadows, the gleam of a plunging knife. And simultaneously he himself moved in a blinding blur of speed. A shift of his whole body avoided the stroke, and as the blade licked past, splitting only thin air, his *kindhjal,* driven with desperate energy, sank it full length in the black torso.

An agonized groan was choked by a rush of blood in the dusky throat. The Negro's knife rang on the marble floor, and the great black figure, checked in its headlong rush, swayed drunkenly and pitched forward. O'Donnell watched with his eyes as hard as flint as the would-be murderer shuddered convulsively and then lay still in a widening crimson pool.

He recognized the man, and as he stood staring down at his victim, a train of associations passed swiftly through his mind, recollections of past events crowding on a realization of his present situation.

Lure of treasure had brought O'Donnell in his disguise to forbidden Shahrazar. Since the days of Genghis Khan, Shahrazar had sheltered the treasure of the long-dead shahs of Khuwarezm. Many an adventurer had sought that fabled hoard, and many had died. But O'Donnell had found it – only to lose it.

Hardly had he arrived in Shahrazar when a band of marauding Turkomans, under their chief, Orkhan Bahadur, had stormed the city and captured it, slaying its prince, the Uzbek Shaibar Khan. And while the battle raged in the streets, O'Donnell had found the hidden treasure in a secret chamber, and his brain had reeled at its splendor. But he had been unable to bear it away, and he dared not leave it for Orkhan. The emissary of an intriguing European power was in Shahrazar, plotting to use that treasure to conquer India. O'Donnell had done away with it forever. The victorious Turkomans had searched for it in vain.

O'Donnell, as Ali el Ghazi, had once saved Orkhan Bahadur's life, and the prince made the supposed Kurd welcome in the palace. None dreamed of his connection with the disappearance of the hoard, unless—O'Donnell stared somberly down at the figure on the marble floor.

That man was Baber, a Soudani servant of Suleiman Pasha, the emissary.

O'Donnell lifted his head and swept his gaze over the black arches, the shadowy columns. Had he only imagined that he heard movement back in the darkness? Bending over quickly, he grasped the limp body and heaved it on his shoulder—an act impossible for a man with less steely thews—and started down the hall. A corpse found before his door meant questions, and the fewer questions O'Donnell had to answer the better.

He went down the broad, silent hall and descended a wide marble stair into swallowing gloom, like an oriental demon carrying a corpse to hell; groped through a tapestried door and down a short, black corridor to a blank marble wall.

When he thrust against this with his foot, a section swung inward, working on a pivot, and he entered a circular, domed chamber with a marble floor and walls hung with heavy gilt-worked tapestries, between which showed broad golden-frieze work. A bronze lamp cast a soft light, making the dome seem lofty and full of shadows, while the tapestries were clinging squares of velvet darkness.

This had been the treasure vault of Shaibar Khan, and why it was empty now, only Kirby O'Donnell could tell.

Lowering the black body with a gasp of relief, for the burden had taxed even his wiry thews to the utmost, he deposited it exactly on the great disk that formed the center of the marble floor. Then he crossed the chamber, seized a gold bar that seemed merely part of the ornamentation, and jerked it strongly. Instantly the great central disk revolved silently, revealing a glimpse of a black opening, into which the corpse tumbled. The sound of rushing water welled up from the darkness, and then the slab, swinging on its pivot, completed its revolution and the floor showed again a smooth unbroken surface.

But O'Donnell wheeled suddenly. The lamp burned

low, filling the chamber with a lurid unreal light. In that
light he saw the door open silently and a slim dark figure
glide in.

It was a slender man with long nervous hands
and an ivory oval of a face, pointed with a short black
beard. His eyes were long and oblique, his garments
dark, even his turban. In his hand a blue, snub-nosed
revolver glinted dully.

'Suleiman Pasha!' muttered O'Donnell tensely.

He had never been able to decide whether this man
was the Oriental he seemed, or a European in masquerade.
Had the man penetrated his own disguise? The emissary's
first words assured him that such was not the case.

'Ali el Ghazi,' said Suleiman, 'you have lost me a
valuable servant, but you have told me a secret. None
other knows the secret of that revolving slab. I did not,
until I followed you, after you killed Baber, and watched
you through the door, though I have suspected that this
chamber was the treasure vault.

'I have suspected you—now I am certain. I know
why the treasure has never been found. You disposed of
it as you have disposed of Baber. You are cup-companion
to Prince Orkhan Bahadur. But if I told him you cast away
the treasure forever, do you suppose his friendship would
prevail over his wrath?

'Keep back!' he warned. 'I did not say that I
would tell Orkhan. Why you threw away the treasure
I cannot guess, unless it was because of fanatical loyalty
to Shaibar Kahn.'

He looked him over closely. 'Face like a hawk, body
of coiled steel springs,' he murmured. 'I can use you, my
Kurdish swaggerer.'

'How use me?' demanded O'Donnell.

'You can help me in the game I play with
Orkhan Bahadur. The treasure is gone, but I can still
use him, I and the *Feringis* who employ me. I will
make him amir of Afghanistan and, after that, sultan
of India.'

'And the puppet of the *Feringis*,' grunted O'Donnell.

'What is that to thee?' Suleiman laughed. 'Time is not to think. I will do the thinking; see thou to the enacting of my commands.'

'I have not said that I would serve you,' growled O'Donnell doggedly.

'You have no other choice,' answered Suleiman calmly. 'If you refuse, I will reveal to Orkhan that which I learned tonight, and he will have you flayed alive.'

O'Donnell bent his head moodily. He was caught in a vise of circumstances. It had not been loyalty to Shaibar Kahn, as Suleiman thought, which had caused him to dump an emperor's ransom in gold and jewels into the subterranean river. He knew Suleiman plotted the overthrow of British rule in India and the massacre of the helpless millions. He knew that Orkhan Bahadur, a ruthless adventurer despite his friendship for the false Kurd, was a pliant tool in the emmissary's hands. The treasure had been too potent a weapon to leave within their reach.

Suleiman was either a Russian or the Oriental tool of the Russians. Perhaps he, too, had secret ambitions. The Khuwarezm treasure had been a pawn in his game; but, even without it, a tool of the emissary's sitting on the throne of Shahrazar, was a living menace to the peace of India. So O'Donnell had remained in the city, seeking in every way to thwart Suleiman's efforts to dominate Orkhan Bahadur. And now he himself was trapped.

He lifted his head and stared murderously at the slim Oriental. 'What do you wish me to do?' he muttered.

'I have a task for you,' answered Suleiman. 'An hour ago word came to me, by one of my secret agents, that the tribesmen of Khuruk had found an Englishman dying in the hills, with valuable papers upon him. I must have those papers. I sent the man on to Orkhan, while I dealt with you.

'But I have changed my plans in regard to you; you

are more valuable to me alive than dead, since there is no danger of your opposing me in the future. Orkhan will desire those papers that the Englishman carried, for the man was undoubtedly a secret-service agent, and I will persuade the prince to send you with a troop of horsemen to secure them. And remember you are taking your real orders from me, not from Orkhan.'

He stepped aside and motioned O'Donnell to precede him.

They traversed the short corridor, an electric torch in Suleiman's left hand playing its beam on his sullen, watchful companion, climbed the stair and went through the wide hall, thence along a winding corridor and into a chamber where Orkhan Bahadur stood near a gold-barred window which opened onto an arcaded court, which was just being whitened by dawn. The prince of Shahrazar was resplendent in satin and pearl-sewn velvet which did not mask the hard lines of his lean body.

His thin dark features lighted at the sight of his cup-companion, but O'Donnell reflected on the wolf that lurked ever below the surface of this barbaric chieftain, and how suddenly it could be unmasked, snarling and flame-eyed.

'Welcome, friends!' said the Turkoman, pacing the chamber restlessly. 'I have heard a tale! Three days' ride to the southwest are the villages of Ahmed Shah, in the valley of Khuruk. Four days ago his men came upon a man dying in the mountains. He wore the garments of an Afghan, but in his delirium he revealed himself as an Englishman. When he was dead they searched him for loot and found certain papers which none of the dogs could read.

'But in his ravings he spoke of having been to Bowhara. It is in my mind that this *Feringi* was an English spy, returning to India with papers valuable to the *sirkar*. Perhaps the British would pay well for these papers, if they knew of them. It is my wish to possess them. Yet I dare not ride forth myself, nor send many men. Suppose the treasure was found in my absence? My own men would bar the gates against me.'

'This is a matter for diplomacy rather than force,' put in Suleiman Pasha smoothly. 'Ali el Ghazi is crafty as well as bold. Send him with fifty men.'

'Can thou do it, brother?' demanded Orkhan eagerly.

Suleiman's gaze burned into O'Donnell's soul. There was but one answer, if he wished to escape flaying steel and searing fire.

'Only in Allah is power,' he muttered. 'Yet I can attempt the thing.'

'*Mashallah!*' exclaimed Orkhan. 'Be ready to start within the hour. There is a Khurukzai in the *suk*, one Dost Shah, who is of Ahmed's clan, and will guide you. There is friendship between me and the men of Khuruk. Approach Ahmed Shah in peace and offer him gold for the papers, but not too much, lest his cupidity be roused. But I leave it to your own judgement. With fifty men there is no fear of the smaller clans between Shahrazar and Khuruk. I go now to choose the men to ride with you.'

As soon as Orkhan left the chamber, Suleiman bent close to O'Donnell and whispered: 'Secure the papers, but do not bring them to Orkhan! Pretend that you have lost them in the hills—anything—but bring them to *me*.'

'Orkhan will be angry and suspicious,' objected O'Donnell.

'Not half as angry as he would be if he knew what became of the Khuwarezm treasure,' retorted Suleiman. 'Your only chance is to obey me. If your men return without you, saying you have fled away, be sure a hundred men will quickly be upon your trail—nor can you hope to win alone through these hostile, devil-haunted hills, anyway. Do not dare to return without the papers, if you do not wish to be denounced to Orkhan. Your life depends on your playing my game, Kurd!'

2

Playing Suleiman's 'game' seemed to be the only thing to do, even three days later as O'Donnell, in his guise of the Kurdish swashbuckler, Ali el Ghazi, was riding along a trail that followed a ledgelike fold of rock ribbing a mile-wide cliff.

Just ahead of him on a bony crowbait rode the Khurukzai guide, a hairy savage with a dirty white turban, and behind him strung out in single file fifty of Orkhan Bahadur's picked warriors. O'Donnell felt the pride of a good leader of fighting men as he glanced back at them. These were no stunted peasants, but tall, sinewy men with the pride and temper of hawks; nomads and sons of nomads, born to the saddle. They rode horses that were distinctive in that land of horsemen, and their rifles were modern repeaters.

'Listen!' It was the Khurukzai who halted, suddenly, lifting a hand in warning.

O'Donnell leaned forward, rising in the wide silver stirrups, turning his head slightly sidewise. A gust of wind whipped along the ledge, bearing with it the echoes of a series of sputtering reports.

The men behind O'Donnell heard it, too, and there was a creaking of saddles as they instinctively unslung rifles and hitched yataghan hilts forward.

'Rifles!' exclaimed Dost Shah. 'Men are fighting in the hills.'

'How far are we from Khuruk?' asked O'Donnell.

'An hour's ride,' answered the Khurukzai, glancing at the mid-afternoon sun. 'Beyond the corner of the cliff we can see the Pass of Akbar, which is the boundary of Ahmed Shah's territory. Khuruk is some miles beyond.'

'Push on, then,' said O'Donnell.

They moved on around the crag which jutted out like the prow of a ship, shutting off all view to the south. The path narrowed and sloped there, so the men dismounted and edged their way, leading the animals which grew half frantic with fear.

Ahead of them the trail broadened and sloped up to a fan-shaped plateau, flanked by rugged ridges. This plateau narrowed to a pass in a solid wall of rock hundreds of feet high; the pass was a triangular gash, and a stone tower in its mouth commanded the approach. There were men in the tower, and they were firing at other men who lay out on the plateau in a wide ragged crescent, concealed behind boulders and rocky ledges. But these were not all firing at the tower, as it presently became apparent.

Off to the left of the pass, skirting the foot of the cliffs, a ravine meandered. Men were hiding in this ravine, and O'Donnell quickly saw that they were trapped there. The men out on the plateau had cast a cordon around it and were working their way closer, shooting as they came. The men in the ravine fired back, and a few corpses were strewn among the rocks. But from the sound of the firing, there were only a few men in the gully, and the men in the tower could not come to their aid. It would have been suicide to try to trust that bullet-swept open space between the ravine and the pass mouth.

O'Donnell had halted his men at an angle of the cliff where the trail wound up toward the plateau, and had advanced with the Khurukzai guide part way up the incline.

'What does this mean?' he asked.

Dost Shah shook his head like one puzzled. 'That is the Pass of Akbar,' he said. 'That tower is Ahmed Shah's. Sometimes the tribes come to fight us, and we shoot them from the tower. It can only be Ahmed's riflemen in the tower and in the ravine. But—'

He shook his head again, and having tied his horse to a straggling tamarisk, he went up the slope, craning his neck and hugging his rifle, while he muttered in his beard as if in uncertainty.

O'Donnell followed him to the crest where the trail bent over the rim of the plateau, but with more caution

than the Khurukzai was showing. They were now within
rifle range of the combatants, and bullets were whistling
like hornets across the plateau.

O'Donnell could plainly make out the forms of the
besiegers lying among the rocks that littered the narrow
plain. Evidently they had not noticed him and the guide,
and he did not believe they saw his men where he had
stationed them in the shade of an overhanging crag. All
their attention was fixed on the ravine, and they yelled
with fierce exultation as a turban thrust above its rim fell
back splashed with crimson. The men in the tower yelled
with helpless fury.

'Keep your head down, you fool!' O'Donnell swore at
Dost Shah, who was carelessly craning his long neck above
a cluster of rocks.

'The men in the tower *must* be Ahmed's men,' muttered
Dost Shah uneasily. 'Yes; it could not be otherwise,
yet—Allah!' The last was an explosive yelp, and he sprang
up like a madman, as if forgetting all caution in some other
overwhelming emotion.

O'Donnell cursed and grabbed at him to pull him
down, but he stood brandishing his rifle, his tattered
garments whipping in the wind like a demon of the hills.

'What devil's work is this?' he yelled. 'That is not—
those are not—'

His voice changed to a gasp as a bullet drilled him
through the temple. He tumbled back to the ground and
lay without motion.

'Now what was he going to say?' muttered O'Donnell,
peering out over the rocks. 'Was that a stray slug, or did
somebody see him?'

He could not tell whether the shot came from the
boulders or the tower. It was typical of hill warfare,
the yells and shooting keeping up an incessant devil's
din. One thing was certain: the cordon was gradually
closing about the men trapped in the ravine. They
were well hidden from the bullets, but the attackers
were working so close that presently they could finish

the job with a short swift rush and knife work at close quarters.

O'Donnell fell back down the incline, and coming to the eager Turkomans, spoke hurriedly: 'Dost Shah is dead, but he has brought us to the borders of Ahmed Shah's territory. Those in the tower are Khurukzai, and these men attacking them have cut off some chief—probably Ahmed Shah himself—in that ravine. I judge that from the noise both sides are making. Then, they'd scarcely be taking such chances to slaughter a few common warriors. If we rescue him we shall have a claim on his friendship, and our task will be made easy, as Allah makes all things for brave men.

'The men attacking seem to me not to number more than a hundred men—twice our number, true, but there are circumstances in our favor, surprise, and the fact that the men in the pass will undoubtedly sally out if we create a diversion in the enemy's rear. At present the Khurukzai are bottled in the pass. They cannot emerge, any more than the raiders can enter in the teeth of their bullets.'

'We await orders,' the men answered.

Turkomans have no love for Kurds, but the horsemen knew that Ali el Ghazi was cup-companion to their prince.

'Ten men to hold the horses!' he snapped. 'The rest follow me.'

A few minutes later they were crawling after him up the short slope. He lined them along the crest, seeing that each man was sheltered among the boulders.

This took but a few minutes, but in that interim the men crawling toward the ravine sprang to their feet and tore madly across the intervening space, yelling like blood-crazed wolves, their curved blades glittering in the sun. Rifles spat from the gully and three of the attackers dropped, and the men in the tower sent up an awful howl and turned their guns desperately on the charging mob. But the range at that angle was too great.

Then O'Donnell snapped an order, and a withering line of flame ran along the crest of the ridge. His men were picked marksmen and understood the value of volleys. Some thirty men were in the open, charging the ravine. A full half of them went down struck from behind, as if by some giant invisible fist. The others halted, realizing that something was wrong; they cringed dazedly, turning here and there, grasping their long knives, while the bullets of the Turkomans took further toll.

Then, suddenly, realizing that they were being attacked from the rear, they dived screaming for cover. The men in the tower, sensing reinforcements, sent up a wild shout and redoubled their fire.

The Turkomans, veterans of a hundred wild battles, hugged their boulders and kept aiming and firing without the slightest confusion. The men on the plateau were kicking up the devil's own din. They were caught in the jaws of the vise, with bullets coming from both ways, and no way of knowing the exact numbers of their new assailants.

The break came with hurricane suddenness, as is nearly always the case in hill fighting. The men on the plain broke and fled westward, a disorderly mob, scrambling over boulders and leaping gullies, their tattered garments flapping in the wind.

The Turkomans sent a last volley into their backs, toppling over distant figures like tenpins, and the men in the tower gave tongue and began scrambling down into the pass.

O'Donnell cast a practised eye at the fleeing marauders, knew that the rout was final, and called for the ten men below him to bring up the horses swiftly. He had an eye for dramatics, and he knew the effect they would make filing over the ridge and out across the boulder-strewn plain on their Turkish steeds.

A few minutes later he enjoyed that effect and the surprised yells of the men they had aided as they saw the Astrakhan *kalpaks* of the riders top the ridge.

The pass was crowded with men in ragged garments, grasping rifles, and in evident doubt as to the status of the newcomers.

O'Donnell headed straight for the ravine, which was nearer the ridge than it was to the pass, believing the Khurukzai chief was among those trapped there.

His rifle was slung on his back, and his open right hand raised as a sign of peace; seeing which the men in the pass dubiously lowered their rifles and came streaming across the plateau toward him, instead of pursuing the vanquished, who were already disappearing among the distant crags and gulches.

A dozen steps from the edge of the ravine O'Donnell drew rein, glimpsing turbans among the rocks, and called out a greeting in *Pashtu*. A deep bellowing voice answered him, and a vast figure heaved up into full view, followed by half a dozen lesser shapes.

'Allah be with thee!' roared the first man.

He was tall, broad, and powerful; his beard was stained with henna, and his eyes blazed like fires burning under gray ice. One massive fist gripped a rifle, the thumb of the other was hooked into the broad silken girdle which banded his capacious belly, as he tilted back on his heels and thrust his beard out truculently. That girdle likewise supported a broad tulwar and three or four knives.

'*Mashallah!*' roared this individual. 'I had thought it was my own men who had taken the dogs in the rear, until I saw those fur caps. Ye are Turks from Shahrazar, no doubt?'

'Aye; I am Ali el Ghazi, a Kurd, brother-in-arms to Orkhan Bahadur. You are Ahmed Shah, lord of Khuruk?'

There was a hyena-like cackle of laughter from the lean, evil-eyed men who had followed the big man out of the gully.

'Ahmed Shah has been in hell these four days,' rumbled the giant. 'I am Afzal Khan, whom men name the Butcher.'

O'Donnell sensed rather than heard a slight stir among
the men behind him. Most of them understood *Pashtu*,
and the deeds of Afzal Khan had found echo in the *serais* of
Turkestan. The man was an outlaw, even in that lawless
land, a savage plunderer whose wild road was lurid with
the smoke and blood of slaughter.

'But that pass is the gateway to Khuruk,' said
O'Donnell, slightly bewildered.

'Aye!' agreed Afzal Khan affably. 'Four days ago
I came down into the valley from the east and drove
out the Khurukzai dogs. Ahmed Shah I slew with my
own hands—so!'

A flicker of red akin to a madness flamed up
momentarily in his eyes as he smashed the butt of
his rifle down on a dead tamarisk branch, shattering it
from the trunk. It was as if the mere mention of murder
roused the sleeping devil in him. Then his beard bristled
in a fierce grin.

'The villages of Khuruk I burned,' he said calmly.
'My men need no roofs between them and the sky. The
village dogs—such as still lived—fled into hills. This day
I was hunting some from among the rocks, not deeming
them wise enough to plant an ambush, when they cut
me off from the pass, and the rest you know. I took
refuge in the ravine. When I heard your firing I thought
it was my own men.'

O'Donnell did not at once answer, but sat his horse,
gazing inscrutably at the fierce, scared countenance
of the Afghan. A sidelong glance showed him the
men from the tower straggling up—some seventy of
them, a wild, dissolute band, ragged and hairy, with
wolfish countenances and rifles in their hands. These
rifles were, in most cases, inferior to those carried
by his own men.

In a battle begun then and there, the advantage was
still with the mounted Turkomans. Then another glance
showed him more men swarming out of the pass—a
hundred at least.

'The dogs come at last!' grunted Afzal Khan. 'They have been gorging back in the valley. I would have been vulture bait if I had been forced to await their coming. Brother!' He strode forward to lay his hand on O'Donnell stirrup strap, while envy of the admiration for the magnificent Turkish stallion burned in his fierce eyes. 'Brother, come with me to Khuruk! You have saved my life this day, and I would reward you fittingly.'

O'Donnell did not look at his Turkomans. He knew they were waiting for his orders and would obey him. He could draw his pistol and shoot Afzal Khan dead, and they could cut their way back across the plateau in the teeth of the volleys that were sure to rake their line of flight. Many would escape. But why escape? Afzal Khan had every reason to show them the face of a friend, and, besides, if he had killed Ahmed Shah, it was logical to suppose that he had the papers without which O'Donnell dared not return to Shahrazar.

'We will ride with you to Khuruk, Afzal Khan,' decided O'Donnell.

The Afghan combed his crimson beard with his fingers and boomed his gratification.

The ragged ruffians closed in about them as they rode toward the pass, a swarm of sheepskin coats and soiled turbans that hemmed in the clean-cut riders in their fur caps and girdled *kaftans*.

O'Donnell did not miss the envy in the glances cast at the rifles and cartridge belts and horses of the Turkomans. Orkhan Bahadur was generous with his men to the point of extravagance; he had sent them out with enough ammunition to fight a small war.

Afzal Khan strode by O'Donnell stirrup, booming his comments and apparently oblivious to everything except the sound of his own voice.

O'Donnell glanced from him to his followers. Afzal Khan was a Yusufzai, a pure-bred Afghan, but his men were a motley mob—Pathans, mostly, Orakzai, Ummer

Khels, Sudozai, Afridis, Ghilzai—outcasts and nameless men from many tribes.

They went through the pass—a knifecut gash between sheer rock walls, forty feet wide and three hundred yards long—and beyond the tower were a score of gaunt horses which Afzal Khan and some of his favored henchmen mounted. Then the chief gave pungent orders to his men; fifty of them climbed into the tower and resumed the ceaseless vigilance that is the price of life in the hills, and the rest followed him and his guests out of the pass and along the knife-edge trail that wound amid savage crags and jutting spurs.

Afzal Khan fell silent, and indeed there was scant opportunity for conversation, each man being occupied in keeping his horse or his own feet on the wavering path. The surrounding crags were so rugged and lofty that the strategic importance of the Pass of Akbar impressed itself still more strongly on O'Donnell.

Only through that pass could any body of men make their way safely. He felt uncomfortably like a man who sees a door shut behind him, blocking his escape, and he glanced furtively at Afzal Khan, riding with stirrups so short that he squatted like a huge toad in his saddle. The chief seemed preoccupied; he gnawed a wisp of his red beard and there was a blank stare in his eyes.

The sun was swinging low when they came to a second pass. This was not exactly a pass at all, in the usual sense. It was an opening in a cluster of rocky spurs that rose like fangs along the lip of a rim beyond which the land fell away in a long gradual sweep. Threading among these stony teeth, O'Donnell looked down into the valley of Khuruk.

It was not a deep valley, but it was flanked by cliffs that looked unscalable. It ran east and west, roughly, and they were entering it at the eastern end. At the western end it seemed to be blocked by a mass of crags.

There were no cultivated patches, or houses to be seen in the valley—only stretches of charred ground. Evidently the destruction of the Khurukzai villages had been thorough. In the midst of the valley stood a square stone inclosure, with a tower at one corner, such as are common in the hills, and serve as forts in times of strife.

Divining his thought, Afzal Khan pointed to this and said: 'I struck like a thunderbolt. They had not time to take refuge in the *sangar*. Their watchmen on the heights were careless. We stole upon them and knifed them; then in the dawn we swept down on the villages Nay, some escaped. We could not slay them all. They will keep coming back to harass me—as they have done this day—until I hunt them down and wipe them all out.'

O'Donnell had not mentioned the papers; to have done so would have been foolish; he could think of no way to question Afzal Khan without waking the Afghan's suspicions; he must await his opportunity.

That opportunity came unexpectedly.

'Can you read *Urdu*?' asked Afzal Khan abruptly.

'Aye!' O'Donnell made no further comment but waited with concealed tenseness.

'I cannot; nor *Pashtu*, either, for that matter,' rumbled the Afghan. 'There were papers on Ahmed Shah's body, which I believe are written in *Urdu*.'

'I might be able to read them for you.'

O'Donnell tried to speak casually, but perhaps he was not able to keep his eagerness altogether out of his voice. Afzal Khan tugged his beard, glanced at him sidewise, and changed the subject. He spoke no more of the papers and made no move to show them to his guest. O'Donnell silently cursed his own impatience; but at least he had learned that the documents he sought were in the bandit's possession, and that Afzal Khan was ignorant of their nature—if he was not lying.

At a growled order all but sixty of the chief's men halted among the spurs overlooking the valley. The rest trailed after him.

'They watch for the Khurukzai dogs,' he explained. 'There are trails by which a few men might get through the hills, avoiding the Pass of Akbar, and reach the head of the valley.'

'Is this the only entrance to Khuruk?'

'The only one that horses can travel. There are footpaths leading through the crags from the north and the south, but I have men posted there as well. One rifleman can hold any one of them forever. My forces are scattered about the valley. I am not to be taken by surprise as I took Ahmed Shah.'

The sun was sinking behind the western hills as they rode down the valley, tailed by the men on foot. All were strangely silent, as if oppressed by the silence of the plundered valley. Their destination evidently was the inclosure, which stood perhaps a mile from the head of the valley. The valley floor was unusually free of boulders and stones, except a broken ledge like a reef that ran across the valley several hundred yards east of the fortalice. Halfway between these rocks and the inclosure, Afzal Khan halted.

'Camp here!' he said abruptly, with a tone more of command than invitation. 'My men and I occupy the *sangar*, and it is well to keep our wolves somewhat apart. There is a place where your horses can be stabled, where there is plenty of fodder stored.' He pointed out a stone-walled pen of considerable dimensions a few hundred yards away, near the southern cliffs. 'Hungry wolves come down from the gorges and attack the horses.'

'We will camp beside the pen,' said O'Donnell, preferring to be closer to their mounts.

Afzal Khan showed a flash of irritation. 'Do you wish to be shot in the dark for an enemy?' he growled. 'Pitch your tents where I bid you. I have told my men at the pass where you will camp, and if any of them come down the valley in the dark, and hear men where no men are supposed to be, they will shoot first and investigate later. Beside, the Khurukzai dogs, if they creep upon the crags and see men sleeping beneath them, will roll down boulders and crush you like insects.'

This seemed reasonable enough, and O'Donnell had no wish to antagonize Afzal Khan. The Afghan's attitude seemed a mixture of his natural domineering arrogance and an effort at geniality. This was what might be expected, considering both the man's nature and his present obligation. O'Donnell believed that Afzal Khan begrudged the obligation, but recognized it.

'We have no tents,' answered the American. 'We need none. We sleep in our cloaks.' And he ordered his men to dismount at the spot designated by the chief. They at once unsaddled and led their horses to the pen, where, as the Afghan had declared, there was an abundance of fodder.

O'Donnell told off five men to guard them. Not, he hastened to explain to the frowning chief, that they feared human thieves, but there were the wolves to be considered. Afzal Khan grunted and turned his own sorry steeds into the pen, growling in his beard at the contrast they made alongside the Turkish horses.

His men showed no disposition to fraternize with the Turkomans; they entered the inclosure and presently the smoke of cooking fires arose. O'Donnell's own men set about preparing their scanty meal, and Afzal Khan came and stood over them, combing his crimson beard that the firelight turned to blood. The jeweled hilts of his knives gleamed in the glow, and his eyes burned red like the eyes of a hawk.

'Our fare is poor,' he said abruptly. 'Those Khurukzai dogs burned their own huts and food stores when they fled before us. We are half starved. I can offer you no food, though you are my guests. But there is a well in the *sangar*, and I have sent some of my men to fetch some steers we have in a pen outside the valley. To-morrow we shall all feast full, *inshallah!*'

O'Donnell murmured a polite response, but he was conscious of a vague uneasiness. Afzal Khan was acting in a most curious manner, even for a bandit who trampled all laws and customs of conventional conduct. He gave them orders one instant and almost apologized for them in the next.

The matter of designating the camp site sounded almost as if they were prisoners, yet he had made no attempt to disarm them. His men were sullen and silent, even for bandits. But he had no reason to be hostile toward his guests, and, even if he had, why had he brought them to Khuruk, when he could have wiped them out up in the hills just as easily?

'Ali el Ghazi,' Afzal Khan suddenly repeated the name. 'Wherefore Ghazi? What infidel didst thou slay to earn the name?'

'The Russian, Colonel Ivan Kurovitch.' O'Donnell spoke no lie there. As Ali el Ghazi, a Kurd, he was known as the slayer of Kurovitch; the duel had occurred in one of the myriad nameless skirmishes along the border.

Afzal Khan meditated this matter for a few minutes. The firelight cast part of his features in shadow, making his expression seem even more sinister than usual. He loomed in the firelit shadows like a somber monster weighing the doom of men. Then with a grunt he turned and strode away toward the *sangar*.

3

Night had fallen. Wind moaned among the crags. Cloud masses moved across the dark vault of the night, obscuring the stars which blinked here and there, were blotted out and then reappearing, like chill points of frosty silver. The Turkomans squatted silently about their tiny fires, casting furtive glances over their shoulders.

Men of the deserts, the brooding grimness of the dark mountains daunted them; the night pressing down in the bowl of the valley dwarfed them in its immensity. They shivered at the wailing of the wind, and peered fearfully into the darkness, where, according to their superstitions, the ghosts of murdered men roamed ghoulishly. They stared bleakly at O'Donnell, in the grip of fear and paralyzing fatalism.

The grimness and desolation of the night had its effect on the American. A foreboding of disaster oppressed him. There was something about Afzal Khan he could not fathom—something unpredictable.

The man had lived too long outside the bounds of ordinary humanity to be judged by the standards of common men. In his present state of mind the bandit chief assumed monstrous proportions, like an ogre out of a fable.

O'Donnell shook himself angrily. Afzal Khan was only a man, who would die if bitten by lead or steel, like any other man. As for treachery, what would be the motive? Yet the foreboding remained.

'To-morrow we will feast,' he told his men. 'Afzal Khan has said it.'

They stared at him somberly, with the instincts of the black forests and the haunted steppes in their eyes which gleamed wolfishly in the firelight.

'The dead feast not,' muttered one of them.

'What talk is this?' rebuked O'Donnell. 'We are living men, not dead.'

'We have not eaten salt with Afzal Khan,' replied the Turkoman. 'We camp here in the open, hemmed in by his slayers on either hand. Aie, we are already dead men. We are sheep led to the butcher.'

O'Donnell stared hard at his men, startled at their voicing the vague fears that troubled him. There was no accusation of his leadership in their voices. They merely spoke their beliefs in a detached way that belied the fear in their eyes. They believed they were to die, and he was beginning to believe they were right. The fires were dying down, and there was no more fuel to build them up. Some of the men wrapped themselves in their cloaks and lay down on the hard ground. Others remained sitting cross-legged on their saddle cloths, their heads bent on their breasts.

O'Donnell rose and walked toward the first outcropping of the rocks, where he turned and stared back at the inclosure. The fires had died down there to a glow. No sound came from the sullen walls. A mental picture formed itself in his mind, resultant from his visit to the redoubt for water.

It was a bare wall inclosing a square space. At the northwest corner rose a tower. At the southwest corner there was a well. Once a tower had protected the well, but now it was fallen into ruins, so that only a hint of it remained. There was nothing else in the inclosure except a small stone hut with a thatched roof. What was in the hut he had no way of knowing. Afzal Khan had remarked that he slept alone in the tower. The chief did not trust his own men too far.

What was Afzal Khan's game? He was not dealing straight with O'Donnell; that was obvious. Some of his evasions and pretenses were transparent; the man was not as clever as one might suppose; he was more like a bull that wins by ferocious charges.

But why should he practice deception? What had he to gain? O'Donnell had smelled meat cooking in the fortalice. There was food in the valley, then, but for some reason the Afghan had denied it. The Turkomans knew that; to them it logically suggested but one thing—he would not share the salt with men he intended to murder. But again, why?

'*Ohai*, Ali el Ghazi!'

At that hiss out of the darkness, O'Donnell wheeled, his big pistol jumping into his hand, his skin pricking. He strained his eyes, but saw nothing; heard only the muttering of the night wind.

'Who is it?' he demanded guardedly. 'Who calls?'

'A friend! Hold your fire!'

O'Donnell saw a more solid shadow detach itself from the rocks and move toward him. With his thumb pressing back the fanged hammer of his pistol, he shoved the muzzle against the man's belly and leaned forward to glare into the hairy face in the dim, uncertain starlight. Even so the darkness was so thick the fellow's features were only a blur.

'Do you not know me?' whispered the man, and by his accent O'Donnell knew him for a Waziri. 'I am Yar Muhammad!'

'Yar Muhammad!' Instantly the gun went out of sight and O'Donnell's hand fell on the other's bull-like shoulder. 'What do you in this den of thieves?'

The man's teeth glimmered in the tangle of his beard as he grinned. *'Mashallah!* Am I not a thief, El Shirkuh?' he asked, giving O'Donnell the name by which the American, in his rightful person, was known to the Moslems. 'Hast thou forgotten the old days? Even now the British would hang me, if they could catch me. But no matter. I was one of those who watch the paths in the hills.

'An hour ago I was relieved, and when I returned to the *sangar* I heard men talking of the Turkomans who camped in the valley outside, and it was said their chief was the Kurd who slew the infidel Kurovitch. So I knew it was El Shirkuh playing with doom again. Art thou mad, sahib? Death spreads his wings above thee and all thy men. Afzal Khan plots that thou seest no other sunrise.'

'I was suspicious of him,' muttered the American. 'In the matter of food—'

'The hut in the inclosure is full of food. Why waste beef and bread on dead men? Food is scarce enough in these hills—and at dawn you die.'

'But why? We saved Afzal Khan's life, and there is no feud—'

'The Jhelum will flow backward when Afzal Khan spares a man because of gratitude,' muttered Yar Muhammad.

'But for what reason?'

'By Allah, sahib, are you blind? Reason? Are not fifty Turkish steeds reason enough? Are not fifty rifles with cartridges reason enough? In these hills firearms and cartridges are worth their weight in silver, and a man will murder his brother for a matchlock. Afzal Khan is a robber, and he covets what you possess.

'These weapons and these horses would lend him great strength. He is ambitious. He would draw to him many more men, make himself strong enough at last to dispute the rule of these hills with Orkhan Bahadur. Nay, he plots some day to take Shahrazar from the Turkoman as he in his turn took it from the Uzbeks. What is the goal of every bandit in these hills, rich or poor? *Mashallah!* The treasure of Khuwarezm!'

O'Donnell was silent, visualizing that accursed hoard as a monstrous loadstone drawing all the evil passions of men from near lands and far. Now it was but an empty shadow men coveted, but they could not know it, and its evil power was as great as ever. He felt an insane desire to laugh.

The wind moaned in the dark, and Yar Muhammad's muttering voice merged eerily with it, unintelligible a yard away.

'Afzal Khan feels no obligation toward you, because you thought it was Ahmed Shah you were aiding. He did not attack you at the Pass because he knew you would slay many of his men, and he feared lest the horses take harm in the battle. Now he has you in a trap as he planned. Sixty men inside the *sangar*; a hundred more at the head of the valley. A short time before moonrise, the men among the spurs will creep down the valley and take position among these rocks. Then when the moon is well risen, so that a man may aim, they will rake you with rifle fire.

'Most of the Turkomans will die in their sleep, and such as live and seek to flee in the other direction will be shot by the men in the inclosure. These sleep now, but sentries keep watch. I slipped out over the western side and have been lying here wondering how to approach your camp without being shot for a prowler.

'Afzal Khan has plotted well. He has you in the perfect trap, with the horses well out of the range of the bullets that will slay their riders.'

'So,' murmured O'Donnell. 'And what is your plan?'

'Plan? Allah, when did I ever have a plan? Nay, that is for you! I know these hills, and I can shoot straight and strike a good blow.' His yard-long Khyber knife thrummed as he swung it through the air. 'But I only follow where wiser men lead. I heard the men talk, and I came to warn you, because once you turned an Afridi blade from my breast, and again you broke the lock on the Peshawar jail where I lay moaning for the hills!'

O'Donnell did not express his gratitude; that was not necessary. But he was conscious of a warm glow toward the hairy ruffian. Man's treachery is balanced by man's loyalty, at least in the barbaric hills where civilized sophistry has not crept in with its cult of time-serving.

'Can you guide us through the mountains?' asked O'Donnell.

'Nay, Sahib; the horses can not follow these paths; and these booted Turks would die on foot.'

'It is nearly two hours yet until moonrise,' O'Donnell muttered. 'To saddle horses now would be to betray us. Some of us might get away in the darkness, but—'

He was thinking of the papers that were the price of his life; but it was not altogether that. Flight in the darkness would mean scattered forces, even though they cut their away out of the valley. Without his guidance the Turkomans would be hopelessly lost; such as were separated from the main command would perish miserably.

'Come with me,' he said at last, and hurried back to the men who lay about the charring embers.

At his whisper they rose like ghouls out of the blackness and clustered about him, muttering like suspicious dogs at the Waziri. O'Donnell could scarcely make out the hawklike faces that pressed close about him. All the stars were hidden by dark clouds. The fortalice was but a shapeless bulk in the darkness, and the flanking mountains were masses of solid blackness. The whining wind drowned voices a few yards away.

'Hearken and speak not,' O'Donnell ordered. 'This is Yar Muhammad, a friend and a true man. We are betrayed. Afzal Khan is a dog, who will slay us for our horses. Nay, listen! In the *sangar* there is a thatched hut. I am going into the inclosure and fire that thatch. When you see the blaze, and hear my pistol speak, rush the wall. Some of you will die, but the surprise will be on our side. We must take the *sangar* and hold it against the men who will come down the valley at moonrise. It is a desperate plan, but the best that offers itself.'

'*Bismillah!*' they murmured softly, and he heard the rasp of blades clearing their scabbards.

'This is work indeed for cold steel,' he said. 'You must rush the wall and swarm it while the Pathans are dazed with surprise. Send one man for the warriors at the horse pen. Be of good heart; the rest is on Allah's lap.'

As he crept away in the darkness, with Yar Muhammad following him like a bent shadow, O'Donnell was aware that the attitude of the Turkomans had changed; they had wakened out of their fatalistic lethargy into fierce tension.

'If I fall,' O'Donnell murmured, 'will you guide these men back to Shahrazar? Orkhan Bahadur will reward you.'

'Shaitan eat Orkhan Bahadur,' answered Yar Muhammad. 'What care I for these *Turki* dogs? It is you, not they, for whom I risk my skin.'

O'Donnell had given the Waziri his rifle. They swung around the south side of the inclosure, almost crawling on their bellies. No sound came from the breastwork, no light showed. O'Donnell knew that they were invisible to whatever eyes were straining into the darkness along the wall. Circling wide, they approached the unguarded western wall.

'Afzal Khan sleeps in the tower,' muttered Yar Muhammad, his lips close to O'Donnell's ear. 'Sleeps or pretends to sleep. The men slumber beneath the eastern wall. All the sentries lurk on that side, trying to watch the Turkomans. They have allowed the fires to die, to lull suspicion.'

'Over the wall, then,' whispered O'Donnell, rising and gripping the coping. He glided over with no more noise than the wind in the dry tamarisk, and Yar Muhammad followed him as silently. He stood in the thicker shadow of the wall, placing everything in his mind before he moved.

The hut was before him, a blob of blackness. It looked eastward and was closer to the west wall than to the other. Near it a cluster of dying coals glowed redly. There was no light in the tower, in the northwest angle of the wall.

Bidding Yar Muhammad remain near the wall, O'Donnell stole toward the embers. When he reached them he could make out the forms of the men sleeping between the hut and the east wall. It was like these hardened killers to sleep at such a time. Why not? At the word of their master they would rise and slay. Until the time came it was good to sleep. O'Donnell himself had slept, and eaten, too, among the corpses of a battlefield.

Dim figures along the wall were sentinels. They did not turn; motionless as statues they leaned on the wall staring into the darkness out of which, in the hills, anything might come.

There was a half-burned faggot dying in the embers, one end a charring stump which glowed redly. O'Donnell reached out and secured it. Yar Muhammad, watching from the wall, shivered, though he knew what it was. It was as if a detached hand had appeared for an instant in the dim glow and then disappeared, and then, a red point moved toward him.

'Allah!' swore the Waziri. 'This blackness is that of Jehannum!'

'Softly!' O'Donnell whispered at him from the pit darkness. 'Be ready; now is the beginning of happenings.'

The ember glowed and smoked as he blew cautiously upon it. A tiny tongue of flame grew, licking at the wood.

'Commend thyself to Allah!' said O'Donnell, and

whirling the brand in a flaming wheel about his head, he
cast it into the thatch of the hut.

There was a tense instant in which a tongue of
flame flickered and crackled, and then in one hungry
combustion the dry stuff leaped ablaze, and the figures of
men started out of blank blackness with startling clarity.
The guards wheeled, their stupid astonishment etched in
the glare, and men sat up in their cloaks on the ground,
gaping bewilderedly.

And O'Donnell yelled like a hungry wolf and began
jerking the trigger of his pistol.

A sentinel spun on his heel and crumpled, discharging
his rifle wildly in the air. Others were howling and
staggering like drunken men, reeling and falling in
the lurid glare. Yar Muhammad was blazing away with
O'Donnell's rifle, shooting down his former companions
as cheerfully as if they were ancient enemies.

A matter of seconds elapsed between the time the blaze
sprang up and the time when the men were scurrying
about wildly, etched in the merciless light and unable
to see the two men who crouched in the shadow of the
far wall, raining them with lead. But in that scant instant
there came another sound—a swift thudding of feet, the
daunting sound of men rushing through the darkness in
desperate haste and desperate silence.

Some of the Pathans heard it and turned to glare
into the night. The fire behind them rendered the
outer darkness more impenetrable. They could not see
the death that was racing fleetly toward them, until the
charge reached the wall.

Then a yell of terror went up as the men along the
wall caught a glimpse of glittering eyes and flickering steel
rushing out of the blackness. They fired one wild, ragged
volley, and then the Turkomans surged up over the wall
in an irresistible wave and were slashing and hacking like
madmen among the defenders.

Scarcely wakened, demoralized by the surprise, and

by the bullets that cut them down from behind, the Pathans were beaten almost before the fight began. Some of them fled over the wall without any attempt at defense, but some fought, snarling and stabbing like wolves. The blazing thatch etched the scene in a lurid glare. *Kalpaks* mingled with turbans, and steel flickered over the seething mob. Yataghans grated against tulwars, and blood spurted.

His pistol empty, O'Donnell ran toward the tower. He had momentarily expected Afzal Khan to appear. But in such moments it is impossible to retain a proper estimate of time. A minute may seem like an hour, an hour like a minute. In reality, the Afghan chief came storming out of the tower just as the Turkomans came surging over the wall. Perhaps he had really been asleep, or perhaps caution kept him from rushing out sooner. Gunfire might mean rebellion against his authority.

At any rate he came roaring like a wounded bull, a rifle in his hands. O'Donnell rushed toward him, but the Afghan glared beyond him to where his swordsmen were falling like wheat under the blades of the maddened Turkomans. He saw the fight was already lost, as far as the men in the inclosure were concerned, and he sprang for the nearest wall.

O'Donnell raced to pull him down, but Afzal Khan, wheeling, fired from the hip. The American felt a heavy blow in his belly, and then he was down on the ground, with all the breath gone from him. Afzal Khan yelled in triumph, brandished his rifle, and was gone over the wall, heedless of the vengeful bullet Yar Muhammad sped after him.

The Waziri had followed O'Donnell across the inclosure and now he knelt beside him, yammering as he fumbled to find the American's wound.

'Aie!' he bawled. 'He is slain! My friend and brother! Where will his like be found again? Slain by the bullet of a hillman! Aie! Aie! Aie!'

'Cease thy bellowing, thou great ox,' gasped O'Donnell, sitting up and shaking off the frantic hands. 'I am
unhurt.'

Yar Muhammad yelled with surprise and relief. 'But
the bullet, brother? He fired at point-blank range!'

'It hit my belt buckle,' grunted O'Donnell, feeling the
heavy gold buckle, which was bent and dented. 'By Allah,
the slug drove it into my belly. It was like being hit with
a sledge hammer. Where is Afzal Khan?'

'Fled away in the darkness.'

O'Donnell rose and turned his attention to the fighting.
It was practically over. The remnants of the Pathans
were fleeing over the wall, harried by the triumphant
Turkomans, who in victory were no more merciful than
the average Oriental. The *sangar* looked like a shambles.

The hut still blazed brightly, and O'Donnell knew
that the contents had been ignited. What had been an
advantage was now a danger, for the men at the head of
the valley would be coming at full run, and in the light
of the fire they could pick off the Turkomans from the
darkness. He ran forward shouting orders, and setting an
example of action.

Men began filling vessels—cooking pots, gourds, even
kalpaks from the well and casting the water on the fire.
O'Donnell burst in the door and began to drag out the
contents of the huts, foods mostly, some of it brightly
ablaze, to be doused.

Working as only men in danger of death can work, they
extinguished the flame and darkness fell again over the
fortress. But over the eastern crags a faint glow announced
the rising of the moon through the breaking clouds.

Then followed a tense period of waiting, in which the
Turkomans hugged their rifles and crouched along the
wall, staring into the darkness as the Pathans had done
only a short time before. Seven of them had been killed
in the fighting and lay with the wounded beside the well.
The bodies of the slain Pathans had been unceremoniously
heaved over the wall.

The men at the valley head could not have been on their way down the valley when the fighting broke out, and they must have hesitated before starting, uncertain as to what the racket meant. But they were on their way at last, and Afzal Khan was trying to establish a contact with them.

The wind brought snatches of shouts down the valley, and a rattle of shots that hinted at hysteria. These were followed by a furious bellowing which indicated that Afzal Khan's demoralized warriors had nearly shot their chief in the dark. The moon broke through the clouds and disclosed a straggling mob of men gesticulating wildly this side of the rocks to the east.

O'Donnell even made out Afzal Khan's bulk and, snatching a rifle from a warrior's hand, tried a long shot. He missed in the uncertain light, but his warriors poured a blast of lead into the thick of their enemies which accounted for a man or so and sent the others leaping for cover. From the reeflike rocks they began firing at the wall, knocking off chips of stone but otherwise doing no damage.

With his enemies definitely located, O'Donnell felt more at ease. Taking a torch he went to the tower, with Yar Muhammad hanging at his heels like a faithful ghoul. In the tower were heaped odds and ends of plunder— saddles, bridles, garments, blankets, food, weapons— but O'Donnell did not find what he sought, though he tore the place to pieces. Yar Muhammad squatted in the doorway, with his rifle across his knees, and watched him, it never occurring to the Waziri to inquire what his friend was searching for.

At length O'Donnell paused, sweating from the vigor of his efforts—for he had concentrated much exertion in a few minutes—and swore.

'Where *does* the dog keep those papers?'

'The papers he took from Ahmed Shah?' inquired Yar Muhammad. 'Those he always carries in his girdle. He cannot read them, but he believes they are valuable. Men say Ahmed Shah had them from a *Feringi* who died.'

4

Dawn was lifting over the valley of Khuruk. The sun that
was not yet visible above the rim of the hills turned the
white peaks to pulsing fire. But down in the valley there
was none who found time to wonder at the changeless
miracle of the mountain dawn. The cliffs rang with the
flat echoes of rifle shots, and whips of smoke drifted
bluely into the air. Lead spanged on stone and whined
venomously off into space, or thudded sickeningly into
quivering flesh. Men howled blasphemously and fouled
the morning with their frantic curses.

O'Donnell crouched at a loophole, staring at the rocks
whence came puffs of white smoke and singing harbingers
of death. His rifle barrel was hot to his hand, and a dozen
yards from the wall lay a huddle of white-clad figures.

Since the first hint of light the wolves of Afzal Khan
had poured lead into the fortalice from the reeflike
ledge that broke the valley floor. Three times they had
broken cover and charged, only to fall back beneath the
merciless fire that raked them. Hopelessly outnumbered,
the advantage of weapons and position counted heavily
for the Turkomans.

O'Donnell had stationed five of the best marksmen
in the tower and the rest held the walls. To reach the
inclosure meant charging across several hundred yards
of open space, devoid of cover. All the outlaws were still
among the rocks east of the *sangar*, where, indeed, the
broken ledge offered the only cover within rifle range
of the redoubt.

The Panthans had suffered savagely in the charges, and
they had had the worst of the long-range exchanges, both
their marksmanship and their weapons being inferior to
the Turkomans'. But some of their bullets did find their
way through the loopholes. A few yards from O'Donnell
a *kaftaned* rider lay in a grotesque huddle, his feet turned

so the growing light glinted on his silver boot heels, his head a smear of blood and brains.

Another lay sprawled near the charred hut, his ghastly face frozen in a grin of agony as he chewed spasmodically on a bullet. He had been shot in the belly and was taking a long time in dying, but not a whimper escaped his livid lips.

A fellow with a bullet hole in his forearm was making more racket; his curses, as a comrade probed for the slug with a dagger point, would have curdled the blood of a devil.

O'Donnell glanced up at the tower, whence wisps of smoke drifting told him that his five snipers were alert. Their range was greater than that of the men at the wall, and they did more damage proportionately and were better protected. Again and again they had broken up attempts to get at the horses in the stone pen. This pen was nearer the inclosure than it was to the rocks, and crumpled shapes on the ground showed of vain attempts to reach it.

But O'Donnell shook his head. They had salvaged a large quantity of food from the burning hut; there was a well of good water; they had better weapons and more ammunition than the men outside. But a long siege meant annihilation.

One of the men wounded in the night fighting had died. There remained alive forty-one men of the fifty with which he had left Shahrazar. One of these was dying, and half a dozen were wounded—one probably fatally. There were at least a hundred and fifty men outside.

Afzal Khan could not storm the walls yet. But under the constant toll of the bullets, the small force of the defenders would melt away. If any of them lived and escaped, O'Donnell knew it could be only by a swift, bold stroke. But he had no plan at all.

The firing from the valley ceased suddenly, and a white turban cloth was waved above the rock of a rifle muzzle.

'*Ohai*, Ali el Ghazi!' came a hail in a bull's roar that could only have issued from Afzal Khan.

Yar Muhammad, squatting beside O'Donnell sneered. 'A trick! Keep thy head below the parapet, sahib. Trust Afzal Khan when wolves knock out their own teeth.'

'Hold your fire, Ali el Ghazi!' boomed the distant voice. 'I would parley with you!'

'Show yourself!' O'Donnell yelled back.

And without hesitation a huge bulk loomed up among the rocks. Whatever his own perfidy, Afzal Khan trusted the honor of the man he thought a Kurd. He lifted his hands to show they were empty.

'Advance, alone!' yelled O'Donnell, straining to make himself heard.

Someone thrust the butt of a rifle into a crevice of the rocks so it stood muzzle upward, with the white cloth blowing out in the morning breeze, and Afzal Khan came striding over the stones with the arrogance of a sultan. Behind him turbans were poked up above the boulders.

O'Donnell halted him within good earshot, and instantly he was covered by a score of rifles. Afzal Khan did not seem to be disturbed by that, or by the blood lust in the dark hawklike faces glaring along the barrels. Then O'Donnell rose into view, and the two leaders faced one another in the full dawn.

O'Donnell expected accusations of treachery—for, after all, he had struck the first blow—but Afzal Khan was too brutally candid for such hypocrisy.

'I have you in a vise, Ali el Ghazi,' he announced without preamble. 'But for that Waziri dog who crouches behind you, I would have cut your throat at moonrise last night. You are all dead men, but siege work grows tiresome, and I am willing to forgo half my advantage. I am generous. As reward of victory I demand either your guns or your horses. Your horses I have already, but you shall have them back, if you wish. Throw down your weapons and you may ride out of Khuruk. Or, if you wish, I will keep the horses, and you may march out on foot with your rifles. What is your answer?'

O'Donnell spat toward him, with a typically Kurdish gesture. 'Are we fools, to be hoodwinked by a dog with scarlet whiskers?' he snarled. 'When Afzal Khan keeps his sworn word, the Indus will flow backward. Shall we ride out, unarmed, for you to cut us down in the passes, or shall we march forth on foot, for you to shoot us from ambush in the hills?

'You lie when you say you have our horses. Ten of your men have died trying to take them for you. You lie when you say you have us in the vise. It is *you* who are in the vise! You have neither food nor water; there is no other well in the valley but this. You have few cartridges, because most of your ammunition is stored in the tower, and *we* hold that.'

The fury in Afzal Khan's countenance told O'Donnell that he had scored with that shot.

'If you had us helpless you would not be offering terms,' O'Donnell sneered. 'You would be cutting our throats, instead of trying to gull us into the open.'

'Sons of sixty dogs!' swore Afzal Khan, plucking at his beard. 'I will flay you all alive! I will keep you hemmed here until you die!'

'If we cannot leave the fortress, you cannot enter it,' O'Donnell retorted. 'Moreover you have drawn all your men but a handful from the passes, and the Krurukzai will steal upon you and cut off your heads. They are waiting, up in the hills.'

Afzal Khan's involuntarily wry face told O'Donnell that the Afghan's plight was more desperate than he had hoped.

'It is a deadlock, Afzal Khan,' said O'Donnell suddenly.

'There is but one way to break it.' He lifted his voice, seeing that the Pathans under the protection of the truce were leaving their coverts and drawing within earshot. 'Meet me there in the open space, man to man,

and decide the feud between us two, with cold steel. If I
win, we ride out of Khuruk unmolested. If you win, my
warriors are at your mercy.'

'The mercy of a wolf!' muttered Yar Muhammad.

O'Donnell did not reply. It was a desperate chance,
but the only one. Afzal Khan hesitated and cast a searching glance at his men; that scowling hairy horde was
muttering among itself. The warriors seemed ill-content,
and they stared meaningly at their leader.

The inference was plain; they were weary of the fighting at which they were at a disadvantage, and they
wished Afzal Khan to accept O'Donnell, challenge. They
feared a return of the Khurukzai might catch them in
the open with empty cartridge pouches. After all, if
their chief lost to the Kurd, they would only lose the
loot they had expected to win. Afzal Khan understood
this attitude, and his beard bristled to the upsurging of
his ready passion.

'Agreed!' he roared, tearing out his tulwar and throwing away the scabbard. He made the bright broad steel
thrum about his head. 'Come over the wall and die, thou
slayer of infidels!'

'Hold your men where they are!' O'Donnell ordered
and vaulted the parapet.

At a bellowed order the Pathans had halted, and the
wall was lined with *kalpaks* as the Turkomans watched
tensely, muzzles turned upward but fingers still crooked
on the triggers. Yar Muhammad followed O'Donnell over
the wall, but did not advance from it; he crouched against
it like a bearded ghoul, fingering his knife.

O'Donnell wasted no time. Scimitar in one hand and
kindhjal in the other, he ran lightly toward the burly
figure advancing to meet him. O'Donnell was slightly
above medium height, but Afzal Khan towered half a
head above him. The Afghan's bull-like shoulders and
muscular bulk contrasted with the rangy figure of the
false Kurd; but O'Donnell's sinews were like steel wires.
His Arab scimitar, though neither so broad nor so heavy

as the tulwar, was fully as long, and the blade was of unbreakable Damascus steel.

The men seemed scarcely within arm's reach when the fight opened with a dazzling crackle and flash of steel. Blow followed blow so swiftly that the men watching, trained to arms since birth, could scarcely follow the strokes. Afzal Khan roared, his eyes blazing, his beard bristling, and wielding the heavy tulwars, as one might wield a camel wand, he flailed away in a frenzy.

But always the scimitar flickered before him, turning the furious blows, or the slim figure of the false Kurd avoided death by the slightest margins, with supple twists and swayings. The scimitar bent beneath the weight of the tulwar, but it did not break; like a serpent's tongue it always snapped straight again, and like a serpent's tongue it flickered at Afzal Khan's breast, his throat, his groin, a constant threat of death that reddened the Afghan's eyes with a tinge akin to madness.

Afzal Khan was a famed swordsman, and his sheer brute strength was more than a man's. But O'Donnell balance and economy of motion was a marvel to witness. He never set a foot wrong or made a false motion; he was always poised, always a threat, even in retreat, beaten backward by the bull-like rushes of the Afghan. Blood trickled down his face where a furious stroke, beating down his blade, had bitten through his silk turban and into the scalp, but the flame in his blue eyes never altered.

Afzal Khan was bleeding, too, O'Donnell's point, barely missing his jugular, had plowed through his beard and along his jaw. Blood dripping from his beard made his aspect more fearsome than ever. He roared and flailed, until it seemed that the fury of his onslaught would overbalance O'Donnell's perfect mastery of himself and his blade.

Few noticed, however, that O'Donnell had been working his way in closer and closer under the sweep of the tulwar. Now he caught a furious swipe near the hilt and the *kindhjal* in his left hand licked in and out. Afzal Khan's bellow caught in a gasp. There was but that fleeting instant of contact, so brief it was like blur of movement, and then O'Donnell, at arm's length again, was slashing and parrying, but now there was a thread of crimson on the narrow *kindhjal* blade, and blood was seeping in a steady stream through Afzal Khan's broad girdle.

There was the pain and desperation of the damned in the Afghan's eyes, in his roaring voice. He began to weave drunkenly, but he attacked more madly than ever, like a man fighting against time.

His strokes ribboned the air with bright steel and thrummed past O'Donnell, ears like a wind of death, until the tulwar rang full against the scimitar's guard with hurricane force and O'Donnell went to his knee under the impact. 'Kurdish dog!' It was a gasp of frenzied triumph. Up flashed the tulwar and the watching hordes gave tongue. But again the *kindhjal* licked out like a serpent's tongue—outward and upward.

The stroke was meant for the Afghan's groin, but a shift of his legs at the instant caused the keen blade to plow through his thigh instead, slicing veins and tendons. He lurched sidewise, throwing out his arm to balance himself. And even before men knew whether he would fall or not, O'Donnell was on his feet and slashed with the scimitar at his head.

Afzal Khan fell as a tree falls, blood gushing from his head. Even so, the terrible vitality of the man clung to life and hate. The tulwar fell from his hand, but, catching himself on his knees, he plucked a knife from his girdle; his hand went back for the throw—then the knife slipped from his nerveless fingers and he crumpled to the earth and lay still.

There was silence, broken by a strident yell from the Turkomans. O'Donnell sheathed his scimitar, sprang swiftly to the fallen giant and thrust a hand into his blood-soaked girdle. His fingers closed on what he had hoped to find, and he drew forth an oilskin-bound packet of papers. A low cry of satisfaction escaped his lips.

In the tense excitement of the fight, neither he nor the Turkomans had noticed that the Pathans had drawn nearer and nearer, until they stood in a ragged semicircle only a few yards away. Now, as O'Donnell stood staring at the packet, a hairy ruffian ran at his back, knife lifted.

A frantic yell from Yar Muhammad warned O'Donnell. There was no time to turn; sensing rather than seeing his assailant, the American ducked deeply and the knife flashed past his ear, the muscular forearm falling on his shoulder with such force that again he was knocked to his knees.

Before the man could strike again Yar Muhammad's yard-long knife was driven into his breast with such fury that the point sprang out between his shoulder blades. Wrenching his blade free as the wretch fell, the Waziri grabbed a handful of O'Donnell's garments and began to drag him toward the wall, yelling like a madman.

It had all happened in a dizzying instant, the charge of the Pathan, Yar Muhammad's leap and retreat. The other Pathans rushed in, howling like wolves, and the Waziri's blade made a fan of steel about him and O'Donnell. Blades were flashing on all sides; O'Donnell was cursing like a madman as he strove to halt Yar Muhammad's headlong progress long enough to get to his feet, which was impossible at the rate he was being yanked along.

All he could see was hairy legs, and all he could hear was a devil's din of yells and clanging knives. He hewed sidewise at the legs and men howled, and then there was a deafening reverberation, and a blast of lead at close range smote the attackers and mowed them down like wheat. The Turkomans had woken up and gone into action.

Yar Muhammad was berserk. With his knife dripping red and his eyes blazing madly he swarmed over the

wall and down on the other side, all asprawl, lugging
O'Donnell like a sack of grain, and still unaware that his
friend was not fatally wounded.

The Pathans were at his heels, not to be halted so
easily this time. The Turkomans fired point-blank into
their faces, but they came on, snarling, snatching at the
rifle barrels poked over the wall, stabbing upward.

Yar Muhammad, heedless of the battle raging along
the wall, was crouching over O'Donnell, mouthing, so
crazy with blood lust and fighting frenzy that he was
hardly aware of what he was doing, tearing at O'Donnell's
clothing in his efforts to discover the wound he was
convinced his friend had received.

He could hardly be convinced otherwise by O'Donnell's lurid blasphemy, and then he nearly strangled
the American in a frantic embrace of relief and joy.
O'Donnell threw him off and leaped to the wall, where
the situation was getting desperate for the Turkomans.
The Pathans, fighting without leadership, were massed in the middle of the east wall, and the men in
the tower were pouring a devastating fire into them,
but the havoc was being wreaked in the rear of the
horde. The men in the tower feared to shoot at the
attackers along the wall for fear of hitting their own
comrades.

As O'Donnell reached the wall, the Turkoman nearest
him thrust his muzzle into a snarling, bearded face and
pulled the trigger, blasting the hillman's head into a red
ruin. Then before he could fire again a knife licked over
the wall and disemboweled him. O'Donnell caught the
rifle as it fell, smashed the butt down on the head of a
hillman climbing over the parapet, and left him hanging
dead across the wall.

It was all confusion and smoke and spurting blood
and insanity. No time to look right or left to see if
the Turkomans still held the wall on either hand. He
had his hands full with the snarling bestial faces which

rose like a wave before him. Crouching on the firing step, he drove the blood-clotted butt into these wolfish faces until a rabid-eyed giant grappled him and bore him back and over.

They struck the ground on the inside, and O'Donnell's head hit a fallen gun stock with a stunning crack. In the moment that his brain swam dizzily the Pathan heaved him underneath, yelled stridently and lifted a knife—then the straining body went suddenly limp, and O'Donnell's face was spattered with blood and brains, as Yar Muhammad split the man's head to the teeth with his Khyber knife.

The Waziri pulled the corpse off and O'Donnell staggered up, slightly sick, and presenting a ghastly spectacle with his red-dabbled face, hands, and garments. The firing, which had lulled while the fighting locked along the wall, now began again. The disorganized Pathans were falling back, were slinking away, breaking and fleeing toward the rocks.

The Turkomans had held the wall, but O'Donnell swore sickly as he saw the gaps in their ranks. One lay dead in a huddle of dead Pathans outside the wall, and five more hung motionless across the wall, or were sprawled on the ground inside. With these latter were the corpses of four Pathans, to show how desperate the brief fight had been. The number of the dead outside was appalling.

O'Donnell shook his dizzy head, shuddering slightly at the thought of how close to destruction his band had been; if the hillmen had had a leader, had kept their wits about them enough to have divided forces and attacked in several places at once—but it takes a keen mind to think in the madness of such a battle. It had been blind, bloody, and furious, and the random-cast dice of fate had decided for the smaller horde.

The Pathans had taken to the rocks again and were firing in a half-hearted manner. Sounds of loud argument drifted down the wind. He set about dressing the wounded as best he could, and while he was so employed, the Pathans tried to get at the horses again. But the effort was without enthusiasm, and a fusillade from the tower drove them back.

As quickly as he could, O'Donnell retired to a corner of the wall and investigated the oilskin-wrapped packet he had taken from Afzal Khan. It was a letter, several sheets of high-grade paper covered with a fine scrawl. The writing was Russ, not *Urdu,* and there were English margin notes in a different hand. These notes made clear points suggested in the letter, and O'Donnell's face grew grim as he read.

How the unknown English secret-service man who had added those notes and had got possession of the letter there was no way of knowing; but it had been intended for the man called Suleiman Pasha, and it revealed what O'Donnell had suspected—a plot within a plot; a red and sinister conspiracy concealing itself in a guise of international policy.

Suleiman Pasha was not only a foreign spy; he was a traitor to the men he served. And the tentacles of the plot which revolved about him stretched incredibly southward into high places. O'Donnell swore softly as he read there the names of men trusted by the government they pretended to serve. And slowly a realization crystallized—this letter must never reach Suleiman Pasha. Somehow, in some way, he, Kirby O'Donnell, must carry on the work of that unknown Englishman who had died with his task uncompleted. That letter must go southward, to lay bare black treachery spawning under the heedless feet of government. He hastily concealed the packet as the Waziri approached.

Yar Muhammad grinned. He had lost a tooth, and his black beard was streaked and clotted with blood which did not make him look any less savage.

'The dogs wrangle with one another,' he said. 'It is always thus; only the hand of Afzal Khan kept them together. Now men who followed him will refuse to follow one of their own number. They fear the Khurukzai. We also have reason to beware of them. They will be waiting in the hills beyond the Pass of Akbar.'

O'Donnell realized the truth of this statement. He believed a handful of Pathans yet held the tower in the pass, but there was no reason to suppose they would not desert their post, now that Afzal Khan was dead. Men trooping down out of the hills told him that the footpaths were no longer guarded. At any time Khurukzai scouts might venture back, learn what was going on, and launch an attack in force.

The day wore on, hot, and full of suffering for the wounded in the inclosure. Only a desultory firing came from the rocks, where continual squabbling seemed to be going on. No further attack was made, and presently Yar Muhammad grunted with gratification.

From the movement among the rocks and beyond them, it was evident that the leaderless outlaw band was breaking up. Men slunk away up the valley, singly or in small bands. Others fought over horses, and one group turned and fired a volley at their former companions before they disappeared among the spurs at the head of the valley. Without a chieftain they trusted, demoralized by losses, short of water and food and ammunition, and in fear of reprisals, the outlaw band melted away, and within an hour from the time the first bolted, the valley of Khuruk was empty except for O'Donnell's men.

To make sure the retreat was real, O'Donnell secured his horse from the pen and, with Yar Muhammad, rode cautiously to the valley head. The spurs were empty. From the tracks the American believed that the bandits had headed southward, preferring to make their way through the pathless hills rather than fight their way through the vengeful Khurukzai who in all probability still lurked among the crags beyond the Pass of Akbar.

He had to consider these men himself and he grinned wryly at the twist of fate which had made enemies of the

very men he had sought in friendship. But life ran that
way in the hills.

'Go back to the Turkomans,' he requested Yar
Muhammad. 'Bid them saddle their horses. Tie the
wounded into the saddles, and load the spare horses with
food and skins of water. We have plenty of spare horses
now, because of the men who were slain. It is dusk now,
and time we are on our way.

'We shall take our chance on the trails in the dark,
for now that the hill paths are unguarded, assuredly the
Khurukzai will be stealing back, and I expect an attack
on the valley by moonrise, at the latest. Let them find it
empty. Perhaps we can make our way through the Pass
and be gone while they are stealing through the hills to
the attack. At least we will make the attempt and leave
the rest to Allah.'

Yar Muhammad grinned widely—the prospect of any
sort of action seemed to gratify him immensely—and
reined his horse down the valley, evidencing all the pride
that becomes a man who rides a blooded Turkish steed.
O'Donnell knew he could leave the preparations for the
journey with him and the Turkomans.

The American dismounted, tied his horse and strode
through the rocky spurs to the point where the trail
wound out of them and along a boulder-littered narrow
level between two slopes. Dusk was gathering, but he
could see any body of men that tried to come along
that trail.

But he was not expecting attack by that route. Not
knowing just what has taken place in the valley, the
Khurukzai even if the men in the tower had deserted
it, would be too suspicious to follow the obvious road.
And it was not attack of any sort that was worrying
him.

He took the packet of papers from his girdle and
stared at it. He was torn by indecision. There were
documents that needed desperately to get to the British
outposts. It was almost sheer suicide for one man to start

through the hills, but two men, with food and water, might make it.

He could take Yar Muhammad, load an extra horse or two with provisions, and slip away southward. Then let Suleiman Pasha do his worst with Orkhan Bahadur. Long before the emissary could learn of his flight, he and the Waziri would be far out of the vengeful Turkoman's reach. But, then, what of the warriors back there in the *sangar*, making ready for their homeward flight, with implicit trust in Ali el Ghazi?

They had followed him blindly, obeyed his every order, demonstrated their courage and faithfulness beyond question. If he deserted them now, they were doomed. They could never make their way back through the hills without him. Such as were not lost to die of starvation would be slaughtered by the vengeful Khurukzai who would not forget their defeat by these dark-skinned riders.

Sweat started out on O'Donnell's skin in the agony of his mental struggle. Not even for the peace of all India could he desert these men who trusted him. He was their leader. His first duty was to them.

But, then, what of that damning letter? It supplied the key to Suleiman Pasha's plot. It told of hell brewing in the Khyber Hills, of revolt seething on the Hindu plains, of a plot which might be nipped in the bud were the British officials to learn of it in time. But if he returned to Shahrazar with the Turkomans, he must give the letter to Suleiman Pasha or be denounced to Orkhan—and that meant torture and death. He was in the fangs of the vise; he must either sacrifice himself, his men, or the helpless people of India.

'*Ohai*, Ali el Ghazi!' It was a soft hiss behind him, from the shadow of a jutting rock. Even as he started about, a pistol muzzle was pressed against his back.

'Nay, do not move. I do not trust you yet.'

Twisting his head about, O'Donnell stared into the dark features of Suleiman Pasha.

'You! How in Shaitan's name—'

'No matter. Give me the papers which you hold in your hand. Give them to me, or, by Allah, I will send you to hell, Kurd!'

With the pistol boring into his back, there was nothing else O'Donnell could do, his heart almost bursting with rage.

Suleiman Pasha stepped back and tucked the papers into his girdle. He allowed O'Donnell to turn and face him, but still kept him covered with the pistol.

'After you had departed,' he said, 'secret word came to me from the North that the papers for which I sent you were more important than I had dreamed. I dared not wait in Shahrazar for your return, lest something go away. I rode for Khuruk with some Ghilzais who knew the road. Beyond the Pass of Akbar we were ambushed by the very people we sought. They slew my men, but they spared me, for I was known to one of their headmen. They told me they had been driven forth by Afzal Khan, and I guessed what else had occurred. They said there had been fighting beyond the Pass, for they had heard the sound of firing, but they did not know its nature. There are no men in the tower in the Pass, but the Khurukzai fear a trap. They do not know the outlaws have fled from the valley.

'I wished to get word with you as soon as possible, so I volunteered to go spying for them alone, so they showed me the footpaths. I reached the valley head in time to see the last of the Pathans depart, and I have been hiding here awaiting a chance to catch you alone. Listen! The Turkomans are doomed. The Khurukzai mean to kill them all. But I can save you. We shall dress you in the clothing of a dead Pathan, and I shall say you are a servant of mine who has escaped from the Turkomans.

'I shall not return to Shahrazar. I have business in the Khyber region. I can use a man like you. We shall return to the Khurukzai and show them how to attack and destroy the Turkomans. Then they will lend us an escort southward. Will you come with me and serve me, Kurd?'

'No, you damned swine!' In the stress of the moment O'Donnell spat his fury in English. Suleiman Pasha's jaw dropped in the staggering unexpectedness of English words from a man he thought to be a Kurd. And in the instant his wits were disrupted by the discovery, O'Donnell, nerved to desperate quickness, was at his throat like a striking cobra.

The pistol exploded once and then was wrenched from the numbed fingers. Suleiman Pasha was fighting in frenzied silence, and he was all steel strings and catlike thews. But O'Donnell's *kindhjal* was out and ripping murderously into him again and again. They went to the earth together in the shadow of the big rock, O'Donnell stabbing in a berserk frenzy; and then he realized that he was driving his blade into a dead man.

He shook himself free and rose, staggering like a drunken man with the red haze of his murder lust. The oilskin packet was in his left hand, torn from his enemy's garments during the struggle. Dusk had given way to blue, star-flecked darkness. To O'Donnell's ears came the clink of hoofs on stone, the creak of leather. His warriors were approaching, still hidden by the towering ledges. He heard a low laugh that identified Yar Muhammad.

O'Donnell breathed deeply in vast content. Now he could guide his men back through the passes to Shahrazar without fear of Orkhan Bahadur, who would never know his secret. He could persuade the Turkoman chief that it would be to his advantage to send this letter on to the British border. He, as Ali el Ghazi, could remain in Shahrazar safely, to oppose subtly what other conspirators came plotting to the forbidden city.

He smiled as he wiped the blood from his *kindhjal* and sheathed it. There still remained the Khurukzai, waiting with murderous patience beyond the Pass of Akbar, but his soul was at rest, and the prospect of fighting his way back through the mountains troubled him not at all. He was as confident of the outcome as if he already sat in the palace at Shahrazar.

FRANCIS X. GORDON (EL BORAK)

The Daughter of Erlik Khan

THE TALL Englishman, Pembroke, was scratching lines on the earth with his hunting knife, talking in a jerky tone that indicated suppressed excitement: 'I tell you, Ormond, that peak to the west is the one we were to look for. Here, I've marked a map in the dirt. This mark here represents our camp, and this one is the peak. We've marched north far enough. At this spot we should turn westward—'

'Shut up!' muttered Ormond. 'Rub out that map. Here comes Gordon.'

Pembroke obliterated the faint lines with a quick sweep of his open hand, and as he scrambled up he managed to shuffle his feet across the spot. He and Ormond were laughing and talking easily as the third man of the expedition came up.

Gordon was shorter than his companions, but his physique did not suffer by comparison with either the rangy Pembroke or the more closely knit Ormond. He was one of those rare individuals at once lithe and compact. His strength did not give the impression of being locked up within himself as is the case with so many strong men. He moved with a flowing ease that advertised power more subtly than does mere beefy bulk.

Though he was clad much like the two Englishmen

except for an Arab headdress, he fitted into the scene as they did not. He, an American, seemed almost as much a part of these rugged uplands as the wild nomads which pasture their sheep along the slopes of the Hindu Kush. There was a certitude in his level gaze, an economy of motion in his movements, that reflected kinship with the wilderness.

'Pembroke and I were discussing that peak, Gordon,' said Ormond, indicating the mountain under discussion, which reared a snow cap in the clear afternoon sky beyond a range of blue hills, hazy with distance. 'We were wondering if it had a name.'

'Everything in these hills has a name,' Gordon answered. 'Some of them don't appear on the maps, though. That peak is called Mount Erlik Khan. Less than a dozen white men have seen it.'

'Never heard of it,' was Pembroke's comment. 'If we weren't in such a hurry to find poor old Reynolds, it might be fun having a closer look at it, what?'

'If getting your belly ripped open can be called fun,' returned Gordon. 'Erlik Khan's in Black Kirghiz country.'

'Kirghiz? Heathens and devil worshipers? Sacred city of Yolgan and all that rot.'

'No rot about the devil worship,' Gordon returned. 'We're almost on the borders of their country now. This is a sort of no man's land here, squabbled over by the Kirghiz and Moslem nomads from farther east. We've been lucky not to have met any of the former. They're an isolated branch off the main stalk which centers about Issik-kul, and they hate white men like poison.

'This is the closest point we approach their country. From now on, as we travel north, we'll be swinging away from it. In another week, at most, we ought to be in the territory of the Uzbek tribe who you think captured your friend.'

'I hope the old boy is still alive.' Pembroke sighed.

'When you engaged me at Peshawar I told you I

feared it was a futile quest,' said Gordon. 'If that tribe did capture your friend, the chances are all against his being still alive. I'm just warning you, so you won't be too disappointed if we don't find him.'

'We appreciate that, old man,' returned Ormond. 'We knew no one but you could get us there with our heads still on our bally shoulders.'

'We're not there yet,' remarked Gordon cryptically, shifting his rifle under his arm. 'I saw hangel sign before we went into camp, and I'm going to see if I can bag one. I may not be back before dark.'

'Going afoot?' inquired Pembroke.

'Yes; if I get one I'll bring back a haunch for supper.'

And with no further comment Gordon strode off down the rolling slope, while the other men stared silently after him.

He seemed to melt rather than stride into the broad copse at the foot of the slope. The men turned, still unspeaking, and glanced at the servants going about their duties in the camp—four stolid Pathans and a slender Punjabi Moslem who was Gordon's personal servant.

The camp with its faded tents and tethered horses was the one spot of sentient life in a scene so vast and broodingly silent that it was almost daunting. To the south, stretched an unbroken rampart of hills climbing up to snowy peaks. Far to the north rose another more broken range.

Between those barriers lay a great expanse of rolling table-land, broken by solitary peaks and lesser hill ranges, and dotted thickly with copses of ash, birch, and larch. Now, in the beginning of the short summer, the slopes were covered with tall lush grass. But here no herds were watched by turbaned nomads and that giant peak far to the southwest seemed somehow aware of that fact. It brooded like a somber sentinel of the unknown.

'Come into my tent!'

Pembroke turned away quickly, motioning Ormond
to follow. Neither of them noticed the burning intensity
with which the Punjabi Ahmed stared after them. In the
tent, the men sitting facing each other across a small
folding table, Pembroke took pencil and paper and began
tracing a duplicate of the map he had scratched in the dirt.

'"Reynolds" has served his purpose, and so has
Gordon,' he said. 'It was a big risk bringing him, but
he was the only man who could get us safely through
Afghanistan. The weight that American carries with the
Mohammedans is amazing. But it doesn't carry with the
Kirghiz, and beyond this point we don't need him.

'That's the peak the Tajik described, right enough,
and he gave it the same name Gordon called it. Using it
as a guide, we can't miss Yolgan. We head due west,
bearing a little to the north of Mount Erlik Khan. We
don't need Gordon's guidance from now on, and we won't
need him going back, because we're returning by the
way of Kashmir, and we'll have a better safe-conduct
even than he. Question now is, how are we going to
get rid of him?'

'That's easy,' snapped Ormond; he was the harder-
framed, the more decisive, of the two. 'We'll simply pick
a quarrel with him and refuse to continue in his company. He'll tell us to go to the devil, take his founded
Punjabi, and head back for Kabul—or maybe some other
wilderness. He spends most of his time wandering around
through countries that are taboo to most white men.'

'Good enough!' approved Pembroke. 'We don't
want to fight him. He's too infernally quick with a
gun. The Afghans call him "El Borak," the Swift. I had
something of the sort in mind when I cooked up an excuse
to halt here in the middle of the afternoon. I recognized
that peak, you see. We'll let him think we're going on to
the Uzbeks, alone, because, naturally, we don't want him
to know we're going to Yolgan—'

'What's that?' snapped Ormond suddenly, his hand
closing on his pistol butt.

In that instant, when his eyes narrowed and his nostrils expanded, he looked almost like another man, as if suspicion disclosed his true—and sinister—nature.

'Go on talking,' he muttered. 'Somebody's listening outside the tent.'

Pembroke obeyed, and Ormond, noiselessly pushing back his camp chair, plunged suddenly out of the tent and fell on some one with a snarl of gratification. An instant later he reentered, dragging the Punjabi, Ahmed, with him. The slender Indian writhed vainly in the Englishman's iron grip.

'This rat was eavesdropping,' Ormond snarled.

'Now he'll spill everything to Gordon and there'll be a fight, sure!' The prospect seemed to agitate Pembroke considerably. 'What'll we do now? What are you going to do?'

Ormond laughed savagely. 'I haven't come this far to risk getting a bullet in my guts and losing everything. I've killed men for less than this.'

Pembroke cried out an involuntary protest as Ormond's hand dipped and the blue-gleaming gun came up. Ahmed screamed, and his cry was drowned in the roar of the shot.

'Now we'll *have* to kill Gordon!'

Pembroke wiped his brow with a hand that shook a trifle. Outside rose a sudden mutter of Pashto as the Pathan servants crowded toward the tent.

'He's played into our hands!' rapped Ormond, shoving the still smoking gun back into his holster. With his booted toe he stirred the motionless body at his feet as casually as if it had been that of a snake. 'He's out on foot, with only a handful of cartridges. It's just as well this turned out as it did.'

'What do you mean?' Pembroke's wits seemed momentarily muddled.

'We'll simply pack up and clear out. Let him try to follow us on foot, if he wants to. There are limits to the abilities of every man. Left in these mountains

on foot, without food, blankets, or ammunition, I don't
think any white man will ever see Francis Xavier Gordon
alive again.'

2.

When Gordon left the camp he did not look behind him.
Any thoughts of treachery on the part of his companions
was furthest from his mind. He had no reason to suppose
that they were anything except what they had represented
themselves to be—white men taking a long chance to find
a comrade the unmapped solitudes had swallowed up.

It was an hour or so after leaving the camp when,
skirting the end of a grassy ridge, he sighted an antelope moving along the fringe of a thicket. The wind,
such as there was, was blowing toward him, away from
the animal. He began stalking it through the thicket,
when a movement in the bushes behind him brought
him around to the realization that he himself was being
stalked.

He had a glimpse of a figure behind a clump of scrub,
and then a bullet fanned his ear, and he fired at the flash
and the puff of smoke. There was a thrashing among the
foliage and then stillness. A moment later he was bending
over a picturesquely clad form on the ground.

It was a lean, wiry man, young, with an ermine-edged
khilat, a fur *calpack*, and silver-heeled boots. Sheathed
knives were in his girdle, and a modern repeating rifle lay
near his hand. He had been shot through the heart.

'Turkoman,' muttered Gordon. 'Bandit, from his
looks, out on a lone scout. I wonder how far he's
been trailing me.'

He knew the presence of the man implied two things:
somewhere in the vicinity there was a band of Turkomans;
and somewhere, probably close by, there was a horse. A
nomad never walked far, even when stalking a victim. He
glanced up at the rise which rolled up from the copse. It

was logical to believe that the Moslem had sighted him from the crest of the low ridge, had tied his horse on the other side, and glided down into the thicket to waylay him while he stalked the antelope.

Gordon went up the slope warily, though he did not believe there were any other tribesmen within earshot— else the reports of the rifles would have brought them to the spot—and found the horse without trouble. It was a Turkish stallion with a red leather saddle with wide silver stirrups and a bridle heavy with goldwork. A scimitar hung from the saddle peak in an ornamented leather scabbard.

Swinging into the saddle, Gordon studied all quarters of the compass from the summit of the ridge. In the south a faint ribbon of smoke stood against the evening. His black eyes were keen as a hawk's; not many could have distinguished that filmy blue feather against the cerulean of the sky.

'Turkoman means bandits,' he muttered. 'Smoke means camp. They're trailing us, sure as fate.'

Reining about, he headed for the camp. His hunt had carried him some miles east of the site, but he rode at a pace that ate up the distance. It was not yet twilight when he halted in the fringe of the larches and sat silently scanning the slope on which the camp had stood. It was bare. There was no sign of tents, men, or beasts.

His gaze sifted the surrounding ridges and clumps, but found nothing to rouse his alert suspicion. At last he walked his steed up the acclivity, carrying his rifle at the ready. He saw a smear of blood on the ground where he knew Pembroke's tent had stood, but there was no other sign of violence, and the grass was not trampled as it would have been by a charge of wild horse-men.

He read the evidence of a swift but orderly exodus. His companions had simply struck their tents, loaded the pack animals, and departed. But why? Sight of distant horsemen might have stampeded the white men, though neither had shown any sign of the white feather before; but certainly Ahmed would not have deserted his master and friend.

As he traced the course of the horses through the grass, his puzzlement increased; they had gone westward.

Their avowed destination lay beyond those mountains in the north. They knew that, as well as he. But there was no mistake about it. For some reason, shortly after he had left camp, as he read the signs, they had packed hurriedly and set off westward, toward the forbidden country identified by Mount Erlik.

Thinking that possibly they had a logical reason for shifting camp and had left him a note of some kind which he had failed to find, Gordon rode back to the camp site and began casting about it in an ever-widening circle, studying the ground. And presently he saw sure signs that a heavy body had been dragged through the grass.

Men and horses had almost obliterated the dim track, but for years Gordon's life had depended upon the keenness of his faculties. He remembered the smear of blood on the ground where Pembroke's tent had stood.

He followed the crushed grass down the south slope and into a thicket, and an instant later he was kneeling beside the body of a man. It was Ahmed, and at first glance Gordon thought he was dead. Then he saw that Punjabi, though shot through the body and undoubtedly dying, still had a faint spark of life in him.

He lifted the turbaned head and set his canteen to the blue lips. Ahmed groaned, and into his glazed eyes came intelligence and recognition.

'Who did this, Ahmed?' Gordon's voice grated with the suppression of his emotions.

'Ormond Sahib,' gasped the Punjabi. 'I listened outside their tent, because I feared they planned treachery to you. I never trusted them. So they shot me and have gone away, leaving you to die alone in the hills.'

'But why?' Gordon was more mystified than ever.

'They go to Yolgan,' panted Ahmed. 'The Reynolds

Sahib we sought never existed. He was a lie they created
to hoodwink you.'

'Why to Yolgan?' asked Gordon.

But Ahmed's eyes dilated with the imminence of death;
in a racking convulsion he heaved up in Gordon's arms;
then blood gushed from his lips and he died.

Gordon rose, mechanically dusting his hands. Immobile
as the deserts he haunted, he was not prone to display his
emotions. Now he merely went about heaping stones over
the body to make a cairn that wolves and jackals could not
tear into. Ahmed had been his companion on many a dim
road; less servant than friend.

But when he had lifted the last stone, Gordon climbed
into the saddle, and without a backward glance he rode
westward. He was alone in a savage country, without
food or proper equipage. Chance had given him a horse,
and years of wandering on the raw edges of the world had
given him experience and a greater familiarity with this
unknown land than any other white man he knew. It was
conceivable that he might live to win his way through to
some civilized outpost.

But he did not even give that possibility a thought.
Gordon's ideas of obligation, of debt and payment, were
as direct and primitive as those of the barbarians among
whom his lot had been cast for so many years. Ahmed
had been his friend and had died in his service. Blood
must pay for blood.

That was as certain in Gordon's mind as hunger is
certain in the mind of a gray timber wolf. He did not know
why the killers were going toward forbidden Yolgan, and
he did not greatly care. His task was to follow them to hell
if necessary and exact full payment for spilled blood. No
other course suggested itself.

Darkness fell and the stars came out, but he did not
slacken his pace. Even by starlight it was not hard to
follow the trail of the caravan through the high grass.
The Turkish horse proved a good one and fairly fresh. He

felt certain of overtaking the laden pack ponies, in spite of their long start.

As the hours passed, however, he decided that the Englishmen were determined to push on all night. They evidently meant to put so much distance between them and himself that he could never catch them, following on foot as they thought him to be. But why were they so anxious to keep from him the truth of their destination?

A sudden thought made his face grim, and after that he pushed his mount a bit harder. His hand instinctively sought the hilt of the broad scimitar slung from the high-peaked horn.

His gaze sought the white cap of Mount Erlik, ghostly in the starlight, then swung to the point where he knew Yolgan lay. He had been there before, himself, had heard the deep roar of the long bronze trumpets that shaven-headed priests blow from the mountains at sunrise.

It was past midnight when he sighted fires near the willow-massed banks of a stream. At first glance he knew it was not the camp of the men he followed. The fires were too many. It was an *ordu* of the nomadic Kirghiz who roam the country between Mount Erlik Khan and the loose boundaries of the Mohammedan tribes. This camp lay full in the path of Yolgan and he wondered if the Englishmen had known enough to avoid it. These fierce people hated strangers. He himself, when he visited Yolgan, had accomplished the feat disguised as a native.

Gaining the stream above the camp he moved closer, in the shelter of the willows, until he could make out the dim shapes of sentries on horseback in the light of the small fires. And he saw something else—three white European tents inside the ring of round, gray felt *kibitkas*. He swore silently; if the Black Kirghiz had killed the white men, appropriating their belongings, it meant the end of his vengeance. He moved nearer.

It was a suspicious, slinking, wolf-like dog that betrayed him. Its frenzied clamor brought men swarming out of the felt tents, and a swarm of mounted sentinels raced toward the spot, stringing bows as they came.

Gordon had no wish to be filled with arrows as he ran. He spurred out of the willows and was among the horsemen before they were aware of him, slashing silently right and left with the Turkish scimitar. Blades swung around him, but the men were more confused than he. He felt his edge grate against steel and glance down to split a broad skull; then he was through the cordon and racing into deeper darkness while the demoralized pack howled behind him.

A familiar voice shouting above the clamor told him that Ormond, at least, was not dead. He glanced back to see a tall figure cross the firelight and recognized Pembroke's rangy frame. The fire gleamed on steel in his hands. That they were armed showed they were not prisoners, though this forbearance on the part of the fierce nomads was more than his store of Eastern lore could explain.

The pursuers did not follow him far; drawing in under the shadows of a thicket he heard them shouting gutturally to each other as they rode back to the tent. There would be no more sleep in that *ordu* that night. Men with naked steel in their hand would pace their horses about the encampment until dawn. It would be difficult to steal back for a long shot at his enemies. But now, before he slew them, he wished to learn what took them to Yolgan.

Absently his hand caressed the hawk-headed pommel of the Turkoman scimitar. Then he turned again eastward and rode back along the route he had come, as fast as he could push the wearying horse. It was not yet dawn when he came upon what he had hoped to find—a second camp, some ten miles west of the spot where Ahmed had been killed; dying fires reflected on one small tent and on the forms of men wrapped in cloaks on the ground.

He did not approach too near; when he could make out the lines of slowly moving shapes that were picketed horses and could see other shapes that were riders pacing about the camp, he drew back behind a thicketed ridge, dismounted and unsaddled his horse.

While it eagerly cropped the fresh grass, he sat cross-legged with his back to a tree trunk, his rifle across his knees, as motionless as an image and as imbued with the vast patience of the East as the eternal hills themselves.

3.

Dawn was little more than a hint of grayness in the sky when the camp that Gordon watched was astir. Smoldering coals leaped up into flames again, and the scent of mutton stew filled the air. Wiry men in caps of Astrakhan fur and girdled *caftans* swaggered among the horse lines or squatted beside the cooking pots, questing after savory morsels with unwashed fingers. There were no women among them and scant luggage. The lightness with which they traveled could mean only one thing.

The sun was not yet up when they began saddling horses and belting on weapons. Gordon chose that moment to appear, riding leisurely down the ridge toward them.

A yell went up, and instantly a score of rifles covered him. The very boldness of his action stayed their fingers on the triggers. Gordon wasted no time, though he did not appear hurried. Their chief had already mounted, and Gordon reined up almost beside him. The Turkoman glared—a hawk-nosed, evil-eyed ruffian with a henna-stained beard. Recognition grew like a red flame in his eyes, and, seeing this, his warriors made no move.

'Yusef Khan,' said Gordon, 'you Sunnite dog, have I found you at last?'

Yusef Khan plucked his red beard and snarled like a wolf. 'Are you mad, El Borak?'

'It is El Borak!' rose an excited murmur from the warriors, and that gained Gordon another respite.

They crowded closer, their blood lust for the instant

conquered by their curiosity. El Borak was a name known from Istanbul to Bhutan and repeated in a hundred wild tales wherever the wolves of the desert gathered.

As for Yusef Khan, he was puzzled, and furtively eyed the slope down which Gordon had ridden. He feared the white man's cunning almost as much as he hated him, and in his suspicion, hate and fear that he was in a trap, the Turkoman was as dangerous and uncertain as a wounded cobra.

'What do you here?' he demanded. 'Speak quickly, before my warriors strip the skin from you a little at a time.'

'I came following an old feud.' Gordon had come down the ridge with no set plan, but he was not surprised to find a personal enemy leading the Turkomans. It was no usual coincidence. Gordon had blood-foes scattered all over Central Asia.

'You are a fool—'

In the midst of the chief's sentence Gordon leaned from his saddle and struck Yusef Khan across the face with his open hand. The blow cracked like a bull whip and Yusef reeled, almost losing his seat. He howled like a wolf and clawed at his girdle, so muddled with fury that he hesitated between knife and pistol. Gordon could have shot him down while he fumbled, but that was not the American's plan.

Keep off!' he warned the warriors, yet not reaching for a weapon. 'I have no quarrel with you. This concerns only your chief and me.'

With another man that would have had no effect; but another man would have been dead already. Even the wildest tribesman had a vague feeling that the rules governing action against ordinary *feringhi* did not apply to El Borak.

'Take him!' howled Yusef Khan. 'He shall be flayed alive!'

They moved forward at that, and Gordon laughed unpleasantly.

'Torture will not wipe out the shame I have put upon your chief,' he taunted. 'Men will say ye are led by a khan who bears the mark of El Borak's hand in his beard. How is such shame to be wiped out? Lo, he calls on his warriors to avenge him! Is Yusef Khan a coward?'

They hesitated again and looked at their chief whose beard was clotted with foam. They all knew that to wipe out such an insult the aggressor must be slain by the victim in single combat. In that wolf pack even a suspicion of cowardice was tantamount to a death sentence.

If Yusef Khan failed to accept Gordon's challenge, his men might obey him and torture the American to death at his pleasure, but they would not forget, and from that moment he was doomed.

Yusef Khan knew this; knew that Gordon had tricked him into a personal duel, but he was too drunk with fury to care. His eyes were red as those of a rabid wolf, and he had forgotten his suspicions that Gordon had riflemen hidden up on the ridge. He had forgotten everything except his frenzied passion to wipe out forever the glitter in those savage black eyes that mocked him.

'Dog!' he screamed, ripping out his broad scimitar. 'Die at the hands of a chief!'

He came like a typhoon, his cloak whipping out in the wind behind him, his scimitar flaming above his head. Gordon met him in the center of the space the warriors left suddenly clear.

Yusef Khan rode a magnificent horse as if it were part of him, and it was fresh. But Gordon's mount had rested, and it was well-trained in the game of war. Both horses responded instantly to the will of their riders.

The fighters revolved about each other in swift curvets and gambados, their blades flashing and grating without the slightest pause, turned red by the rising sun. It was less like two men fighting on horseback than like a pair of centaurs, half man and half beast, striking for one another's life.

'Dog!' panted Yusef Khan, hacking and hewing like a man possessed of devils. 'I'll nail your head to my tent pole—ahhhh!'

Not a dozen of the hundred men watching saw the stroke, except as a dazzling flash of steel before their eyes, but all heard its crunching impact. Yusef Khan's charger screamed and reared, throwing a dead man from the saddle with a split skull.

A wordless wolfish yell that was neither anger nor applause went up, and Gordon wheeled, whirling his scimitar about his head so that the red drops flew in a shower.

'Yusef Khan is dead!' he roared. 'Is there one to take up his quarrel?'

They gaped at him, not sure of his intention, and before they could recover from surprise of seeing their invincible chief fall, Gordon thrust his scimitar back in its sheath with a certain air of finality and said:

'And now who will follow me to plunder greater than any of ye ever dreamed?'

That struck an instant spark, but their eagerness was qualified by suspicion.

'Show us!' demanded one. 'Show us the plunder before we slay thee.'

Without answering, Gordon swung off his horse and cast the reins to a mustached rider to hold, who was so astonished that he accepted the indignity without protest. Gordon strode over to a cooking pot, squatted beside it and began to eat ravenously. He had not tasted food in many hours.

'Shall I show you the stars by daylight?' he demanded, scooping out handfuls of stewed mutton. 'Yet the stars are there, and men see them in the proper time. If I had the loot would I come asking you to share it? Neither of us can win it without the other's aid.'

'He lies,' said one whom his comrades addressed as Uzun Beg. 'Let us slay him and continue to follow the caravan we have been tracking.'

'Who will lead you?' asked Gordon pointedly.

They scowled at him, and various ruffians who considered themselves logical candidates glanced furtively at one another. Then all looked back at Gordon, unconcernedly wolfing down mutton stew five minutes after having slain the most dangerous swordsman of the black tents.

His attitude of indifference deceived nobody. They knew he was dangerous as a cobra that could strike like lightning in any direction. They knew they could not kill him so quickly that he would not kill some of them, and naturally none wanted to be first to die.

That alone would not have stopped them. But that was combined with curiosity, avarice roused by his mention of plunder, vague suspicion that he would not have put himself in a trap unless he held some sort of a winning hand, and jealousy of the leaders of each other.

Uzun Beg, who had been examining Gordon's mount, exclaimed angrily: 'He rides Ali Khan's steed!'

'Aye,' Gordon assented tranquilly. 'Moreover this is Ali Khan's sword. He fired at me from ambush, so he lies dead.'

There was no answer. There was no feeling in that wolf pack except fear and hate, and respect for courage, craft, and ferocity.

'Where would you lead us?' demanded one named Orkhan Shah, tacitly recognizing Gordon's dominance. 'We be all free men and sons of the sword.'

'Ye be all sons of dogs,' answered Gordon. 'Men without grazing lands or wives, outcasts, denied by thine own people—outlaws whose lives are forfeit, and who must roam in the naked mountains. You followed that dead dog without question. Now ye demand this and that of me!'

Then ensued a medley of argument among themselves, in which Gordon seemed to take no interest. All his attention was devoted to the cooking pot. His attitude was no pose; without swagger or conceit the man was so sure of himself that his bearing was no more self-conscious among a hundred cutthroats hovering on the hair line of murder than it would have been among friends.

Many eyes sought the gun butt at his hip. Men said his skill with the weapon was sorcery; an ordinary revolver became in his hand a living engine of destruction that was drawn and roaring death before a man could realize that Gordon's hand had moved.

'Men say thou hast never broken thy word,' suggested Orkhan. 'Swear to lead us to this plunder, and it may be we shall see.'

'I swear no oaths,' answered Gordon, rising and wiping his hands on a saddle cloth. 'I have spoken. It is enough. Follow me, and many of you will die. Aye, the jackals will feed full. You will go up to the paradise of the prophet and your brothers will forget your names. But to those that live, wealth like the rain of Allah will fall upon them.'

'Enough of words!' exclaimed one greedily. 'Lead us to this rare loot.'

'You dare not follow where I would lead,' he answered. 'It lies in the land of the Kara Kirghiz.'

'We dare, by Allah!' they barked angrily. 'We are already in the land of the Black Kirghiz, and we follow the caravan of some infidels, whom, *inshallah*, we shall send to hell before another sunrise.'

'*Bismillah,*' said Gordon. 'Many of you shall eat arrows and edged steel before our quest is over. But if you dare stake your lives against plunder richer than treasures of Hind, come with me. We have far to ride.'

A few minutes later the whole band was trotting westward. Gordon led, with lean riders on either hand; their attitude suggested that he was more prisoner than guide, but he was not perturbed. His confidence in his destiny had again been justified, and the fact that he had not the slightest idea of how to redeem his pledge concerning treasure disturbed him not at all. A way would be opened to him, somehow, and at present he did not even bother to consider it.

4.

The fact that Gordon knew the country better than the
Turkomans did aided him in his subtle policy to gain
ascendancy over them. From giving suggestions to giving
orders and being obeyed is a short step, when delicately
taken.

He took care that they kept below the sky lines as
much as possible. It was not easy to hide the progress of
a hundred men from the alert nomads; but these roamed
far and there was a chance that only the band he had seen
were between him and Yolgan.

But Gordon doubted this when they crossed a track
that had been made since he rode eastward the night
before. Many riders had passed that point, and Gordon
urged greater speed, knowing that if they were spied by
the Kirghiz instant pursuit was inevitable.

In the late afternoon they came in sight of the *ordu*
beside the willow-lined stream. Horses tended by young-
sters grazed near the camp, and farther away the riders
watched the sheep which browsed through the tall grass.

Gordon had left all his men except half a dozen in a
thicket-massed hollow behind the next ridge, and he now
lay among a cluster of boulders on a slope overlooking
the valley. The encampment was beneath him, distinct
in every detail, and he frowned. There was no sign of the
white tents. The Englishmen had been there. They were
not there now. Had their hosts turned on them at last, or
had they continued alone toward Yolgan?

The Turkomans, who did not doubt that they were to
attack and loot their hereditary enemies, began to grow
impatient.

'Their fighting men are less than ours,' suggested Uzun
Beg, 'and they are scattered, suspecting nothing. It is long
since an enemy invaded the land of the Black Kirghiz.
Send back for the others, and let us attack. You promised
us plunder.'

'Flat-faced women and fat-tailed sheep?' Gordon jeered.

'Some of the women are fair to look at,' the Turkoman maintained. 'And we could feast full on the sheep. But these dogs carry gold in their wagons to trade to merchants from Kashmir. It comes from Mount Erlik Khan.'

Gordon remembered that he had heard tales of a gold mine in Mount Erlik before, and he had seen some crudely cast ingots the owners of which swore they had them from the Black Kirghiz. But gold did not interest him just then.

'That is a child's tale,' he said, at least half believing what he said. 'The plunder I will lead you to is real, would you throw it away for a dream? Go back to the others and bid them stay hidden. Presently I will return.'

They were instantly suspicious, and he saw it.

'Return thou, Uzun Beg,' he said, 'and give the others my message. The rest of you come with me.'

That quieted the hair-trigger suspicions of the five, but Uzun Beg grumbled in his beard as he strode back down the slope, mounted and rode eastward. Gordon and his companions likewise mounted behind the crest and, keeping below the sky line, they followed the ridge around as it slanted toward the southwest.

It ended in sheer cliffs, as if it had been sliced off with a knife, but dense thickets hid them from the sight of the camp as they crossed the space that lay between the cliffs and the next ridge, which ran to a bend in the stream, a mile below the *ordu*.

This ridge was considerably higher than the one they had left, and before they reached the point where it began to slope downward toward the river, Gordon crawled to the crest and scanned the camp again with a pair of binoculars that had once been the property of Yusef Khan.

The nomads showed no sign that they suspected the presence of enemies, and Gordon turned his glasses farther eastward, located the ridge beyond which his men were concealed, but saw no sign of them. But he did see something else.

Miles to the east a knife-edge ridge cut the sky, notched with a shallow pass. As he looked he saw a string of black dots moving through that notch. It was so far away that even the powerful glasses did not identify them, but he knew what the dots were—mounted men, many of them.

Hurrying back to his five Turkomans, he said nothing, but pressed on, and presently they emerged from behind the ridge and came upon the stream where it wound out of sight of the encampment. Here was the logical crossing for any road leading to Yolgan, and it was not long before he found what he sought.

In the mud at the edges of the stream were the prints of shod hoofs and at one spot the mark of a European boot. The Englishmen had crossed here; beyond the ford their trail lay west, across the rolling table-land.

Gordon was puzzled anew. He had supposed that there was some particular reason why this clan had received the Englishmen in peace. He had reasoned that Ormond would persuade them to escort him to Yolgan. Though the clans made common cause against invaders, there were feuds among themselves, and the fact that one tribe received a man in peace did not mean that another tribe would not cut his throat.

Gordon had never heard of the nomads of this region showing friendship to any white man. Yet the Englishmen had passed the night in that *ordu* and now plunged boldly on as if confident of their reception. It looked like utter madness.

As he meditated, a distant sputter of rifle fire jerked his head up. He splashed across the stream and raced up the slope that hid them from the valley, with the Turkomans at his heels working the levers of their rifles. As he topped the slope he saw the scene below him crystal-etched in the blue evening.

The Turkomans were attacking the Kirghiz camp. They had crept up the ridge overlooking the valley, and then swept down like a whirlwind. The surprise had been almost, but not quite, complete. Outriding shepherds had been shot down and the flocks scattered, but the surviving nomads had made a stand within the ring of their tents and wagons.

Ancient matchlocks, bows, and a few modern rifles answered the fire of the Turkomans. These came on swiftly, shooting from the saddle, only to wheel and swerve out of close range again.

The Kirghiz were protected by their cover, but even so the hail of lead took toll. A few saddles were emptied, but the Turkomans were hard to hit on their prancing horses, as the riders swung their bodies from side to side.

Gordon gave his horse the rein and came galloping across the valley, his scimitar glittering in his hand. With his enemies gone from the camp, there was no reason for attacking the Kirghiz now as he had planned. But the distance was too great for shouted orders to be heard.

The Turkomans saw him coming, sword in hand, and mistook his meaning. They thought he meant to lead a charge, and in their zeal they anticipated him. They were aided by the panic which struck the Kirghiz as they saw Gordon and his five Turkomans sweep down the slope and construed it as an attack in force on their flank.

Instantly they directed all their fire at the newcomers, emptying the clumsy matchlocks long before Gordon was even within good rifle range. And as they did, the Turkomans charged home with a yell that shook the valley, preceded by a withering fire as they blazed away over their horses' ears.

This time no ragged volleys could stop them. In their panic the tribesmen had loosed all their firearms at once, and the charge caught them with matchlocks and muskets empty. A straggling rifle fire met the oncoming raiders and knocked a few out of their saddles, and a flight of arrows accounted for a few more, but then the charge burst on the makeshift barricade and crumpled it. The howling Turkomans rode their horses in among the tents, flailing right and left with scimitars already crimson.

For an instant hell raged in the *ordu*, then the demoralized nomads broke and fled as best they could, being cut down and trampled by the conquerors. Neither women nor children were spared by the blood-mad Turks. Such as could slipped out of the ring and ran wailing for the river. An instant later the riders were after them like wolves.

Yet, winged by the fear of death, a disorderly mob reached the shore first, broke through the willows and plunged screaming over the low bank, trampling each other in the water. Before the Turkomans could rein their horses over the bank, Gordon arrived, with his horse plastered with sweat and snorting foam.

Enraged at the wanton slaughter, Gordon was an incarnation of berserk fury. He caught the first man's bridle and threw his horse back on its haunches with such violence that the beast lost its footing and fell, sprawling, throwing its rider. The next man sought to crowd past, giving tongue like a wolf, and him Gordon smote with the flat of his scimitar. Only the heavy fur cap saved the skull beneath, and the man pitched, senseless, from his saddle. The others yelled and reined back suddenly.

Gordon's wrath was like a dash of ice-cold water in their faces, shocking their blood-mad nerves into stinging sensibility. From among the tents cries still affronted the twilight, with the butcherlike chopping of merciless sword blows, but Gordon gave no heed. He could save no one in the plundered camp, where the howling warriors were ripping the tents to pieces, overturning the wagons and setting the torch in a hundred places.

More and more men with burning eyes and dripping blades were streaming toward the river, halting as they saw El Borak barring their way. There was not a ruffian there who looked half as formidable as Gordon did in that instant. His lips snarled and his eyes were black coals of hell's fire.

There was no play acting about it. His mask of immobility had fallen, revealing the sheer primordial ferocity of

the soul beneath. The dazed Turkomans, still dizzy from
the glutting of their blood lust, weary from striking great
blows, and puzzled by his attitude, shrank back from him.

'Who gave the order to attack?' he yelled, and his voice
was like the slash of a saber.

He trembled in the intensity of his passion. He was
a blazing flame of fury and death, without control or
repression. He was as wild and brute-savage in that
moment as the wildest barbarian in that raw land.

'Uzun Beg!' cried a score of voices, and men pointed at
the scowling warrior. 'He said that you had stolen away
to betray us to the Kirghiz, and that we should attack
before they had time to come upon us and surround us.
We believed him until we saw you riding over the slope.'

With a wordless fierce yell like the scream of a striking
panther, Gordon hurled his horse like a typhoon on Uzun
Beg, smiting with his scimitar. Uzun Beg catapulted from
his saddle with his skull crushed, dead before he actually
realized that he was menaced.

El Borak wheeled on the others and they reined back
from him, scrambling in terror.

'Dogs! Jackals! Noseless apes! Forgotten of God!' he
lashed them with words that burned like scorpions. 'Sons
of nameless curs! Did I not bid you keep hidden? Is my
word wind—a leaf to be blown away by the breath of a
dog like Uzun Beg? Now you have lapped up needless
blood, and the whole countryside will be riding us down
like jackals. Where is your loot? Where is the gold with
which the wagons were laden?'

'There was no gold,' muttered a tribesman, mopping
blood from a sword cut.

They flinched from the savage scorn and anger in
Gordon's baying laughter.

'Dogs that nuzzle in the dung heaps of hell! I should
leave you to die.'

'Slay him!' mouthed a tribesman. 'Shall we eat of an
infidel? Slay him and let us go back whence we came.
There is no loot in this naked land.'

The proposal was not greeted with enthusiasm. Their rifles were all empty, some even discarded in the fury of sword strokes. They knew the rifle under El Borak's knee was loaded and the pistol at his hip. Nor did any of them care to ride into the teeth of that reddened scimitar that swung like a live thing in his right hand.

Gordon saw their indecision and mocked them. He did not argue or reason as another man might have done. And if he had, they would have killed him. He beat down opposition with curses, abuses, and threats that were convincing because he meant every word he spat at them. They submitted because they were a wolf pack, and he was the grimmest wolf of them all.

Not one man in a thousand could have bearded them as he did and lived. But there was a driving elemental power about him that shook resolution and daunted anger—something of the fury of an unleashed torrent or a roaring wind that hammered down will power by sheer ferocity.

'We will have no more of thee,' the boldest voiced the last spark of rebellion. 'Go thy ways, and we will go ours.'

Gordon barked a bitter laugh. 'Thy ways lead to the fires of Jehannum!' he taunted bitterly. 'Ye have spilled blood, and blood will be demanded in payment. Do you dream that those who have escaped will not flee to the nearest tribes and raise the countryside? You will have a thousand riders about your ears before dawn.'

'Let us ride eastward,' one said nervously. 'We will be out of this land of devils before the alarm is raised.'

Again Gordon laughed and men shivered. 'Fools! You cannot return. With the glasses I have seen a body of horsemen following our trail. Ye are caught in the fangs of the vise. Without me you cannot go onward; if you stand still or go back, none of you will see another sun set.'

Panic followed instantly which was more difficult to fight down than rebellion.

'Slay him!' howled one. 'He has led us into a trap!'

'Fools!' cried Orkhan Shah, who was one of the five Gordon had led to the ford. 'It was not he who tricked you into charging the Kirghiz. *He* would have led us on to the loot he promised. He knows this land and we do not. If ye slay him now, ye slay the only man who may save us!'

That spark caught instantly, and they clamored about Gordon.

'The wisdom of the sahibs is thine! We be dogs who eat dirt! Save us from our folly! Lo, we obey thee! Lead us out of this land of death, and show us the gold whereof thou spokest!'

Gordon sheathed his scimitar and took command without comment. He gave orders and they were obeyed. Once these wild men, in their fear, turned to him, they trusted him implicitly. They knew he was somehow using them ruthlessly in his own plans, but that was nothing more than any one of them would have done had he been able. In that wild land only the ways of the wolf pack prevailed.

As many Kirghiz horses as could be quickly caught were rounded up. On some of them food and articles of clothing from the looted camp were hastily tied. Half a dozen Turkomans had been killed, nearly a dozen wounded. The dead were left where they had fallen. The most badly wounded were tied to their saddles, and their groans made the night hideous. Darkness had fallen as the desperate band rode over the slope and plunged across the river. The wailing of the Kirghiz women, hidden in the thickets, was like the dirging of lost souls.

5.

Gordon did not attempt to follow the trail of the Englishmen over the comparatively level table-land. Yolgan was his destination and he believed he would find them there, but there was desperate need to escape the tribesmen who he was certain were following them, and who would be lashed to fiercer determination by what they would find in the camp by the river.

Instead of heading straight across the table-land, Gordon swung into the hills that bordered it on the south and began following them westward. Before midnight one of the wounded men died in his saddle, and some of the others were semidelirious. They hid the body in a crevice and went on. They moved through the darkness of the hills like ghosts; the only sounds were the clink of hoofs on stone and the groans of the wounded.

An hour before dawn they came to a stream which wound between limestone ledges, a broad shallow stream with a solid rock bottom. They waded their horses along it for three miles, then climbed out again on the same side.

Gordon knew that the Kirghiz, smelling out their trail like wolves, would follow them to the bank and expect some such ruse as an effort to hide their tracks. But he hoped that the nomads would be expecting them to cross the stream and plunge into the mountains on the other side and would therefore waste time looking for tracks along the south bank.

He now headed westward in a more direct route. He did not expect to throw the Kirghiz entirely off the scent. He was only playing for time. If they lost his trail, they would search in any direction first except toward Yolgan, and to Yolgan he must go, since there was now no chance of catching his enemies on the road.

Dawn found them in the hills, a haggard, weary band. Gordon bade them halt and rest and, while they did so, he climbed the highest crag he could find and patiently scanned the surrounding cliffs and ravines with his binoculars, while he chewed tough strips of dried mutton which the tribesmen carried between saddle and saddle-cloth to keep warm and soft. He alternated with cat naps of ten or fifteen minutes' duration, storing up concentrated energy as men of the outlands learn to do, and between times watching the ridges for signs of pursuit.

He let the men rest as long as he dared, and the sun was high when he descended the rock and stirred them into wakefulness. Their steel-spring bodies had recoverd some of their resilience, and they rose and saddled with alacrity, all except one of the wounded men, who had died in his sleep. They lowered his body into a deep fissure in the rocks and went on, more slowly, for the horses felt the grind more than the men.

All day they threaded their way through wild gorges overhung by gloomy crags. The Turkomans were cowed by the grim desolation and the knowledge that a horde of bloodthirsty barbarians were on their trail. They followed Gordon without question as he held them, turning and twisting, along dizzy heights and down into the abysmal gloom of savage gorges, then up turreted ridges again and around windswept shoulders.

He had used every artifice known to him to shake off pursuit and was making for his set goal as fast as possible. He did not fear encountering any clans in these bare hills; they grazed their flocks on the lower levels. But he was not familiar with the route he was following as his men thought.

He was feeling his way, mostly by the instinct for direction that men who live in the open possess, but he would have been lost a dozen times but for glimpses of Mount Erlik Khan shouldering up above the surrounding hills in the distance.

As they progressed westward he recognized other landmarks, seen from new angles, and just before sunset he glimpsed a broad shallow valley, across the pine-grown slopes of which he saw the walls of Yolgan looming against the crags behind it.

Yolgan was built at the foot of a mountain, overlooking the valley through which a stream wandered among masses of reeds and willows. Timber was unusually dense. Rugged mountains, dominated by Erlik's peak to the south, swept around the valley to the south and west, and in the north it was blocked by a chain of hills. To the east it was open, sloping down from a succession of uneven ridges. Gordon and his men had followed the ranges in their flight, and now they looked down on the valley from the south.

El Borak led the warriors down from the higher crags and hid them on one of the many gorges debouching on the lower slopes, not more than a mile and a half from the city itself. It ended in a cul-de-sac and suggested a trap, but the horses were ready to fall from exhaustion, the men's canteens were empty, and a spring gurgling out of the solid rock decided Gordon.

He found a ravine leading out of the gorge and placed men on guard there, as well as at the gorge mouth. It would serve as an avenue of escape if need be. The men gnawed the scraps of food that remained, and dressed their wounds as best they could. When he told them he was going on a solitary scout they looked at him with lack-luster eyes, in the grip of the fatalism that is the heritage of the Turkish races.

They did not mistrust him, but they felt like dead men already. They looked like ghouls, with their dusty, torn garments, clotted with dried blood, and sunken eyes of hunger and weariness. They squatted or lay about, wrapped in their tattered cloaks, unspeaking.

Gordon was more optimistic than they. Perhaps they had not completely eluded the Kirghiz, but he believed it would take some time for even those human bloodhounds to ferret them out, and he did not fear discovery by the inhabitants of Yolgan. He knew they seldom wandered into the hills.

Gordon had neither slept nor eaten as much as his men, but his steely frame was more enduring than theirs, and he was animated by a terrific vitality that would keep his brain clear and his body vibrant long after another man had dropped in his tracks.

It was dark when Gordon strode on foot out of the gorge, the stars hanging over the peaks like points of chilled silver. He did not strike straight across the valley, but kept to the line of marching hills. So it was no great coincidence that he discovered the cave where men were hidden.

It was situated in a rocky shoulder that ran out into the valley, and which he skirted rather than clamber over. Tamarisk grew thickly about it, masking the mouth so effectually that it was only by chance that he glimpsed the reflection of a fire against a smooth inner wall.

Gordon crept through the thickets and peered in. It was a bigger cave than the mouth indicated. A small fire was going, and three men squatted by it, eating and conversing in guttural Pashto. Gordon recognized three of the camp servants of the Englishmen. Farther back in the cave he saw the horses and heaps of camp equipment. The mutter of conversation was unintelligible where he crouched, and even as he wondered where the white men and the fourth servant were, he heard some one approaching.

He drew back farther into the shadows and waited, and presently a tall figure loomed in the starlight. It was the other Pathan, with his arms full of firewood.

As he strode toward the natural ramp which led up to the cave mouth, he passed so close to Gordon's hiding place that the American could have touched him with an extended arm. But he did not extend an arm; he sprang on the man's back like a panther on a buck.

The firewood was knocked in all directions and the two men rolled together down a short grassy slope, but Gordon's fingers were digging into the Pathan's bull throat, strangling his efforts to cry out, and the struggle made no noise that could have been heard inside the cave above the crackle of the tamarisk chunks.

The Pathan's superior height and weight were futile against the corded sinews and wrestling skill of his opponent. Heaving the man under him, Gordon crouched on his breast and throttled him dizzy before he relaxed his grasp and let life and intelligence flow back into his victim's dazed brain.

The Pathan recognized his captor and his fear was the greater, because he thought he was in the hands of a ghost.

His eyes glimmered in the gloom and his teeth shone in the black tangle of his beard.

'Where are the Englishmen?' demanded Gordon softly. 'Speak, you dog, before I break your neck!'

'They went at dusk toward the city of devils!' gasped the Pathan.

'Prisoners?'

'Nay; one with a shaven head guided them. They bore their weapons and were not afraid.'

'What are they doing here?'

'By Allah, I do not know!'

'Tell me all you do know,' commanded Gordon. 'But speak softly. If your mates hear and come forth, you will suddenly cease to be. Begin where I went forth to shoot the stag. After that, Ormond killed Ahmed. That I know.'

'Aye; it was the Englishman. I had naught to do with it. I saw Ahmed lurking outside Pembroke Sahib's tent. Presently Ormond Sahib came forth and dragged him in the tent. A gun spoke, and when we went to look, the Punjabi lay dead on the floor of the tent.

'Then the sahibs bade us strike the tents and load the pack horses, and we did so without question. We went westward in great haste. When the night was not yet half over, we sighted a camp of pagans, and my brothers and I were much afraid. But the sahibs went forward, and when the accursed ones came forth with arrows on string, Ormond Sahib held up a strange emblem which glowed in the light of the torches, whereupon the heathens dismounted and bowed to the earth.

'We abode in their camp that night. In the darkness some one came to the camp and there was fighting and a man slain, and Ormond Sahib said it was a spying Turkoman, and that there would be fighting, so at dawn we left the pagans and went westward in haste, across the ford. When we met other heathens, Ormond showed them the talisman, and they did us honor. All day we hastened, driving the beasts hard, and when night fell we did not halt, for Ormond Sahib was like one mad. So before the night was half gone, we came into this valley, and the sahibs hid us in this cave.

'Here we abode until a pagan passed near the cavern this morning, driving sheep. Then Ormond Sahib called to him and showed him the talisman and made it known that he wished speech with the priest of the city. So the man went, and presently he returned with the priest who could speak Kashmiri. He and the sahibs talked long together, but what they said I know not. But Ormond Sahib killed the man who had gone to fetch the priest, and he and the priest hid the body with stones.

'Then after more talk, the priest went away, and the sahibs abode in the cave all day. But at dusk another man came to them, a man with a shaven head and camel's hair robes, and they went with him toward the city. They bade us eat and then saddle and pack the animals, and be ready to move with great haste between midnight and dawn. That is all I know, as Allah is my witness.'

Gordon made no reply. He believed the man was telling the truth, and his bewilderment grew. As he meditated on the tangle, he unconsciously relaxed his grip, and the Pathan chose that instant to make his break for freedom. With a convulsive heave he tore himself partly free of Gordon's grasp, whipped from his garments a knife he had been unable to reach before, and yelled loudly as he stabbed.

Gordon avoided the thrust by a quick twist of his body; the edge slit his shirt and the skin beneath, and stung by its bite and his peril, he caught the Pathan's bull neck in both hands and put all his strength into a savage wrench. The man's spinal column snapped like a rotten branch, and Gordon flung himself over backward into the thicker shadows as a man bulked black in the mouth of the cavern. The fellow called a cautious query, but Gordon waited for no more. He was already gone like a phantom into the gloom.

The Pathan repeated his call and then, getting no response, summoned his mates in some trepidation. With weapons in their hands they stole down the ramp, and presently one of them stumbled over the body of their companion. They bent over it, muttering affrightedly.

'This is a place of devils,' said one. 'The devils have slain Akbar.'

'Nay,' said another. 'It is the people of this valley. They mean to slay us one by one.' He grasped his rifle and stared fearsomely into the shadows that hemmed them in. 'They have bewitched the sahibs and led them away to be slain,' he muttered.

'We will be next,' said the third. 'The sahibs are dead. Let us load the animals and go away quickly. Better die in the hills than wait like sheep for our throats to be cut.'

A few minutes later they were hurrying eastward through the pines as fast as they could urge the beasts.

Of this Gordon knew nothing. When he left the slope below the cave he did not follow the trend of hills as before, but headed straight through the pines toward the lights of Yolgan. He had not gone far when he struck a road from the east leading toward the city. It wound among the pines, a slightly less dark thread in a bulwark of blackness.

He followed it to within easy sight of the great gate which stood open in the dark and massive walls of the town. Guards leaned carelessly on their matchlocks. Yolgan feared no attack. Why should it? The wildest of the Mohammeddan tribes shunned the land of the devil worshipers. Sounds of barter and dispute were wafted by the night wind through the gate.

Somewhere in Yolgan, Gordon was sure, were the men he was seeking. That they intended returning to the cave he had been assured. But there was a reason why he wished to enter Yolgan, a reason not altogether tied up with vengeance. As he pondered, hidden in the deep shadow, he heard the soft *clop* of hoofs on the dusty road behind him. He slid farther back among the pines; then with a sudden thought he turned and made his way back beyond the first turn, where he crouched in the blackness beside the road.

Presently a train of laden pack mules came along, with men before and behind and at either side. They bore no torches, moving like men who knew their path. Gordon's eyes had so adjusted themselves to the faint starlight of the road that he was able to recognize them as Kirghiz herdsmen in their long cloaks and round caps. They passed so close to him that their body-scent filled his nostrils.

He crouched lower in the blackness, and as the last man moved past him, a steely arm hooked fiercely about the Kirghiz's throat, choking his cry. An iron fist crunched against his jaw and he sagged senseless in Gordon's arms. The others were already out of sight around the bend of the trail, and the scrape of the mules' bulging packs against the branches along the road was enough to drown the slight noises of the struggle.

Gordon dragged his victim in under the black branches and swiftly stripped him, discarding his own boots and kaffiych and donning the native's garments, with pistol and scimitar buckled on under the long cloak. A few minutes later he was moving along after the receding column, leaning on his staff as with the weariness of long travel. He knew the man behind him would not regain consciousness for hours.

He came up with the tail of the train, but lagged behind as a straggler might. He kept close enough to the caravan to be identified with it, but not so close as to tempt conversation or recognition by the other members of the train. When they passed through the gate none challenged him. Even in the flare of the torches under the great gloomy arch he looked like a native, with his dark features fitting in with his garments and the lambskin cap.

As he went down the torch-lighted street, passing unnoticed among the people who chattered and argued in the markets and stalls, he might have been one of the many Kirghiz shepherds who wandered about, gaping at the sights of the city which to them represented the last world in the metropolitan.

Yolgan was not like any other city in Asia. Legend said it was built long ago by a cult of devil worshipers who, driven from their distant homeland, had found sanctuary in this unmapped country, where an isolated branch of the Black Kirghiz, wilder than their kinsmen, roamed as masters. The people of the city were a mixed breed, descendants of these original founders and the Kirghiz.

Gordon saw the monks who were the ruling caste in Yolgan striding through the bazaars—tall, shaven-headed men with Mongolian features. He wondered anew as to their exact origin. They were not Tibetans. Their religion was not a depraved Buddhism. It was unadulterated devil worship. The architecture of their shrines and temples differed from any he had ever encountered anywhere.

But he wasted no time in conjecture, nor in aimless wandering. He went straight to the great stone building squatted against the side of the mountain at the foot of which Yolgan was built. Its great blank curtains of stone seemed almost like part of the mountain itself.

No one hindered him. He mounted a long flight of steps that were at least a hundred feet wide, bending over his staff as with the weariness of a long pilgrimage. Great bronze doors stood open, unguarded, and he kicked off his sandals and came into a huge hall the inner gloom of which was barely lighted by dim brazen lamps in which melted butter was burned.

Shaven-headed monks moved through the shadows' like dusky ghosts, but they gave him no heed, thinking him merely a rustic worshipper come to leave some humble offering at the shrine of Erlik, Lord of the Seventh Hell.

At the other end of the hall, the view was cut off by a great divided curtain of gilded leather that hung from the lofty roof to the floor. Half a dozen steps that crossed the hall led up to the foot of the curtain, and before it a monk sat cross-legged and motionless as a statue, arms folded and head bent as if in communion with unguessed spirits.

Gordon halted at the foot of the steps, made as if to prostrate himself, then retreated as if in sudden panic. The monk showed no interest. He had seen too many nomads from the outer world overcome by superstitious awe before the curtain that hid the dread effigy of Erlik Khan. The timid Kirghiz might skulk about the temple for hours before working up nerve enough to make his devotions to the deity. None of the priests paid any attention to the man in the caftan of a shepherd who slunk away as if abashed.

As soon as he was confident that he was not being watched, Gordon slipped through a dark doorway some distance from the gilded curtain and groped his way down a broad unlighted hallway until he came to a flight of stairs. Up this he went with both haste and caution and came presently into a long corridor along which winked sparks of light, like fireflies in a tunnel.

He knew these lights were tiny lamps in the small cells that lined the passage, where the monks spent long hours in contemplation of dark mysteries, or pored over forbidden volumes, the very existence of which is not suspected by the outer world. There was a stair at the nearer end of the corridor, and up this he went, without being discovered by the monks in their cells. The pin points of light in the chambers did not serve to illuminate the darkness of the corridor to any extent.

As Gordon approached a crook in the stair he renewed his caution, for he knew there would be a man on guard at the head of the steps. He knew also that he would be likely to be asleep. The man was there—a half-naked giant with the wizened features of a deaf mute. A broad-tipped tulwar lay across his knees and his head rested on it as he slept.

Gordon stole noiselessly past him and came into an upper corridor which was dimly lighted by brass lamps hung at intervals. There were no doorless cells here, but heavy bronze-bound teak portals flanked the passage. Gordon went straight to one which was particularly ornately carved and furnished with an unusual fretted arch by way of ornament. He crouched there listening intently, then took a chance and rapped softly on the door. He rapped nine times, with an interval between each three raps.

There was an instant's tense silence, then an impulsive rush of feet across a carpeted floor, and the door was jerked open. A magnificent figure stood framed in the soft light. It was a woman, a lithe, splendid creature whose vibrant figure exuded magnetic vitality. The jewels that sparkled in the girdle about her supple hips were no more scintillant than her eyes.

Instant recognition blazed in those eyes, despite his native garments. She caught him in a fierce grasp. Her slender arms were strong as pliant steel.

'El Borak! I knew you would come!'

Gordon stepped into the chamber and closed the door behind him. A quick glance showed him there was no one there but themselves. Its thick Persian rugs, silk divans, velvet hangings, and gold-chased lamps struck a vivid contrast with the grim plainness of the rest of the temple. Then he turned his full attention again to the woman who stood before him, her white hands clenched in a sort of passionate triumph.

'How did you know I would come, Yasmeena?' he asked.

'You never failed a friend in need,' she answered.

'Who is in need?'

'I!'

'But you are a goddess!'

'I explained it all in my letter!' she exclaimed bewilderedly.

Gordon shook his head. 'I have received no letter.'

'Then why are you here?' she demanded in evident puzzlement.

'It's a long story,' he answered. 'Tell me first why Yasmeena, who had the world at her feet and threw it away for weariness to become a goddess in a strange land, should speak of herself as one in need.'

'In desperate need, El Borak.' She raked back her dark locks with a nervously quick hand. Her eyes were shadowed with weariness and something more, something which Gordon had never seen there before—the shadow of fear.

'Here is food you need more than I,' she said as she sank down on a divan and with a dainty foot pushed toward him a small gold table on which were chupaties, curried rice, and broiled mutton, all in gold vessels, and a gold jug of kumiss.

He sat down without comment and began to eat with unfeigned gusto. In his drab camel's-hair caftan, with the wide sleeves drawn back from his corded brown arms, he looked out of place in that exotic chamber.

Yasmeena watched him broodingly, her chin resting on her hand, her somber eyes enigmatic

'I did not have the world at my feet, El Borak,' she said presently. 'But I had enough of it to sicken me. It became a wine which had lost its savor. Flattery became like an insult; the adulation of men became an empty repetition without meaning. I grew maddeningly weary of the flat fool faces that smirked eternally up at me, all wearing the same sheep expressions and animated by the same sheep thoughts. All except a few men like you, El Borak, and you were wolves in the flock. I might have loved you, El Borak, but there is something too fierce about you; your soul is a whetted blade on which I feared I might cut myself.'

He made no reply, but tilted the golden jug and gulped down enough stinging kumiss to have made an ordinary man's head swim at once. He had lived the life of the nomads so long that their tastes had become his.

'So I became a princess, wife of a prince of Kashmir,' she went on, her eyes smoldering with a marvellous shifting of clouds and colors. 'I thought I knew the depths of men's swinishness. I found I had much to learn. He was a beast. I fled from him into India, and the British protected me when his ruffians would have dragged me back to him. He still offers many thousand rupees to any one who will bring me alive to him, so that he may soothe his vanity by having me tortured to death.'

'I have heard a rumor to that effect,' answered Gordon.

A recurrent thought caused his face to darken. He did not frown, but the effect was subtly sinister.

'That experience completed my distaste for the life I knew,' she said, her dark eyes vividly introspective. 'I remembered that my father was a priest of Yolgan who fled away for love of a stranger woman. I had emptied the cup and the bowl was dry. I remembered Yolgan through the tales my father told me when I was a babe, and a great yearning rose in me to lose the world and find my soul. All the gods I knew had proved false to me. The mark of Erlik was upon me—' she parted her pearl-sewn vest and displayed a curious starlike mark between her firm breasts.

'I came to Yolgan as well as you know, because you brought me, in the guise of a Kirghiz from Issik-kul. As you know, the people remembered my father, and though they looked on him as a traitor, they accepted me as one of them, and because of an old legend which spoke of the star on a woman's bosom, they hailed me as a goddess, the incarnation of the daughter of Erlik Khan

'For a while after you went away I was content. The people worshiped me with more sincerity than I had ever seen displayed by the masses of civilization. Their curious rituals were strange and fascinating. Then I began to go further into their mysteries; I began to sense the essence below the formula—' She paused, and Gordon saw the fear grow in her eyes again.

'I had dreamed of a calm retreat of mystics, inhabited by philosophers. I found a haunt of bestial devils, ignorant of all but evil. Mysticism? It is black shamanism, foul as the tundras which bred it I have seen things that made me afraid. Yes, I, Yasmeena, who never knew the meaning of the word, I have learned fear. Yogok, the high priest, taught me. You warned me against Yogok before you left Yolgan. Well had I heeded you. He hates me. He knows I am not divine, but he fears my power over the people. He would have slain me long ago had he dared.

'I am wearied to death of Yolgan. Erlik Khan and his devils have proved no less an illusion than the gods of India and the West. I have not found the perfect way. I have found only awakened desire to return to the world I cast away.

'I want to go back to Delhi. At night I dream of the noise and smell of the streets and bazaars. I am half Indian, and all the blood of India is calling me. I was a fool. I had life in my hands and did not recognize it.'

'Why not go back, then?' asked Gordon.

She shuddered. 'I cannot. The gods of Yolgan must remain in Yolgan forever. Should one depart, the people believe the city would perish. Yogok would be glad to see me go, but he fears the fury of the people too much either to slay me or aid me to escape. I knew there was but one man who might help me. I wrote a letter to you and smuggled it out by a Tajik trader. With it I sent my sacred emblem—a jeweled gold star—which would pass you safely through the country of the nomads. They would not harm a man bearing it. He would be safe from all but the priests of the city. I explained that in my letter.'

'I never got it,' Gordon answered. 'I'm here after a couple of scoundrels whom I was guiding into the Uzbek country, and who for no apparent reason murdered my servant Ahmed and deserted me in the hills. They're in Yolgan now, somewhere.'

'White men?' she exclaimed. 'That is impossible! They could never have got through the tribes—'

'There's only one key to the puzzle,' he interrupted. 'Somehow your letter fell into their hands. They used

your star to let them through. They don't mean to rescue
you, because they got in touch with Yogok as soon as
they reached the valley. There's only one thing I can
think of—they intend kidnapping you to sell to your
former husband.'

She sat up straight; her white hands clenched on the
edge of the divan and her eyes flashed. In that instant
she looked as splendid and as dangerous as a cobra when
it rears up to strike.

'Back to that pig? Where are these dogs? I will speak a
word to the people and they shall cease to be!'

'That would betray yourself,' returned Gordon. 'The
people would kill the stranger, and Yogok, too, maybe,
but they'd learn that you'd been trying to escape from
Yolgan. They allow you the freedom of the temple, don't
they?'

'Yes; with shaven-headed skulkers spying on my every
move, except when I am on this floor, from which only a
single stair leads down. That stair is always guarded.'

'By a guard who sleeps,' said Gordon. 'That's bad
enough, but if the people found you were trying to escape,
they might shut you up in a little cell for the rest of your
life. People are particularly careful of their deities.'

She shuddered, and her fine eyes flashed the fear an
eagle feels for a cage. 'Then what are we to do?'

'I don't know—yet. I have nearly a hundred Turkoman
ruffians hidden up in the hills, but just now they're more
hindrance than help. There's not enough of them to do
much good in a pitched battle, and they're almost sure
to be discovered tomorrow, if not before. I brought them
into this mess, and it's up to me to get them out—or as
many as I can. I came here to kill these Englishmen,
Ormond and Pembroke. But that can wait now. I'm going
to get you out of here, but I don't dare move until I know
where Yogok and the Englishmen are. Is there any one in
Yolgan you can trust?'

'Any of the people would die for me, but they won't
let me go. Only actual harm done me by the monks

would stir them up against Yogok. No; I dare trust none of them.'

'You say that stair is the only way up onto this floor?'

'Yes. The temple is built against the mountain, and galleries and corridors on the lower floors go back far into the mountain itself. But this is the highest floor, and is reserved entirely for me. There's no escape from it except down through the temple, swarming with monks. I keep only one servant here at night, and she is at present sleeping in a chamber some distance from this and is senseless with bhang as usual.'

'Good enough!' grunted Gordon. 'Here, take this pistol. Lock the door after I go through and admit no one but myself. You'll recognize me by the nine raps, as usual.'

'Where are you going?' she demanded, staring up and mechanically taking the weapon he tendered her, butt first.

'To do a little spying,' he answered. 'I've got to know what Yogok and the others are doing. If I tried to smuggle you out now, we might run square into them. I can't make plans until I know some of theirs. If they intend sneaking you out tonight, as I think they do, it might be a good idea to let them do it, and then swoop down with the Turkomans and take you away from them, when they've got well away from the city. But I don't want to do that unless I have to. Bound to be shooting and a chance of your getting hit by a stray bullet. I'm going now; listen for my rap.'

6.

The mute guard still slumbered on the stair as Gordon glided past him. No lights glinted now as he descended into the lower corridor. He knew the cells were all empty, for the monks slept in chambers on a lower level. As he hesitated, he heard sandals shuffling down the passage in the pitch blackness.

Stepping into one of the cells he waited until the unseen traveler was opposite him, then he hissed softly. The tread halted and a voice muttered a query.

'Art thou Yatub?' asked Gordon in the gutturals of the Kirghiz. Many of the lower monks were pure Kirghiz in blood and speech.

'Nay,' came the answer. 'I am Ojuh. Who art thou?'

'No matter; call me Yogok's dog if thou wilt. I am a watcher. Have the white men come into the temple yet?'

'Aye. Yogok brought them by the secret way, lest the people suspect their presence. If thou art close to Yogok, tell me—what is his plan?'

'What is thine own opinion?' asked Gordon.

An evil laugh answered him, and he could feel the monk leaning closer in the darkness to rest an elbow on the jamb.

'Yogok is crafty,' he murmured. 'When the Tajik whom Yasmeena bribed to bear her letter showed it to Yogok, our master bade him do as she had instructed him. When the man for whom she sent came for her, Yogok planned to slay both him and her, making it seem to the people that the white man had slain their goddess.'

'Yogok is not forgiving,' said Gordon at a venture.

'A cobra is more so.' The monk laughed. 'Yasmeena has thwarted him too often in the matter of sacrifices for him to allow her to depart in peace.

'Yet such is now his plan!' asserted Gordon.

'Nay; thou art a simple man, for one who calls himself a watcher. The letter was meant for El Borak. But the Tajik was greedy and sold it to these sahibs and told them of Yogok. They will not take her to India. They will sell her to a prince in Kashmir who will have her beaten to death with a slipper. Yogok himself will guide them through the hills by the secret route. He is in terror of the people, but his hate for Yasmeena overcomes him.'

Gordon had heard all he wished to know, and he was in a sudden rush to be gone. He had abandoned his tentative plan of letting Ormond get the girl outside the city before rescuing her. With Yogok guiding the Englishmen through hidden passes, he might find it impossible to overtake them.

The monk, however, was in no hurry to conclude the conversation. He began speaking again, and then Gordon saw a light moving like a glowworm in the blackness, and he heard a swift patter of bare feet and a man breathing heavily. He drew farther back into the cell.

It was another monk who came up the corridor, carrying a small brass lamp that lighted his broad, thin-lipped face and made him look something like a Mongolian devil.

As he saw the monk outside the cell, he began hastily: 'Yogok and the white men have gone to Yasmeena's chamber. The girl, her servant who spied upon her, has told us that the white devil El Borak is in Yolgan. He talked with Yasmeena less than half an hour agone. The girl sped to Yogok as swiftly as she dared, but she dared not stir until he had left Yasmeena's chamber. He is somewhere in the temple. I gather men to search. Come with me, thou, and thou also—'

He swung the lamp about so that it shone full on Gordon, crouching in the cell. As the man blinked to see the garments of a shepherd instead of the familiar robes of a monk, Gordon lashed out for his jaw, quick and silent as the stroke of a python. The monk went down like a man shot in the head, and even as the lamp smashed on the floor, Gordon had leaped and grappled with the other man in the sudden darkness.

A single cry rang to the vaulted roof before it was strangled in the corded throat. The monk was hard to hold as a snake, and he kept groping for a knife, but as they crashed into the stone wall, Gordon smashed his opponent's head savagely against it. The man went limp and Gordon flung him down beside the other senseless shape.

The next instant Gordon was racing up the stairway. It was only a few steps from the cell where he had hidden, its upper portion dim in the subdued light of

the upper corridor. He knew no one had gone up or
down while he talked with the monk. Yet the man with
the lamp had said that Yogok and the others had gone to
Yasmeena's chamber, and that her treacherous servant
girl had come to them.

He rounded the crook with reckless haste, his scimitar
ready, but the slumping figure at the stairhead did not
rise to oppose him. There was a new sag in the mute's
shoulders as he huddled on the steps. He had been stabbed
in the back, so fiercely that the spinal column had been
severed with one stroke.

Gordon wondered why the priest should kill one of his
own servants, but he did not pause; premonition gripping
his heart, he hurled himself down the corridor and in
through the arched doorway, which was unbolted. The
chamber was empty. Cushions from the divan were strewn
on the floor. Yasmeena was not to be seen.

Gordon stood like a statue in the center of the room, his
scimitar in his hand. The blue sheen of the light on steel
was no more deadly than the glitter of his black eyes. His
gaze swept the room, lingering no longer on a slight bulge
in the hangings on the rear wall than anywhere else.

He turned toward the door, took a step—then wheeled
and raced across the chamber like a gust of wind,
slashing and hacking at the tapestry before the man
hiding there realized he was discovered. The keen edge
ribboned the velvet arras and blood spurted; out of the
tatters a figure toppled to the floor—a shaven monk,
literally cut to pieces. He had dropped his knife and
could only grovel and moan, clutching at his spurting
arteries.

'Where is she?' snarled Gordon, panting with passion
as he crouched over his hideous handiwork. 'Where is
she?'

But the man only whimpered and yammered and died
without speaking.

Gordon ran to the walls and began ripping the hangings
away. Somewhere he knew there must be a secret door.

But the walls showed blank, resisting his most violent efforts. He could not follow Yasmeena by the route her abductors had obviously carried her. He must escape from the city and hasten to the cave, where the servants were hidden, and to which the Englishmen would undoubtedly return. He was sweating with the violence of his rage, which almost submerged caution. He ripped off the camel's hair robe, feeling in his frenzy that it cramped and hampered him.

But the action brought a thought born of cold reason. The garments of the senseless monks in the corridor below would furnish him a disguise which would aid him to pass unhindered through the temple, where he knew scores of shaven-headed murderers were hunting him.

He ran silently from the chamber, passed the sprawling corpse, rounded the turn of the stair—then he stopped short. The lower corridor was a blaze of light, and at the foot of the stairs stood a mass of monks, holding torches and swords. He saw rifles in the hands of a dozen.

Details sprang out in startling clarity in the instant that the monks yelled and raised their rifles. Beyond them he saw a round-faced slant-eyed girl crouching by the wall. She grasped a rope which hung down the wall and jerked, and Gordon felt the stairs give way beneath him. The rifles roared in a ragged volley as he shot down the black opening which gasped beneath his feet, and the bullets whined over his head. A fierce cry of triumph rose from the monks.

7.

After Gordon left her, Yasmeena made fast the door and returned to her divan. She idly studied the big pistol he had left with her, fascinated by the blue gleam of the light on its dully polished steel.

Then she tossed it aside and lay back with her eyes closed. There was a certain sophistication or innate mysticism in her which refused to let her put much faith in material weapons. Hers was that overrefinement of civilization which instinctively belittles physical action. With all her admiration for Gordon, he was, after all, to her, a barbarian who put his thrust in lead and steel.

She undervalued the weapon he had left with her, and so it was out of her reach when the noise of a swishing tapestry roused her. She turned and stared at the rear wall with eyes suddenly dilated. Behind the hanging she knew—or thought she knew—was solid stone wall, built hard against the sheer mountainside.

But now that hanging lifted, grasped in a yellow clawlike hand. The hand was followed by a face—an evil, leering, grayish face, with slanted eyes and lank hair falling over a narrow forehead. A thin gash of a mouth gaped, revealing pointed teeth.

She was so astounded that she sat frozen, unable to supply the simple explanation of the phenomenon, until the man entered the room with a slithering silence repulsively suggestive of a snake. Then she saw that a black opening gaped in the wall behind the lifted arras, and two faces were framed in it—white men's faces, hard and inexorable as stone.

She sprang up then and snatched for the revolver, but it was at the other end of the divan. She ran around for it, but the slant-eyed man, with a motion incredibly quick, was before her and crushed her cruelly in his lean arms, clapping a hand over her mouth. He heeded the twisting and writhing of her supple body no more than the struggles of a child.

'Swift!' he ordered in harsh gutturals. 'Bind her!'

The white men had followed him into the chamber, but it was a monk who obeyed, adding a velvet gag. One of the white men picked up the pistol.

'See to the mute who slumbers on the stairs,' her captor ordered. 'He is not our man, but a creature set

by the people to guard her. Even a mute can speak by
gestures sometimes.'

The evil-faced monk bowed deeply and, unbolting the
door, went out, thumbing a long knife. Another monk
stood in the secret entrance.

'You did not know of the hidden door,' jeered the
slant-eyed man. 'You fool! The mountain below this
temple is honeycombed with tunnels. You have been
spied on constantly. The girl whom you thought drunk on
bhang watched tonight while you talked with El Borak.
That will not alter my plans any, though, except that I
have set my monks to slay El Borak.

'Then we will show the people his body and tell them
that you have returned to your father in the Seventh
Hell because Yolgan has been polluted by the presence
of a Feringhi. In the meantime these sahibs will be well
on their way to Kashmir with you, my lovely goddess!
Daughter of Erlik! Bah!'

'We're wasting time, Yogok,' broke in Ormond roughly. 'Once in the hills, you say, we won't meet any of the
Kirghiz, but I want to be far from Yolgan by daylight.'

The priest nodded and motioned to the monk who
came forward and lifted Yasmeena onto a litter he carried.
Pembroke took the other end. At that moment the other
monk glided back into the chamber, wiping blood from
his curved blade.

Yogok directed him to hide behinds the hangings. 'El
Borak might return before the others find him.'

Then they passed through the hidden door into darkness
lighted by a butter lamp in Yogok's hand. The priest slid
to the heavy section of stone that formed part of the wall
and made it fast with a bronze bar. Yasmeena saw by the
small light of the lamp that they were in a narrow corridor
which slanted downward at a pitch which grew steeper
until it ended in a long narrow stair cut out of solid rock.
At the bottom of this stair they struck a level tunnel
which they followed for some time, the Englishmen and

the monk alternating with the litter. It ended at last in a wall of rock, in the center of which was a stone block which worked on a pivot. This turned, they emerged into a cave, at the mouth of which stars were visible through a tangle of branches.

When Yogok pushed the block back in place its rough exterior looked like part of a solid wall. He extinguished the lamp and a moment later was pushing aside the massed willows which masked the cave mouth. As they emerged into the starlight, Yasmeena saw that these willows stood on the bank of a stream.

When her captors had pushed through the trees, waded the shallow channel, and ascended the farther bank, she saw a cluster of lights off to her right. Those lights were Yolgan. They had followed tunnels out into the solid rock of the mountain and had come out at its foot less than half a mile from the city. Directly ahead of her the forest lifted in rows of black ramparts, and off to the left the hills climbed in marching lines.

Her captors set off through the starlight, their apparent objective a jutting shoulder less than half a mile to the east. The distance was covered in silence. The nervousness of the white men was no more evident than that of Yogok. Each man was thinking what his fate would be if the common people of Yolgan discovered them kidnapping their goddess.

Yogok's fear was greater than that of the Englishmen. He had covered his tracks with corpses—the shepherd who had brought him Ormond's message, the mute guardian of the stairs; his teeth chattered as he conjured up possibilities. El Borak must die without speaking, also; that, he had drilled into the monks.

'Faster! Faster!' he urged, a note of panic in his voice as he glared at the black forest walls about him. In the moan of the night wind he seemed to hear the stealthy tread of pursuers.

'Here's the cave,' grunted Ormond. 'Set her down; no use lugging her up that slope. I'll go get the servants and the horses. We'll mount her on one of the pack animals. Have to leave some of our stuff behind, anyhow. Ohai, Akbar!' he called softly.

There was no answer. The fire had gone out in the cave and the mouth gaped black and silent.

'Have they gone to sleep?' Ormond swore irritably, 'I'll jolly well wake 'em. Wait!'

He ran lightly up the rough ramp and vanished in the cave. A moment later his voice reached them, echoing hollowly between the rocky walls. The echoes did not disguise the sudden fear in his voice.

8.

When Gordon fell through the treacherous stairs, he shot downward in utter blackness to land on solid stone. Not one man in a hundred could have survived the fall with unsmashed bones, but El Borak was all knit wires and steel springs. He landed on all fours, catlike, with bent joints absorbing the shock. Even so his whole body was numbed, and his limbs crumpled under him, letting his frame dash violently against the stone.

He lay there half stunned for a space, then pulled himself together, cursing the stinging and tingling of his hands and feet, and felt himself for broken bones.

Thankful to find himself intact, he groped for and found the scimitar which he had cast from him as he fell. Above him the trap had closed. Where he was he had no idea, but it was dark as a Stygian vault. He wondered how far he had fallen, and felt that it was farther than any one would ever believe, supposing he escaped to tell of it. He felt about in the darkness and found that he was in a square cell of no great dimensions. The one door was locked on the outside.

His investigations took him only a matter of seconds, and it was while he was feeling the door that he heard someone fumbling at it on the other side. He drew back, believing that those who dropped him into the cell would scarcely have had time to reach it by a safer way. He believed it was someone who had heard the sound of his fall and was coming to investigate, doubtless expecting to find a corpse on the floor.

The door was cast open and light blinded him, but he cut at the vague figure which loomed in the open door. Then his eyes could see and they saw a monk lying on the floor of a narrow lamp-lighted corridor with his shaven head split to the temples. The passage was empty except for the dead man.

The floor of the corridor sloped slightly, and Gordon went down it, because to go up it would obviously be returning toward his enemies. He momentarily expected to hear them howling on his heels, but evidently they considered that his fall through the trap, riddled, as they thought, with bullets, was sufficient and were in no hurry to verify their belief. Doubtless it was the duty of the monk he had killed to finish off victims dropped through the trap on the stairs.

The corridor made a sharp turn to the right and the lamps no longer burned along the walls. Gordon took one of them and went on, finding that the pitch of the slope grew steeper until he was forced to check his descent with a hand braced against the wall. These walls were solid rock, and he knew he was in the mountain on which the temple was built.

He did not believe any of the inhabitants of Yolgan knew of these tunnels except the monks; certainly Yasmeena was ignorant of them. Thought of the girl made him wince. Heaven alone knew where she was, just then, but he could not aid her until he had escaped himself from these rat-runs.

Presently the passage turned at right angles into a broader tunnel which ran level, and he followed it hastily but cautiously, holding his lamp high. Ahead of him he saw the tunnel end at last against a rough stone wall in which a door was set in the shape of a ponderous square block. This, he discovered, was hung on a pivot, and it revolved with ease, letting him through into a cave beyond.

As Yasmeena had seen the stars among the branches not long before, Gordon now discovered them. He put out his lamp, halted an instant to let his eyes get used to the sudden darkness, and then started toward the cavern mouth.

Just as he reached it, he crouched back. Somebody was splashing through the water outside, thrashing through the willows. The man came panting up the short steep slope, and Gordon saw the evil face of Yogok in the starlight before the man became a shapeless blob of blackness as he plunged into the cavern.

The next instant El Borak sprang, bearing his man to the floor. Yogok let out one hair-raising yell, and then Gordon found his throat and crouched over him, savagely digging and twisting his fingers in the priest's neck.

'Where is Yasmeena?' he demanded.

A gurgle answered him. He relaxed his grip a trifle and repeated the question. Yogok was mad with fear of this attack in the dark, but somehow—probably by the body-scent or the lack of it—he divined that his captor was a white man.

'Are you El Borak?' he gasped.

'Who else? Where is Yasmeena?' Gordon emphasized his demand by a wrench which brought a gurgle of pain from Yogok's thin lips.

'The Englishmen have her!' he panted.

'Where are they?'

'Nay; I know not! Ahhh! Mercy, sahib! I will tell!'

Yogok's eyes glimmered white with fear in the darkness. His lean body was shaking as with an ague.

'We took her to a cave where the sahibs' servants were hidden. They were gone, with the horses. The Englishmen accused me of treachery. They said I had made away with their servants and meant to murder them. They lied. By Erlik, I know not what became of their cursed Pathans!

The Englishmen attacked me, but I fled while a servant of mine fought with them.'

Gordon hauled him to his feet, faced him toward the cave mouth and bound his hands behind him with his own girdle.

'We're going back,' he said grimly. 'One yelp out of you and I'll let out your snake's soul. Guide me as straight to Ormond's cave as you know.'

'Nay; the dogs will slay me!'

'I'll kill you if you don't,' Gordon assured him, pushing Yogok stumbling before him.

The priest was not a back-to-the-wall fighter. Confronted by two perils he chose the more remote. They waded the stream and on the other side Yogok turned to the right. Gordon jerked him back.

'I know where I am now,' he growled. 'And I know where the cave is. It's in that jut of land to the left. If there's a path through the pines, show it to me.'

Yogok surrendered and hurried through the shadows, conscious of Gordon's grasp on his collar and the broad edge of Gordon's scimitar glimmering near. It was growing toward the darkness that precedes dawn as they came to the cave which loomed dark and silent among the trees.

'They are gone!' Yogok shivered.

'I didn't expect to find them here,' muttered Gordon. 'I came here to pick up their trail. If they thought you'd set the natives on them, they'd pull out on foot. What worries me is what they did with Yasmeena.'

'Listen!'

Yogok started convulsively as a low moan smote the air.

Gordon threw him and lashed together his hands and feet. 'Not a sound out of you!' he warned, and then stole up the ramp, sword ready.

At the mouth he hesitated unwilling to show himself against the dim starlight behind him. Then he heard the moan again and knew it was not feigned. It was a human being in mortal agony.

He felt his way into the darkness and presently stumbled over something yielding, which evoked another moan. His hands told him it was a man in European clothing. Something warm and oozy smeared his hands as he groped. Feeling in the man's pockets he found a box of matches and struck one, cupping it in his hands.

A livid face with glassy eyes stared up at him.

'Pembroke!' muttered Gordon.

The sound of his name seemed to rouse the dying man. He half rose on an elbow, blood trickling from his mouth with the effort.

'Ormond!' he whispered ghastily. 'Have you come back? Damn you, I'll do for you yet—'

'I'm not Ormond,' growled the American. 'I'm Gordon. It seems somebody has saved me the trouble of killing you. Where's Yasmeena?'

'He took her away.' The Englishman's voice was scarcely intelligible, choked by the flow of blood. 'Ormond, the dirty swine! We found the cave empty—knew old Yogok had betrayed us. We jumped him. He ran away. His damned monk stabbed me. Ormond took Yasmeena and the monk and went away. He's mad. He's going to try to cross the mountains on foot, with the girl, and the monk to guide him. And he left me to die, the swine, the filthy swine!'

The dying man's voice rose to a hysterical shriek; he heaved himself up, his eyes glaring; then a terrible shudder ran through his body and he was dead.

Gordon rose, struck another match and swept a glance over the cave. It was utterly bare. Not a firearm in sight. Ormond has evidently robbed his dying partner. Ormond, starting through the mountains with a captive woman, and a treacherous monk for a guide, on foot and with no provisions—surely the man must be mad.

Returning to Yogok he unbound his legs, repeating Pembroke's tale in a few words. He saw the priest's eyes gleam in the starlight.

'Good! They will all die in the mountains! Let them go!'

'We're following them,' Gordon answered. 'You know the way the monk will lead Ormond. Show it to me.'

A restoration of confidence had wakened insolence and defiance.

'No! Let them die!'

With a searing curse Gordon caught the priest's throat and jammed his head back between his shoulders, until his eyes were glaring at the stars.

'Damn you!' he ground between his teeth, shaking the man as a dog shakes a rat. 'If you try to balk me now I'll kill you the slowest way I know. Do you want me to drag you back to Yolgan and tell the people what you plotted against the daughter of Erlik Khan? They'll kill me, but they'll flay you alive!'

Yogok knew Gordon would not do that, not because the American feared death, but because to sacrifice himself would be to remove Yasmeena's last hope. But Gordon glaring eyes made him cold with fear; he sensed the abysmal rage that gripped the white man and knew that El Borak was on the point of tearing him limb from limb. In that moment there was no bloody deed of which Gordon was not capable.

'Stay, sahib!' Yogok gasped. 'I will guide you.'

'And guide me right!' Gordon jerked him savagely to his feet. 'They have been gone less than an hour. If we don't overtake them by sunrise, I'll know you've led me astray, and I'll tie you head down to a cliff for the vultures to eat alive.'

9.

In the darkness before dawn Yogok led Gordon up into the hills by a narrow trail that wound among ravines and windy crags, climbing ever southward. The eternal lights of Yolgan fell away behinds them, growing smaller and smaller with distance.

They left half a mile to the east of the gorge where the

Turkomans were concealed. Gordon ardently wished to get his men out of that ravine before dawn, but he dared not take the time now. His eyes burned from lack of sleep and moments of giddiness assailed him, but the fire of his driving energy burned fiercer than ever. He urged the priest to greater and greater speed until sweat dripped like water from the man's trembling limbs.

'He'll practically have to drag the girl. She'll fight him every step of the way. And he'll have to beat the monk every now and then to make him point out the right path. We ought to be gaining on them at every step.'

Full dawn found them climbing a ledge that pitched up around a gigantic shoulder where the wind staggered them. Then, off to the left, sounded a sudden rattle of rifle fire. The wind brought it in snatches. Gordon turned, loosing his binoculars. They were high above the ridges and hills that rimmed the valley.

He could see Yolgan in the distance, like a huddle of toy blocks. He could see the gorges that debouched into the valley spread out like the finger of a hand. He saw the gorge in which his Turkomans had taken refuge. Black dots which he knew were men scattered among the boulders at the canyon mouth and up on the rims of the walls; tiny white puffs spurted.

Even before he brought his glasses into play he knew that the pursuing Kirghiz had at last smelled his men out. The Turkomans were bottled in the gorge. He saw puffs of smoke jetting from the rocks that from the mountainside overhung the ravine leading out of the canyon. Strings of dots moved out of the gates of Yolgan, which were men coming to investigate the shooting. Doubtless the Kirghiz had sent riders to bring the men of the city.

Yogok shrieked and fell down flat on the ledge. Gordon felt his cap tugged from his head as if by an invisible hand, and there came to him the flat sharp crack of a rifle.

He dropped behind a boulder and began scanning the narrow, sheer-walled plateau upon which the ledge debouched. Presently a head and part of a shoulder rose above a shelf of rock, and then a rifle came up and spoke flatly. The bullet knocked a chip out of the boulder near Gordon's elbow.

Ormond had been making even poorer time than Gordon hoped, and seeing his pursuers gaining, had turned to make a fight of it. That he recognized Gordon was evident from his mocking shouts. There was a hint of hysteria in them.

Yogok was too helpless with terror to do anything but hug the ledge and moan. Gordon began working his way toward the Englishman. Evidently Ormond did not know that he had no firearm. The sun was not yet above the peaks when it turned to fire, and the light and atmosphere of those altitudes make for uncertain shooting.

Ormond blazed away as Gordon flitted from ridge to boulder and from rock to ledge, and sometimes his lead whispered perilously close. But Gordon was gliding ever nearer, working his way so that the sun would be behind him when it rose. Something about that silent shadowy figure that he could not hit began to shake Ormond's nerve; it was more like being stalked by a leopard than by a human being.

Gordon could not see Yasmeena, but presently he saw the monk. The man took advantage of a moment when Ormond was loading his rifle. He sprang up from behind the ledge with his hands tied behind his back, and scudded across the rock like a rabbit. Ormond, like a man gone mad, jerked a pistol and put a bullet between his shoulders, and he stumbled and slid screaming over the thousand-foot edge.

Gordon broke cover, too, and came ripping across the treacherous rock like a gust of hill wind. As he came the sun burst up over a ridge behind him, full in Ormond's eyes. The Englishman yelled incoherently, trying to shade his eyes with his left arm, and began firing half blindly. The bullets ripped past Gordon's head or knocked up splinters of stone at his speeding feet. Panic had Ormond, and he was firing without proper aim.

Then the hammer clicked on an empty chamber. Another stride and Gordon would reach him with that hovering arc of steel that the sun turned crimson. Ormond hurled the pistol blindly, yelling 'You damned werewolf! I'll cheat you yet!' and bounded far out, arms outspread.

His feet struck the sloping lip of a fissure and he shot down and vanished so suddenly it was like the unreality of a dream.

Gordon reached the crevice and glared down into echoing darkness. He could see nothing, but the chasm seemed bottomless. With an angry shrug he turned away, disappointed.

Behind the stony shelf Gordon found Yasmeena lying with her arms bound, where Ormond had flung her down. Her soft slippers hung in tatters, and the bruises and abrasions on her tender flesh told of Ormond's brutal attempts to force her at top speed along the rocky path.

Gordon cut her cords and she caught his arms with all her old fierceness of passion. There was no fear in her eyes now, only wild excitement.

'They said you were dead!' she cried. 'I knew they lied! They cannot kill you any more than they can kill the mountains or the wind that blows across them. You have Yogok. I saw him. He knows the secret paths better than the monk Ormond killed. Let us go, while the Kirghiz are killing the Turkomans! What if we have no supplies? It is summer. We shall not freeze. We can starve for a while if need be. Let us go!'

'I brought those men to Yolgan with me for my own purposes, Yasmeena,' he replied. 'Even for you I can't desert them.'

She nodded her splendid head. 'I expected that from you, El Borak.'

Ormond's rifle lay near by but there were no cartridges for it. He cast it over the precipice and, taking Yasmeena's hand, led her back to the ledge where Yogok lay yammering.

Gordon hauled him erect and pointed to the gorge where the white puffs spurted.

'Is there a way to reach that gorge without returning to the valley? Your life depends on it.'

'Half these gorges have hidden exits,' answered Yogok, shivering. 'That one has. But I cannot guide you along that route with my arms tied.'

Gordon unbound his hands, but tied the girdle about the priest's waist and retained the other end in his hand. 'Lead on,' he ordered.

Yogok led them back along the ledge they had just traversed to a point where, halfway along it, it was cut by a great natural causeway of solid stone. They made their way along it, with dizzy depths echoing on either hand, to a broad ledge which skirted a deep canyon. They followed this ledge around a colossal crag and after a while Yogok plunged into a cave which opened upon the narrow path.

This they traversed in semidarkness relieved by light which filtered in from a ragged crevice in the roof. The cave wound steeply downward, following a fault in the rock, and they came out at last in a triangular cleft between towering walls. The narrow slit which was the cave mouth opened in a side of the cleft and was masked from outer view by a spur of rock that looked like part of a solid wall. Gordon had looked into that cleft the day before and failed to discover the cave.

The sound of firing had grown louder as they advanced along the twisting cave, and now it filled the defile with thundering echoes. They were in the gorge of the Turkomans. Gordon saw the wiry warriors crouching among the boulders at the mouth, firing at the fur-capped heads which appeared among the rocks of the outer slopes.

He shouted before they saw him, and they nearly shot him before they recognized him. He went toward them, dragging Yogok with him, and the warriors stared in silent amazement at the shivering priest and the girl in her tattered finery. She scarcely noticed them; they were wolves whose fangs she did not fear; all her attention was centered on Gordon. When a bullet whined near her she did not flinch.

Men crouched at the mouth of the ravine, firing into it. Bullets hummed back up the gut.

'They stole up in the darkness,' grunted Orkhan, binding up a bleeding bullet hole in his forearm. 'They had the gorge mouth surrounded before our sentries saw them. They cut the throat of the sentry we had stationed down the ravine and came stealing up it. Had not others in the gorge seen them and opened fire, they would have cut all our throats while we slept. Aye, they were like cats that see in the dark. What shall we do, El Borak? We are trapped. We cannot climb these walls. There is the spring, and grass for the horses, and we have slept, but we have no food left and our ammunition will not last forever.'

Gordon took a yataghan from one of the men and handed it to Yasmeena.

'Watch Yogok,' he directed. 'Stab him if he seeks to escape.'

And from the flash of her eyes he knew that she at last realized the value of direct action in its proper place, and that she would not hesitate to carry out his order. Yogok looked like a singed serpent in his fury, but he feared Yasmeena as much as he did Gordon.

El Borak collected a rifle and a handful of cartridges on his way to the boulder-strewn gorge mouth. Three Turkomans lay dead among the rocks and others were wounded. The Kirghiz were working their way up the outer slope on foot from rock to rock, trying to get in to close quarters where their superior numbers would count, but not willing to sacrifice too many lives to get there. Up from the city a ragged line of men were streaming through the pines.

'We've got to get out of this trap before the monks come up with the Kirghiz and lead them up in the hills and down through that cave,' Gordon muttered.

He could see them already toiling up the first ridges

of the hills, shouting frantically to the tribesmen as they came. Working in fierce haste he told off half a dozen men on the best horses, and mounting Yogok and Yasmeena on spare steeds, he ordered the priest to lead the Turkomans back through the cave. To Orkhan Shah he gave instructions to follow Yasmeena's orders, and so imbued with trust was the Turkoman that he made no objections to obeying a woman.

Three of the men remaining with him Gordon stationed at the ravine, and with the other three he held the mouth of the canyon. They began firing as the others urged their horses down the defile. The men on the lower slopes sensed that the volleys were diminishing and came storming up the acclivities, only to take cover again as they were swept by a hail of lead, the deadly accuracy of which made up for its lack of volume. Gordon's presence heartened his men and they put new spirit in their rifle work.

When the last rider had disappeared into the cleft, Gordon waited until he thought the fugitives had time enough to traverse the winding cave, and then he fell back swiftly, picked up the men at the ravine, and raced for the hidden exit. The men outside suspected a trap in the sudden cessation of the firing, and they held back for long minutes, during which time Gordon and his men were galloping through the twisting cavern, their hoofs filling the narrow gut with thunder.

The others awaited them on the ledge skirting the ravine and Gordon sent them hurrying on. He cursed because he could not be at two places at once—at the head of the column bullying Yogok, and at the rear watching for the first of the pursuers to ride out on the ledge. But Yasmeena, flourishing the knife at the priest's throat, was guarantee against treachery at the front. She had sworn to sink the blade in his breast if the Kirghiz came within rifle range, and Yogok sweated with fear and himself urged the band onward.

They moved around the corner of the crag and out across the ridge, a knife-edged causeway half a mile in length, with a sheet of rock slanting steeply down for a thousand feet on either hand.

Gordon waited alone at the angle of the ledge. When his party was moving like insects along the crest of the ridge, the first of the Kirghiz came racing out on the ledge. Sitting his horse behind a jutting spur of rock, Gordon lined his sights carefully and fired. It was a long range, even for him; so long that he missed the first rider and hit the horse instead.

The stricken beast reared high, screaming, and plunged backward. The ledge was narrow where the cave opened on it. The screams and plunges of the maddened animal, before it toppled over the edge, put the horses in confusion behind it. Three more got out of control and were carried over the cliff with their riders, and the other Kirghiz retreated into the cave. After a while they tried again, but a bullet spattering on the rock sent them scurrying back.

A glance over his shoulder showed Gordon his horsemen just dropping off the ridge onto the farther ledge. He reined about and sent his horse flying along the path. If he loitered, the Kirghiz might venture out again, find no one opposing them, and reach the bend of the trail in time to pick him off the causeway.

Most of his hardened band had dismounted, leading their horses at a walk. Gordon rode at a gallop with death yawning on either hand if the horse slipped or put a single foot wrong. But the beast was sure-footed as a mountain sheep.

Gordon's head swam from lack of sleep as he glanced down into the blue haze of the abyss, but he did not slacken his pace. When he dropped down the slope onto the ledge where Yasmeena stood, white-faced and her nails biting into her pink palms, the Kirghiz had not yet appeared.

Gordon pushed his riders as hard as he dared, making them from time to time change to the spare horses, to save the animals as much as possible. Nearly a dozen of these still remained. Many of the men were giddy with dizziness caused by hunger and the altitude. He himself was mad for sleep and kept himself awake only by an effort of will that made the hills reel to his gaze.

He kept his grip on clarity of purpose as only a man toughened by a savagely hard life can do, and led them on, following the paths Yogok pointed out. They skirted ledges that hovered over ravines the bottoms of which were lost in shadowy gloom. They plunged through defiles like a knife cut where sheer walls rose up to the skies on either hand.

Behind them from time to time they heard faint yells, and once, when they toiled up over the shoulder of a breathtaking crag on a path where the horses fought for footing, they saw their pursuers far below and behind them. The Kirghiz and monks were not mantaining such a suicidal pace; hate is seldom as desperate as the will to live.

The snowy crest of Mount Erlik loomed higher and higher before them, and Yogok, when questioned, swore that the way to safety lay through the mountain. More he would not say; he was green with fear, and his mind held to but one thought—to keep the trail that would buy his life. He feared his captors no more than he feared that his pursuing subjects would overtake them and learn of his duplicity in regard to their goddess.

They pushed on like men already dead, beginning to stagger with weakness and exhaustion. The horses drooped and stumbled. The wind was like whetted steel. Darkness was gathering when they followed the backbone of a giant ridge which ran like a natural causeway to the sheer slope of Mount Erlik Khan.

The mountain towered gigantically above them, a brutish mass of crags and dizzy escarpments and colossal steeps, with the snow-clad pinnacle, glimpsed between the great spurs, dominating all. The ridge ended at a ledge high up among the cliffs, and in the sheer rock there stood a bronze door, thickly carved with inscriptions that

Gordon could not decipher. It was heavy enough to have resisted an attack of artillery.

'This is sacred to Erlik,' said Yogok, but he showed about as much reverence as one of the Mohammedans. 'Push against the door. Nay; fear not. On my life, there is no trap.'

'On your life it is,' Gordon assured him grimly, and himself set a shoulder to the door, almost falling as he dismounted.

10.

The ponderous portal swung inward with a smoothness that showed the antique hinges had recently been oiled. A makeshift torch reveald the entrance to a tunnel, cut in solid rock. A few feet from the door the tunnel opened out like the neck of a bottle, and the flickering torch, held at the entrance, only hinted at the vastness of its dimensions.

'This tunnel runs clear through the mountain,' said Yogok. 'By dawn we can be out of reach of those who follow, because even if they climb over the mountain by the most direct route, they must go by foot and it will take them all the rest of the night and all of another day. If they skirt the mountain and work their way through the passes of the surrounding hills, it will take them even longer; and their horses are weary, too.

'That is the way I was going to guide Ormond. I was not going to take him though the mountain. But it is the only way of escape for you. There is food here. At certain seasons of the year the monks work here. In that cell there are lamps.'

He pointed to a small chamber cut in the rock just inside the doorway. Gordon lighted several of the butter lamps, and gave them to the Turkomans to carry. He dared not follow the course which caution suggested and ride ahead to investigate before he led his men into the tunnel. The pursuers were too close behind them. He must bar the big door and plunge on, trusting the priest's desire to save his own skin.

When the men were all in the tunnel, Yogok directed the barring of the door—giant bronze bars, thick as a man's leg. It took half a dozen of the weakened Turkomans to lift one, but once they were in place, Gordon was certain that nothing short of siege guns could force the ton-heavy door, with its massive bronze sills and jambs set deep in the living rock.

He made Yogok ride between him and Orkhan, the Turkoman holding a lamp. There was no use trusting Yogok, even though the priest was getting some satisfaction out of the thought that he was at least ridding himself of the 'goddess' he feared and hated, although it meant foregoing his vengeance on her.

Even with all his faculties occupied in a savage battle to keep from falling senseless with exhaustion, Gordon found space to be amazed at what the light showed him. He had never dreamed of the existence of such a place. Thirty men could have ridden abreast in the cavernlike passage, and the roof soared out of sight in some places; in others stalactites reflected the light in a thousand scintillant colors.

The floors and walls were as even as man-shaped marble, and Gordon wondered how many centuries had been required for the hand-cutting and smoothing of them. Cells appeared at irregular intervals, cut in the rock at the sides, and presently he saw marks of pick work, and then caught glints of dull yellow.

The light showed him the incredible truth. The tales of Mount Erlik Khan were true. The walls were patterned with veins of gold that could be dug out of the rock with a knife point.

The Turkomans, who smelled loot as vultures smell carrion, woke suddenly out of their daze of fatigue and began to take an almost painfully intense interest.

'This is where the monks get their gold, sahib,' said Orkhan, his eyes blazing in the lamplight. 'Let me twist the old one's toes for a space, and he will tell us where they have hidden that which they have dug out of the walls.'

But 'the old one' did not need persuasion. He pointed out a square-hewn chamber in which stood stacks of peculiarly shaped objects that were ingots of virgin gold. In other, larger cells were the primitive contrivances with which they smelted the ore and cast the metal.

'Take what ye will,' said Yogok indifferently. 'A thousand horses could not carry away the gold we have cast and stored, and we have scarcely dipped into the richness of the veins.'

Thin lips were licked greedily, drooping mustaches twisted in emotion, and eyes that burned like hawks' were turned questioningly on Gordon.

'Ye have spare horses,' he suggested, and that was enough for them.

After that nothing could have convinced them that everything which had passed had not been planned by Gordon in order to lead them to the gold which was the plunder he had promised them. They loaded the extra ponies until he interfered, to save the animals' strength. Then they hacked off chunks of the soft gold and stuffed their pouches and belts and girdles, and even so they had scarcely diminished the stacks. Some of the raiders lifted up their voices and wept when they saw how much they must leave behind.

'Assuredly,' they promised each other, 'we shall return with wagons and many horses and secure every crumb of it, *inshallah!*'

'Dogs!' swore Gordon. 'Ye have each man a fortune beyond your dreams. Are ye jackals to feast on carrion until your bellies burst? Will ye loiter here until the Kirghiz cross the mountain and cut us off? What of gold then, you crop-eared rogues?'

Of more interest to the American was a cell where barley was stored in leather sacks, and he made the tribesmen load some of the horses with food instead of gold. They grumbled, but they obeyed him. They would obey him now, if he ordered them to ride with him into Jehannum.

Every nerve in his body shrieked for sleep, submerging

hunger, but he gnawed a handful of raw barley and flogged his failing powers with the lash of his driving will. Yasmeena drooped in her saddle wearily, but her eyes shone unclouded in the lamplight, and Gordon was dully aware of a deep respect for her that dwarfed even his former admiration.

They rode on through that glittering, dream-palace cavern, the tribesmen munching barley and babbling ecstatically of the joys their gold would buy, and at last they came to a bronze door which was a counterpart of the one at the other end of the tunnel. It was not barred. Yogok maintained that none but the monks had visited Mount Erlik in centuries. The door swung inward at their efforts and they blinked in the glow of a white dawn.

They were looking out on a small ledge from which a narrow trail wound along the edge of a giant escarpment. On one side the land fell away sheer for thousands of feet, so that a stream at the bottom looked like a thread of silver, and on the other a sheer cliff rose for some five hundred feet.

The cliff limited the view to the left, but to the right Gordon could see some of the mountains which flanked Mount Erlik Khan, and the valley far below them wandered southward away to a pass in the distance, a notch in the savage rampart of the hills.

'This is life for you, El Borak,' said Yogok, pointing to the pass. 'Three miles from the spot where we now stand this trail leads down into the valley where there is water and game and rich grass for the horses. You can follow it southward beyond the pass for three days' journey when you will come into country you know well. It is inhabited by marauding tribes, but they will not attack a party as large as yours. You can be through the pass before the Kirghiz round the mountain, and they will not follow you through it. That is the limit of their country. Now let me go.'

'Not yet; I'll release you at the pass. You can make

your way back here easily and wait for the Kirghiz, and tell them any lie you want to about their goddess.'

Yogok glared angrily at Gordon. The American's eyes were bloodshot, the skin stretched taut over the bones of his face. He looked like a man who had been sweated in hell's fires, and he felt the same way. There was no reason for Yogok's strident objections, except a desire to get out of the company of those he hated as quickly as possible.

In Gordon's state a man reverts to primitive instincts, and the American held his thrumming nerves in an iron grip to keep from braining the priest with his gun butt. Dispute and importunities were like screaming insults to his struggling brain.

While the priest squawked, and Gordon hesitated between reasoning with him or knocking him down, the Turkomans, inspired by the gold and food, and eager for the trail, began to crowd past him. Half a dozen had emerged on the ledge when Gordon noticed them, and ordering Orkhan to bring Yogok along, he rode past those on the ledge, intending to take the lead as usual. But one of the men was already out to the path, and could neither turn back nor hug the wall close enough to let Gordon by.

The American, perforce, called to him to go ahead, and he would follow, and even as Gordon set his horse to the trail a volley of boulders came thundering down from above. They hit the wretched Turkoman and swept him and his horse off the trail as a broom sweeps a spider from a wall. One of the stones, bouncing from the ledge, hit Gordon's horse and broke its leg, and the beast screamed and toppled over the side after the other.

Gordon threw himself clear as it fell, landed half over the edge, and clawed a desperate way to safety with Yasmeena's screams and the yells of the Turkomans ringing in his ears. There was nothing seen to shoot at, but some of them loosed their rifles anyway, and the volley was greeted by a wild peal of mocking laughter from the cliffs above.

In no way unnerved by his narrow escape, Gordon

drove his men back into the shelter of the cave. They were like wolves in a trap, ready to strike blind right and left, and a dozen tulwars hovered over Yogok's head.

'Slay him! He has led us into a trap! Allah!'

Yogok's face was a green, convulsed mask of fear. He squalled like a tortured cat.

'Nay! I led you swift and sure! The Kirghiz could not have reached this side of the mountain by this time!'

'Were there monks hiding in these cells?' asked Gordon. 'They could have sneaked out when they saw us coming in. Is that a monk up there?'

'Nay; as Erlik is my witness! We work the gold three moons in the year; at other times it is death to go near Mount Erlik. I know not who it is.'

Gordon ventured out on the path again and was greeted by another shower of stones, which he barely avoided, and a voice yelled high above him:

'You Yankee dog, how do you like that? I've got you now, damn you! Thought I was done for when I fell into that fissure, didn't you? Well, there was a ledge a few feet down that I landed on. You couldn't see it because the sun wasn't high enough to shine down into it. If I'd had a gun I'd have killed you when you looked down. I climbed out after you left.'

'Ormond!' snarled Gordon.

'Did you think I hadn't wormed anything out of that monk?' the Englishman yelled. 'He told me all about the paths and Mount Erlik after I'd caved in some of his teeth with a gun barrel. I saw old Yogok with you and knew he'd lead you to Erlik. I got here first. I'd have barred the door and locked you out to be butchered by the fellows who're chasing you, but I couldn't lift the bars. But, anyway, I've got you trapped. You can't leave the cave; if you do I'll mash you like insects on the path. I can see you on it, and you can't see me. I'm going to keep you here until the Kirghiz come up. I've still got Yasmeena's symbol. They'll listen to me.

'I'll tell them Yogok is helping you to kidnap her;

they'll kill you all except her. They'll take her back, but I don't care now. I don't need that Kashmiri's money. I've got the secret of Mount Erlik Khan!'

Gordon fell back into the doorway and repeated what the Englishman had said. Yogok turned a shade greener in his fear, and all stared silently at El Borak. His bloodshot gaze traveled over them as they stood blinking, disheveled, and haggard, with lamps paled by the dawn, like ghouls caught above earth by day-break. Grimly he marshaled his straying wits. Gordon had never reached the ultimate limits of his endurance; always he had plumbed a deeper, hidden reservoir of vitality below what seemed the last.

'Is there another way out of here?' he demanded.

Yogok shook his head, chattering again with terror. 'No way that men and horses can go.'

'What do you mean?'

The priest moved back into the darkness and held a lamp close to the flank of the wall where the tunnel narrowed for the entrance. Rusty bits of metal jutted from the rock.

'Here was once a ladder,' he said. 'It led far up to a crevice in the wall where long ago one sat to watch the southern pass for invaders. But none has climbed it for many years, and the handholds are rusty and rotten. The crevice opens on the sheer of the outer cliffs, and even if a man reached it, he could scarcely climb down the outside.'

'Well, maybe I can pick Ormond off from the crevice,' muttered Gordon, his head swimming with the effort of thinking.

Standing still was making infinitely harder his fight to keep awake. The muttering of the Turkomans was a meaningless tangle of sound, and Yasmeena's dark anxious eyes seemed to be looking at him from a vast distance. He thought he felt her arms cling to him briefly, but he could not be sure. The lights were beginning to swim in a thick mist.

Beating himself into wakefulness by striking his own

face with his open hand, he began the climb, a rifle slung to his back. Orkhan was plucking at him, begging to be allowed to make the attempt in his stead, but Gordon shook him off. In his dazed brain was a conviction that the responsibility was his own. He went up like an automaton, slowly, all his muddled faculties concentrating grimly on the task.

Fifty feet up, the light of the lamps ceased to aid him, and he groped upward in the gloom, feeling for the rusty bolts set in the wall. They were so rotten that he dared not put his full weight on any one of them. In some places they were missing and he clung with his fingers in the niches where they had been. Only the slant of the rock enabled him to accomplish the climb at all, and it seemed endless, a hell-born eternity of torture.

The lamps below him were like fireflies in the darkness, and the roof with its clustering stalactites was only a few yards above his head. Then he saw a gleam of light, and an instant later he was crouching in a cleft that opened on the outer air. It was only a couple of yards wide, and not tall enough for a man to stand upright.

He crawled along it for some thirty feet and then looked out on a rugged slant that pitched down to a crest of cliffs, a hundred feet below. He could not see the ledge where the door opened, nor the path that led from it, but he saw a figure crouching among the boulders along the lip of the cliff, and he unslung his rifle.

Ordinarily he could not have missed at that range. But his bloodshot eyes refused to line the sights. Slumber never assails a weary man so fiercely as in the growing light of dawn. The figure among the rocks below merged and blended fantastically with the scenery, and the sights of the rifle were mere blurs.

Setting his teeth, Gordon pulled the trigger, and the bullet smashed on the rock a foot from Ormond's head. The Englishman dived out of sight among the boulders.

In desperation Gordon slung his rifle and threw a leg over the lip of the cleft. He was certain that Ormond had no firearm. Down below the Turkomans were clamoring

like a wolf pack, but his numbed faculties were fully
occupied with the task of climbing down the ribbed pitch.
He stumbled and fumbled and nearly fell, and at last he
did slip and came sliding and tumbling down until his rifle
caught on a projection and held him dangling by the strap.

In a red mist he saw Ormond break cover, with a tulwar
that he must have found in the cavern, and in a panic
lest the Englishman climb up and kill him as he hung
helplessly, Gordon braced his feet and elbows against the
rock and wrenched savagely, breaking the rifle strap. He
plunged down like a plummet, hit the slope, clawed at
rocks and knobs, and brought up on shalving stone a
dozen feet from the cliff edge, while his rifle, tumbling
before him, slid over and was gone.

The fall jolted his numbed nerves back into life again,
knocked some of the cobwebs out of his dizzy brain.
Ormond was within a few steps of him when he scrambled
up, drawing his scimitar. The Englishman was as savage
and haggard in appearance as was Gordon, and his eyes
blazed with a frenzy that almost amounted to madness.

'Steel to steel, now, El Borak!' Ormond gritted. 'We'll
see if you're the swordsman they say you are!'

Ormond came with a rush and Gordon met him, fired
above his exhaustion by his hate and the stinging frenzy
of battle. They fought back and forth along the cliff
edge, with a foot to spare between them and eternity
sometimes, until the clangor of the swords wakened the
eagles to shrill hysteria.

Ormond fought like a wild man, yet with all the craft
the sword masters of his native England had taught him.
Gordon fought as he had learned to fight in grim and
merciless battles in the hills and the steppes and the
deserts. He fought as an Afghan fights, with the furious
intensity of onslaught that gathers force like a rising hurricane as it progresses.

Beating on his blade like a smith on an anvil, Gordon
drove the Englishman staggering before him, until the
man swayed dizzily with his heels over the edge of the cliff.

'Swine!' gasped Ormond with his last breath, and spat in his enemy's face and slashed madly at his head.

'This for Ahmed!' roared Gordon, and his scimitar whirled past Ormond's blade and crunched home.

The Englishman reeled outward, his features suddenly blotted out by blood and brains, and pitched backward into the gulf without a sound.

Gordon sat down on a boulder, suddenly aware of the quivering of his leg muscles. He sat there, his gory blade across his knees and his head sunk in his hands, his brain a black blank, until shouts welling up from below roused him to consciousness.

'Ohai, El Borak! A man with a cleft head had fallen past us into the valley! Art thou safe? We await orders!'

He lifted his head and glanced at the sun which was just rising over the eastern peaks, turning to crimson flame the snow of Mount Erlik Khan. He would have traded all the gold of the monks of Yolgan to be allowed to lie down and sleep for an hour, and climbing up on his stiffened legs that trembled with his weight was a task of appalling magnitude. But his labor was not yet done; there was no rest for him this side of the pass.

Summoning the shreds of his strength, he shouted down to the raiders.

'Get upon the horses and ride, sons of nameless dogs! Follow the trail and I will come along the cliff. I see a place beyond the next bend where I can climb down to the trail. Bring Yogok with you; he has earned his release, but the time is not yet.'

'Hurry, El Borak,' floated up Yasmeena's golden call. 'It is far to Delhi, and many mountains lie between!'

Gordon laughed and sheathed his scimitar, and his laugh sounded like the ghastly mirth of a hyena; below him the Turkomans had taken the road and were already singing a chant improvised in his honor, naming 'Son of the Sword' the man who staggered along the cliffs above them, with a face like a grinning skull and feet that left smears of blood on the rock.